PENGUIN BOOKS

the
Ruby Circle

Richelle Mead, the *New York Times* bestselling author of the Vampire Academy series and the Bloodlines series, lives in Seattle in the USA.

www.richellemead.com

D0278038

the Ruby Circle

A *Bloodlines* NOVEL

RICHELLE MEAD

PENGUIN BOOKS

PENGUIN BOOKS

UK | USA | Canada | Ireland | Australia
India | New Zealand | South Africa

Penguin Books is part of the Penguin Random House group of companies
whose addresses can be found at global.penguinrandomhouse.com.

First published in the USA by Razorbill, a division of Penguin Young Readers Group, 2015
Published in Great Britain by Penguin Books 2015
001

Copyright © Richelle Mead, 2015

The moral right of the author has been asserted

Set in Fairfield LT Std
Printed in Great Britain by Clays Ltd, St Ives plc

A CIP catalogue record for this book is available from the British Library

TRADE PAPERBACK ISBN: 978–0–141–36145–1

PAPERBACK ISBN: 978–0–141–36131–4

www.greenpenguin.co.uk

MIX
Paper from
responsible sources
FSC® C018179

Penguin Random House is committed to a
sustainable future for our business, our readers
and our planet. This book is made from Forest
Stewardship Council® certified paper.

For the #VAFamily

CHAPTER 1
ADRIAN

MARRIED LIFE WASN'T WHAT I'D EXPECTED.

Don't get me wrong: I had no regrets about the woman I'd married. In fact, I loved her more than I'd ever imagined it was possible to love a person. The reality we lived in, though? Well, let's just say I'd never really imagined anything like that either. In all our previous fantasies, we'd dreamed of exotic locations and, most importantly, freedom. Being cooped up in a small suite of rooms had never been part of any escape plan, let alone a romantic getaway.

But I was never one to back down from a challenge.

"What's this?" asked Sydney, startled.

"Happy anniversary," I said.

She'd just finished getting showered and dressed and now stood in the bathroom's doorway, staring around at the transformation I'd wrought in our living room. It hadn't been easy doing so much in so little time. Sydney was an efficient person, and that extended to showers as well. Me? You could have conducted full demolition and remodeling in the time it took me to shower. With Sydney, there'd been barely enough time to decorate the place in candles and flowers. But I'd managed.

A smile crept over her face. "It's only been one month."

"Hey, don't say 'only,'" I warned. "It's still monumental. And I'll have you know that I plan on celebrating every month for the rest of our lives."

Her smile turned into a full-on grin as she ran her fingers over the petals of a vase full of flowers. It made my heart ache. I couldn't remember the last time I'd seen such a genuine smile on her. "You even got peonies," she said. "How'd you manage that?"

"Hey, I have my ways," I stated loftily.

Though it's probably better she doesn't know what those ways are, a voice in my head warned.

Sydney strolled around and assessed the rest of my handiwork, which included a bottle of red wine and a box of chocolate truffles artfully set out on the kitchen table. "Isn't it a little early in the day?" she teased.

"Depends on whom you're asking," I said, nodding toward the dark window. "For you, it's technically evening."

Her smile dimmed a little. "Honestly, I hardly ever know what time it is anymore."

This lifestyle is taking its toll on her, my inner voice warned. *Just look at her.*

Even in the flickering light of the candles, I could see signs of the stress Sydney was feeling. Dark shadows under her eyes. A perpetually weary look—born more of despair than fatigue. She was the only human at the royal Moroi Court who wasn't here specifically to feed us vampires. She was also the only human in any civilized Moroi place to have married one of us. Doing so had meant incurring the wrath of her own people and cutting herself off from friends and family (the ones who were still speaking to her, at least) in the outside world. And thanks to the scorn and prying looks she received around Court, Sydney had pretty much cut herself off from people here as well, narrowing her whole world down to our suite of rooms.

"Wait, there's more," I said quickly, hoping to distract her. With a button push, classical music began playing through the living room's sound system. I extended my hand to her. "Since we didn't get to dance at our wedding."

That brought the smile back. She took my hand and let me draw her close. I twirled her around the room, careful not to bump any of the candles, and she regarded me with amusement. "What are you doing? It's a waltz. It has three beats. Can't you hear it? One-two-three, one-two-three."

"Really? That's what a waltz is? Huh. I just picked something that sounded fancy. Since we don't really have a song or anything." I pondered that for a second. "I guess we've failed as a couple in that regard."

She scoffed. "If that's our biggest failing, then I think we're doing okay."

Long moments passed as I danced her around the room, then I suddenly said, "'She Blinded Me With Science.'"

"What?" Sydney asked.

"That could be our song."

She laughed outright, and I realized I hadn't heard that sound in a very long time. It somehow managed to make my heart both ache and leap. "Well," she said. "I guess that's better than 'Tainted Love.'"

We both laughed then, and she rested her cheek against my chest. I kissed the top of her golden head, taking in the mingled scents of her soap and skin. "It feels wrong," she said quietly. "To be happy, I mean. When Jill's out there . . ."

At that name, my heart sank, and a heavy darkness threatened to descend on me and shatter this small moment of joy I'd created. I had to forcibly push away the darkness, making myself step back from a dangerous precipice I knew all too well these days. "We'll find her," I whispered, tightening my hold on Sydney. "Wherever she is, we'll find her."

If she's still alive, that inner voice said nastily.

It's probably worth pointing out that the voice that kept speaking in my head wasn't part of some mental exercise. It was actually a very distinct voice, belonging to my dead aunt Tatiana, former queen of the Moroi. She wasn't with me in any ghostly form, though. Her voice was a delusion, born out of the increasing grip insanity was taking on me, thanks to the rare type of magic I used. A quick prescription would have shut her up, but it also would've cut me off from my magic, and our world was too unpredictable right now for me to do that. And so this phantom Aunt Tatiana and I had become roommates in my mind. Sometimes that delusional presence terrified me, making me wonder how long it would be until I completely lost it. At other times, I found myself taking her in stride—and that scared me even more, that I was coming to regard her as normal.

For now, I managed to ignore Aunt Tatiana as I kissed Sydney again. "We'll find Jill," I said more firmly. "And in the meantime, we have to keep living our lives."

"I suppose so," said Sydney with a sigh. I could tell she was trying to summon back that earlier cheer. "If this is supposed to make up for our lack of a wedding dance, I feel kind of underdressed. Maybe I should go dig out that gown."

"No way," I said. "Not that that dress wasn't great. But I kind of like you underdressed. In fact, I wouldn't mind if you were a lot more underdressed . . ."

I stopped waltzing (or whatever dance move it was I'd been attempting to do) and brought my mouth down to hers in a very different sort of kiss than the one I'd just given her. Heat filled me as I felt the softness of her lips, and I was surprised to sense an answering passion in her. In light of our recent circumstances, Sydney hadn't been feeling particularly physical, and honestly, I couldn't blame her. I'd respected her wishes and kept my distance . . . not realizing how much I'd missed that fire in her until now.

We found ourselves sinking down onto the couch, arms wrapped tightly around each other, still kissing passionately. I paused to study her, admiring the way the candlelight shone on her blond hair and brown eyes. I could've drowned in that beauty, that and the love I could feel radiating off of her. It was a perfect, much-needed romantic moment . . . at least, it was until the door opened.

"Mom?" I exclaimed, leaping off Sydney like I was a high school kid and not a married man of twenty-two.

"Oh, hello, dear," my mother said, strolling into the living room. "Why are all the lights off? It looks like a mausoleum in here. Was the power out?" She flipped on a light switch, making both Sydney and me wince. "It's back now. But you really shouldn't have lit so many candles. It's dangerous." She helpfully blew a cluster out.

"Thanks," said Sydney flatly. "It's nice to know you're taking safety seriously." Her expression reminded me of the time my mother had "helpfully" pulled out a bunch of sticky notes that were "cluttering up" a book Sydney had spent hours painstakingly notating.

"Mom, I thought you were going to be gone a couple of hours," I said pointedly.

"I was, but it was just getting too awkward over at the feeders' salon. You'd think everyone would be busy at the council meeting, but no. So many stares. I couldn't relax. So they just let me bring one with me." She glanced around. "Where'd he go? Ah, there." She stepped back out into the hallway and steered in a dazed-looking human who was a little older than me. "Sit over there on that chair, and I'll be right with you."

I leapt to my feet. "You brought a feeder here? Mom, you know how Sydney feels about that."

Sydney made no comment but blanched at the sight of the feeder sitting across the room. His eyes—dazed and happy from the endorphins he received from letting vampires feed off of him—stared around blankly.

My mother sighed in exasperation. "What do you expect me to do, darling? There was absolutely *no way* I could feed with Maureen Tarus and Gladys Dashkov sitting there and gossiping right beside me."

"I expect you to have a little consideration for my wife!" I exclaimed. Since Sydney and I had gotten married and sought refuge at Court, most people—including my own father—had turned their backs on us. My mom had stood by us, even going so far as to live with us—which wasn't without its complications.

"I'm sure she can just wait in your bedroom," my mother said, leaning over to blow out more candles. Spotting the truffles on the table, she paused to pop one in her mouth.

"Sydney doesn't have to go hide away in her own home," I argued.

"Well," said my mother, "neither do I. It's my home too."

"I don't mind," said Sydney, getting to her feet. "I'll wait."

I was so frustrated, I wanted to rip my hair out. Passion was no longer the issue. All traces of that earlier happiness I'd seen in Sydney were gone. She was retreating back into herself, back to that hopeless feeling of being a human stuck in a world of vampires. And then, impossibly, things got worse. My mother had noticed one of the peony vases.

"These are beautiful," she said. "Melinda must have been so grateful for that healing."

Sydney froze mid-step. "What healing?"

"It's not important," I said hastily, hoping my mother would get the hint. At other times, Daniella Ivashkov was a remarkably astute woman. Today, however, she seemed to be in fully oblivious mode.

"Melinda Rowe, the Court florist," my mother explained. "Adrian and I ran into her the last time we were out at a feeding. She was having a terrible acne flare-up, and Adrian was nice enough to speed along its healing. She promised to help get some peonies in stock in return."

Sydney turned on me, speechless in her fury. Needing to calm this situation immediately, I grabbed hold of her arm and pulled her into our bedroom. "Make it fast," I called to my mom, just before I shut the door.

Sydney lashed out immediately. "Adrian, how could you?

7

You promised! You promised no more spirit, unless it was to help find Jill!"

"It was nothing," I insisted. "It hardly took any power at all."

"It adds up!" Sydney cried. "You know it does. Every little bit. You can't waste it on stuff like this . . . on someone's acne!"

Although I understood why she was upset, I couldn't help but feel a bit hurt. "I did it for us. For our anniversary. I thought you'd like it."

"What I'd like is for my husband to stay sane," she snapped back.

"Well, we're long past that," I said.

She doesn't know the half of it, remarked Aunt Tatiana.

Sydney crossed her arms and sat on the bed. "See? There you go. Making a joke of everything. This is serious, Adrian."

"And I'm being serious. I know what I can handle."

She met my gaze levelly. "Do you? I still think you'd be better off stopping spirit altogether. Go back on your pills. It's safest."

"What about finding Jill?" I reminded her. "What if we need my spirit magic for that?"

Sydney looked away. "Well, it hasn't been of much use so far. No one's magic has."

That last remark was a condemnation of herself as much as of me. Our friend Jill Mastrano Dragomir had been kidnapped a month ago, and so far, our efforts to find her had been for nothing. I hadn't been able to reach Jill in spirit dreams, nor had Sydney—an adept student of human witchcraft—been able to locate her using the spells at her disposal. The best Sydney's magic had been able to tell us was that Jill was still alive, but that was it. The general belief was that wherever she was, Jill was being drugged—which could effectively hide someone from both human and Moroi magic. It didn't stop us from both feeling useless, though. We both cared about Jill immensely—and my relationship with her was particularly intense since I'd once used spirit magic to bring her back from the brink of death. Not knowing what had happened to her now had cast a shadow over Sydney and me—and any attempts at happiness we'd mustered while under this self-imposed house arrest.

"It doesn't matter," I said. "When we do find her, I need my magic. There's no telling what I'll need to do."

"Like fix her acne?" asked Sydney.

I flinched. "I told you, it was nothing! Let me worry about me and how much spirit I can use. It's not your job."

She turned incredulous. "Of course it is! I'm your wife, Adrian. If I'm not going to worry about you, who will? You need to keep spirit in check."

"I can handle it," I said through gritted teeth.

"Is your aunt still talking to you?" she demanded.

I looked away, refusing to meet her eye. In my head, Aunt Tatiana sighed. *You never should have told her about me.*

At my silence, Sydney said, "She is, isn't she? Adrian, that's not healthy! You have to know that!"

I spun around in anger. "I can handle it. Okay? I can handle it, and I can handle her!" I shouted. "So stop telling me what to do! You don't know everything—no matter how much you want everyone to think you do!"

Stricken, Sydney took a step back. The pain in her eyes hurt me a lot more than her earlier words had. I felt terrible. How had this day gone so wrong? It was supposed to have been perfect. Suddenly, I needed to get out. I couldn't stand these four walls anymore. I couldn't stand my mother's control. I couldn't stand feeling like I was always disappointing Sydney—and Jill. Sydney and I had come to Court to seek protection from our enemies, hiding here so we could be together. Lately, it seemed like this arrangement was in danger of tearing us apart.

"I have to get out," I said.

Sydney's eyes widened. "To where?"

I raked a hand through my hair. "Anywhere. Anywhere to get some air. Anywhere but here."

I turned before she could say anything and stormed out through the living room, past where my mom was drinking from the feeder. She gave me a quizzical look, but I ignored it and kept on going until I was out our door and through the lobby of the guest-housing building. It wasn't until I emerged outside, until the balmy summer air hit my skin, that I paused to evaluate my actions—and pop a piece of gum, which was my current way to avoid smoking when stressed. I stared back up at the building, feeling guilty and cowardly for running out on our fight.

Don't feel bad, Aunt Tatiana said. *Marriage is hard. That's why I never did it.*

It is hard, I agreed. *But that's not an excuse to run away. I need to go back. I need to apologize. I need to work things out.*

You're never going to work things out as long as you're locked up here and Jill's still missing, warned Aunt Tatiana.

Two guardians walked past me just then, and I caught a piece of their conversation, mentioning extra patrols for the council meeting going on. I remembered my mom's earlier comment about that meeting, and inspiration suddenly hit. Turning away from the building, I began hurrying toward what served as the royal palace here at Court, hoping I could get to the meeting in time.

I know what to do, I told Aunt Tatiana. *I know how to get us out of here and fix things with Sydney and me. We need a purpose, a goal. And I'm going to get us one. I need to talk to Lissa. If I can make her understand, I can fix everything.*

That phantom made no response as I walked. Around me, midnight had clothed the world in darkness—bedtime for humans, prime time for those of us on a vampiric schedule. The Moroi Court was set up like a university: forty or so venerable brick buildings arranged around beautifully landscaped quads and courtyards. It was high summer, warm and humid, and there were a fair number of people out and about. Most were too consumed with their own affairs to notice me or realize who I was. Those who did shot me those same curious looks.

They're just jealous, Aunt Tatiana declared.

I don't think that's what it is, I told her. Even knowing she was a delusion, it was hard not to respond sometimes.

Of course it is. The Ivashkov name has always inspired awe and envy. They're all underlings, and they know it. In my day, this never would've been tolerated. It's that child queen of yours letting things run amok.

Even with the intrusive looks, I found I enjoyed my walk. It really wasn't healthy being shut indoors so much—something I never thought I'd admit. Despite the thickness of the humid air, it felt light and refreshing to me, and I found myself wishing Sydney could be out here too. A moment later, I decided that wasn't right. She needed to be outside later, when the sun was up. That was the time for humans. Being on our schedule was probably just as hard on her as the isolation. I made a mental note to suggest a walk with her later on. Sun didn't kill us like it did Strigoi—evil, undead vampires—but it wasn't always comfortable for Moroi either. Most slept or stayed in during the day, and Sydney would be less likely to run into anyone if we timed our outing correctly.

The thought cheered me as I popped in another piece of gum and reached the royal palace. Outside, it looked like all the other buildings, but inside, it was decorated with all the grandeur and opulence you'd expect from the royalty of an ancient civilization. The Moroi elected their monarchs from among twelve royal families, and massive portraits of those illustrious figures lined the corridors, illuminated by the light of glittering chandeliers. Crowds of people walked the halls, and when I reached the council's chamber, I saw that I'd arrived at the end of the meeting. People were leaving as I entered, and many of them, too, stopped to stare at me. I heard whispers of "abomination" and "human wife."

I ignored them and kept my focus on my real goal, up near the front of the room. There, near the council's platform, stood Vasilisa Dragomir—the "child queen" Aunt Tatiana had referred to. Lissa, as I called her, stood ringed by dark-suited dhampir guardians: half-human, half-Moroi warriors whose race had originated from a time long ago, when Moroi and humans had intermarried without scandal. Dhampirs couldn't have children with each other, but through a genetic quirk, their race continued by reproducing with Moroi.

Standing just beyond Lissa's bodyguards, Moroi press shouted questions at her that she answered in that same calm way of hers. I summoned a bit of spirit magic in order to view her aura, and she lit up in my vision. She shone with gold, indicating she was a spirit user like me, but her other colors had dimmed, and there was a tremulous quality to it all, showing she was uneasy. I released the magic as I hurried up to the crowd and waved my hand in her direction, shouting to be heard among the noise. "Your Majesty! Your Majesty!"

Somehow, she heard my voice through the others and beckoned me forward once she finished answering someone else's questions. Her guardians parted to let me get close. That triggered everyone's interest—especially when the onlookers saw whom she'd allowed into her personal space. I could see they were dying to know what we were discussing, but the guardians kept them back, and there was too much noise in the room anyway.

"Well, this is an unexpected surprise. You couldn't have scheduled an appointment?" she asked me in a low voice, still keeping that public smile on her face. "It would've attracted a lot less attention."

I shrugged. "Everything I do attracts attention these days. I've stopped noticing."

A spark of legitimate amusement flashed in her eyes, so I felt good for at least bringing that about. "What can I do for you, Adrian?"

"It's what I can do for you," I said, still fired up by the idea that had hit me earlier. "You need to let Sydney and me go look for Jill."

Her eyes widened, and the smile slipped. "*Let you go?* You begged me to let you stay here a month ago!"

"I know, I know. And I'm grateful. But your people haven't found Jill yet. You need to call in some special help with special abilities."

"If I recall," she said, "you and Sydney have already tried those special abilities—and failed."

"Which is why you need to let us get out there!" I exclaimed. "Go back to Palm Springs and—"

"Adrian," Lissa interrupted. "Do you hear yourself? You came here because the Alchemists were trying to hunt you two down. And now you want to walk right back out there into their clutches?"

"Well, not when you put it that way. I figured we'd sneak out when they didn't know and—"

"No," she interrupted again. "Absolutely not. I have enough to worry about without you two getting caught by the Alchemists. You wanted me to protect you, and that's what I'm going to do. So don't get any ideas about sneaking out—I'm having the gates watched. You're both staying here, where you're safe."

Safe and starting to lose it, I thought, recalling the bleak look in Sydney's eyes.

Darling, Aunt Tatiana whispered to me, *you were starting to lose it long before this.*

"I have good people looking for Jill," Lissa continued when I didn't answer her. "Rose and Dimitri are out there."

"Why haven't they found her? And if someone wanted to remove you, why haven't they—"

I couldn't finish, but the sadness in Lissa's jade-green eyes told me she knew. Thanks to a law she was trying to change, Lissa's throne required her to have one living relative. Anyone wanting to remove Lissa would have simply had to kill Jill and show proof. The fact that it hadn't happened yet was a blessing but also deepened the mystery around this. Why else would someone have taken Jill?

"Go home, Adrian," said Lissa gently. "We'll talk more

later—in private—if you want. Maybe we'll come up with some other options."

"Maybe," I agreed. But I didn't really believe it.

I left Lissa to her admirers and slipped back out through the gawking crowd, as a dark and all-too-familiar mood began to settle on me. Going to Lissa had been an impulse, one that had given me momentary hope. When Sydney and I had sought sanctuary, we'd had no idea what was about to happen to Jill. It was true that Lissa had good people looking for Jill—and even the reluctant help of Sydney's old organization, the Alchemists. Still, I couldn't shake the guilt-ridden feeling that if Sydney and I were out there, instead of hiding away, we'd find Jill. There was something going on that we didn't understand yet. Otherwise, Jill's abductors would have—

"Well, well, well. Look who decided to show his cowardly face."

I came to a halt and blinked, barely aware of where I was. My thoughts had been churning so furiously that I'd made it halfway home and now stood on a stone path that cut between two buildings—a quiet, out-of-the-way path that was perfect for an ambush. Wesley Drozdov, a royal Moroi who'd become a nemesis of mine recently, stood blocking my way, with several cronies around him.

"That's more than you usually travel with, Wes," I said mildly. "Dig up a few more, and maybe you'll finally have a fair fight to—"

A fist struck me from behind, in my lower back, knocking the wind out of me and causing me to stumble forward. Wesley surged toward me and caught me with a right hook before I could respond. I realized dimly, through my pain, that the

15

comment I'd been about to make to him was actually spot-on: Wesley was traveling with a group because it was the only way he could combat my spirit magic. As someone's foot struck my knee, forcing me to the ground, I realized I had, in fact, been an idiot to reveal myself so publicly. Wesley had been waiting for a chance to get back at me for past grievances, and now he had it.

"What's the matter?" Wesley asked, kicking me hard in the stomach as I lay on the ground, struggling to get up. "Your feeder wife not here to save you?"

"Yeah," someone else chided. "Where's your human whore?"

I couldn't respond through the pain. More kicks followed, from more people than I could keep track of. Their faces swam above me, and I was shocked to recognize a number of them. They weren't all Wesley's usual tagalongs. Some of them were people I knew, had partied with in the past . . . people I might have once counted as friends.

A blow to my head caused stars to dance before my eyes, momentarily blurring their faces in my vision. Their taunts blended into an unintelligible cacophony as hit followed upon hit. I curled up in agony, struggling to breathe. Suddenly, through the din, a clear voice demanded, "What the hell is going on?"

Blinking, trying to bring the world back into focus, I just barely saw strong hands rip Wesley away and hurl him against the side of a nearby building. It took a second and then a third of his toadies following suit before they realized something had gone wrong. They backed away like the scared sheep they were, and a familiar face suddenly appeared as Eddie Castile stood over me.

"Anyone else feel like sticking around?" I croaked. "You still outnumber us."

Their numbers were nothing compared to one Eddie, and they knew it. I couldn't see them all run off, but I imagined it, and it was glorious. Silence fell, and a moment later, someone else was helping me stand. I glanced back and saw another familiar face, Neil Raymond, slipping his arm through mine.

"Can you walk?" asked Neil, his voice lightly touched by a British accent.

I winced as I put weight on my foot but nodded. "Yeah. Let's just get home now and see if anything's broken later. Thanks, by the way," I added, as Eddie supported my other side and we began to walk. "Nice to know this Moroi-in-distress can count on such gallant knights to follow me around."

Eddie shook his head. "Total coincidence, actually. We just happened to be on our way to your place with some news."

A chill ran through me, and I stopped my halting steps. "What news?" I demanded.

A smile crossed Eddie's features. "Relax—it's good news. I think. Just unexpected. You and Sydney have a visitor at the front gate. A human visitor."

If I hadn't been in so much pain, my jaw would've dropped. That *was* unexpected news. In marrying me and seeking sanctuary among the Moroi, Sydney had cut herself off from most of her human contacts. One of them showing up here was weird, and it couldn't be an Alchemist. An Alchemist would've been turned away.

"Who is it?" I asked.

Eddie's smile turned into an outright grin. "Jackie Terwilliger."

CHAPTER 2
SYDNEY

"OH, ADRIAN."

There was nothing more I could say as I helped wipe blood and dirt from Adrian's face with a damp cloth, brushing aside wayward pieces of chestnut hair. He gave me his devil-may-care smile and still managed to look dashing, despite his bedraggled state.

"Hey, don't sound so down, Sage. It wasn't that hopeless of a fight." He glanced over at Neil and said in a stage whisper, "Right? Tell her it wasn't that hopeless of a fight. Tell her I really held my own."

Neil managed a wan smile, but Adrian's mother spoke before he could. "Adrian, dear, this is no time for jokes."

My vampire mother-in-law and I didn't agree on many things, but this was a topic we were in perfect harmony about. The pall from our earlier fight still hung over us, and I couldn't help but feel a little guilty that I hadn't worked harder to get him to stay. At the very least, I should've told him to bring a guardian, since this wasn't his first encounter with troublemakers. Usually, guardians only accompanied Moroi out in the world, where Strigoi were a real danger. But here, with the rest of Adrian's people thinking we were freaks of nature for getting married, antagonism hit a little closer to home. We'd faced plenty of threats and slander, though never outright violence before. It was a stroke of good—albeit weird—luck that Eddie and Neil had found him.

Eddie was gone, having hurried off to the front gates to escort Ms. Terwilliger to us. It was a sign of my distress over Adrian's condition that I'd barely spared a moment to ponder what in the world could've brought my former history teacher and magical mentor to the royal stronghold of a secretive race of vampires. Even though some troubled part of me worried her visit couldn't be for any good reason, I still couldn't help but be excited at the prospect of seeing her. It had been months since we'd been together in person. I loved Adrian and didn't mind Daniella—but was dying for some other sort of interaction.

"Nothing's broken," Adrian insisted. "I probably won't even have a scar from any of this. Too bad. I think a well-placed scar right about here"—he touched the side of his face—"could really accentuate my already-perfect cheekbones while adding a rugged touch of manliness to my features. Not that I need any more manliness—"

"Adrian, enough," I said wearily. "I'm just glad you're okay. That could've been a lot worse. And you should still see a doctor after this, just to be safe."

He looked as though he had another snarky comment ready and then, wisely, said, "Yes, dear."

He attempted an angelic expression that only strengthened

my suspicion that he had no intention of actually following through. I shook my head, smiling in spite of myself, and then gave him a kiss on the cheek. Adrian. My husband. If anyone had told me a year ago that I'd be married, I would've said they were joking. If they'd told me I'd be married to a vampire, I would've said they were delusional. Looking at Adrian now, I felt a surge of love well up within me, despite our earlier tension. I could no longer imagine a life without him in it. It was impossible. Could I imagine a life with him that didn't involve us being trapped in a suite of rooms with his mother while both our peoples reviled us and made plans against us? Definitely. There were any number of futures I'd love to have for us, but this was our current path until something spectacular happened. Outside the Court's gates, my people wanted to imprison me. Inside them, his people wanted to assault him. At least in this suite, we were safe. Most importantly, we were together.

A knock at the door saved Adrian from any more chastisement. Daniella opened it, and Eddie appeared in the doorway. Seeing him almost always brought a smile to my face. In Palm Springs, we'd passed ourselves off as twins, sharing similar dark blond hair and brown eyes. But over time, he'd truly come to feel like a brother to me. I knew few others with such courage and loyalty. I was proud to call him my friend, and as such, it hurt me to see all the pain he felt over Jill's disappearance. There was always a haunted look about him now, and sometimes I worried whether he was really taking care of himself. He hardly ever shaved anymore, and I had a feeling the only reason he bothered eating was so that he could keep training and stay in shape for when he located Jill's abductors.

But my concerns for Eddie were put on hold when I saw the next person entering our suite. I sprinted across the room and wrapped her in a big embrace that caught her by surprise. Ms. Terwilliger—I could never bring myself to call her Jackie, even if I wasn't her student anymore—had changed my life in so many ways. She'd taken on the role my father used to have: teaching me secrets of an ancient art. Unlike him, though, she never made me feel bad about myself. She'd encouraged me and supported me, making me feel worthwhile and capable, even if I wasn't always perfect. She and I had communicated by phone since I'd come to Court, but it wasn't until now that I realized how much I'd missed her.

"My, my," she said with a chuckle, trying to return the hug. "I didn't expect such a welcome." Her efforts were made a little awkward due to the fact that she was holding a satchel in one hand and what looked like a small animal carrier in the other.

"Will you finally let me take this?" insisted Eddie, pulling the carrier from her. She yielded it, allowing for a proper hug. The mingled scents of patchouli and nag champa surrounded her, reminding me of more carefree times, when she and I would huddle together to work on spells. I felt tears spring to my eyes and quickly stepped back to wipe them away.

"I'm glad you're here," I said, trying to become businesslike again. "Surprised, but glad. This couldn't have been an easy trip for you."

"What I have to say could only be said in person." She pushed her glasses up her nose and surveyed the others in the room. "Neil, nice to see you again. And Adrian, I'm glad Sydney finally made an honest man of you."

He grinned at that and introduced Daniella. She was polite

21

but remained a little aloof. Moroi like her, who generally lived secluded lives at Court, didn't have many human friends. The whole concept of magic-using humans was just as weird for Moroi as for Alchemists, but I had to give Daniella credit for trying to come to terms with it all. She might have terrible timing and not be able to take a hint during would-be romantic interludes, but I couldn't deny that her life had also certainly undergone a lot of upheaval in the last year.

"Come in, come in," I said, beckoning Ms. Terwilliger forward. We received so few guests that I'd nearly forgotten basic hospitality. "Sit down, and I'll get you something to drink. Or eat?"

She shook her head as she went with me toward the kitchen. The others followed, except for Eddie, still awkwardly holding the carrier. "I'm fine," she said. "And we may not have the time. As it is, I hope I'm not too late."

Her words made the hairs on my neck rise, but before I could respond, Eddie cleared his throat and lifted the carrier, which I could now see held a cat. "Um, would you like me to do anything special with her?"

"Him," corrected Ms. Terwilliger. "And Mr. Bojangles will be just fine waiting in there while we talk. Besides, if I'm correct, we're going to need him."

Adrian shot me a questioning look at that, but I could only shrug in response.

We all gathered around the kitchen table. I sat, and Adrian stood behind me, resting his hands on my shoulder. In my peripheral vision, the rubies and white gold of his wedding band glittered. Ms. Terwilliger took the spot opposite me and produced an ornate wooden box from her satchel. It was covered in a floral design that appeared to have been hand-carved. She set the box on the table's surface and slid it over to me.

"What's this?" I asked.

"I was hoping you could tell me," she said. "It arrived a few weeks ago, left on my doorstep. At first, I thought it was some sort of gift from Malachi—even though this isn't his style."

"Right," agreed Adrian. "Grenades, camo vests . . . those are his usual gifts of choice." Malachi Wolfe was a questionably stable self-defense instructor Adrian and I had taken classes with and who had inexplicably won Ms. Terwilliger's heart.

She smiled briefly at Adrian's comment but never took her eyes from the box as she continued. "I soon learned the box is magically sealed. I tried all sorts of unlocking spells, common and rare, with no luck. Whoever did this cast something extremely powerful. I spent the last few weeks exhausting my resources and finally took it to Inez. You remember her, of course?"

"She's hard to forget," I said, thinking back on the venerable and quirky old witch back in California who had decorated every single item in her house with roses.

"Indeed. She told me she had a powerful spell that could probably bust it open but I'd failed because this enchantment is keyed to a specific person." Ms. Terwilliger looked chagrined. "I hadn't detected that. Obviously, that person isn't me. Inez speculated whoever the box was intended for would be able to open it with little difficulty, and from there, I concluded that *you* were the recipient."

I started at that. "But why would they give it to you for me?"

Ms. Terwilliger glanced around with a wry look. "This isn't

exactly an easy address to deliver to. I just wish I'd learned this sooner. Hopefully, whatever's inside isn't time sensitive."

I regarded the box in a new light, feeling myself fill with both eagerness and trepidation. "What should I do?"

"Open it," said Ms. Terwilliger simply. "Although I'd advise the rest of you to step back."

Daniella complied quickly, but Adrian and the dhampirs obstinately stayed put. "Do what she says," I said.

"What if it's a bomb?" demanded Eddie.

"I can most likely minimize any damage to Sydney but make no guarantees to the rest of you," said Ms. Terwilliger.

"'Most likely'?" asked Adrian. "Maybe this is the Alchemists' way of finally getting to you."

"Maybe, but they're not fans of human magic. I can't imagine they'd turn to it." I sighed. "Please. Just move back. I'll be fine."

I didn't know that for sure, but after a little more coaxing, the guys yielded. Ms. Terwilliger took out a small pouch and sprinkled a yellow, spicy-smelling powder on the table. She murmured a Greek incantation, and I felt magic—my kind of magic—burn in the air around us. It had been a very long time since I'd sensed it in another, and I was surprised at the rush it gave me. With the protective spell in place, she nodded encouragingly at me.

"Go ahead, Sydney. If just opening it doesn't work, then try a basic unlocking spell."

I rested my fingertips on the lid and took a deep breath. Nothing happened when I lifted it, but that was to be expected. Even if Ms. Terwilliger was right about this being intended for me, that didn't mean it was going to be entirely easy. As

I summoned the words of an unlocking spell, the obvious questions nagged at the edges of my mind: Was this really for me? If so, from whom? And most importantly, why?

I spoke the spell, and though the box didn't change, we all heard a small *pop* sound. I tried the lid again, and this time it lifted easily. Even better, no bomb went off inside. After a moment of hesitation, the guys all crowded forward to see what the box held. Looking down, I saw some folded pieces of paper with a single hair on top. I lifted it carefully, holding it up to the light. It was blond.

"Probably yours," said Ms. Terwilliger. "To key a spell like this to a specific person, you need something that's part of the recipient. Hair. Nail. Skin."

I wrinkled my nose at that as I opened up the first piece of paper and tried not to think about how someone would have obtained one of my hairs. The paper turned out to be a flyer for a robot museum in Pittsburgh. That would've been comical if not for the chilling words written over the picture of one of the museum's featured exhibits, the Raptorbot 2000: *COME PLAY, SYDNEY.* My breath caught, and I looked up sharply. Everyone else looked as bewildered as I felt. The writing was none I recognized.

"What's the other piece of paper?" asked Neil.

It too was folded and had a sheen to it, like it was from a magazine. At a glance, it appeared to be some sort of travel ad. I opened it up and found myself looking at a picture of a bed-and-breakfast in Palo Alto. "What's this have to do with a robot museum in Pittsburgh?"

Ms. Terwilliger stiffened. "I don't think that's the page you're meant to see."

I flipped the paper over and gasped at what—or more importantly, whom—I saw.

Jill.

I'd nearly forgotten about this ad. Ages ago—or at least it felt that way—Jill had briefly done some modeling for a Palm Springs fashion designer. I should've never allowed it, seeing what a security breach it was. The picture I now looked at was one that had been done in secret, against my wishes. Jill wore a pair of large, gilt sunglasses and a peacock-colored scarf wrapped around her abundant curly hair. She was gazing off at a cluster of palm trees, and unless someone knew her well, it would be difficult to realize this was her. In fact, it would be difficult for most people to even recognize she was Moroi.

"What the hell is this?" demanded Eddie. He looked as though he might rip the page away from me. Few things could make him lose his cool and collected nature. Jill's safety was one of them.

I shook my head in disbelief. "Your guess is as good as mine."

Adrian leaned over me and picked up the first page. "Surely it doesn't mean Jill's being held prisoner at some robot museum? In Pittsburgh?"

"We have to go," said Eddie fiercely. He turned as though he might walk out the door then and there.

"*I* have to go," I said, pointing at the flyer Adrian held. "The box was intended for me. This note is even addressed to me."

"You're not going alone," Eddie retorted.

"You're not going anywhere," said Adrian. He set the paper back down. "Before my little, uh, fallout with Wesley, I had a chat with Her Majesty, who made it very clear you and I are not allowed to leave Court."

Sorrow and guilt filled me as I gazed at Jill's profile. Jill. Missing for almost a month. We'd waited desperately for some lead, and now it had come to us. But as Ms. Terwilliger had speculated: Was it too late? What had happened while this box sat around?

"I have to," I said. "There's no way I can ignore this. Adrian, you know that."

Our eyes met. So many feelings churned between us, and he finally nodded. "I do."

"You don't think Lissa would really forcibly have security stop me?"

He sighed. "I don't know. But she—correctly—pointed out that after all the trouble we gave her by staying here, it'd cause even more if you left and were caught by the Alchemists. We could try to sneak out . . . but I wouldn't be surprised if they're checking cars at the gates."

"I thought something like that might be going on," said Ms. Terwilliger. She'd overcome her shock and was slipping into her let's-get-things-done mode, which I found immensely reassuring. "Which is why I came prepared. I have a way to smuggle you out, Sydney, if you're willing." Her gaze lifted to Adrian. "Just Sydney, I'm afraid."

"No way," he said promptly. "If she goes, I go."

"No," I said slowly. "She's right."

His eyebrows rose. "Look, you risk a lot more than I do by going out there. I'm not going to let you go and endanger yourself while I stay safe, so don't—"

"It's not that," I interrupted. A moment later, I amended that. "I mean, I want you safe, yes, but listen to what you just said. If I go out there, I risk more because the Alchemists are looking for me. Except they aren't looking right now because they think I'm safely locked away with you. And so long as they keep thinking that, they aren't going to be actively looking for me. No one sees me here around Court, but they do see you every once in a while for feeder visits. If we both suddenly disappear, word might get out to the Alchemists that we've left. But if people still see you . . ."

Adrian grimaced. "Then they'll think you're still here too, just hiding away from the mean vampires."

"You'd be part of my cover," I said, placing my hand over his. "I know you don't like that, but this really would help. It'd let me move around more freely in the world and try to figure out how that"—I nodded at the robot flyer—"is tied to Jill."

He took a few moments to answer. I could tell he knew the truth of my argument—but still didn't like it. "It just bothers me to think of you out there alone while I sit around."

"She won't be alone," said Eddie. "I don't have any assignment, and no one's after me. I can come and go freely from Court."

"Me too," said Neil.

"One of you needs to stay with Adrian," I argued. "Just in case there's another repeat of today. Neil, would you? And Eddie, you'll come with me to check this out?"

I made it sound like a request, a favor even, but knew there was nothing on earth Eddie would rather do right now than search for Jill.

"Here's the deal," said Adrian, once the dhampirs had agreed. "I'll stay here and cover for you, but as soon as there's a way I can join you without blowing our cover, I will."

I met his eyes again, wishing I could tell him so much. Like that I was sorry about our earlier fight, that I wasn't trying to control him. I was worried. I loved him so much that I just wanted him to be safe. I hoped he knew all of that. All I could do now, with so many witnesses, was nod in agreement.

Ms. Terwilliger regarded us all with dry amusement. "Has everyone decided which brave roles they'll be taking on?" she asked. She shot me a smile. "You don't seem very concerned about how I plan on getting you out of here yet, Sydney."

I shrugged. "I have faith in you, ma'am. If you say you've got a way, I believe it. What's it involve?"

After she told me, silence fell in the room. We all stared at her, dumbfounded, until Adrian finally spoke. "Wow," he said. "I can't say I saw that coming."

"I don't think anyone could have," admitted Eddie.

Ms. Terwilliger's focus was on me. "Are you up for it, Sydney?"

I swallowed. "I guess I have to be. And we shouldn't waste any more time."

"First," said Adrian, "can I have a word with my wife before the hilarity ensues?"

"Of course," said Ms. Terwilliger, gesturing grandly.

Adrian steered me away and called to the others, "Talk amongst yourselves." He led me to our bedroom, not saying anything else until the door shut behind us. "Sydney, you realize this is crazy, right? And I don't say that lightly."

I smiled and drew him to me. "I know. But we both also know there's no way I can't *not* follow a lead that might take us to Jill."

His expression darkened. "I wish I could do more than be your cover," he said. "But if that's what it takes . . ." He sighed.

"What also seems crazy is you leaving after we fought so hard to get here and be together."

"Yeah, but . . ." I hesitated, hating to say my next words. "You can't say this has exactly been what we imagined."

"What do you mean?" he asked, but I could tell he already knew.

"Adrian, there's no question I love you and want a life with you. But this particular life . . . hiding away from both our people . . . having your mother hovering over us . . . I don't know. Maybe some space is a good thing."

His green eyes widened. "You want to get away from me?"

"No, of course not! But I want to revaluate things, to figure out how we can get that life we've been wanting." I sighed. "And of course, even more than that . . ."

"We need to find Jill," he finished.

I nodded and rested my head on his chest, listening to the steady rhythm of his heartbeat. That earlier emotion rose up within me as I thought about the last year and all we'd gone through. We'd had to keep our relationship a secret, and then once it was discovered, the Alchemists had held me prisoner and tried to brainwash me into coming back into their fold. Every moment I had now with Adrian was a precious gift, but reveling in that, turning my back on Jill . . . well, that would be selfish.

"Finding her is bigger than us right now," I said.

"I know," he said, pressing a kiss to my forehead. "And part of why I love you is that there's no question you have to do this. And that you'd let me if our roles were reversed."

"It's what we do," I said simply.

"I swear it, as soon as I feel like I can sneak out safely, I'll come to you. You won't be alone."

I touched my heart. "I never am. I always feel you in here."

He brought his lips down to mine in a long, exquisite kiss, the kind that sent heat all the way to my fingers and toes and made me very conscious of the fact that there was a bed behind us. I pulled back before we accidentally got distracted.

"I'll be back before you know it," I said, giving him one more hug. "And if all goes as planned, Jill will be with me."

"If all goes as planned," he countered, "we'll get a call any minute now that whoever's holding her has released her after the law change and she's on her way home."

I smiled at that, but there was no true joy in it. "That would be nice."

We kissed again and returned to the others. I realized then that although Adrian and I were on good terms again, we hadn't exactly resolved the fight from before. There were still a lot of issues to deal with—the biggest one being his continued flirtation with spirit. I'd missed my chance, and now I could only hope for the best with him.

Meanwhile, Ms. Terwilliger had already made herself busy converting our kitchen into a spell workshop. Bottles and bags of components were set out on the table, and she was busily boiling water on the stove. She sprinkled something into it, and the steam soon took on the fragrance of star anise.

"Good, good," she said, barely looking up. "You're back. Would you measure two teaspoons of that beetroot powder for me?"

I fell in beside her and had a brief sense of déjà vu. It was easy, momentarily, to feel like I had slipped back into those old days together. Not that they'd been exactly stress free. Learning magic from her had been difficult both mentally and physically, and I'd always had the added pressures of my struggles with Adrian and the others. Still, the familiarity was nice, particularly since I'd missed this sort of magic-working. I still practiced but rarely cast anything of this magnitude here at Court. The spell she had in mind to make my escape work required both of us and a few hours of labor. Adrian and the others tried to distract themselves as best they could, and Eddie left once to grab an overnight bag, since none of us knew exactly what would happen in Pittsburgh.

Jill, I hoped silently. *Please just let us get to that robot museum and find Jill there selling tickets.*

Somehow, I doubted it'd be that easy.

Around four in the morning, Ms. Terwilliger and I completed our work. This was still practically midday on the vampiric schedule, which I'd adjusted to, but she was showing signs of fatigue. I knew she was dying for coffee, but caffeine reduced the effectiveness of magic, and she'd had to cast small spells along the way. The final one in the process was mine, however, and as the end neared, I began to question just what I was about to do.

"Maybe it would be easier to just smuggle me in the trunk," I said, holding a cup of the brew we'd crafted.

"Good chance they'll be searching cars as you leave," said Adrian. "Especially hers. Lissa made it clear she didn't want us leaving."

I started to carry the potion over to where Ms. Terwilliger was setting up a mirror. A new worry fell over me. "Do you think she'll let me back in when she finds out I left?"

No one had an answer for that right away until Ms. Terwilliger said pragmatically, "We can always get you back in the same way we're getting you out."

I grimaced and glanced down at the cup in my hands, wondering how I'd feel about that later. In the living room, Ms. Terwilliger had helpfully propped up a full-length mirror from Daniella's bedroom. She now hauled the pet carrier over to it and opened the door. A white cat with tabby patches—Mr. Bojangles—came out and calmly sat in front of the mirror. If I hadn't known any better, I would've said he was admiring himself.

"You know the words?" asked Ms. Terwilliger.

I nodded and knelt down by the cat. I'd memorized the spell throughout our work time today. "Anything I should know before this happens?"

"Just remember to look at the cat once the spell is cast," Ms. Terwilliger said.

I glanced at the others one last time. "See you soon, I guess."

"Good luck," said Neil.

Adrian met my eyes for a long moment, saying nothing aloud yet somehow conveying a million messages. I felt a lump form in my throat as that earlier sentiment returned. We'd fought so hard to get here, and here I was, walking away. *Not walking away*, I told myself. *Going to save Jill*. What Adrian and I had talked about earlier was true. We loved each other but weren't so selfish about our love that we could simply turn our backs on someone we cared about.

I gave him a small smile and then drank the potion. It had a faintly peppery taste, not entirely unpleasant but also not something I'd really drink for fun. When the cup was empty, I set it aside and then focused on the mirror—particularly the cat's reflection beside mine. Mr. Bojangles was still sitting contentedly, and I assumed Ms. Terwilliger had picked this particular cat for his good nature. I called upon the magic within me, tuning out the rest of the world and focusing only on the spell at hand. I spoke the Latin words, still gazing at the cat. Aside from the physical labor involved, the spell required a fair amount of personal strength, and when I finished speaking, I felt exhausted as the magic surged through me and went to work.

My eyes were on the cat, but slowly, my vision of him changed. In fact, my eyesight changed completely. The cat's orange color muted to gray in my vision while the pattern on his coat suddenly sharpened. I noticed more nuance and detail in the tabby pattern than I had before. Meanwhile, everything looked incredibly bright, as though the lights had been turned up. I blinked a few times to try to clear up that sensation and noticed I was getting closer and closer to the ground. Something fell over my face, obscuring my sight, and I wiggled out from under it. It was my shirt. Looking back at the mirror, I found myself regarding the reflections of two cats.

One of them was me.

"Well, I'll be damned."

I didn't recognize the voice as Adrian's right away. I was still human enough to understand language, but my new ears processed sounds in an entirely different way. In particular, I heard more of them, and ordinary noises from before seemed louder. I had little time to ponder this as two hands suddenly scooped me up and pushed me into the cat carrier. The door shut.

"We don't want to get them mixed up," Ms. Terwilliger said.

"Where are you going to put the other one?" asked Daniella.

"Wherever you like," said Ms. Terwilliger. "I can't take him with me. The guards saw me come in with one cat. They'll see me leave with one."

"What?" My mother-in-law's voice came out extra shrill to my ears. "That creature's staying?" It figured. Her daughter-in-law transforming into an animal? No problem. Having to take care of a cat? Crisis.

"I'll pick you guys up a litter box and some cat food," said Neil helpfully.

Through the metal grating on my carrier door, Adrian's face suddenly appeared, peering in at me. "What's new, pussycat? You okay in there?"

Out of habit, I tried to answer, but all that came out was a half meow.

The world suddenly whirled around me as the carrier lifted in the air, forcing me to scramble to keep my balance with both feet and senses that were foreign. "No time for chitchat," said Ms. Terwilliger. "We need to move."

Adrian must have followed her because his face appeared again through the door. "Be careful, Sage. I love you."

Ms. Terwilliger and Eddie made their farewells and headed out the door. We walked through the building and then outside. I knew from an earlier clock that it was still nighttime, but the world I was able to see through the gaps in the carrier looked wholly different from what I was used to. The scattered lampposts more than lit up the darkness to my enhanced vision, and even if I didn't see a full range of colors, I could see much farther than my human eyes ever could have. We had at least an hour on the spell's longevity, but my companions kept up a good pace, walking briskly through the Court's grounds to visitor parking.

There, Ms. Terwilliger reclaimed the rental car she'd driven in and set my carrier in the backseat. It gave me a poor view of our surroundings but still allowed me to hear everything. At the main gate, guardians interrogated Ms. Terwilliger about her visit, wanting to know why Eddie was with her.

"I'm currently on leave," he responded in a way that was brisk but not defensive. "I've got personal matters to take care of, and she offered me a ride."

"I know the roads outside your Court aren't always friendly in the dark," Ms. Terwilliger added. "So I don't mind the company."

"Wait, and the sun'll be up in less than an hour," said the guardian.

"No time," she replied. "I have a flight to catch."

As Adrian had predicted, the guardians searched the car thoroughly, and I heard one of them whisper to the other, "Make sure there are no stowaways."

My anxiety rose, and I found myself experiencing the strange sensation of whipping my tail back and forth.

A dhampir face appeared before me, and he made some clicking sounds. "Hey, kitty, kitty."

I made no response, afraid it might come out as a hiss.

The guardians finally cleared us, and like that, we were on the road, free of the place that had been both a sanctuary and prison for the last month. Ms. Terwilliger drove us another half hour to put distance between us and Court, and then pulled the car off on the shoulder of a rural highway. Once parked, she opened up the carrier so that I could come out onto the backseat, and she set a pile of clothes beside me. Beyond her, I could barely discern the sky lightening.

"There you go," she said, moving back to the front seat. "I should probably have told you before . . . it's a lot easier going into this spell than it is coming out of it."

CHAPTER 3

ADRIAN

MINUTES FELT LIKE HOURS AFTER SYDNEY'S DEPARTURE. I paced the length of our small suite, a knot in my chest, as I braced myself for the worst. Any second now, I feared, I would get word that the plan had gone awry and guardians had intercepted Sydney trying to escape Court.

"Darling, must you do that?" my mother asked at last. "You're agitating the animals."

I paused and glanced down to where Mr. Bojangles was keeping a wary eye on Hopper—the small, enchanted dragon that Sydney had summoned earlier this year. Hopper had become a pet of sorts and was regarding the cat with an excitement that clearly wasn't reciprocated.

"I don't think it's me, Mom. They're just—"

A chime from my phone interrupted me, and I dove for it, startling both cat and dragon. On my phone's display, a text message from Eddie was clear and succinct: *Made it out of Court. All is well.*

I texted back: *Am I still married to a cat?*

Yes, came the response, followed a moment later by: *But Ms. T swears it's temporary.*

Some of my anxiety lessened, but not all. I wrote: *Let me know when she's back.*

Twenty minutes later, a new message came in, this one from Sydney herself: *Back in human form. Everything seems to be normal.*

Everything? I questioned.

Well, aside from a weird urge to chase laser pointers, she responded.

If that's the worst effect, I'll take it. Keep me posted. I love you.

I meow you too, she wrote back. It was promptly corrected with: *I mean, I love you.*

I smiled as I put the phone away but found I was still a long way from feeling as though all was right in the world. I couldn't shake the feeling that things weren't entirely settled between Sydney and me, and that wasn't even taking into consideration the physical threats she now faced. She'd made it outside of Court . . . but was now potentially facing all the same dangers that had driven us to seek sanctuary here.

Only if they know she's out, Aunt Tatiana's voice reminded me, in a rare moment of legitimate helpfulness. *As long as no one's looking for her—and she doesn't get discovered—she'll be safe. So don't blow it.*

Right, I agreed. *And no one will have any reason to think she's not here. She never leaves our suite, and we don't really have that many visitors.*

Later that day, of course, we had a visitor.

Thankfully, it wasn't a regiment of guardians demanding to know Sydney's whereabouts. Instead, I found Sonya Karp Tanner standing outside our door, smiling when she saw me. Whatever relief I found at seeing her was quashed by an anxious Aunt Tatiana.

Don't let your guard down at any cost! she hissed.

Sonya's our friend, I silently replied.

Aunt Tatiana disagreed. *It doesn't matter. No one can know Sydney's gone, no matter how friendly you think they are. All it takes is one little slip, no matter how good the intention. The fewer the people who know a secret, the better.*

With a pang, I realized she was right. Meanwhile, Sonya's congenial expression had turned puzzled as I conducted my mental conversation with a phantom.

"Are you okay, Adrian?" asked Sonya.

"Fine, fine," I said, beckoning her in. "Just tired. I had kind of a rough morning." I gestured vaguely at my face, which still bore the signs of scuffling with Wesley and his crew.

As I'd hoped, Sonya was effectively deflected. Concern lit her features. "What happened?"

"Oh, the usual. Just some idiots jealous of me being married to the hottest human around."

"Where is she?" asked Sonya, glancing around the empty suite. "And your mother?"

"Mom went to bed," I replied. "And Sydney . . . she's out for a walk."

Sonya's sharp eyes focused back on me. "She's out after you were attacked this morning?"

"Well, it's daylight out, so there's less of a threat. And . . .

Neil's with her." I nearly said Eddie but wasn't sure if Sonya might have heard about him leaving Court. Knowing my luck now, Neil would stop by unannounced and ruin the story. "She needed some air," I added, seeing Sonya's skeptical look. "Staying cooped up inside is really getting to her." That, at least, wasn't a lie.

Sonya held my gaze a few more moments before finally deciding to let the topic go. She could probably tell from my aura and body language that I wasn't being entirely honest, but it was unlikely she could guess the truth—that Sydney had transformed into a cat and been smuggled out of Court in a far-fetched attempt to find Jill.

"Well, it's you I came to see," Sonya said at last. "I need to discuss something with you. Or rather someone."

I sat down at our kitchen table and nodded for her to do the same. Discuss someone? I could do that, as long as it wasn't Sydney. "Who do you have in mind?" I asked.

Sonya laced her fingers together and took a deep breath. "Nina Sinclair."

I winced. Perhaps not as problematic as Sydney right now, but Nina was by no means a welcome topic. She was a spirit user, like me, one I'd been pretty good friends with while Sydney had been in captivity. Unfortunately, Nina had wanted to be *much* better friends and had been reading more into our relationship than there was. She'd taken my rejection badly—and had responded even worse when she found out I'd married a human. On the rare times I'd passed her since returning to Court, I was constantly reminded of the old "if looks could kill" adage.

"What about Nina?" I asked carefully. "Is she still working for you?"

Sonya was the leader on a project attempting to use spirit to prevent people from turning Strigoi. Nina had inadvertently helped with this initially when she'd restored her sister, Olive, from being a Strigoi. With several of us working together, we'd managed to transfer that spirit magic to Neil's blood, effectively creating a vaccine that protected Neil from ever being forcibly turned. Sonya's victory had been short-lived, however, as she was unable to replicate that effect in anyone else. But she was still tirelessly working toward that goal.

"Technically, yes, but it's been a while since she truly offered anything of value." Sonya's expression darkened. "Nina's been a little . . . off lately."

I couldn't help a small laugh at that. "We're spirit users. We're *all* a little off."

Sonya didn't return my smile. "Not like this. If you could see her . . . well, you'd understand. I sent her home yesterday because she wasn't making any sense. She also looked as though she hadn't slept in weeks. The only spirit user I've seen in such bad shape was . . . well, the time I interviewed Avery Lazar."

That drew me up short. Avery, another spirit user, was currently in the mental facility of a Moroi prison. "Avery used ridiculous amounts of spirit," I reminded her. "I mean, *ridiculous*. And on a regular basis." Bringing back Jill had taken its toll on me, temporarily draining me of spirit, but it had been a one-time thing. Avery had attempted a number of high-power feats, over and over, landing her in her current state when her mind finally couldn't take any more. "Nina would have to be doing some pretty serious magic to end up like that."

"That's exactly what I'm afraid of," said Sonya grimly.

I gasped, thinking of Avery. "That she's trying to acquire shadow-kissed bondmates?"

"No, not that . . . but something that takes almost as much power and is being done on a regular basis. Whenever I try to get an answer out of her, she evades me or just starts babbling nonsense." Sonya sighed. "I'm worried about her, Adrian. She needs help, but she won't talk to me."

As the pointed silence grew, I suddenly caught on to what Sonya was getting at. "What? You think she'll talk to *me*?"

Sonya shrugged. "I don't know who else to ask."

"Well, not me!" I exclaimed. "She was furious when I turned her down. If she's got something going on and needs help, I'm not the one she's going to turn to. You need to ask someone else."

"There *is* no one else! Her sister's still missing. And did you know Nina quit her office job? Or . . . actually, I think she was fired, but it's hard to get a straight answer out of her. As far as I know, you and I are the only ones around who care about what she's doing to herself—and we need to step up and help her."

"She won't talk to me," I reiterated.

Sonya raked a hand through her dark red hair. "You might be surprised. Even though things . . . fell out . . . between you, she clearly still felt as though there was some connection. Please, Adrian. Please just try. If she sends you away, fine. So be it. I won't ask you again."

I started to say no once more, but a closer look at Sonya stopped me. She truly was agitated by this. It was in her voice and eyes . . . even in the colors of her aura. I knew Sonya wasn't the type to overreact. I also knew she wouldn't ask this of me if she wasn't truly concerned, especially since she was the one who'd advised me to stay away from Nina to protect her feelings.

I glanced at the time. It was growing late by our standards. Most Moroi would be going to bed. "Okay if I wait to see her until tomorrow?"

Sonya considered and then gave a small nod. "I'm sure that'll be fine. Of course, I'm also sure she probably won't be asleep anytime soon. But it may be best if you wait for Sydney to get back before leaving, so that Neil can accompany you."

For a moment, I nearly said that Eddie was with Sydney, not Neil, and then I remembered the cover story. I'd have to get in touch with Neil to make sure he backed up what I said. If I wasn't careful, things could get very complicated very quickly. It was what I hated most about lying: It rarely stayed simple.

"Sounds good," I said, standing as Sonya did. "I'll let you know how it goes."

"Thank you. I know this isn't—" She bit her words off as Mr. Bojangles came tearing through the room, with Hopper in hot pursuit. Sonya turned to me, startled. "When did you get a cat?"

"Uh, today, actually. Jackie Terwilliger—Sydney's old teacher?—left it when she visited."

That was obviously news to Sonya. "She was here? At Court? How long did she stay?"

"Not long," I said, immediately wishing I hadn't mentioned it at all. "Just checking up on Sydney."

"That's a lot of effort just to check up on someone. A phone call would've been simpler."

I hoped I looked guileless. "Yeah, but then she wouldn't have been able to give us the cat. Belated wedding gift."

"Adrian," said Sonya, using the voice she must have used to chastise countless students when she was a high school biology teacher, "what aren't you telling me?"

"Nothing, nothing," I said, steering her to the door. "Relax, we're all fine. The only thing you need to worry about is how fast Nina's going to send me packing."

"Adrian—"

"Everything's fine," I said cheerily. I opened the door for her. "Thanks for stopping by. Say hi to Mikhail for me."

It was clear from her expression that I'd completely failed in convincing her of my innocence, but at least she looked like she wasn't going to compel me to tell her what was really going on—for now. We made our farewells, and I breathed a sigh of relief when she was gone, hoping no one else would come by and force me to fumble for another excuse about why Sydney wasn't around.

I went to bed soon thereafter and was awakened midday by a new text message from Sydney. She reported that she, Eddie, and Jackie had made it to Pittsburgh but wouldn't be truly investigating the museum until nightfall. She assured me everything was fine, and I assured her of the same, deciding it was probably best if she didn't know I'd agreed to go talk to a potentially crazy girl who was either in love with me or despised everything about me. Sydney had enough to worry about.

When the Moroi Court began waking up later in the day, I managed to get Neil to come back and walk me over to Nina's. It was early enough that not too many people were out, but I figured it was better to be safe than sorry. Neil, driven by duty, was happy to help me regardless, but I knew he had an ulterior interest in going with me to see Nina. Months ago, he and her sister, Olive, had had the beginnings of a romance blossoming. None of us were entirely sure how far it had gone, but things had ended abruptly when Olive had taken off with little contact with Nina and none with Neil. I doubted Nina had any new details on her sister's whereabouts, but Neil was probably hoping for some scrap of info.

The late summer sun was still well above the horizon, even around six, when we reached Nina's door. She lived in a section of bare-bones apartments inhabited by other Court employees (or ex-employees, as it turned out), far from the much more posh lodgings that royals like my father lived in. I took a deep breath as I stared at that door, summoning my courage.

"It won't get any easier if you put it off," Neil told me, unhelpfully.

"I know." Resolved, I gave two short raps to the door, secretly hoping Nina was asleep or not at home. Then I could honestly tell Sonya I'd tried and leave it at that. Unfortunately, Nina opened the door almost immediately, as though she'd been waiting right by it.

"Hello, Adrian," she said warily. Her gray eyes lifted beyond me. "Neil."

He gave a nod of greeting, but I was momentarily stunned. Nina didn't come from a rich or royal background, but that had never affected her beauty, and she'd always presented herself in an immaculate manner.

At least, she *used* to.

That Nina I'd known was nowhere in sight. Her dark, curly hair looked as though it hadn't been brushed recently. In fact, I wasn't sure it had been washed in a while either. A rumpled blue plaid skirt clashed with an orange T-shirt, over which she wore an inside-out gray cardigan. One of her feet was covered with a white ankle sock. Her other sock—adorned with red and white stripes—came up to her knee.

And yet, it wasn't the bizarre wardrobe choice that was most alarming; instead, it was the look on her face that told me Sonya hadn't been exaggerating. Dark circles hung under Nina's eyes, though the eyes themselves were bright and almost too alert, glittering feverishly. It was a look I'd seen before in spirit users pushed to the edge. It was a look I'd seen on Avery Lazar's face.

I swallowed. "Hello, Nina. Can we come in?"

Her eyes narrowed. "Why? So you can tell me again how totally unsuitable we are? So you can tell me how we can never, ever possibly work out—seeing as I'm not human and you apparently only hook up with people who double as dinner?"

My temper started to flare at the slight, but then I reminded myself that she wasn't well. "I'm sorry for what I said last time—I mean it. I'd met Sydney long before I met you. But that's not what I'm here to talk about. Please—can we come in?"

Nina stared at me wordlessly for a long time, and I used the opportunity to call on spirit and sneak a glimpse of her aura. Like Lissa's yesterday, Nina's aura was filled with the pale gold of a spirit user. Unlike Lissa's, however, Nina's gold had a weak, almost watery quality to it. It didn't burn like a flame. The other colors were equally frail, flickering in and out.

"Okay," she said at last.

She stepped aside and let us pass. What I found inside was nearly as disconcerting as her appearance. I'd been to her place before, back when she and I had done a lot of party-hopping together. The tiny apartment was actually more of a studio, with bedroom and living room merged into one. Despite the small size, Nina had always gone to great pains to keep her home tidy and well decorated. Much like the care given to her physical exterior, though, that upkeep seemed to be a thing of the past.

Crusty, smelly dishes were piled high in the kitchen sink, where a couple of flies buzzed lazily. Laundry, books, and cans of energy drink were piled everywhere—tables, floor, even the bed. Weirdest of all was a stack of magazines on the floor with a pile of shredded paper next to them.

"How do you sleep?" I asked, unable to help myself.

"I don't," she said, clasping her hands behind her back. "I don't. There's no time. I can't risk it."

"You have to sleep sometime," said Neil pragmatically.

She shook her head frantically. "I *can't*! I have to keep trying to find Olive. I mean, I've found her. Kind of. Depends on how you look at it. But I can't *get* to her, you see? That's the problem. That's why I have to keep trying. Why I can't sleep. Understand?"

I didn't understand at all, but Neil's breath had caught at the mention of Olive's name. "You've found her? You know where she is?"

"No," said Nina, sounding slightly irritated. "I just told you that."

Without warning, she flounced down on the floor beside the magazine pile. She picked a magazine up at random and began tearing it, page by page, into tiny little pieces, building up the pile of shreddings.

"What are you doing?" I asked.

"Thinking," she replied.

"No, I mean with the magazines."

"This helps me think," she explained.

Neil and I exchanged glances. "Nina," I said carefully, "I think maybe you should go visit a doctor. Neil and I can go with you, if you'd like."

"I *can't*," she protested, still methodically shredding the magazine. "Not until I reach Olive."

I crouched down beside her, wishing I had a better idea of how to talk to someone so clearly unstable. You'd think I'd be an expert. "How are you trying to reach her? By phone?"

"By dream," said Nina. "I succeeded. A couple of times. But then she blocked me. She turned the dream against me. I'm trying to fight through it, but I can't."

I could tell from Neil's expression that he was hoping that had made sense to me, but I was more confused than ever. A particularly resistant person *could* make it difficult for a spirit user to form a dream connection, but the rest made no sense. "Olive's not a spirit user," I told her. "She can't do anything to the dream without your permission. You wield the ultimate control."

"She can, she can, she can." Nina began tearing up the magazine with renewed energy. "Each time I try to talk to her, she throws up some obstacle! Things I never even thought of. Her nightmares, my nightmares. Someone's. I fight them. I do. Really, I do. But it takes so much spirit." She abruptly stopped the shredding and stared off into space bleakly. "It's exhausting. And by the time I get through, she's slipped away. She wakes herself up, and I can't talk to her. Can't ask her why she left me. Do you know?" Nina's eyes flitted from me to Neil. "Do you know why she left?"

"No," I said gently. "All I know is that you need some serious rest." I started to put a hand on her shoulder, and she jerked away, anger glinting in her eyes.

"Don't torment me," she said in a low voice. "Don't come here and act like you're my friend."

"I *am* your friend, Nina. No matter what happened—or didn't happen—between us, I'm your friend. I want to help you."

Her anger instantly flipped to despair. "No one can help me. No one can—Wait." Unexpectedly, she grabbed my arm, her fingers digging in with astonishing—and uncomfortable—strength. "Maybe you can help me. You're the best dreamer. Come with me the next time I visit Olive. Then you'll see—you'll see how she's controlling the dream! If we combine our powers, maybe we'll be strong enough to stop her! Then we can talk to her!"

I shook my head. "Nina, there's no way she can—"

Those fingers bit deeper into my arm. "She *is*, Adrian! Join me, and you'll see."

I thought carefully before responding. Nina was right about me being the best spirit dreamer (that we knew of), and I'd never seen any sign of a non–spirit user being able to take control of a dream. Nina clearly believed that was the case and that it was preventing her from making contact with Olive. I didn't dare say it, but I wondered if Nina had been using so much spirit lately that her control was faltering. That would explain why she was having difficulty forging a dream connection, and in her addled state, she'd come up with the idea that Olive was interfering.

Yes, but what has she been using so much spirit on? asked Aunt Tatiana.

It was a good question. Looking over Nina and her state of disarray, I found myself at a loss. Even if she tried to form a spirit dream connection with Olive every day, there was no way that alone could've driven Nina to this state. What else was she using magic on? Or was her mental deterioration being accelerated by something more than the magic? Was it a culmination of that and personal stress—like Olive's disappearance and my rejection?

"Adrian?" asked Neil tentatively. "Isn't there any way you'd consider helping?"

Not knowing my thoughts, he believed my hesitation was over a refusal to offer assistance. The truth was, I just didn't know how. And honestly, Nina needed a *lot* more than help with a spirit dream. She needed help with her life.

"Okay," I said at last. "I'll help you connect to her in a dream—but only if you get some sleep."

Immediately, Nina began shaking her head. "I can't. I'm too excited. I have to keep looking. I have to—"

"You *will* get some sleep," I ordered. "I'm getting Sonya here, and she's going to bring you a sedative. You will take it. And you will sleep."

"Later I will. Right now, we need to reach Olive. She's on a human schedule. She'll go to bed soon, and I can't be asleep. We'll reach her first and—"

"No. No deal." I made my voice as firm and harsh as I could. "If she's waited this long, she'll keep waiting. Sleep first. For God's sake, Nina! Look at yourself. You're—"

"What? What?" she demanded, that earlier feverish look returning. "A mess? Ugly? Not good enough for you?"

"Exhausted." I sighed. "Now, please. Let me call Sonya.

You'll sleep today, and we'll look for Olive tomorrow. If you're rested, you'll be better able to, uh, fight her control." I still didn't buy that, but Nina did, and she finally conceded.

"Okay," she said. "You can call Sonya."

I did, and Sonya was relieved to hear I'd made progress, small though it was. She promised to come over with something to help Nina sleep, and I promised to hang around until then. When I disconnected, Nina returned to her shredding and began humming what sounded like "Sweet Caroline."

"It's really nice of you to help her," Neil murmured, coming to stand beside me across the room. "Sleep will do her good. And for my own selfish reasons . . . well, I admit I'm eager for you to have contact with Olive too. Not that that's your primary reason for doing this."

"Hey, it's a good enough reason. They all are." I tried to keep my voice light, not letting on just how bothered I was by Nina's state. Because if I had to be honest, I wasn't doing this just for Neil, Sonya, or Nina. Watching Nina as she sat there humming, so clearly out of her mind . . . well, the truth was, it wasn't that hard to imagine myself in that state someday. And if it came to that, I hoped desperately that someone would help me too.

CHAPTER 4
SYDNEY

I DON'T RECOMMEND TURNING INTO A CAT.

The actual experience of being a cat isn't too bad. But coming out of it? Awful. I felt as though I were being torn in two. My bones and skin stretched and twisted in ways that nature had never intended, and when it was all over, I felt beaten and bruised—like the time I'd fallen down a full flight of stairs as a child. A vaguely nauseous feeling settled in the pit of my stomach, and for a panicked moment, I thought I would throw up. Forced vomiting had been one of many punishments the Alchemists had inflicted on me while I was in their captivity, and the very idea of it triggered a flood of unwelcome memories. Fortunately, the sensation soon passed, and I felt more or less like my former self.

"There's a great place to get coffee about twenty miles from here," Ms. Terwilliger said once I was settled and had my seat belt on. "We'll stop there and get some gas before pushing on to Pittsburgh."

I nodded, finished a text to Adrian, and stretched my legs, still coming to terms with the return to my old body. Beside me in the seat sat the wooden box Ms. Terwilliger had brought, and I picked it up for a closer look. Free of its sealing enchantment, there was nothing extraordinary about it now. In the month since Jill's disappearance, there'd been a lot of speculation about who would've taken her. Almost always, we'd laid the blame on some Moroi dissident who didn't support Lissa. Yet, this clearly showed evidence of human magic, which kind of turned everything we'd believed upside down. Aside from me, we knew of no magic-using humans working with Moroi.

I could only hope this museum offered some answers, as unlikely as it seemed. Inside the box, the words on that flyer glared up at me: *COME PLAY, SYDNEY.*

Once we had our coffee, the drive passed uneventfully, with our only slowdown being summertime construction scattered along the highway. Honestly, it would have been a pleasant road trip, if not for the fact we were all still keyed up with worry and tension. I was worried Adrian might do something reckless back at Court. And, of course, I was worried about Jill. Eddie clearly was too, and rather than make him feel better, this new lead had only increased his agitation. He barely said two words to us the whole drive. We still made good time overall, rolling up to the Pittsburgh Robot Museum in late afternoon. A hand-painted sign declared that it was "world famous," but none of us had ever heard of it. Judging from the empty parking lot, not many people had.

"We're usually busier on weekends," explained the attendant at the admission window. We bought three tickets and stepped inside.

"Please come in, please come in," boomed a robot standing near the entrance. It didn't move and had been patched with duct tape in a number of places. In its arms, it held a long, rectangular welcome sign.

The bulk of the museum was contained inside one large gallery that displayed a motley assortment of robots used in both entertainment and practical business applications. Most of the displays were static, but a few were animated, like a mini assembly line showing a robot that checked for manufacturing quality control. A conveyor belt on an endless loop sent ceramic mugs around and around past a boxy-looking device that paused and scanned each one, flashing either red or green lights, depending on whether it found a defect.

An adjacent room displayed "A History of Robotics" along its walls. It included mythological origins, like automatons that served the Greek god Hephaestus, which I thought was a nice touch. The bulk of the timeline focused on developments in the twentieth and twenty-first centuries and then ended with *THE FUTURE*: ???

I stared at those question marks a moment, thinking they might as well be a label for my own future. What did my life hold? Would I ever manage the college and world-travel dreams I'd harbored for so long? Or would my life be limited to a suite of rooms surrounded by vampires? Was being on the run the best outcome I could hope for?

"Sydney?"

Ms. Terwilliger's voice drew me from the timeline room, and I returned to the main gallery. She and Eddie were standing by a huge glass display case featuring what looked like a metal dinosaur more than twice my height. I recognized it as the one from the flyer, beside which my name had been written. Ms. Terwilliger's hand rested on the glass. "Can you feel this?" she asked me.

I placed my hand next to hers and waited. After several seconds, I sensed some kind of buzzing energy. Eddie imitated us but then shook his head. "I don't feel anything," he said.

"There's an enchantment on this display," Ms. Terwilliger explained, stepping back.

"Can you tell anything about it?" I asked. She was more sensitive to that sort of thing than I was. It was a skill that required practice.

"No. I need to open this case."

There was a small metal lock on the glass case that either of us probably could have opened with a spell. From what I could tell, there was no other security or electronic alarm on this display or the others, and I honestly wasn't surprised. Something told me this place didn't have the budget for anything too high tech, ironically enough. As it was, it didn't even have air conditioning, making it hot and stuffy inside with only a few screened windows to provide ventilation.

"Ah," said the attendant, striding over to us. He'd probably grown bored at his post. "I see you're admiring the Raptorbot."

I glanced up at its metal teeth and red eyes. "It's something else," I said honestly.

"Are you fans of the movie?" he asked.

"What movie?" I asked.

"*Raptorbot Rampage*," said the attendant.

"Yes," said Eddie, almost reluctantly. Ms. Terwilliger and I turned to him in surprise. He flushed under our scrutiny. "What? It . . . well, it was kind of awesome. I saw it with Micah and Trey."

The attendant nodded eagerly. "It's about a scientist whose wife is dying of an incurable disease. Just before she dies, he builds this robot raptor and manages to transfer her soul into it. Only things go unexpectedly awry when she goes off on a rampant killing spree."

"It couldn't have been that unexpected," I argued. "I mean, why did he build a dinosaur body for her? Why not something more human? Or at least a more friendly animal?"

"Because then there wouldn't have been much of a movie," said Eddie.

"There's still got to be a plausible backstory . . ." I said.

A wry smile crossed Eddie's features, and although the entire topic was absurd, I realized I'd hardly ever seen anything but a grim expression on his face since Jill had been taken. "I don't think you can really sit down with a movie called *Raptorbot Rampage* and expect a plausible backstory," he said.

The attendant looked offended. "What are you suggesting? It was a fine piece of film. When the sequel comes out, people will be lined up out the doors to see this exhibit!"

"Sequel?" Eddie and I asked in unison.

Ms. Terwilliger cleared her throat. "I'm sorry to interrupt, but how long are you open today?"

"Until five," said the attendant, still looking put out that I wasn't showing proper respect for the Raptorbot.

"Thank you," she said. "I think we've seen all we need. It's been an enjoyable visit. Let's go, Sydney, Eddie."

Puzzled over her actions, we followed her out but didn't speak until we were in the car. "What's going on?" I asked.

"We need to come back tonight, after they're closed, and bust into that display." She spoke in a prim and proper tone, not at all like she was suggesting breaking and entering. "I figured there was no point in sticking around and making ourselves more memorable."

"We were probably his only customers today," I remarked. "That'll make us memorable—that and having someone who's actually seen and liked *Raptorbot Rampage*."

"Hey," warned Eddie. "Don't judge until you've watched it."

We went into downtown Pittsburgh and booked a hotel, since presumably we'd be staying there overnight. A number of restaurants were within walking distance, and we found a nice place for dinner where we could almost pretend we were living a normal life. Even still, I could tell Eddie was restless. He offered to go on a walk with me after dinner, and for a moment, I was tempted. The historic part of downtown looked like it'd be fun to explore, and it was a perfect summer evening, warm and breezy. Then, I thought about the Alchemists finding me and locking me away again, forcing me to repeat their rhetoric and undergo their tortures. My chest grew tight, and I shook my head.

"I'll just wait in our room until we go back to the museum."

"They don't know you're here," he said softly, watching me with a careful eye. "And I wouldn't let any of them get near you anyway."

I shook my head. "Better play it safe."

When it was fully dark outside, we drove back to the robot museum and parked a few blocks away, making the rest of the journey on foot. Metal grates had been closed and locked in front of all the windows and doors, and a sign warned that there was an electronic alarm on the door.

"No sign that the windows are rigged with an alarm," said

Eddie, after inspecting it closely. "In fact, you can see that one of them's still open behind its metal grate—probably to air the place out." Even though it was well into night, the summer heat and humidity were still going strong.

"No cameras inside, and none that I see here either," added Ms. Terwilliger.

"I guess they sunk all their budget into the Raptorbot," I said. "Not that it seems to be bringing in the customers."

Eddie's brief moment of levity earlier was long gone, and he made no response to my barb. Instead, he examined the metal grate in front of the open window, his expression steely. "If I pull hard enough, I might be able to break this lock."

"No need to use up your strength," said Ms. Terwilliger. "I'm sure I have a spell to open it."

"And no need to use up your magic," I said, stepping forward. From the depths of my large purse, I pulled out a small vial. My time cooped up in our suite at Court hadn't been entirely wasted. Thanks to our questionably moral friend Abe, I'd been able to get my hand on a number of the components that went into some of the Alchemists' more common chemical compounds. I'd spent my long confinement building up a stockpile of useful things—including this one, which dissolved metal pretty handily.

The metal grating was like a little gate that slid out from one side of the window and latched to a lock on the opposite side. It actually might have been tough for Eddie to break it, but a few drops of the solution on the latch melted it away, releasing the gate easily. We slid it open, exposing the window. Its glass was up, with only a screen between the contents of the museum and us. Eddie took out a pocketknife, quickly and efficiently cutting open the screen. I winced in spite of myself.

"I feel kind of bad," I admitted. "This place isn't doing so well, and now we're damaging their property."

"That's what insurance is for," said Ms. Terwilliger. "Besides, if it helps us find Jill, I'm sure your queen can make an anonymous donation to this place."

Eddie helped the two of us climb up and get through the window, and then he followed deftly on his own. Inside, the gallery was empty and quiet—exactly how it was during regular business hours. The dim glow from the exit signs, as well as illumination from the streetlamps outside, provided enough light for us to see by, once we gave our eyes some time to adjust. We went immediately to the Raptorbot exhibit, and this time, I let Ms. Terwilliger cast an unlocking spell on the glass door. After she finished, I wondered for a moment if there might be some kind of spell on it that was keyed to me again. Then we heard an audible click, and the door swung open. Inside the case, the Raptorbot rested on top of a large stand that also had a door and an interior compartment.

"No lock," I said, reaching to pull open the smaller door.

"Sydney, wait—" began Ms. Terwilliger, but she was too late. I'd already opened it. I froze, expecting the entire thing to explode. But, after several tense seconds, nothing happened. I exhaled in relief.

"Sorry, I wasn't thinking."

She nodded, still ill at ease. "I can still sense that there's some sort of magic here."

"Maybe it's the object inside this," I said. I couldn't make out the interior compartment's belongings and tentatively reached my hand into the dark space, half-expecting a scorpion to sting me. Instead, my fingertips touched a large manila envelope, which I slowly pulled out. My name was written across it.

"Same handwriting," Eddie observed.

I nodded in agreement. "Yeah, too bad we don't have an easy way to trace—do you hear that?"

I could tell from Eddie's face that his quicker hearing had already picked it up. Ms. Terwilliger took a little longer to notice. "Like buzzing . . ." She glanced up into the Raptorbot's metal face. "From that."

The buzzing grew louder and louder, and Eddie hurried forward to put himself between the display case and us. "Get back!" he shouted, just as the Raptorbot's mouth opened and several dozen glowing objects came flying out. They came at us with unbelievable force, and I fell backward, landing awkwardly on my side. I held up my hands to block the glowing swarm, but some of them still grazed my face as they passed by. I cried out at the contact, which stung like a million paper cuts.

"What are they?" I managed to exclaim.

"Fotianas," Ms. Terwilliger called back. She too had hit the floor and was covering her face as the swarm came by for another pass.

"Foti-what?" asked Eddie.

"They're from the same realm Hopper comes from, but they're much less friendly." She cautiously removed her hands from her face so she could get a line of sight on the creatures. "Think of them as mutant fireflies."

Eddie, ever ready to improvise, grabbed the welcome sign from the robot standing at the doorway. Wielding it like a baseball bat, he swung it toward the fotianas as they came toward him. As though they shared one mind, the swarm parted so that his

"bat" hit mostly open air. Only a couple of the fotianas were too slow. They disintegrated into sparks as they were struck. That was encouraging, at least, but we had a lot more of them to get through. Things grew more complicated when the swarm split into three and came after each of us.

I had just gotten to my feet, but as I saw the group targeting me—in an arrow formation, even—I tore across the room and managed to duck under the conveyor belt's table just in time. "What's the best way to get rid of them?" I yelled to Ms. Terwilliger. "Fire?" Across the room, I could see Eddie continuing to nick away at them with his sign, but their speed and agility kept him from making significant progress.

"I don't want to burn this place down," she called back, trying to dodge as the swarm chasing her passed nearby. They swiped her arm, leaving tears in her sleeve and small bloody cuts visible on the skin beneath. As soon as she had some distance between her and them, she held up her hands and chanted a Latin incantation I'd never heard before. A hundred tiny sparkling crystals appeared in the air before her, and with another command, she sent them flying into the fotianas. Where the crystals struck, the "mutant fireflies" vanished into sparks.

The swarm chasing me flew low, trying to run me out from under my table. I waved them off, getting my hand stung in the process, as I parsed Ms. Terwilliger's spell. It had been very similar in word and feel to my old friend the fireball spell, with just a few notable differences. It was an ice spell, I realized. Thrown with enough force, bits of ice could have the impact of little razors.

I scurried out from under my table and tried to put some

space between my swarm and me. Behind me, I heard Ms. Terwilliger once again reciting the spell. Hoping I had the words memorized, I attempted the same feat, using the same motions and gestures I would for the fireball spell. Power coursed through me, and ice crystals shot forward at my command. But my aim wasn't as good as Ms. Terwilliger's. Although the spell's structure was similar to that of the fireball, the feel of it was different and required practice. I only managed to take out a few of the fotianas that time but had more success on my second and third attempts. Whenever I paused to recast, they wasted no chance to come at me, causing more irritation and pain. I would wave them off and cast the spell again, gradually picking off their numbers.

I lost track of time until I caught sight of a second cluster of ice crystals joining mine as I sent them into the significantly smaller fotiana flock. Out of the corner of my eye, I saw Ms. Terwilliger waving her hands. A moment later, Eddie came striding forward as well, still wielding that sign. They'd both defeated their respective swarms. Mine was the only one left, and within minutes, my friends helped me finish off the last of them.

Without the buzzing, the room suddenly took on an eerie silence. We all stood still, chests rising and falling heavily, as we looked around the dim room for any further signs of danger. Eddie and Ms. Terwilliger's faces both showed cuts and scrapes where the fotianas had touched them, and from the stinging of my own skin, I assumed I looked the same. We were alive, though, and the threat seemed to be neutralized for now.

"Where's the envelope?" Eddie asked at last.

I hurried over to where I'd dropped it, back by the Raptorbot, who had just surveyed our altercation from his lofty display. The ice crystals had melted into puddles on the floor, and one corner of the envelope was soaked as a result. Otherwise, it seemed undamaged. I carried it over to my friends and turned to Ms. Terwilliger before opening it.

"Do you sense anything?" I asked.

"If there's a spell, it's very cleverly concealed." She held up her hand and a small burst of fire appeared in her palm. "I'll be ready, just in case."

The envelope was heavy and bulky, so I wasn't entirely surprised when I found a brick inside, even though I had no clue what its purpose could be. It appeared to be made out of some sort of sandstone. I glanced at my companions to see if it made sense to them, but they looked as puzzled as I felt. I reached back into the envelope and pulled out a map of the Missouri Ozarks.

"I *really* didn't expect that," I remarked, scanning it for any writing or clues. There were none.

Anger filled Eddie's features, laced with something I felt too: disappointment. I hadn't known what we'd discover here, but there'd been a secret part of me that had hoped for a miracle and that we'd find Jill herself. Instead, all we had to show for this trip were some cuts and more cryptic clues. I shook the envelope. It felt empty.

"What on earth could this mean?" mused Ms. Terwilliger, taking the map from me.

"It means someone's playing with us," growled Eddie. He wiped a hand over his sweaty forehead, smearing blood in the process. "For all we know, Jill isn't even involved in this, and someone's just making us think they have her."

I peered inside the envelope, and my heart sank when I realized it wasn't empty after all. "I'm afraid not." I reached into it and pulled out the envelope's last item. Even in the poor lighting, there was no mistaking what this was: a lock of long, curling, light brown hair. And there was no question to whom it belonged. "Whoever's doing this, they definitely have Jill."

CHAPTER 5

ADRIAN

IT TOOK EVERY BIT OF MY ALREADY QUESTIONABLE self-control not to constantly text and call Sydney for updates. I hadn't realized how hard her absence would hit me. It wasn't just missing her—though that was certainly part of it. I'd gotten used to waking up to her every morning, to seeing her around for meals and other ordinary parts of life. Now, I didn't just have to pass the time without her; I had to also constantly reassure myself that she wasn't in the clutches of the Alchemists.

"I shouldn't have let her go alone," I told my mom the next day.

She glanced up from her cross-stitching. It was a hobby she'd taken up to pass the time and was only slightly less astonishing than everything else going on in our lives recently. "You worry too much, darling. If there's one thing I can say about my human daughter-in-law, it's that she's shockingly resourceful."

I stopped my pacing. "You really think so?"

A wry smile played over my mom's lips. "Are you surprised that I'd have something nice to say about her?"

"A little, yeah," I admitted. My mother had never openly protested my relationship with Sydney. Really, there'd been no chance. I'd simply shown up at Court with a bride in tow, and no one had been able to put asunder those whom the state of Nevada had brought together. My mom hadn't exactly embraced Sydney with open arms, but she'd also stood with us when others—including my own father—had turned their backs on us. I'd always assumed my mom didn't approve but was simply making the best of a bad situation.

"I'd be lying if I said that I'd ever, at any point in my life, wished for you to marry a human," she said after a moment of consideration. "I do, however, know that the road you walk in life isn't an easy one. It never has been. It never will be. I've realized that since you were a child. And I've also known that whomever you end up with would have to be someone very special, someone capable of facing those challenges with you. This girl? Sydney? She's someone like that. I've gathered that much in this last month. And I'd rather you have a worthy partner who's a human than a Moroi who can't help you share your burdens."

My jaw nearly hit the floor. "Mom, I think that's the most sentimental thing I've ever heard you say."

"Hush," she said. "And stop worrying. She's competent and talented. And she's not alone. She's got a guardian and that strange human woman with her."

I managed a faint smile but couldn't bring myself to tell my mom that Sydney, no matter how competent and talented, hadn't been able to elude the Alchemists before. In fact, when she'd initially been captured, Eddie had been with her. He'd been deadly and fierce as usual . . . but it hadn't been enough.

A knock at the door saved me from further rumination but presented a host of other new problems. I'd promised Nina we could go looking for Olive later, but that was still a few hours away. Sonya had assured me the sedative she'd given Nina to help her sleep would last a while, but for all I knew, it had worn off and I'd find Nina outside my door with those crazy eyes, demanding we go dreaming *right now*.

But when I opened the door, it was Rose I found instead. I wasn't sure whether to feel relieved or be on my guard. Last I'd known, she'd been away from Court.

"Hey," I said. "What's up?"

She was clearly off-duty now, dressed casually in jeans and a T-shirt as opposed to the black and white suits guardians wore for formal occasions. She tossed her mane of dark brown hair over one shoulder and grinned. "I heard how you've been locked away up here, so I thought I'd come spring you guys."

I tried not to wince at *you guys*.

"I thought you and Dimitri were away looking for Jill," I said, hoping to deflect the attention off of us.

Some of her enthusiasm dimmed at that. "We were . . . but we weren't having much luck. So Lissa had us come back and look into a few royals who've always been against her, in case they might have abducted Jill."

That was news. "You think there's any truth to it?"

"Probably not," said Rose. "And Lissa knows it's a long shot too. But she wants to exhaust every lead."

I stepped back. "Well, I don't want to hold you up from that . . ."

Her grin returned. "You aren't. We already put in some hours today and can't do anything else until one of the lords in question gets back tomorrow. So now we're doing something else productive. Grab Sydney, and I'll show you."

"She's, um, asleep right now," I lied.

"Asleep? It's the middle of the day."

"Our day," I corrected. "She's still on a human schedule."

Rose looked understandably floored. "Really? Last time I was here, I thought she'd adapted pretty nicely."

"She misses the sun," I explained.

"Does she actually go out?"

"Well, no . . . but it's the principle of the matter. It's a human thing." Judging from Rose's increasingly baffled expression, I really wasn't doing a good job of covering for us here, so I decided to cut my losses. "Look, why don't you show me whatever you've got, and I'll leave a note for Sydney." I figured that was better than Rose possibly offering to wait around until Sydney woke up.

"Sure," said Rose. "We can get her out another time."

I gestured her toward the hallway. "After you."

"Don't you need to leave the note?" she asked pointedly.

"Uh, right. Hang on." I stepped back inside and left Rose out in the hall. After standing there for about half a minute, I opened the door again and joined her. "All set."

Rose took me to a section of Court generally reserved for guardian activities. It was near their headquarters and some of their housing. More importantly, it was where they trained, and it was to one of their training fields she led me now. Only, when we arrived, it wasn't a group of dhampirs we found. It was a group of warrior Moroi.

"Well, I'll be damned," I said. I meant it as a compliment.

Ages ago, during the time humans and Moroi had intermarried, Moroi had also done a lot of their own self-defense. They'd used elemental magic as a weapon, fighting the Strigoi themselves. Over time, dhampirs had taken over protective duties, and using magic for anything more than parlor tricks had become taboo among the Moroi. Among many of the other changes recently suggested in Moroi politics, taking on self-defense once more with magical means often came up for discussion. Now I was seeing it implemented.

There were about two dozen Moroi here now, divided into four groups, each wearing a different color. They were doing drills that could've come straight out of Malachi Wolfe's school, defensive maneuvers and hand-to-hand combat. A couple of guardians were advising them, and one I immediately recognized, even with his back to me, thanks to his height and brown leather duster. Dimitri Belikov strode over, offering his hand to me in greeting.

"Adrian," he said warmly. "We don't have a spirit cadre yet. Would you like to lead one? Find some recruits?"

The first person who came to mind was Nina, who was already potentially losing her mind from spirit use. The thought of leading her into combat was discomfiting.

Finally, a leadership role for you, remarked Aunt Tatiana.

I shook my head. "Thanks, but no thanks. I've already got plenty on my plate."

"Where's Sydney?" he asked. "I thought she'd like to see this."

"She's asleep," said Rose helpfully.

Seeing Dimitri's surprise, I explained, "She's on a human

schedule. But you're right—she would've liked to see this. Another time."

"Another time," agreed Dimitri. "Look—they're about to start."

"Start what?" I asked.

A guardian I didn't know had just finished setting up some practice dummies on one end of the field. He called each group up, and I watched in amazement as each one demonstrated just how deadly the elements could be. Water users sent high-powered blasts of water at their dummies, knocking them over in one blow. Earth users made the ground unstable and also called upon rocks and dirt as weapons. Air users called up blasts of wind that would have knocked a live opponent over. Some of them were even able to use air to lift objects as weapons. And fire users—well, their destructive ability was pretty obvious as one of the dummies completely went up in flames.

"Just a demo, please," called the guardian wearily. "We don't need to wipe out our supply of dummies yet."

"Sorry," called a cheerful voice I recognized. Christian Ozera was standing there among the red-clad fire users, and he vanquished the flames with a glance.

After the separate demonstrations of elemental power, the warriors then showed how they might use the elements together. Air users helped freeze water summoned by water users. Earth users trapped dummies in the ground, letting fire users swoop in for the kill. (This resulted in another near destruction of a dummy when Christian again got too zealous with his flames. "Sorry," he repeated, not sounding sorry in the least.)

Finally, they concluded with a demonstration of the hand-to-hand maneuvers I'd seen them practicing when I arrived.

Moroi weren't as physically strong as dhampirs, but it was clear this group had put in a lot of training. I wouldn't have wanted to go up against any of them in a fight. They demonstrated moves any guardian would've been proud to master and even showed how to work in elemental attacks. All in all, it was a stunning display.

"Well?" demanded Christian afterward. He came striding over to us on the sidelines when the display finished. "Think that'll win them over?"

A small blond girl in blue walked beside him, and I was pleased—though not surprised—that Mia Rinaldi was a leader among the water users. "That was flawless," she agreed. "There's no way they can't approve a program now."

"What are you talking about?" I asked.

"This was just a warm-up," Christian explained. "No pun intended. We're going to show this to the Moroi Council in the hopes they'll approve a program we can take to all the Moroi schools, in order to recruit and train more people for the cause."

Mia's blue eyes gleamed. "We also want to get approval to launch some private Strigoi hunting parties."

"Well, you'd have my vote," I said honestly. "You seem like you might put the guardians out of business."

"Let's not get carried away," teased Rose. "But you're right—they've come a long way. Now we just have to get the council to agree. Lissa's already on board."

"Of course she is," I said. "Because she's young and progressive. The others . . . might be more resistant to change. Even with a display as impressive as this."

Rose nodded, perfectly understanding how even the most well-intentioned Moroi clung to tradition. "I'd hoped Sydney might have some logical arguments we could use to plead our case."

I chuckled at that. "I'm sure she would."

"Where is Sydney anyway?" asked Christian.

"Asleep," Rose and I said in unison.

As fascinating as these Moroi warriors were, I feared more questions about Sydney were coming my way. That and a glance at my watch told me it'd soon be time to go dream walking with Nina. "I should head back," I said. "Thanks for letting me see this."

"Happy to," said Rose, steering me back toward the main part of Court. "Find out what would be a good day for Sydney, and we'll set this up again—at a more human-friendly time."

I gritted my teeth, hating the lies. "I'll talk to her and get back to you."

Rose walked me back, and I could tell she thought it was strange that I made a point of keeping her out of the suite. I blamed it on Sydney being a light sleeper, which Rose mostly seemed to accept. When she finally left, I found the excitement of the demo and the further deepening of lies had me restless and uneasy, making it difficult to fall asleep when I crawled into bed. It was also the middle of the vampiric day for me, further muddling things, but Nina had said Olive was on a human schedule, so she would be asleep now. When thirty minutes went by of tossing and turning in bed, I received a text from Nina, saying she couldn't reach me in a dream.

Having trouble sleeping, I wrote back.

I've got plenty of sedatives from Sonya if you need one, came the joking response. *Happy to share.*

I smiled, wistful for a moment of the easy friendship I used to have with Nina. *No thanks. Just give me a little more time.*

Eventually, I managed to relax and drift off to sleep on my own. It had been a while since any spirit user pulled me into a dream. Usually, I was the dream's creator, calling the shots and inviting others to join me with spirit's power. My surroundings materialized around me, solidifying into a pastoral setting in front of a cute white house. Beyond it, a fence enclosed a pasture where horses idly grazed in the purple and orange light of a setting sun. Birds sang evening songs, and a warm breeze brushed my skin.

"My dad's house in Wisconsin," a voice behind me said.

I turned and found Nina approaching me through the long grass of the house's front yard. She looked a million times better than the last time I'd seen her, with her curly hair pulled into a loose bun and a lavender sundress on her slim frame. I hoped this reflected some improvement in the waking world and wasn't simply an illusion of the dream.

"It's nice," I said honestly. "The kind of place kids dream of growing up."

She smiled at that. "We could only come in the summer. We had some family friends who were minor royals, and they'd join us with their guardians. Otherwise, it would've been too dangerous out here. It's pretty remote . . . but you never know."

She didn't have to finish that thought. Nina and Olive were half sisters, sharing their Moroi father. Because he wasn't royal, he'd received no guardian protection, so dhampir Olive had made herself his protection—and gotten herself turned Strigoi during an attack. Nina's spirit magic had brought her back. It was a rare distinction Olive shared with only a couple of others—Dimitri and Sonya, to be precise.

"Shall we bring Olive here?" I asked, not wanting Nina to dwell on ugly topics from the past. At my question, though, her frown grew.

"It's not quite that simple . . . you'll see. I mean, maybe it'll be different with you here. I hope so."

I still didn't entirely understand what the problem was but decided to wait and see what happened. Really, if Olive was asleep, this should've been a piece of cake. Nina should've been able to use spirit to bring Olive to this country house, just as she'd brought me. Nina grew still, gazing off at the horse pasture, and I sensed the spirit magic welling up in her as she attempted a dream connection with her sister. So far, so good.

A few moments later, a translucent form started to materialize near us. I recognized Olive's shorter stance, her dark hair and coppery skin. A billowing cloak swirled around her, obscuring what I knew was a more muscular build than her sister's. Olive's eyes widened as she realized what was happening. "No, Nina. Please. Not again."

Normally, this would be the point where Olive would've completely solidified and been standing with us. Instead, the country scenery began to fade in the distance, growing increasingly insubstantial. I jerked my gaze back to Nina.

"What are you doing?"

She sighed. "I'm not doing anything. That's what I've been trying to tell you."

The beautiful green landscape disappeared, replaced by a black, ashen terrain that was dotted with rocks. A jagged mountainside rose steeply before us, climbing into a sky growing gray with thunderclouds. Occasional flashes of lightning danced between the clouds. There was no sign of Olive.

"What is this?" I exclaimed. "Did we get transported into a dystopian movie?"

Nina's expression was grim. "We're in Hawaii."

I glanced around. "I hate to disagree, but when I think *Hawaii*, I think *palm trees* and *bikinis*."

Nina glanced down at her feet, and a moment later, her sandals transformed into sneakers. She began hiking up the slope. "It's a volcano we visited when we were kids on vacation."

"That doesn't seem so bad," I said, cautiously following her. "But why change it? The farm was nice."

"I *didn't* change it," she said, clearly frustrated. "Olive did."

"Olive's not a spirit user," I protested. "She can change her outfit, yeah, but not something this big."

"Somehow, she took control of the dream from me. She does it every time. I mean, I can do small things like this." She paused to gesture to her shoes. "But I can't send us back or bring Olive out."

"Where is she?"

"Hiding somewhere." Nina scanned around and pointed to a dark hole in the volcano's side. "Probably there. That wasn't part of the real volcano we saw. She must've created it."

My mind was reeling as I approached the cave with her. What she was saying was impossible. Olive couldn't have power in this dream unless Nina ceded it to her.

"How?" I asked. "How is she doing this? Do you think it has something to do with her being restored from being a Strigoi? From being infused with spirit?"

Nina shook her head. "I don't think so. I don't actually feel her using spirit. It's almost like she's controlling it by . . . her will."

I tried to wrap my head around that as we came to a halt in front of the cave. "Now what?"

"Now," said Nina, "she's probably hiding from us in there. But if it's like other places she's brought me to in dreams, we probably can't just walk in and—"

A roar from within the cave's depths cut off her words. Instinctively, I took a few steps back. "What the hell is that?"

Nina looked more weary than frightened. "I don't know. Something terrible. Something to scare us off."

Her words were realized as a huge manlike figure made of black rocks came lumbering out of the cave, its eyes burning red. It was a full head taller than me and twice as broad. It came to a halt before us, beat its chest, and let out another roar.

"Have you seen this before?" I exclaimed.

"Not exactly," said Nina. "Last time she sent a swarm of bats. Before that it was some kind of werewolf creature."

"You made this dream," I insisted, backing up further as the lava monster (for lack of a better term) approached. "Get rid of it."

"I can't. Not with my thoughts, at least. We have to do this the old-fashioned way." I felt spirit magic surge within her again, and a cudgel appeared in her hands. Without further warning, she charged forward and swung the weapon at the monster. As she did, I felt more spirit flare inside her. In fact, it was the spirit magic that seemed to lash out at the monster, more than the cudgel. The creature roared in pain, and cracks appeared where the cudgel hit.

"You said you'd help me!" she yelled, clearly annoyed.

I *had* said that, but I certainly hadn't expected it to be in this manner. Before I signed on for senseless beating, though, I summoned my own magic and attempted to change the setting into something more hospitable. But when I tried it, I met firm resistance and understood better what Nina had meant. It wasn't exactly spirit I felt keeping the dream in place . . . but very much like will or intention, just as she'd said.

Unable to alter the dream's larger context, I imitated her and used a small burst of spirit to create a cudgel of my own. I wasn't usually violent in nature, and as I swung toward the lava monster—on which Nina had made significant progress—I reminded myself that he was just a dream creation and not a real living thing. When my cudgel struck the creature's stony hide, I nearly fell backward at the jolt of the impact. It rattled my bones and teeth . . . and didn't seem to make a difference to the lava monster. Nina paused to glare at me.

"You need to fill yourself up with spirit when you hit it," she explained in frustration. "That's the way to fight through."

She was certainly practicing what she preached. Brimming with magic, she was like a spirit torch beside me, and I was a bit taken aback by the amount she was wielding. It wasn't quite as severe as the burst used in restoring a Strigoi or bringing back the dead, but it was a notable amount to be holding and sustaining over an extended period of time. Reluctantly, I summoned some of my own—not nearly the amount she was using—and used it to blast the creature when I swung my cudgel. This time, I too cracked the surface.

"More, more!" Nina cried.

"There's no need," I said. "This still has impact—without as much magic. It just takes a little longer."

"We don't have the time!"

I didn't understand what she meant until our collective

efforts finally defeated the lava monster, and it crumbled to dust before us. Nina sprinted into the cave, and with the creature gone, she seemed to have regained control of the dream. The setting around us changed, and suddenly we were running into the white country house in Wisconsin. I just barely caught sight of Olive in the shadowy corner of a living room, her body obscured by that same billowing cloak from earlier.

"Olive!" screamed Nina. "Show me where you are!" More power surged through her, and the room started to flicker. I could feel a little of what she was doing, and I was astonished. She was trying to make the dream reflect Olive's surroundings—something even I hadn't known was possible.

But Olive was fading before our eyes. "I'm sorry, Nina. Please—please stop trying to find me. It's better this way."

"Olive!"

It was too late. Olive faded, and the room stopped flickering. It stabilized, firmly remaining a little country living room and offering no clues as to where Olive was. Defeated, Nina slumped into a wicker chair, tears in her eyes. "She woke herself up. That's what happens every time. She throws up some obstacle for me to fight against, and it distracts me from making the dream show where she's at. By the time I fight through, she's managed to wake herself and escape from the dream." Nina turned her gaze on me accusingly. "If we'd defeated her faster, she wouldn't have had time to wake up! You should've used more spirit to blast that monster away!"

Nina, though obviously upset, looked mostly stable here in the dream world. Thinking back to the other day, however, I knew her real-world self was another matter. "I don't think that's a good idea," I said slowly. "I think using all this spirit has been having a, um, detrimental effect on you over time."

"If you'd help me—*really* help me—we'd only have to do it once. If we can corner her, we can make the dream show us where she's at."

"Yeah, about that," I said, sitting beside her. "Where'd you learn to do that? Make the dream show where she's at?" That would've been incredibly useful when I'd been trying to find Sydney.

Nina shrugged. "You can make a person appear as they are in real life, right? I was experimenting one day and channeled the spirit through her in a way that made the dream's setting simply mirror the place she was in."

"I'm not sure 'simply' is the word I'd use," I remarked. "That involved a lot of spirit too. And I wonder . . . did she start controlling the dream afterward? Did you inadvertently give her control?"

It was obvious Nina hadn't thought of that. "I . . . I don't know. Maybe I did . . . but how else am I supposed to find out where she is?"

"Try talking to her?" I suggested.

She slammed her fist on the wicker armrest. "I have! She won't see me. This is the only way. Something's wrong, and we need to find out what. We need to try again. Only next time—"

"Whoa, whoa. There can't be a next time," I warned. "You'll burn yourself out. You've done this every day for how long?"

Her gaze grew distant. "I don't know. Months."

I winced. No wonder she was losing it. "No more spirit."

She looked up at me, her gaze pleading. "I have to. Can't you understand that? Do you know what it's like to not know what's happened to someone you care so much about?"

Jill, I thought with a pang. Nina must have seen something in my expression because she suddenly lit up.

"Help me! Help me, Adrian, and together we'll have enough spirit to overcome her. I can stop doing this every day. I'll find out what's happened to her. Please."

I thought of Sonya's worries for Nina. Then I thought of Sydney, cautioning me to be careful with spirit. I'd be in enough trouble already if she found out about this burst of spirit use. I slowly shook my head. "I can't. I shouldn't have even done this."

"If we work together, it won't require as much from either of us," Nina begged. "Please help me. I'll help you in return. Is there something you need? Help me find Olive, and I'll do anything."

I started to shake my head again, then paused as an idea hit me. "No," I said, more to myself than her. "No."

She jumped to her feet. "There is something, isn't there? Tell me!"

I hesitated, knowing I really shouldn't be going down this path. But her offer of help had made me think of one thing I did want very badly: getting back to Sydney. "I need to sneak out of Court without anyone knowing. And then I need to make people think I'm still here, back with my mom."

"Done," said Nina. "I can do that. Easy."

"Nina—"

"Look," she said. "I can help you right now—right this minute—get you out of Court. It'd be an easy compulsion spell. Then you can meet me in a dream to find Olive, wherever you are."

"That's nice of you," I said wearily. "But that's not going to convince people I'm still living here."

A mischievous smile crossed her lips. "I can do that too. If your mom'll let me stay with her. I'll compel anyone who comes looking for you into thinking they saw you. I'll make the workers at guest housing think they see you coming and going. No one'll suspect a thing. Please, Adrian." She squeezed my hand. "Let's help each other."

I took my hand back, unwilling to admit how tempted I was. She was offering me the only shot I had at joining Sydney, something I wanted badly enough to consider ignoring all warnings about spirit use. But how could I subject either of us to more magic? Especially her. It was selfish. "It's too dangerous," I told her.

"I don't care," she said obstinately. "I'll just keep trying whether you help me or not. Olive is everything to me."

And Sydney's everything to me, I thought. Desperately, I tried to find a way to reconcile the guilt I felt about taking Nina's help. She'd said she'd keep going after Olive, right? Well . . . if I helped her find Olive and made her stop, it'd result in Nina actually using less spirit. That was a good thing . . . right?

I took a deep breath and looked her squarely in the eyes. "If we try this again . . . let me wield the bulk of the spirit."

"But we both—"

"We both will," I said. "And we're only doing it once—not every day. If I do the heavy lifting once, it won't affect me as badly. You augment—a little. But that's it. You can't keep hurting yourself."

She reached her hand toward mine again, then drew it back, though her expression had softened. "You do care about me, don't you? I knew it. Even though you're married—"

"Nina," I said firmly. "It's not like that. I care about you, but

I love Sydney. And if we're going to do this again, we're doing it my way."

Her eyes remained dreamy a few moments longer, and then she gave a reluctant nod. "Your way," she reiterated. "And I really will help you."

"I'm counting on it," I admitted. "But hopefully you can pull off what we need using as little spirit as possible."

She gave a meek nod and then turned curious. "Okay . . . but are you sure you aren't worried about *your* sanity in all of this?"

I hesitated. If Sydney were here, I knew she'd tell me this was foolish, that I was frivolously using spirit I didn't need to and possibly damaging myself. But there was no way I could abandon Nina to insanity, especially if there really was something wrong with Olive. And I certainly had to seize a chance to get out in the world to help both Sydney and Jill. I just hoped what I'd told Nina earlier, that a one-time use wouldn't hurt me, would prove true. I managed a stiff smile.

"Hey, I'm not showing any signs of insanity yet," I told her. "I'm sure I'll be fine."

Me too, whispered Aunt Tatiana. *I'm sure you'll be fine too.*

CHAPTER 6

SYDNEY

WE HAD NO IDEA WHAT THE SANDSTONE BRICK MEANT. There was no enchantment that we could detect on it, no indication of what its role in this mystery was. The only thing we knew for sure was that we needed to get to the Ozarks or, at the very least, Missouri. Once Ms. Terwilliger had settled things with her rental car company to prolong her lease, she suggested we drive to St. Louis and then make a plan of attack. Instantly, my stomach sank.

"Not there," I said swiftly. "There's an Alchemist facility in St. Louis. I didn't go to all this trouble just to walk right back into their hands."

Eddie's eyebrows rose in consideration. "Maybe that's part of the plan? What if this scavenger hunt is part of an Alchemist plot to lure you out and has nothing to do with Jill at all?"

It was a sobering thought, one made more alarming when Ms. Terwilliger suggested, "Or what if it does have to do with Jill? There is the lock of hair, after all, which certainly looks like Jill's. Would the Alchemists have taken her as a way to trap you?"

For a moment, I dared give the idea credence. Jill *was* taken right when Adrian and I had managed to escape and hide at Court. The Alchemists were among the few people who knew Jill's location, so they could have easily sent someone after her. I pondered the possibility and analyzed it every way I could with lingering Alchemist logic. At last, I shook my head.

"I don't think so," I said. "They might have had the means, but not the motivation. The Alchemists are guilty of a lot of things, but they don't want the Moroi turning on each other— which would happen with the death of a royal princess, one whose life influenced the throne. I also can't see the Alchemists resorting to human magic, even to get to me. It goes against too much of their doctrine."

Even if this wasn't some elaborate Alchemist trap, I still didn't want to risk walking into an Alchemist on their lunch break in St. Louis. With that in mind, we set a new destination. It took an entire day of driving, but we finally called a halt the following night in Jefferson City, Missouri, putting us well past St. Louis. It also positioned us toward the Ozarks in a slightly out-of-the-way trajectory that we hoped might throw off someone waiting for our approach. Of course, we still didn't know exactly where we were going. The Ozarks consisted of a very large expanse of land, and thus far, our brick hadn't yielded any clues.

We went out to dinner after checking into a hotel, all three of us weary in that way you got from sitting in a car all day. It was nearing midnight, but we'd skipped dinner in order to make better driving time. I was tired more than anything else, with food simply being a formality. Across the table, Ms. Terwilliger stifled a yawn, and even Eddie, despite his perpetual vigilance, seemed like he was looking forward to bed as well. We had the brick sitting on our table as we waited for our food to arrive, all of us staring at it as though we could make it yield some answers through sheer force of will.

I finally dragged my gaze away from it and glanced at my cell phone, hoping I'd missed a text from Adrian in response to one I'd sent earlier with our status. There'd been little communication from him throughout the day, which seemed odd after yesterday, when he'd sent almost constant updates. I knew it was unreasonable to expect him to do nothing except sit by the phone to talk to me, but I couldn't shake the difference. After the troubling way things had been between us this last month, I found myself getting caught up in weird fits of paranoia, thinking that maybe once the shock of having me gone was over, Adrian found he kind of liked the freedom.

The waitress arrived with our food just then, and I tucked the phone back into my purse. As she set down our plates, her breath caught at the sight of the sandstone brick.

"Did you guys steal that from Ha Ha Tonka?"

We stared her as though she were speaking another language.

"I mean, that's cool if you did," she added hastily, unnerved by our silence. "It's a sweet place. I see lots of people going to and from there. Wouldn't mind a souvenir myself."

Ms. Terwilliger recovered herself first. "Can you say that name again? Ha Ha Wonka?"

"Ha Ha *Tonka*," the girl corrected. She glanced between our faces. "You really haven't been there? That brick looks just like the one the ruins are made of. You should check it out if you're going into the Ozarks."

The instant she was gone, I looked up Ha Ha Tonka on my phone. "No way," I said. "There's a castle in Missouri!"

"Do you think Jill's being held there?" Eddie asked, eyes aglow. I could already tell he was envisioning himself rescuing her from some tall tower, possibly battling a dragon or a robot dinosaur in the process.

"Not likely. She was right about the 'ruins' part." I showed them a picture of Ha Ha Tonka, which was an impressive structure, despite having seen better days. It had no roof, and some sections of the walls were gone, making it all open-air and easy to walk through. The building was technically a mansion, not a castle, and the whole area had been turned into a state park full of trails and other natural attractions. If Jill was there, it wasn't obvious where she could be held captive . . . but at least we had a destination now, because the waitress was right about one thing: Our brick looked exactly like those from the ruins.

The new knowledge reinvigorated us, and we nearly forgot our food as we began making plans. According to the park's website, it opened at seven in the morning. We decided to get there as soon as we could get in and do some preliminary scouting. If there was a chance we might have some showdown akin to what we'd faced at the robot museum, then we'd go to the trouble of sneaking in after hours. With the way this weird scavenger hunt was unfolding, there was really no telling what we might be facing or what the person running it expected of us.

We woke up energized the next morning, even after only

five hours of sleep, eager to get on the road and see what secrets Ha Ha Tonka held. The park was only an hour away, but we stopped at a gas station to fill up the car before getting on the highway. While Eddie took care of refueling, I headed inside the station to make sure Ms. Terwilliger and I had more coffee for the road. As I was approaching the door, I came to a screeching halt when I saw someone familiar inside.

My dad.

He was standing at the counter, taking money out of his wallet. His body was angled away from me, so he couldn't see me on the other side of the glass door. Yesterday's conversation came back to me, and I suddenly wondered if this really was all some Alchemist plot to catch me.

For a moment, I was so paralyzed with fear that I couldn't react. Despite the awkwardness of my living situation at the Moroi Court this last month, there was no question that it was a million times better than what I'd faced in re-education. I'd thought that I'd been able to put that awful experience behind me, but as I stood there, staring at my dad's back, I suddenly found it hard to breathe. For all I knew, fifty Alchemists were about to spring out from all directions, dragging me back to a tiny dark room and sentencing me to a lifetime of physical and psychological torture.

Move, Sydney, move! some part of my brain shouted at me.

But I couldn't. All I kept thinking about was how the Alchemists had overwhelmed me before, and that was with Eddie by my side. What chance did I stand here, all by myself?

MOVE, I told myself again. *Stop feeling helpless!*

That spurred me to action. I began breathing again and slowly backed away, not wanting to do anything that might catch attention in his periphery. When I couldn't see him anymore, I spun around and prepared to make a mad dash back to the car.

Instead, I ran into my sister Zoe.

She'd been walking toward the gas station, and my panic shot back up as I looked at her. Then, as I studied her expression of complete shock, I realized something: I was the last person she'd expected to see here. This wasn't some sort of elaborate trap. At least, it hadn't been until I walked into it.

"Zoe," I squeaked. "What are you doing here?"

Her eyes were impossibly wide as she attempted her own recovery. "We're on our way to the St. Louis facility. I'm starting an internship there."

Last I knew, she'd been in Salt Lake City with my dad, and I couldn't help but pull up a mental road map. This wasn't a direct route between the two places. "Why didn't you take I-70?" I demanded suspiciously.

"There was construction and—" She shook her head, almost angrily. "What are *you* doing here? You're supposed to be stashed away with the Moroi!" Increasing my astonishment, she grabbed my sleeve and began steering me farther from the station. "You have to get out of here!"

Cue more astonishment. "Are you . . . helping me?"

Before she could answer, I heard Eddie's voice. "Sydney?"

It was all he said, but as Zoe and I turned around, I could see the apprehension and battle readiness all over him. He stayed where he was but looked as though he could instantly leap up and throw Zoe against the building if she tried to hurt me. I really hoped it wouldn't come to that, because no matter what had happened between us, no matter how much she'd betrayed me, she was still my sister. I still loved her.

"Is it true?" she whispered. "Did they really torture you in re-education?"

I nodded and cast another anxious glance at the gas station. "In more ways than you can imagine."

She blanched but drew a resolved breath. "Then get out of here. Hurry—before he comes out. Both of you."

I was stunned at this complete reversal in her behavior, but Eddie didn't need to be told twice. He took hold of my arm and nearly dragged me to the car. "We're going—now," he ordered.

I caught one last glimpse of Zoe before Eddie shoved me in the car, where Ms. Terwilliger sat waiting for us. A thousand emotions played over Zoe's face as we peeled out, but I could only interpret a few. Sadness. Longing. As we quickly got back on the road, I found myself shaking. Eddie was driving and kept anxiously checking the rearview mirror.

"No sign of pursuit," he said. "She must not have been able to see which direction we went to tell him."

I slowly shook my head. "No . . . she didn't tell him at all. She helped us."

"Sydney," said Eddie, in a stern-but-trying-to-sound-kind voice, "she's the one who turned you in the first time! The one who started that whole re-education nightmare."

"I know, but . . ."

I thought back to Zoe's face just now, looking so serious and upset about the notion of me being tortured. I thought back also to the day Adrian and I had first arrived at Court, when we'd been hauled in front of the queen and found a group of Alchemists already waiting there to try to get me back. My father and Ian, another Alchemist we knew, had spoken plenty about the wrongness of what I'd done and how I needed to be removed from the Moroi. Zoe had stayed silent, her face stricken, and I'd been too overwhelmed to think much about what she might be feeling. I'd assumed she'd been too outraged by my marriage to speak—not to mention the fact that my dad didn't really let anyone else get a word in edgewise.

Now I suddenly realized there might have been something I'd missed altogether: regret.

"I really think she was trying to help," I insisted, knowing how crazy the words sounded—especially to Eddie. He'd been there the night I was taken, the night she'd betrayed me. "Something's changed."

He didn't contradict me but was still on edge. "I wonder if we should change our plans, in case they start scouting the area for us."

"No," I said firmly, feeling more and more confident of my suspicions. "She's not going to turn us in. Unless you see active signs of someone coming after us, we're pushing on to Ha Ha Tonka."

I was reeling as the drive continued, still in awe at this new revelation that Zoe might be having doubts—if not about the Alchemists, then at least about what had been done to me. Once I recovered from my initial shock, I found myself feeling an emotion I hadn't felt about her in a very long time: hope.

Clouds were thinning out when we reached Ha Ha Tonka State Park, and the early morning temperatures were already promising a sweltering day ahead. We parked and stopped by the visitors' center, clustering around a map of the park. Although there were extensive grounds and trails, we decided the ruins of the massive stone building—which even the park referred to as the "castle"—were the place to start, seeing as that's what our clue directly connected to.

No one else was out this early, aside from the staff at the visitors' center. Ms. Terwilliger and I walked around the stone ruins, looking for signs of magic and occasionally casting detection spells. Eddie stayed near us protectively, doing his own searching as well, but mostly relying on us to find whatever it was we were looking for. The part of me that had long loved art and architecture couldn't help but get caught up in the ruined grandeur around us, and I wished Adrian was with me. We hadn't officially had a honeymoon after our wedding, but we'd often talked about all the potential places we'd like to go, if only we had the freedom. Italy was still high on my list, as was Greece. But honestly, I would've gladly settled for Missouri, if only Adrian could be with me, free from pursuit.

After a few hours of searching, we were hot and sweaty but had yielded no results. Eddie, still not convinced of Zoe's intentions, was growing nervous about us lingering and wanted to be on the road soon. As lunchtime neared and we contemplated calling a break, something flashed in my periphery. I turned and looked up at one of the castle's dilapidated towers and saw something small and golden shining in the afternoon sunlight. I touched Eddie's arm and pointed.

"What's that gold thing?"

He put a hand above his eyes and squinted. "What gold thing?"

"On the tower there. Right below the top window opening."

Eddie looked again and then dropped his hand. "I don't see anything."

I beckoned Ms. Terwilliger over and tried to show her. "Do

you see that? Below that window on the tallest tower?"

"It looks golden," she said promptly.

Eddie was incredulous and turned back to where we indicated. "What are you guys talking about? There's nothing there." I could understand his disbelief. Dhampir vision was superior to that of a human.

Ms. Terwilliger scrutinized him for a moment before fixing her gaze back on the tower. "It's possible we're looking at something that can only be seen by those who perceive magic. This could be what we need."

"Then how do we get to it?" I wondered aloud. The tower itself was little more than a high stone wall, and I wasn't confident it offered great footholds for climbing. It was also in a section of the castle behind a fence, warning visitors to stay on the outside. With a few more tourists wandering through, plus the occasional park ranger, I knew there was no way we could covertly jump the fence.

Eddie surprised us both with a magical suggestion. "I could climb it. Can't you guys do an invisibility spell?"

"Yes . . ." I began. "But it won't do much good if you can't see what you're looking for. I wish I could climb it . . . but I think it's a bit beyond my abilities."

"Can we both be invisible?" he asked. "You stand at the bottom and spot me. Tell me where to go."

Ms. Terwilliger turned Eddie invisible, and I then cast the same spell on myself. It wasn't a particularly strong invisibility spell, and anyone looking for us would be able to detect us. We didn't want to cast a stronger spell, in case we had to defend ourselves later, and we were taking it on faith no tourist or ranger was expecting to find someone climbing the ruin walls.

Unseen, Eddie and I easily hopped the fence and approached the tower in question. Up close, I now had a better sense for what the golden object was. "It looks like a brick," I told him.

He followed my gaze, still unable to see what I saw. "I'll take your word for it."

The tower's surface was rough and irregular, with erratic handholds and other openings left behind for long-gone windows. I wouldn't have been able to climb it, but Eddie managed it deftly, the strong muscles in his body working as he grappled for places to rest feet and hands as he slowly made his way up. When he arrived at the top window, he at least had a place to rest and stand on the opening's edge. Reaching up, he placed his hand on a brick at random. "Now what?"

"It's three bricks to your left and two up," I called.

He counted and moved his hand, setting it on what I saw as a golden brick. "Is this it? It's loose. I can pull it out."

"That's the one."

I tensed as he pried the brick from the wall. I sensed no obvious traps from this distance, but for all I knew the entire structure would crumble down around us when he removed it. With a little wriggling, it came free. Both Eddie and I froze, waiting for a deadly fotiana swarm or some other disaster. When nothing happened, he tossed the brick to the ground beside me and began scaling his way down. Once he was safely back, we hurried out of the enclosed area and took the brick to Ms. Terwilliger.

All three of us crowded around it, hoping for revelation— but got nothing. We cast more spells on it and tried pairing it with the original brick we'd brought from Pittsburgh. Still nothing. Wondering if there might be more gold bricks around, we did another search of the property but came up empty. Hot and hungry by this point, we decided to call a break and get some lunch. We went to a German restaurant and were surprised to see how crowded it and other restaurants in the park's small town were.

"There's a fishing convention in town," our waiter told us. "Hope you've got a hotel if you were planning on staying."

We hadn't gotten one yet, actually, though we had been discussing staying overnight to possibly search the park again tomorrow. "Maybe we can find another nearby town," I mused.

The waiter brightened. "My uncle runs a campground that has vacancies right now. He'll even rent tents and everything. Cheaper than a hotel."

Cost wasn't an issue, but after a brief discussion, we decided to follow up on the offer and go out to the campground, simply because of its proximity to the park. We were able to rent what we needed, get set up, and then make another trip to Ha Ha Tonka before it closed for the night. Once more, we found no answers in either the park or the brick. We tried to tell ourselves that morning would bring fresh perspective, but none of us would give voice to the burning question hanging between us: What were we going to do if we weren't able to find the gold brick's secrets?

I longed to discuss it with Adrian, but there'd still been no communication since my last update. Dutifully, I sent him another report about what was going on and then prepared for bed, unwilling to admit how much his radio silence bothered me. Exhausted from a long day, I soon fell asleep in the rented tent . . .

. . . and was awakened a few hours later by a panicked Eddie.

"Sydney! Jackie! Get up!"

I opened my eyes and instantly sat upright. "What? What is it?"

He was standing in the unzipped opening of the tent, pointing outward. Ms. Terwilliger and I scrambled to his side and looked where he indicated. There, out in the moonlight, a glowing puddle of what seemed like molten gold was oozing over the ground, coming toward us. Where it touched, it left scorched grass and earth behind.

"What is that?" I exclaimed.

"The brick," said Eddie. "I was on watch inside and noticed it starting to glow. I picked it up, and it nearly burned my hand. I threw it outside, and it melted into that."

Ms. Terwilliger murmured a quick incantation as the blob nearly reached our tent. An invisible wave of power shot out and knocked the golden glob back a few feet. Then it began making its way back toward us.

"Wonderful," I muttered. She repeated the spell, but it was clear that was only a temporary fix.

"Can we trap it?" I asked. "There are a lot of stones around. We could make some kind of enclosure?"

"It's burning right through the stones in its path," said Eddie grimly.

Ms. Terwilliger gave up on the force spells and cast a freezing spell similar to what she'd used in the robot museum. She directed a blast of bitter cold toward the molten puddle, which halted in its tracks. Half of the blob began to solidify, though the other half was still liquid and mobile and tried to wriggle away, dragging its frozen half with it.

"Sydney, get to the other side!" Ms. Terwilliger said.

I hurried to obey, running out of the tent and standing on the other side of the blob, which had liquefied now that she'd momentarily dropped the spell. The ooze moved toward the tent again, and Ms. Terwilliger held up her hands to cast. "On the count of three," she ordered. "One . . . two . . . three!"

Simultaneously, we released freezing spells, attacking the molten gold from opposite sides. The mass wriggled and writhed in the grip of the magic but slowly began to solidify. I'd never sustained the spell for a long time, but Ms. Terwilliger wasn't letting go of the magic. I followed her lead until, at last, the gold was still, completely solidified into an irregularly shaped puddle. We let go of the magic and carefully walked up to it. The gold stayed as it was.

"That was weird," I said. "Not quite as bad as the last attack." I still had a few cuts from the little magical fireflies that had come after us in Pittsburgh.

"Only because it didn't get to us," warned Ms. Terwilliger. "I hate to think what would've happened if we'd all been asleep in that tent when it liquefied."

I shuddered, knowing she was right. "But what does it mean?"

No one had an immediate answer, but Eddie surprised us when he spoke a few seconds later. "I've seen this before."

"A golden brick that turned into a deadly, rampaging puddle of molten metal?" I asked.

He shot me a wan smile. "No. Look at that shape. Doesn't it seem familiar?"

I tilted my head to study the golden form before us. There didn't seem to be any design to the shape. It was an amorphous, vaguely ovalish shape that looked like it had hardened that way by coincidence. Eddie's intense look of concentration said he believed otherwise. After a few more moments of concentration, revelation lit his features. He pulled out his cell phone and tapped in something. With shoddy coverage in the park, it took a little while for the phone to find what Eddie needed, but when it did, he was triumphant.

"There, take a look."

Ms. Terwilliger and I peered at his screen and found a map of the greater Palm Springs area. Instantly, I realized what he'd tuned into.

"It's the Salton Sea," I breathed. "Good recall, Eddie."

The Salton Sea was a saline lake outside of Palm Springs, and the metal puddle before us was exactly the same shape as that body of water. Ms. Terwilliger shook her head and gave a snort of dismay.

"Wonderful. I left Palm Springs to warn you, got caught up in a magical scavenger hunt, and am now, after all that effort, simply taking you back home."

"But why?" asked Eddie. "Has Jill been there the whole time? And who's the one pulling the strings behind all—"

"Get back!" cried Ms. Terwilliger, holding her hands in a warding gesture.

Not even Eddie could move fast enough from what she'd spotted. The golden blob had begun to tremble, like it was suddenly filled with energy that needed to get out. I tried to cast a shielding spell, but even as the words formed on my lips, I knew I wasn't going to be fast enough. The blob exploded into a hundred little golden razor blades that came flying toward us—and then stopped. They hit an invisible barrier and fell harmlessly to the ground.

I stared at where they lay, my heart pounding as I thought of the terrible damage they would have caused if Ms. Terwilliger hadn't been fast enough. So it was a surprise to me when she said, "Excellent reflexes, Sydney. I couldn't manage it in time."

I jerked my gaze up from the blades. "You didn't cast that?"

She frowned. "No. I thought you did."

"I did," a voice behind us said.

I spun around and gasped as, incredibly, Adrian emerged from the trees. Forgetting the tragedy that had nearly taken place, I ran into his arms, letting him lift me off my feet. "What are you doing here?" I exclaimed. "Never mind." I kissed him hard, so overwhelmed that I didn't even care that Eddie and Ms. Terwilliger were nearby. Being away from him these last couple of days had made my heart ache more than I'd expected, and I think we were both surprised when he was the one who finally broke the kiss off.

"I told you I'd find a way to get here," he said, grinning. His gaze fell on the blades, and his smile faded. "Not a moment too soon, I guess."

With his arm still around me, I turned back to the razors, which glittered ominously in the grass. A memory slowly surfaced within me. "I've seen those before," I said, sounding much like Eddie had earlier.

Ms. Terwilliger exhaled a shaking breath. "It's a nasty spell. Not one to be cast lightly."

"I know," I said softly. "I cast it once."

Everyone turned to me in astonishment. "When?" she asked. "Where?"

"At your house . . . your old house, before it burned down," I corrected. A thousand memories crushed down on me, and the world swayed a little as I suddenly made connection after connection. I'd thought I didn't know anyone capable of using this kind of human magic—anyone who'd want to come after me, at least. I'd been wrong. I met my friends' expectant gazes. "It's the spell I used to kill Alicia," I explained.

CHAPTER 7

ADRIAN

ALICIA DEGRAW WAS ALIVE.

It was shocking to me, so I could only imagine how Sydney must feel. She thought she'd killed Alicia. Alicia had been the apprentice of Jackie's sister, Veronica, but had gone rogue. That was no small thing, seeing as Veronica herself was certainly no role model. She'd been obsessed with stealing youth and power from other witches, effectively leaving them in comas for the rest of their lives. Alicia had turned on her mentor, taken her power, and then gone after Jackie. Sydney and I had been involved in a showdown at Jackie's house at the end of last year—a showdown that had resulted in said house burning to the ground. We hadn't known for sure if Alicia had made it out, but now we had our answer.

"I'm kind of torn," Sydney admitted, stirring the coffee she had yet to drink. We'd left the campground to go discuss matters in a twenty-four-hour restaurant, and it was a sign of her worry that the coffee was untouched. I was pretty sure I'd never seen her pass on caffeine in all our time together. "Part of me's relieved I didn't actually kill someone. On the other hand . . . well, this kind of complicates things."

"You're certain?" Jackie asked from across the table. "Those are the same ones?"

Sydney held up a golden razor blade, the only one she'd saved from the campsite. The rest had been destroyed. "Positive. You don't forget something like that. That night I fought her, I transformed some perpetual-motion balls into blades just like these."

"I remember those," Jackie murmured, almost wistfully. "They were an end-of-the-year gift from a former student. I think he hoped I'd raise his grade."

Sydney seemed not to have heard. There was a haunted look in her eyes. "I sent the blades toward Alicia. It was just instinct. She fell down your basement stairs, and I couldn't stick around to see what had happened—not with everything on fire."

I put my hand over hers. "You did what you had to do. It was the right thing. She was—*is*—an evil person."

"I suppose," Sydney said with a sigh. "And I guess this answers our questions. We've been trying to figure out who would have a vendetta against me and could use human magic. She's the perfect fit."

"Now that we know she's behind this, let's go after her and get Jill," growled Eddie. This life on the road had made him shave even less, and he was well on his way to a beard. "She left that clue: She's in Palm Springs. She needs to be stopped once and for all."

"Agreed," Sydney said, snapping out of her earlier malaise. "We need to finish this and get Jill. None of us are going to sleep anytime soon—we might as well hit the road now and go to Palm Springs."

"Not you," said Jackie. "I don't want you anywhere near Palm Springs right now."

"What?" exclaimed Sydney. Her intensity was a match for Eddie's. "But that's the next piece of this! Alicia all but told us."

"And that's why we're not going to rush into this—at least not right away."

"But Jill—" Eddie began.

Jackie shook her head. "We don't yet know the extent of Jill's involvement in this. What we do know is that Alicia is baiting Sydney and wants her to come to Palm Springs, where there's probably a very neatly laid trap. Alicia's also following her old pattern of wearing out an enemy first. This 'scavenger hunt' wasn't just for her amusement. It was to weaken Sydney magically. If you run off to Palm Springs now, after the magic you've wielded these last few days, you might very well succumb to whatever she has in store. Then we lose you and never find out what's become of Jill."

I felt conflicted and tightened my hold on Sydney's hand. I could understand why Jackie wanted to keep Sydney away from danger. I wanted that too. But I also felt the increasing pressure that everyone else did. Each passing day put Jill at greater risk. How could we not take action when we had a lead?

"But," continued Jackie, as though reading my mind, "that's not to say I have any intention of just abandoning Jill. I want to conduct a search in Palm Springs—specifically the Salton Sea area—but I plan on doing it with appropriate backup."

Eddie and I were both confused, but Sydney, as usual, caught on fastest. "The Stelle," she said, referring to the coven of witches she'd joined.

Jackie nodded. "Them and others. Alicia isn't just your problem—she represents a problem for the entire magical community. And so the entire community will deal with her. I'll get them together, and we'll conduct a search, using magical and conventional means. You, meanwhile, will stay somewhere safe—somewhere far away."

"And I'll stay with you," I said, feeling a little bit better knowing that Jill wasn't being abandoned. It was tough, almost like I had to choose between Sydney and Jill, but it sounded like Jackie wouldn't be sitting around idly.

"I'll go with you," Eddie told Jackie. Then he turned to Sydney and me. "That is . . ." The conflict on his face mirrored what I felt inside.

"Go," I said. "We'll be okay. No one knows we're gone yet. We'll disappear somewhere and be fine."

Eddie hesitated again. He hated to have his loyalties torn, but at last he nodded. "As long as you think you'll be okay. How *did* you get away without anyone knowing?"

"I'll tell you some other time," I said.

I could tell from Sydney's expression she was interested in that story too. She looked at Jackie instead. "But I want you to call me as soon as you and the other witches have things secure. As soon as you think it's safe, I want to be a part of the hunt for Jill."

"Unless we find her first and defeat Alicia," insisted Eddie.

Sydney gave him a small smile that suggested she didn't think it'd be that easy. "I would love that."

The four of us hashed out a few more details before finally parting ways. I could tell it still bothered Eddie to be leaving us, and he was full of advice on how we should lie low and not attract any attention. He also wanted to send for Neil to guard us, but Sydney dismissed that idea, saying it'd be easier for us to just slip away now. We all agreed Neil might be handy in Palm Springs when we closed in on Alicia, so Eddie promised to make that happen.

"Don't worry," I assured Eddie, clapping him on the back after a few more of his well-intentioned pieces of caution. "I have no intention of doing anything that's going to let Alchemists or Moroi know we've left Court. You go do your thing, we'll do ours, and then you can let us know when it's safe to join you."

Jackie and Eddie both agreed they didn't want to know where Sydney and I were going. The less they knew, the less they could accidentally reveal to others. They were both filled with advice on the kinds of places we should go, however, and I finally had to send them both on their way and tell them we'd be fine.

That left Sydney and me in our rental car, suddenly faced with infinite possibilities. It was also the first time we'd truly been alone in a very long time.

"It's a little overwhelming," she admitted to me as we sat in the restaurant's parking lot. "It's like we could suddenly live out any of our escape plans."

"Well, not any," I remarked. "We're in the middle of the United States and need to be safely lodged somewhere in five hours so that I can, um, meet up with Nina in a dream."

Sydney's eyes widened. "What?"

I sighed and started the car. "Let me explain."

I'd known it would all have to come out . . . I just hadn't expected it to come out this soon. So we got on a highway headed north, and I briefed Sydney on what had happened in the days we'd been apart. Nina had made good on her word about covering for me. She'd driven me out of Court in her own car, using compulsion on the gate guard so that he wouldn't remember seeing me. After she'd dropped me off at a small regional airport, she'd promised to go to our rooms in guest housing and stay with my mom. In the twenty-four hours it had taken me to catch connecting flights and drive to Sydney's location in the Ozarks, I'd heard updates from both Nina and my mom. No one had come looking for me, and Nina had strolled down to the lobby and had a compulsion-filled conversation that convinced the desk attendant she'd seen me leave and come back for a feeding.

"And now I've got to uphold my part of the bargain," I explained to Sydney, once I'd recapped the backstory.

"By engaging in a bunch of spirit use that's burning her out?" cried Sydney. "Adrian, you told me you'd back off!"

She doesn't understand, snarled Aunt Tatiana. *You did this for her!*

I felt my anger rise in response. "It was the only way I could get away from Court!"

"You didn't *have* to get away from Court," Sydney argued. "We were fine. You just needed to stay safe and cover for us."

"Fine? I saved you from getting sliced up by those blades!"

Sydney crossed her arms over her chest and stared obstinately out the passenger side window. "We don't know how bad the damage would've been, and Ms. Terwilliger and

I might have gotten off a spell at the last second. But this . . . this spirit walking with Nina! We *do* know the kind of damage it can do! You just said she's in bad shape."

"My helping her will prevent her from getting worse," I retorted. "One time isn't going to hurt me."

Sydney turned back to me, incredulous. "No! Not one time. Not any time! You can't do this! I can't let you!"

Since when does she control you? demanded Aunt Tatiana, raging. *Barely married a month, and she's already dictating your life! You can't stand for that. Tell her. Tell her that she can't control you!*

I was as worked up as the phantom in my head, and I opened my mouth, ready to snap something harsh back at Sydney. Then, glancing over, I caught sight of her face in the passing glow of another car's headlights. The concern and love I saw in her features pierced my heart, and like that, the anger went out of me.

She's deceiving you, insisted Aunt Tatiana.

No, I replied back. *She just cares about me. She wants to help.*

To Sydney, I said, "Okay. You're right. It's not a good idea. I won't engage in the dream. I'll just find . . . some way . . . to explain things to Nina." I felt guilty going back on my word to Nina, but I had greater vows binding me to Sydney. When I saw the relief those words brought to her, I knew I'd made the right choice.

Nina isn't going to like this, hissed Aunt Tatiana.

I'm not married to Nina, I retorted.

Sydney moved her hand over mine. "Thank you, Adrian. I know it's not easy. I know you just want to help."

"I do," I admitted, still conflicted by the decision. The instinct to help Nina was so, so strong. "But there's a cost to it. My sanity's not worth it." I squeezed Sydney's hand back. "Our relationship's not worth it."

I told you, Nina isn't going to like this, warned Aunt Tatiana again. *You can pat yourself on the back for protecting your sanity, but hers is long gone. She's not just going to let you walk out of your deal.*

I'll deal with Nina. For now, it's worth it just to have some alone time with Sydney and not be fighting for a change.

It was true. Sydney and I hadn't had anything even remotely close to this kind of freedom in a long time, and even if we were stuck in the middle of the United States instead of some tropical island, the options before us suddenly seemed limitless. After mulling over some internet maps, we finally made our way to Council Bluffs, Iowa. It didn't exactly scream excitement, but that was kind of the point. Most importantly, it was far away from the Alchemists in St. Louis and even farther from Palm Springs, where Alicia was hoping Sydney would show up. We debated checking into a large chain hotel and finally settled on a small country inn just outside the town. We pulled up to it late in the morning and were greeted by a sign proclaiming, WELCOME TO THE BLACK SQUIRREL LODGE.

"Oh no," groaned Sydney. "Please don't let this be like that place in Los Angeles. I don't know if I can handle a room full of squirrel decor."

I grinned, thinking back to the time Sydney and I had investigated another bed-and-breakfast that had taken rabbits to an unprecedented height in tacky decorating. "Hey, come on, after everything else we've been through, that'd be the least of our worries."

But when we stepped inside, we were pleasantly surprised to see everything was actually pretty tastefully decorated in neutral colors and modern decor. No quilts with squirrels on them or squirrel-shaped wicker sculptures in sight. The innkeeper, though surprised to see guests this early in the day, was happy to welcome us and get us into a room.

"What's with the inn's name?" I asked as I paid for the room.

The innkeeper, a kindly middle-aged woman, beamed. "Oh, that's in honor of Cashew."

"Cashew?" asked Sydney.

The innkeeper nodded. "Our resident black squirrel. I'd call him our pet . . . but, well, he's so much more than that."

I peered farther into the lobby. "Does he have a cage here or something?"

"Oh, no," she said. "That'd be cruel. Also illegal. He's . . ." She shrugged and gestured vaguely with her hand. "Well, he's around somewhere."

"What do you mean 'around'?" asked Sydney uneasily. "Like, outside?"

"Oh, no," said the innkeeper. "Poor thing wouldn't know what to do out there."

Sydney's eyes widened. "Wait. If he's not outside, then does that mean—"

"Let's get you two into your room," said the innkeeper sunnily. "I've got your key right here."

The room she took us to had a cozy sitting area and access to a private porch, as well as a big, plush bed. After an uncomfortable day of travel, I was looking forward to catching up on sleep and finally getting some real rest. Before I could throw myself on the mattress, however, I knew I needed to get in touch with Nina and tell her the deal was off. When Sydney said she wanted to take a shower, I saw the perfect opportunity. It was just around the time Nina would be asleep, waiting for me to contact her through a spirit dream. I didn't have to be asleep for that, simply in a meditative state.

I sat on the bed, calming myself and closing my eyes, calling on just enough spirit to reach across the dream world to Nina. My tranquil state was shattered, however, when I heard a scream from the bathroom. I opened my eyes and tore across the room, flinging the door open.

"Adrian, look out!" cried Sydney.

A small, furry black form leapt off the counter, landing right on my chest. Out of instinct, I swatted it off. It landed on the floor and went scurrying off across the room. Sydney, wrapped in a towel, stepped out and stood beside me.

"I think it went under the bed," she said.

"That thing better not get on me again," I muttered, walking gingerly over to the edge of the bed.

You've faced much worse than this, Aunt Tatiana said scornfully. *Stop being foolish.*

Sydney followed, and when I lifted a corner of the bed frame up, she waved her hand in what I recognized as a gesture for casting spells. Seconds later, I felt a breeze stir and blow under the bed. Moments later, the squirrel—Cashew, I presumed— came tearing out and began frantically racing around the room. Sydney, courageously overcoming her earlier shock, darted over to the door that led to the porch and opened it. After a few circuits of the room, the squirrel noticed and ran out. Sydney slammed the door shut behind him, and for several seconds, we both just stood there.

"Why," she asked at last, "can't anything ever just be simple for us?"

"Look at you," I teased, walking over to her. "Fearlessly vanquishing Cashew the Deranged Squirrel."

"I wasn't so fearless initially," she admitted. "Not when he jumped out at me when I was about to get in the shower."

I pulled her to me, suddenly very aware of how little she was wearing and how gorgeous she looked—even after a close call with a squirrel. "Hey, you were braver than me. And look, you did it all without losing that towel."

Amusement lit Sydney's features as she let me draw her near. She patted the top of the towel, where it wrapped around her chest. "It's all in how you fold it," she said practically. "Do it the right way, and nothing will get it off."

"Challenge accepted," I murmured, bringing my lips down to hers.

She melted into me, warm and vibrant and smelling exquisitely of Sydney. I pressed her against the wall, bringing us closer together, and she wrapped a leg around my hip. I ran a hand over the smooth, perfect skin of her thigh, and it hit me that we were truly alone for the first time in a very long while. My mother wasn't outside our door. We didn't have an entire Court of Moroi surrounding us, waiting for us to step outside, or a team of Alchemists hunting us beyond its walls. We'd lost ourselves. We'd made an escape plan. No one knew we were here. If we'd wanted to, the power to simply disappear was right before us.

I think that knowledge, that we were truly and really free for the first time, sparked an extra intensity between us. There was a heat in Sydney as she kissed me back and entwined her fingers in my hair that reminded me of our early days together. I lifted her easily in my arms and carried her over to the bed, amazed at how the strongest women I knew could feel so light in my arms.

I was also amazed at how difficult that towel was to get off.

Sydney laughed softly, trailing her fingers along my cheek. The sunlight peeping in around the window blinds made her look like she was made of gold. "Uh-oh," she said. "Are you going to fail in your challenge?"

I finally untwisted the fold and removed the towel, tossing it as far from the bed as I could. "No way," I said, as always in awe of her body. "It takes a lot more than that to keep me away. You'll have to try harder next time."

She helped pull my shirt off over my head. "Now why would I want to do that?"

We kissed again, and as we became entangled in each other, I found all the worries that had chased me in the rest of the world disappearing. Nina, the Alchemists, Alicia . . . even Aunt Tatiana. There was no one in the world but Sydney and me just then, and the only things that mattered were our love and the way I felt in her arms. It was a joy that went beyond just physical pleasure, though I'd be lying if I said there wasn't plenty of that.

Afterward, sweaty and exhausted, we curled up with each other in a much calmer way. She rested her head on my chest, and I kissed her forehead contentedly. I decided then that the best thing that could happen would be if Jackie called and told us Alicia had been dealt with, Jill was free, and Sydney and I could live happily ever after in Council Bluffs. I drifted off to sleep, happily dreaming about that fantasy.

It was short-lived, however, as I was soon pulled into a very different kind of dream. Aunt Tatiana's warning came back to me, about how Nina wasn't going to just let me walk out on our deal.

"Where have you been?" exclaimed Nina. The farmhouse in Wisconsin materialized before us. "You were supposed to find me."

I stared around, trying to gather my bearings at this unexpected change in venue. "I, uh, sorry. I got distracted in the real world and fell asleep."

"Well, no problem," she said briskly. "I'll just lead the dream. Remember, you've got to wield more spirit this time."

My eyes widened. "No, Nina—wait—"

But Nina wasn't listening. She was too caught up in her obsessive mission of finding Olive. I felt Nina call on spirit and bring another person to join us. Moments later, Olive began materializing in the room before us, as shadowy and cloaked as before. And just like before, panic seized Olive, and she began to wrest the dream away from Nina. This time, knowing what to expect, I was more aware of it happening.

Since that last attempt, I'd looked into dream walking as much as I could, though there really wasn't much to go off of. I'd even chatted with Sonya, and we'd decided it came down to Olive's will. If her motivation was great enough, she could overcome the spirit user who was controlling the dream she was in. And clearly, that was happening now.

You're a stronger dream walker than Nina, Aunt Tatiana reminded me. *The strongest of any dream walker.*

I know, I told her. And as I saw the setting dissolving, I made an impulse decision, going against what I told Sydney I'd do.

"Let go of the dream," I said to Nina.

Understanding my intent, she complied. I was ready, channeling spirit, and I swooped in to become the dream's new master. The farmhouse, which had been crumbling, began to rematerialize. Likewise, Olive also began solidifying.

"No!" she cried.

Nina hurried toward her. "Olive! I've missed you so much!"

Olive's face was filled with fear, and she backed up quickly, wrapping the cloak more tightly around her. "No . . . no. Please leave me alone!"

And like that, I started to feel the dream slipping away from me. Despite my hold, Olive's will was still winning out. Cracks appeared in the wooden walls. The wicker furniture crumbled to dust. The windows filled with sunlight went dark. I called on spirit's power, pulling more magic through me in order to fight back against Olive's usurpation. Spirit burned within my body, but she'd already changed the face of the dream. The house was gone, replaced by what looked like a hotel parking lot. A flickering streetlamp cast weak light down on us, eerily supplemented by the red glow of a neon sign hanging in the lobby's window. What normally might have been busy streets surrounded us, but no traffic flowed on them in this dream. Eerie silence dominated until I spoke.

"I'm sorry, she was too fast," I said to Nina. "Where are we?"

She took a step closer to me, her face filled with fear. "This is where we were attacked with our dad. When Olive was turned. There were Strigoi—"

Before she could finish, two menacing figures emerged from behind the dark shape of a parked Buick. The phantom lighting made their pale white skin look even more gruesome. I couldn't see the red in their eyes, but the evil within came through plainly, no matter the dim conditions. They snarled, revealing fangs similar to mine, save that their only intent was to kill.

I gripped Nina's hand and slowly backed up. "They can't kill us in a dream," I said, my mouth suddenly dry. "Not really."

"No, but we'll wake up," she said. "And Olive will be gone again."

"Not if we annihilate them first."

Terror filled me, even though I knew the Strigoi were only part of the dream. I'd been too conditioned against them my entire life to feel anything except fear. But what I'd said was true: You couldn't die in a spirit dream. You would simply wake up. And before that, you'd feel deep, excruciating pain. *They aren't real*, I told myself. *This is a dream, and I still have some control.*

Olive had taken charge of big things—like the setting—but little things were within my grasp. Here, I could wield fire as deftly as Christian or Sydney. A fireball appeared in my hand, fueled by spirit magic. I felt magic surge in Nina too, and I was quick to chastise her.

"No—let me handle this." If I was caught in this dream, I might as well fulfill the original goal of keeping her away from the brunt of spirit. "Just assist. Don't wield too much."

I hurled the fireball toward one of the Strigoi, and it went wide, missing him by about two feet. Okay—maybe I couldn't wield fire quite as deftly as Christian or Sydney. It had always looked so easy when Sydney did it, and I realized I was thinking in those terms, imitating her throw. But relying on my physical abilities wasn't the way to go. I had to be much more intentional. I summoned another fireball and this time used spirit to specifically guide it toward the Strigoi. My aim proved true, but the Strigoi, even in a dream, moved quickly. He dodged the brunt of the fireball and only ended up singeing his arm. It was enough to inspire me, though. I called on spirit again, summoning two more fireballs, one to keep going after this target and another to keep the other Strigoi at a distance.

I also managed to anticipate the way the Strigoi would dodge this time, so I adjusted accordingly, sending the fireball right into his chest. Flames engulfed him, and I used spirit to summon a silver stake. Moving to where he writhed on the ground, I called on spirit to shield me from the fire as I plunged the stake into what I hoped was his heart. Either I was right or the fire had already done its job, because the creature suddenly stopped moving and vanished into nothing.

The other Strigoi had tried to advance on Nina while I was distracted. She threw a fireball of her own and experienced the same learning curve I had, missing with her first attempt. It was enough to distract the Strigoi until I could swoop in.

"Hold off," I reminded Nina. I hit the second Strigoi squarely with another fireball, and then I once again finished the job with a silver stake. As I did, I felt my triumph falter as four more Strigoi suddenly stepped forward. I hastily retreated back to Nina.

"No problem," I told her. "We'll get rid of them too." Seeing four of them was daunting, but my method seemed to be working. In a dream, at least, I could be as badass as any guardian.

"There's no time!" Nina exclaimed. Spirit swelled within her—a lot of spirit. I turned on her in alarm.

"What are you doing? That's too much!"

She ignored me and, impossibly, called on even more spirit. I was reminded of a balloon, ready to burst. "We need them gone, and we need them gone now!"

"Stop it!" I cried. I shook her arm, hoping I could get her to lose her concentration. She shook me off and continued building up spirit to impossible, dizzying heights.

"I won't let Olive escape again!" Nina said.

Fire shot out from her fingertips. It wasn't a compact little ball like I'd formed. Nina was wielding sheets and sheets of fire. Substantial amounts of fire. Flames lit up the night, wrapping around the three Strigoi. There was no need to stake them; I think they were killed almost instantly.

I shook her again. "Let go! Let the magic go!"

What she'd done, to create that ridiculous amount of fire, hadn't been a small change to the dream. She'd not only had to break through Olive's control, she'd also had to break through mine at the dream's foundation. The spirit that had required—to blast all those Strigoi away in one fell swoop—was staggering. It was at least twice as much as I'd seen her wielding when we were in the dream together before.

The fire vanished (as did the incinerated Strigoi), and Nina dropped to her knees. She rested her hands on the side of her head and began to scream. And scream. Around us, the dark parking lot transformed to the sunny Getty Villa as my control of the dream returned—thanks to her efforts. I knelt beside her and gently rested my hands on her shoulders. Her eyes stared blankly ahead, lost, as she kept screaming.

"Nina, Nina . . . it's okay. It's okay."

But I didn't know if it was. She wasn't screaming because of the Strigoi. There was something else going on, the terrible aftereffects of all that spirit use. Week after week of so much use, now followed by this . . . it was too much. The final straw. I had no idea how much damage had been done, but something was seriously wrong. I needed to wake us up and find out how she was in real life. With a thought, I let the dream begin to disintegrate.

"Nina . . ."

The small voice jerked my attention up. I hadn't realized that Olive was back with us in the Getty Villa. When Nina had blasted through the Strigoi, she'd wrested control back from Olive and temporarily from me. Now Olive was left with nothing, no more control, no ability to escape. She was fading, though, just like Nina and me as I sent us to the waking world.

Before we all disappeared, however, I saw a few things very clearly. One was concern on Olive's features as she stared at Nina. No matter what had passed between them, Olive loved her sister and wasn't trying to purposely hurt her with these obstacles.

The other thing I noticed was that Olive's cloak was gone. With no control left of the dream, Olive now appeared as she did in the waking world. The clothes she wore were old and threadbare, as though they'd been passed around a few times. Around her neck was a small, circular wooden pendant edged in green. I'd never seen it before and didn't know what it meant.

But as I got my last glimpse of her before waking, I saw something else about her that I recognized immediately.

The dream completely shattered, and I found myself alert and sitting up in the inn's bed. As I blinked and tried to focus, Sydney clutched my arm and tried to calm me.

"Adrian," she exclaimed, and I knew it wasn't the first time she'd said my name. "What's wrong?"

"Olive's pregnant," I gasped out.

CHAPTER 8

SYDNEY

"OLIVE?" I REPEATED STUPIDLY. I was a little addled myself, having been woken out of a deep sleep by Adrian's cries. "What are you talking about?"

He shook his head, regret on his features. "I'm sorry, Sydney. I didn't mean to. Nina found me in a spirit dream, and I got pulled into looking for Olive. And this time we got to her. She was pregnant."

I was so stunned to hear that he'd gone through with the dream that I couldn't process the rest of what he was saying immediately. But the regret on his face was so sincere, I believed that it had been against his will. "She can't be pregnant," I said at last. "I mean . . . I guess she can. But I thought she was involved with Neil. If she's pregnant, then . . ."

Adrian swallowed and slowly seemed to be recovering himself. "I know, I know. If she's pregnant, then it was by someone other than Neil."

Soap opera drama with Olive wasn't dire in the grand

scheme of things—especially when compared to what was happening with Jill—but it was still a surprise. Olive and Neil had seemed so close. "Do you know for certain she is?"

He gave a shaky nod. "We did it. Nina and I broke through Olive's defenses and saw her as she truly is in the waking world. No question—she was pregnant. I guess that's why she kept trying to hide herself in the dream." He paused to consider. "I guess that's why she's hiding herself in real life too."

"I suppose I can understand her wanting to hide from Neil . . ." I began, my mind spinning. Because she was a dhampir, only a Moroi could have gotten her pregnant. Well, a human could have as well, but most people in the mainstream Moroi world weren't taking after Adrian and me. "But why Nina? Especially since they were so close? Unless . . . oh." My heart sank. "Maybe . . . maybe whatever happened wasn't consensual."

It took Adrian a moment to catch on, and anger darkened his features. "If some Moroi forced her, then why wouldn't she tell Nina? And everyone else?"

I laced my fingers through his. "Because unfortunately not all girls think like that. Look at my sister Carly, when Keith raped her. She thought it was her fault. She was mortified at the thought of anyone finding out and judging her."

"Nina wouldn't judge her," said Adrian adamantly. "Olive should know that. Nina might be crazy, but—"

I did a double take at the alarm that suddenly filled his face. "What's wrong?"

"Nina." He reached over and grabbed his cell phone. He dialed a number and put the phone to his ear. I could just barely hear the sound of ringing and eventually voice mail picking up.

"Nina, it's me. Call me. Immediately." When he'd disconnected, he turned back to me with a sigh. "What we did . . . whatever happened to break through to Olive, it didn't go so well for Nina. She took control from me and ended up wielding most of the spirit. I'm not entirely sure what happened to her—it was just a sense I got before the dream disbanded, but I feel like something went horribly wrong. Like she got injured." He glanced at his phone, as though staring long enough might make her call back.

"She might still be asleep," I warned. I wouldn't say so aloud—and I hoped Nina hadn't been harmed—but a part of me was relieved Adrian hadn't wielded all the spirit he'd planned. "She'll probably be fine when she wakes up. And you'll have a lot to tell her."

Adrian sighed. "Not sure I will. I mean, I suppose I could tell her the pregnancy part. But the rest? I'm still not sure where she is. She was dressed strangely . . ." He got up and found a pen and some inn stationery. After some quick sketching, he showed me a drawing of a circle filled with abstract designs. "Does this mean anything to you?"

I studied it with a frown. "No. Should it?"

"Olive was wearing it on a necklace. I thought it might mean something." He sat back beside me and stifled a yawn. "I hope Nina and I haven't gone through all of this and not found any way to help Olive. Worse, if we don't get any answers, I'm afraid Nina's going to keep doing it." He cast another anxious glance at his cell phone, but there was still no response from Nina.

I put an arm around him and drew him near. "Just hope for the best. That symbol may mean something to her. Be patient until she gets back to you."

I tried to keep my tone light and hide the fear within me. I wasn't afraid for Nina. I worried Adrian would help her again, putting her and Olive's needs above his own, no matter the dangers. My heart clenched at the thought, and conflicting emotions stirred in my chest. I admired Adrian for wanting to help them. But I also loved him and selfishly wanted to protect him.

He tried calling Nina one more time and then finally heeded my words when I said we should try to get some rest while we could. I hated seeing him so worried and worked up, and at last, he managed to put his worries aside and relax. We fell asleep wrapped in each other's arms and were jolted awake a few hours later by a phone ringing. Adrian grabbed for his, nearly falling out of bed in the process, and stared at the screen in dismay. "Crap. My battery died. I forgot to charge it."

"It's my phone," I said, making my way groggily to my purse. A jolt of panic helped push me awake as I braced myself for news from Ms. Terwilliger. But when I picked up the phone, I was surprised to see Sonya's name on the display. "Hello?"

"Hello, Sydney," came her familiar voice. "I trust you're doing well."

"Yes," I said cautiously, puzzled as to why she was calling me. We were friendly, but usually she dealt with Adrian. "How about you?"

"I'm fine. I can't say the same for Nina Sinclair," she replied, making my heart stop. "I tried calling Adrian, but it went to voice mail."

"His phone's dead," I explained. "What's wrong with Nina?" At that, Adrian jerked his head up.

"I figured you two would already know, seeing as she was found in your rooms at guest housing."

"We stepped out," I said uneasily. "What do you mean, 'found'?" It was the kind of terminology you used when people died.

"She's alive," said Sonya, guessing my thoughts. "She's been taken to the medical center, but she's practically comatose. The one time she did come to, she babbled incoherently before lapsing back into unconsciousness. The doctors haven't been able to rouse her since. Perhaps you'd like to come by and see her."

"Um, I'll have to talk to Adrian and see when we can get a chance to—"

"Save the subterfuge, Sydney." There was something both weary and exasperated in Sonya's voice. "We know you aren't here."

"Well, yeah, like I said, we stepped out—"

"We know you aren't at Court," she interrupted. "After Nina's fit, a Court-wide search was conducted, and then Daniella Ivashkov finally caved and admitted you both were gone. She won't tell us where you are, though, and I think she's trying to confuse us by giving us some outlandish story about you turning into a cat."

I really didn't know how to respond to any of that.

"A number of people would like to speak to you," Sonya continued. "Both of you. I don't suppose you have the means to do a video call?"

My eyes fell on Adrian's laptop bag, which he'd brought along. "We do . . ." Honestly, I was kind of afraid of what this conference call might entail, but I could see Adrian was having to restrain himself from tearing the phone away from me to get answers about Nina. A group call might be the best solution, especially since our cover was blown. There was also a good chance we could be traced by such a call, but I wasn't quite as nervous about the Moroi finding us as the Alchemists.

When I disconnected with Sonya, I found Adrian was in agreement. He was dying to know more about Nina, and we decided it'd be worth the risk. We were both still naked, so the first order of business was hastily tossing on some clothes so it wouldn't be entirely obvious what we'd been doing.

Adrian eyed me wistfully as I searched for my shirt. "If we made sure only our heads were in the shot, I don't think anyone would notice." I answered him with a warning look, and after a great deal of dramatic sighing, he reluctantly put on his own clothes too.

We still stayed on the bed, however, opening up the laptop there. Once we had everything set up and connected, we leaned in together over the laptop and found Sonya's worried face looking back at us. Before Adrian could even ask her about Nina, Sonya moved away, and another face filled the screen.

"Really, Adrian?" Lissa exclaimed, outrage written all over her. "How could you guys do this to me? You *begged* me to protect you! I risked the wrath of my own people and the Alchemists to take you in, and this is how you repay me?"

She looked truly frustrated, and uneasily, I wondered just how much trouble we might have caused. I forgot sometimes what a precarious position Lissa was in, constantly being pulled in different directions as she worked hard to do the impossible and please everyone. Adrian and I had done what we needed to do for ourselves—but hadn't considered the fallout for others.

"It was for Jill," Adrian said resolutely. "We had to go after her."

Lissa shook her head angrily. "And I told you, as much as it's appreciated, we don't need you out there looking for Jill. We've already got people on it."

"No, no . . . it's not like that," Adrian protested. "It wasn't just some impulsive trip. Sydney had a real lead."

Lissa's green eyes focused on me expectantly. I launched into a retelling of what I knew so far, about how Alicia was behind Jill's disappearance and how my contacts in Palm Springs were currently looking for leads. As I spoke, I saw Lissa's expression grow more and more incredulous.

"How am I just learning about this? You guys should have told me immediately!"

"We didn't know all the facts then," said Adrian. Despite his outward confidence, I could tell he too was second-guessing our actions. "Still don't. But Jackie Terwilliger's good. She'll turn up something." He hesitated. "Who knows we're gone?"

"The Alchemists don't, if that's what you're worried about," said Lissa. "So far, only a handful of people here at Court know, and you'd better hope it stays that way. The Alchemists have made it very clear to me that Sydney won't be returned to us if they catch her." I flinched at the words.

"Enough, Liss." Rose suddenly pushed her way into the picture, wriggling in beside her friend, like Lissa wasn't the ruler of all Moroi. "They get it. They screwed up."

"We didn't screw up," said Adrian obstinately. "Finding Jill is the most important thing we can do right now."

Lissa's anger diminished a bit. "It is. And I want to find her too. Why didn't you come to me once you had that box?"

Adrian shrugged. "We only know about the connection to Jill and Alicia now, after going through all those hoops. At the time, it didn't seem certain, and we honestly didn't know if you'd let us go. We felt the most important thing was to get Sydney out of Court to go after the lead. Me joining her was an afterthought."

Surprisingly, Lissa nodded and conceded the point. "You're right. I probably would've wanted more proof if all you'd had was the box with Jill's picture. And no one I sent would've learned what you uncovered, Sydney."

It wasn't exactly an apology, but Adrian still took it as such. "Thank you," he said.

"You still should've told me afterward," she warned.

"Or me," piped in Rose.

"Now that you're done scolding me," Adrian said, "will someone please tell me more about Nina?"

"They can catch you up," said Lissa, gesturing to those beside her. "I need to go make sure your secret escape from Court stays a secret. Unless you guys plan on coming back and letting Eddie and your human friend handle things? It's not too late to return to the way things were."

Adrian and I exchanged glances briefly before turning back to Lissa. We both shook our heads.

"I didn't think so," Lissa said, with a small, rueful laugh. "Let me go see what I can do to keep this quiet. In the meantime, please, don't you guys do anything that'll get yourselves caught."

She left the screen, and a moment later, Sonya moved in beside Rose. "There's not much more to tell than what I already did. Maybe you could help by telling me what happened."

"It was from spirit use," Adrian said, casting me an apologetic glance. "I joined her in a dream and helped her blast down the barriers Olive had put up."

"I suspected as much," said Sonya grimly.

"Do you know when Nina will wake up?" Adrian demanded. "Will she be okay?"

"It depends on how you define 'okay,'" Sonya replied. "The doctor thinks her difficulties with waking up are due to exhaustion. She'll hopefully come around with a little more rest. But as for what state she'll be in . . ."

"If she's so worn out, that would explain why she's not making any sense," Adrian said quickly. I could tell he very, very badly wanted to believe that. "Hell, you should see me after pulling an all-nighter. I make her sound totally articulate and lucid."

Sonya didn't laugh at the joke. "It's possible . . . but I don't think it's that simple. I've seen her aura. That tells its own tale, and it's not a good one. Plus, I've spent a lot of time with Avery Lazar, Adrian. I've seen what spirit did to her—and this has a very similar feel."

"So what are you saying?" I asked, surprised at the lump in my throat. I didn't even know Nina that well, but there was something chilling in listening to this grim prognosis—maybe because I feared one day, we'd be talking about Adrian.

Sonya suddenly looked tired, as though she were the one who'd expended so much power and energy and needed to sleep. "I'm saying, when Nina comes around, she may not be the same Nina we knew. What happened? I thought you were going to keep her from using excessive spirit?"

"I tried. I really did." Adrian leaned against me, and I rested my arm on his back. "I led the dream. I did most of the work when Olive took control—but Nina got impatient and took over. She blew through everything before I could stop her."

Sonya nodded wearily. "Were you able to talk to Olive at least?"

"Not really," he said carefully. I kept my own face schooled to neutrality, lest I give away that he wasn't telling the whole truth. He held up the piece of paper he'd sketched on for me. "Does this mean anything to you?"

"No, I'm sorry." Sonya looked down and grimaced. "I'm getting a text from the doctor monitoring Nina. They have some more questions for me. I'll be in touch if I learn more."

Adrian gave a weak nod, and I clutched his hand. I knew he felt terrible, like he was personally responsible for Nina's state. With Sonya gone from the call too, that left Rose, looking dismayed at the news.

"Well, I'm glad we got a lead on Jill," she said. "But you guys really should have been more careful about—"

"What was that you showed Sonya?"

Dimitri suddenly joined Rose on the screen. She shot him an amused look. "Easy, comrade. You'll get your chance to lecture them too."

"Geez," said Adrian. "How many other people are there lurking off-screen?"

"What was that you showed her?" Dimitri reiterated, his face hard as he peered at us. Even through a computer screen, he was intimidating.

Adrian held up the piece of paper again. "This?" He leaned forward eagerly. "Do you know what it is?"

"Yes, it's—" Dimitri bit off his words and glanced at Rose,

then back at the drawing. "It's a kind of marker worn by women in, uh, dhampir communes."

Rose had no problem stating what his delicate sensibilities had held back from. "A blood whore camp?" Her eyes widened, and suddenly, she turned as angry as Lissa had been earlier. "Adrian Ivashkov! You should be ashamed of yourself, going to a place like that, especially now that you're married—"

Adrian scoffed. "Both of you, calm down. I've never set foot in one of those places, nor do I really want to." He looked back at Dimitri. "What do you mean, it's a marker?"

I could tell from Dimitri's face that it wasn't a topic he liked discussing, and frankly, I didn't blame him. Moroi society hadn't always treated dhampir women well. They could only have children with Moroi fathers, fathers who often viewed those women as little more than playthings. The standard practice for dhampir women who had children was to turn those children over early to one of the schools, like St. Vladimir's, while the mother returned to guardian services. A lot of dhampir women didn't like doing that, however. They wanted to raise their own children. Some would go off and blend into human society, but that was discouraged. Even if dhampirs looked identical to humans, dhampirs often demonstrated extraordinary physical abilities that called too much attention to them. Without other options, these dhampir women often banded together in "communes," some more civilized than others. Some dhampir women found perfectly ordinary ways to survive . . . others turned to more desperate paths, which Dimitri confirmed.

"Members of these communes wear markers that show what their role is," he explained. "Some are residents, some are guests. Some are women making themselves available to interested men—selling their bodies."

"Disgusting," said Rose.

I glanced at Adrian's drawing, and a horrible, terrible thought occurred to me about Olive. Had she become that desperate? "Do you know what kind this is?" I asked.

Dimitri shook his head. "Not without color. These marks identify which commune it is. There's usually a color on it to signify the person's status."

"It was green," said Adrian.

"Green marks a guest," Dimitri said. Both Adrian and I exhaled in relief. "Someone living there temporarily. Maybe visiting a relative. Maybe seeking sanctuary."

"So not someone selling herself?" I clarified. I couldn't stand the thought of poor Olive doing that.

"No," said Dimitri, looking puzzled. Rose did as well.

"What's this all about?" she asked.

Adrian didn't answer right away. Instead, he held up the paper again for them to see. "Do you know which commune this belongs to? Where it's at?"

Dimitri studied the drawing a moment before shaking his head. "No . . . but I could probably find out. Why?"

Adrian hesitated again. "Is Lissa still there somewhere? Or is anyone else lurking?"

"No," said Rose. "It's just us. Why?"

Adrian glanced at me, and just like that, I knew what he was thinking. "We're supposed to be lying low," I reminded him. "Staying out of trouble."

"Olive could be in a lot of trouble. And if she won't talk in a dream, maybe going to her in person is the only option we have," Adrian said. "That and, I mean, come on. If we can't help Jackie, we might as well help someone else . . ."

Once again, I was torn. My logic said to stay here and stay safe. But my heart—especially when it feared Olive might have been raped like Carly—wanted to go off and help. "There's no telling what we could be walking into," I said. "From what I've heard, some of those dhampir communes are like the Wild West."

Adrian grinned at that. "Good thing we've got our own cowboy."

"Um, hello," said Rose from the screen, her face lined with irritation at being left out of the conversation. "Do you guys want to fill us in on what you're talking about?"

Adrian looked up, glancing between her and Dimitri. "How would you two like to take a trip with us?"

CHAPTER 9

ADRIAN

"SO THIS IS CANADA," I SAID, looking outside my car door.

"For the last time, it's not Canada," Sydney replied, rolling her eyes. "It's northern Michigan."

I glanced around, seeing nothing but enormous trees in every direction. Despite it being a late August afternoon, the temperature could've easily passed for something in autumn. Craning my head, I just barely caught a glimpse of gray waters beyond the trees to my right: Lake Superior, according to the map I'd seen.

"Maybe it's not Canada," I conceded. "But it's exactly how I always imagined Canada would look. Except I thought there'd be more hockey."

Sydney gave me an indulgent smile as she slid out of the backseat and stood beside me. "It's a lot different from Iowa."

"That's for sure," I agreed, slipping my arm around her as we admired the scenery.

It was crazy to think how far we'd come in less than twenty-four hours. After convincing Rose and Dimitri to go with us to the dhampir commune, we'd had to wait for Dimitri to use his resources and confirm where Olive's medallion was linked to. He'd gotten back to us fairly quickly, revealing that the symbol on the necklace was used by a commune in Michigan's upper peninsula. He and Rose had then begun a series of convoluted flights to get there from Court. Sydney and I had chosen the more direct route, hopping back in the car and driving twelve hours. It had been exhausting, given how little sleep we'd gotten, but we'd traded off driving and napping. It had also given us little opportunity to discuss the larger issues that still loomed over us. I didn't know if that was a good or bad thing.

"Come on," said Rose, hopping out of the SUV's passenger seat. "It looks like the entrance is that way." We'd rendezvoused with her and Dimitri in Houghton and then taken their more rugged rental vehicle out here to the packed-earth parking lot we now found ourselves in. Several other cars with Michigan plates were parked beside our rental, most of them the kind of heavy-duty models needed for life out in the wilderness. Admittedly, we were only an hour from Houghton, but it was hardly what you'd call a major metropolitan area. It had the basics—grocery stores, a hospital, Starbucks, even a university—but that was about it. Once you left the city limits, you were almost immediately out in the woods again. That was all I could see right now, and it took me a moment to spot the opening to the trailhead that Rose indicated.

"Narrow," I remarked as Sydney and I followed her and Dimitri over to it. The trail itself was clear, but around it, the thick forest was difficult to pass through.

"By design," he said, setting off like he did this sort of hike all the time. Probably it was how he'd gotten to school every day in Siberia. "Makes it harder for Strigoi to come through."

"I bet it's a real bitch to get through in the winter," I added. I swore as a low branch snagged my coat.

Careful, warned Aunt Tatiana. *That's Italian leather.*

"I wouldn't be surprised if a lot of them left for the winter," Dimitri remarked. "This is an ideal summer location—somewhat high latitude. In peak summer, there's probably only five hours without daylight. If you've got that and some solid wards, you can hold out relatively well against attacks—especially when it's a group of dhampirs we're talking about. They put up a good fight."

I could believe that and stayed silent as I focused on paying attention to my footing and not eating any gnats. My muscles were stiff from so much time in the car, and the movement actually felt good. When Dimitri had said the medallion symbol was linked to a place called Wild Pine Intentional Community, I'd had no idea what we'd be getting into. Apparently, "intentional community" was the modern name for a commune, and they were something that humans still formed nowadays too. I'd also learned—thanks to Sydney's endless knowledge on the drive here—that a lot of communes weren't just hippie love fests à la the 1960s. Some were very modern but embraced green ways of living. Some were little more than campgrounds. Dimitri had told us in Houghton that this particular dhampir community likely fell somewhere in the middle. I was crossing my fingers for something on the more modern side, maybe like a secret wooded resort. Images of the Ewok village from *Return of the Jedi* came to mind.

"I just hope they have plumbing," Rose said. "That was the rough part about staying with the Keepers."

"I was actually okay with that," Sydney said unexpectedly. "It was the questionable meat I had a problem with."

"Whoa, no plumbing?" I exclaimed. My brain had trouble wrapping itself around how you'd even function in such a scenario.

"Better get used to the idea," Rose teased, glancing back at me. "Liss may not let you guys come back. When this is all over, you two may end up living with the Keepers."

"I'm sure we can find some alternative before resorting to that," I said loftily, not wanting to admit how uncertain I was about our future.

Dimitri didn't share Rose's amusement. "If the Alchemists are still after her, I'm sure Lissa will let you return to your suite."

Won't that be fun, noted Aunt Tatiana. *More close quarters with your mother, none of you ever wanting to go out and face the other Moroi.*

"That's no kind of life," I murmured, thinking of how trapped both Sydney and I had felt. I hadn't fully realized it until we'd left and had some breathing room. Even when we were fighting, the vibe between us was more electric when we had our freedom. Meeting Sydney's eyes, I knew she was thinking the same thing and was full of the same questions I had about what our future held. Unfortunately, we weren't likely to get any answers right away. We could only focus on the immediate concerns. Jill. Olive.

Dimitri came to a halt and pointed off toward the woods. "Look. The beginning of the wards."

I followed his motion and caught a glimpse of silver in the underbrush. A charmed silver stake. The dhampirs in this commune would have them placed strategically around their settlement, creating a magical barrier to keep Strigoi out. The undead couldn't cross that kind of power, but it required constant maintenance. If the bonds weakened or someone moved a stake out of place, Strigoi would be able to come through. It was a concern all Moroi and dhampir communities had. The wards at Court were checked several times a day.

We had just passed the stake when a figure suddenly stepped out of the woods and onto the path in front of Dimitri, who struck a defensive stance at the sight of the newcomer and then relaxed when he saw it was a dhampir. She too wore a tough, ready-for-anything expression, along with both a gun and a silver stake at her belt. A medallion around her neck was an exact copy of Olive's—save that it was edged in blue, not green. The woman's face softened a little as she took in Rose and Dimitri, then hardened again at the sight of me.

"Greetings," she said. "You're looking for Wild Pine?"

Rose squeezed up beside Dimitri, which wasn't easy on the narrow path. "We're looking for a friend of ours," she said. "We think she's staying with you."

After assessing Rose and Dimitri, the dhampir woman nodded congenially at Sydney and then turned downright hostile when she looked me over. "And him? What's *he* looking for?"

"The girl we're looking for is my friend too," I said, surprised at her reaction. "I told her sister I'd find her."

Our hostess looked skeptical, and I wondered what was up with that. I'd think it was dhampir solidarity, except that she'd seemed fine with Sydney. Probably the woman had seen Sydney's lily tattoo and assumed she was doing some routine Alchemist visit. That still didn't explain my cold welcome.

"What's your friend's name?" the woman asked.

"Olive Sinclair," I replied.

Immediately, a look of distaste filled the woman's eyes, but it was clearly in regard to me, not Olive. "So you're the one who got her in trouble."

"The one who . . ." The meaning became clear, and I found myself blushing—something I'd maybe done twice in my life. "What? No! Of course not. I mean, if I did, I'd never—that is—I'm not the kind of guy who—"

"No," said Dimitri bluntly. "Adrian's not responsible. His intentions are honorable here. I'll vouch for him. I'm Dimitri Belikov. This is Rose Hathaway, Sydney Ivashkov."

Normally, a human introduced with a royal Moroi last name would have warranted a double take. But it was clear this woman never heard anything past Rose and Dimitri's names. I saw it clearly in her eyes: the same awe and worship I'd observed in so many other faces whenever this dynamic duo introduced itself. And like that, the woman turned from fiercely protective doorkeeper to swooning fangirl.

"Omigod," she gushed. "I thought you looked familiar! I've seen your pictures! I should've known right away! I'm so embarrassed. Come on, come on. I'm Mallory, by the way. Let's not stand around in the woods! You must have done a lot of traveling to get here. Come rest. Get something to eat. Omigod."

We followed her down the narrow trail, which eventually opened up to a huge clearing in the forest. It turned out Wild Pine really was kind of a cross between a camp and a resort. Actually, it kind of reminded me of a Wild West town after all. I could totally picture a shoot-out happening. Nice-looking cabins were arranged in orderly rows and seemed to be divided into business and residential areas. Dhampirs, almost entirely women and children, moved about their business, some pausing to give us speculative looks. Mallory led us toward a large cabin that was situated between the business and residential areas, bouncing with each step she took.

We entered what seemed to be a sort of office, and the first thing I noticed was that they had electricity. I took that as a good omen for plumbing. An older dhampir woman, her blond hair streaked with silver, sat at a desk, clicking something on a computer. She too wore a blue-edged medallion. When she saw us, she stood up and looped her fingers through the belt on her jeans as she leaned against the wall, showing off tooled leather boots that further reinforced my Wild West stereotypes.

"Well, what did you turn up, Mallory?" she asked with amusement.

"Lana, you'll never believe who this is," exclaimed Mallory. "It's "

"Rose Hathaway and Dimitri Belikov," supplied Lana. Her eyes then fell on Sydney and me, and she arched an eyebrow. "And Adrian Ivashkov and his infamous wife. I've been to Court. I know who the celebrities are."

"We're not celebrities," I assured her, putting my arm around Sydney and nodding toward Rose and Dimitri. "Not like those two."

Lana's eyes crinkled at the corners as she smiled at us. "Aren't you? Your marriage has been the source of a lot of speculation."

"I think that makes us more of a source of a gossip than

celebrities." Although, as soon as the words left my mouth, I wondered whether there was any real difference between the two.

"Well, I'm delighted to meet you. All of you." Lana walked forward and shook our hands. "I've also heard from Olive how you've done some pretty fancy work to create a Strigoi vaccine, Lord Ivashkov."

I started to say we weren't having much luck on the vaccine, but something more important in her words drew my attention. "You know Olive."

"Of course," Lana said. "I know everyone here."

"Lana's our leader," explained Mallory.

Lana actually guffawed. "I'm more of an administrator. I assume it's Olive you're here to see?"

"If you'll allow it," said Dimitri politely. "We'd be grateful for any assistance you can offer."

"Not up to me. It's up to Olive." Lana held us in her gaze for a few moments, as though deciding something. At last, she gave a small nod. "I'll take you to her myself. But first, have some dinner and relax. I know it's not easy getting here."

We thanked her for her hospitality, but it was hard to relax, knowing we were so close to finding Olive. I'd given Rose and Dimitri the full rundown on her story when we'd met up in Houghton—at least as much as I knew about it. They were as concerned as I was and also concurred that there was probably something sinister going on if she felt such a strong need to hide her pregnancy. I got the impression that if she had been taken advantage of—and Dimitri found out who was responsible— there were going to be some serious consequences.

Dinner turned out to be chicken salad sandwiches, a

surprisingly ordinary meal to be eating in a wilderness resort of half vampires. Sydney didn't even hesitate before biting into hers, which I thought spoke legions about how far she'd come in dealing with Moroi. Lana meanwhile made it clear to me there were no official feeders around here and that I shouldn't even think of soliciting blood from any of the Wild Pine dhampirs. There was a catch in her voice as she spoke, however, and combined with what I knew about these communes, I suspected there were dhampirs here who sold their blood to Moroi as freely as they sold their bodies for sex. It was the dark side of these camps, what had given them such a bad reputation. It certainly wasn't a practice they all engaged in, but it happened frequently enough.

After dinner, Lana was true to her word and led us out herself, giving us a brief tour of the community. As I'd suspected, some of the buildings doubled as businesses.

"We make regular runs into Houghton for supplies," she explained. "But we also try to be as self-sustaining as we can. We grow a lot of our own food and even make some of our own clothes." She nodded to one cabin where two dhampir women sat sewing on the porch by lantern light, now that twilight was fast moving in. They waved back in greeting. She pointed out other buildings as we passed them. "That's Jody's shop—she can fix anything. And that right there's our medical center, such as it is. April's in charge of it, but she's out of town getting supplies. The things she needs are a little harder to make. Over there is Briana's school."

"You've got some solar panels over there," Sydney remarked. "Smart idea out here."

Lana beamed, clearly proud. "That was Talia's idea. We

get some electricity wired in, but she felt we should have a renewable source on hand."

I noted all the women's names and also noted that aside from some of the children, everyone in this community was female. So, it was kind of a shock when I caught a glimpse of a Moroi man walking between a group of cabins set off a bit from the others. Seeing my gaze, Lana scowled and gave a resigned sigh.

"Yes. That's where the girls who want to 'entertain' male guests live."

"Why don't you keep them out?" asked Dimitri, his expression dark.

"Because there are some girls who would do it anyway. They'd sneak off, live somewhere unsafe. I'd rather keep everything under my control. Some guys just want a good time, and there are girls who accept that and expect nothing more . . ." As she spoke, Lana watched the Moroi guy I'd seen. A dhampir girl hung on his arm, and they were laughing as they walked past us, caught up in some private conversation. She appeared to be walking him to the community's exit, and I noted her medallion was ringed in red. Lana turned back to us when they were gone. "Other guys are nothing but trouble. Those are the ones I need to keep an eye on—and sometimes the ones we have to forcibly remove."

"Any idea what kind of guy Olive was involved with?" I asked.

Lana began walking again, leading us to a section of residential cabins away from the one the Moroi guy had been in. "No. It's her business, so I haven't pushed. She hasn't had any gentleman callers, I can tell you that. Doesn't seem to have any romantic interests."

"She's got a pretty decent dhampir guy interested in her," I said. "But she cut off ties with him. And everyone else."

"Damn shame," said Lana. We came to a halt in front of a cute cabin with green shutters. "But who am I to judge? We're all fighting our own battles, the best way we can."

Pretty wise for a backwoods wannabe sheriff, said Aunt Tatiana.

I mulled Lana's words over as she knocked on the cabin's door. A dhampir woman with wildly curly hair answered, grinning when she saw Lana. "Hey, Mom."

"Hey, Diana." Lana kissed her on the cheek. "Is Olive around?"

Diana studied our group, her gaze lingering on me the longest. I hated that everyone around here assumed the worst. It was a sad state of affairs when even an Alchemist didn't get the suspicion a Moroi guy did. "Sure," she said. "I'll go get her."

Diana disappeared inside the cabin. I found I was holding my breath as we waited to see what would happen. Sensing my anticipation, Sydney squeezed my hand.

"I just can't believe we're about to see her after everything that's happened. No lava monsters. No spirit battles." I had to pause as my voice caught. "I feel like if I can connect with Olive here, help her, then I won't have failed Nina . . ."

Sydney's hold on me tightened. "You didn't fail her, Adrian. She made those choices."

Maybe if you'd been stronger, maybe if you'd used more spirit in the dream . . . Aunt Tatiana's voice paused in my head as she let me ponder that thought. *Well, maybe Nina wouldn't be in her current state.*

Be quiet, I snapped back to the phantom voice. *Sydney's right. It's not my fault. Nina made those choices.*

If you say so, said Aunt Tatiana.

Olive stepped out onto the porch just then, wearing the same homemade clothes I'd seen in the dream. And also just like in the dream, she was very obviously pregnant. She started to smile when she saw Lana, then froze when she caught sight of the rest of us.

"No," she said, backing up. "No, no, no."

Rose leapt forward. "Olive, wait. Please. We want to talk to you. We want to help you."

Olive shook her head frantically, and Lana put an arm around her. "Honey, you really should talk to them."

"I don't want to!" Olive exclaimed. She glanced from face to face, looking like a trapped animal as we all gathered around, and my heart went out to her. When her gaze fell on Sydney, she did a double take. "An Alchemist!"

"I'm not with them anymore," Sydney said. "I'm here to help you, just like everyone else."

"You know Sydney," I reminded Olive. "You can trust her."

Olive still looked frightened but at last dragged her attention from Sydney. "I don't have anything to say to any of you!"

"Then don't say anything," I said. "Just listen. Take a walk with me. Just me. Let me tell you what's been going on with Nina. I'll do all the taking."

Her sister's name drew Olive back from where she'd been about to retreat inside the cabin. She brushed long strands of black hair out of her face, peering at me with tear-filled eyes. "Nina? Is she okay? In that dream . . ."

I gestured past me. "Let's take a walk. I'll tell you everything."

After several moments of hesitation, Olive nodded and stepped off the porch. Sydney understood my cautious approach and quietly kept her distance. Rose, on the other hand, clearly wanted to come with Olive and me, but I gave her a quick shake of the head. Dimitri rested his hand on her arm to emphasize the point. I knew Olive liked Rose and Dimitri, and they certainly meant well, but right now, they were too much. Fear of being interrogated by a group was probably the reason she'd sought refuge here in the woods. I gave her a reassuring smile and nearly used a touch of compulsion to calm her but decided against it at the last minute. If she'd grown up around a spirit-using sister, she might recognize the signs and feel like I was trying to take advantage of her.

"Nice place," I remarked as we set out down a trail between the cabins. Tall trees created a canopy above us, and birds sang to the sunset up in the branches.

"Tell me about Nina," Olive said, wasting no time with small talk. "Is she okay?"

I hesitated. "Kind of. What she did in that last dream we were in . . . well, it involved a lot of spirit. A *lot*." I tried to find a delicate way to put it, without saying that Nina had burned herself out or possibly lost her mind. "That much spirit takes a toll on you. They tell me right now she's, uh, sleeping a lot and not making much sense. But that may change. She may be fine once she has time to recover."

Olive stared bleakly ahead. "Why couldn't she just leave me alone? Why'd she insist on trying to find me? She should never have put herself at risk like that!"

"She loves you," I said. "And I think Neil does too."

Tears filled Olive's eyes again. "Oh, Neil. How can I tell him what's happened?"

I stopped and faced her. "Look, whatever it is, he'll understand. He won't care what some other guy did to you—well, I mean, he'll want to kick that guy's ass—but he's not going to judge you or hold it against you. He's crazy about you. He'll help you and support you. We all will."

Confusion replaced her despair. "'Some other guy'?"

"Well . . . yeah." I glanced down at her rounded stomach. "I mean, there was obviously some Moroi guy involved. And if he did this against your will, you need to let us know. He needs to be brought to justice."

It felt ludicrous using the term "brought to justice" in this faux Wild West town, but Olive's puzzled look said it was lost on her. "No, no. You . . . you don't understand. You don't understand at all."

"Then help me," I said, catching hold of her hands. "Help me to understand so that I can help you. I promised Nina I would."

"Adrian? Is that you?"

The voice calling me wasn't immediately familiar, and I slowly turned from Olive to see who was speaking. We'd set out walking at random, and the place we'd stopped gave us a good vantage on what I thought of as the "Red Light District Cabins." Another Moroi guy appeared to be leaving one of those cabins, and from the stagger in his steps, he'd been enjoying happy hour out in the woods.

"It *is* you!" the man exclaimed, smacking his leg in triumph. "I knew it."

A few more seconds, and recognition set in. "Uncle Rand?" I asked in disbelief.

He strode on up to us and grinned. "The same."

I could hardly believe it. In my life, I'd come to expect any number of fantastic and wondrous things to happen in day-to-day affairs. Spirit battles? No problem. My wife turning into a cat? Sure, go for it. So it was astonishing that the sight of a relative I hadn't thought about in years would so completely floor me. Rand Ivashkov was my dad's older brother, someone I'd neither seen nor thought about since I was a child. Rand hadn't been disowned—not officially—but it had been clear to me from an early age that everyone preferred it when he wasn't around. My father had assumed his responsibilities at Court and sent Rand out of the country on errands that were mostly meant to keep him out of the way and give him things he couldn't screw up. Once, when I'd gotten in trouble as a teen at an illicit party, my mother had urged my father to go easy on punishing me. "After all," she'd said, "it's not like he's as bad as your brother."

He's a screwup, whispered Aunt Tatiana. *A disgrace. More consumed with women and wine than family honor.*

Doesn't sound that different from me, I admitted.

She scoffed. *Hardly. Your family never shipped you off to keep you out of the way.*

Last I'd known, Rand was somewhere in Europe. I certainly hadn't expected to find my uncle in northern Michigan. "What are you doing here?" I asked.

"Same thing you are," he said, giving me a wink. He had the same dark green eyes I had, and though there was some silver in his brown hair, it was nowhere near the amount my dad had. Maybe living a life of women and wine was less stressful than living a respectable one on the Moroi Council. Rand was tall, even among Moroi, and had to lean down to leer at Olive, making her cringe against me. "She's cute," he said. "And I see you've got your own little sideline family going, eh? I've got a couple of those myself. These dhampir girls breed like—"

"It's not like that," I interrupted, getting tired of explaining this. "I'm not—that is, Olive's just a friend I'm checking up on."

Uncle Rand perked up. "So she's available? I haven't seen her around—"

"No," I said through gritted teeth. "She's *not* available. Look, it's nice to see you and everything, but this really isn't the time or place. I have things to do."

I started to turn away, indicating to Olive that we should head back to Diana's cabin. To my astonishment, Rand grabbed my arm and turned me back around. That close, the scent of vodka coming off of him nearly knocked me over.

"Don't be like that!" he said hotly. "A snob like the rest of your family. Your dad and his holier-than-thou wife always acted like I wasn't good enough to hang out with the rest of you. But look at you now. You're here, no better than me. And I hear all kinds of things about you too—do you see me judging? We have a lot in common."

I jerked my arm away. "I don't think so."

"You *are* just like the rest of them!" He lunged toward me, his steps faltering drunkenly. I didn't know if he was trying to hit me or just grab me again, but I never found out because a tall figure suddenly stepped in between us and sent him flying with a right hook. I looked up and saw Dimitri regarding my uncle, who was now lying sprawled on the grass, with an expression of intense disgust. Rose, Sydney, and Lana came hurrying up to us.

"What the hell's going on?" exclaimed Rose.

"Thanks," I told Dimitri. "Though I don't think we needed quite that much intervention. I was holding my own."

"He's an animal," growled Dimitri. "He has no business being here."

"Well, I suppose it—" I stopped and reconsidered Dimitri's words. "Do you know him or something?"

Dimitri eyed me. "Yes. Do you?"

"Yeah," I said. "He's my uncle. Rand Ivashkov."

"Oh?" Dimitri's hardened expression didn't change. "He's my father."

CHAPTER 10
SYDNEY

AND JUST LIKE THAT, Olive Sinclair's pregnancy was no longer the most astonishing thing going on. Or, well, at least it had some serious competition for bizarreness.

We all stood there awkwardly in the middle of the path, with the birds singing merrily around us, making this unexpected family revelation that much more surreal. Even Rose, who was rarely at a loss for words, stood there gaping. The Moroi man—Rand Ivashkov, according to Adrian—blinked at Dimitri as though he were seeing a ghost. Some of Rand's cocky swagger diminished a little, and he took an uneasy step back.

"Well, I'll be damned. It *is* you, Dimka." He wet his lips and tried to smile. "You look pretty good for a guy who used to be undead, am I right?" He glanced around at the rest of us, looking for us to laugh at the joke. We stayed silent. Dimitri turned to Lana.

"Is he causing you trouble?" he asked her politely. "Are you having difficulty removing him? I'll be happy to do it for you."

"We can take care of ourselves," she shot back, though not unkindly. As though summoned by some unspoken signal, Mallory and another dhampir woman who looked like a guard appeared on the path behind her. Mallory no longer seemed like a dreamy fangirl. In that moment she was as formidable as any guardian I'd met.

Rand relaxed a little. "Yeah, see? No need to do anything hasty."

Lana fixed her glare on him. "That does *not* mean you are welcome here."

"Hey," he said, confidence returning, "I have every right to be here. I was visiting Elaine. She's a resident. She can have guests."

"She can have guests at my discretion," Lana corrected, fists on her hips. "And I've told you before, I don't want you here drinking."

He held up his hands in what was apparently supposed to be a pacifying gesture. "Fine, I won't have another drop. I swear it. But you can't kick me out now—not when my son and nephew are here. This is practically a family reunion."

Rose finally found her voice and turned on Dimitri. "Really? This guy? Are you sure?" I shared her disbelief.

Dimitri's gaze was cool as it rested unblinkingly on Adrian's uncle. "Positive. Though I thought he was off wandering Europe."

Rand shook his head. "Haven't been there in years. That business Nate hooked me up with said they didn't need my consulting services anymore. How's Olena doing these days?"

"Do not ever speak my mother's name to me again," growled Dimitri.

"Really?" repeated Rose. "This guy?"

The mention of Dimitri's mother and Adrian's father—whom I'd never, ever heard called Nate—suddenly triggered the most astonishing revelation of all. Adrian's jaw dropped as understanding hit him as well. "Are we . . . does that mean . . . are we *cousins*?" he exclaimed, turning toward Dimitri.

Rose's eyes widened even more.

Near us, Olive shifted uncomfortably and rested a hand on the small of her back, wincing as she did. As mind-boggling as this family drama was for the rest of us, I had to imagine it was of small concern to her, what with everything else going on in her life. Dimitri immediately swooped in and linked his arm through hers. "You're tired. There's no need for you to stand around and endure all this. I'll escort you back." He began leading Olive toward Diana's cabin but paused to glance at Lana. "Whatever you do with him is your choice, but I'm more than happy to get rid of him for you, if you wish."

"We'll deal with it," she replied.

Dimitri gave her a nod of acknowledgment and then escorted Olive away, like a knight from a chivalrous, albeit surreal, fairy tale. Rose appeared torn about whether to go with them or stay and finally followed the twosome down the path. Lana turned to Adrian and me.

"Will you vouch for him if he stays?"

"My uncle?" Adrian asked. "Hell no. I haven't seen him in years. I don't know anything about him."

"Oh, come on," cried Rand. "We're family. And Lana, you can't really turn me out. It'll be sunset soon. There've been reports of local Strigoi sightings this week."

I wondered if he was exaggerating for his own benefit, but

Lana's grave face suggested otherwise. "Fine. You can spend the night in our guest quarters at the front of the community."

He gestured back to the private cabins. "No need to put yourself out. I'm sure Elaine would—"

"Guest quarters," Lana repeated more loudly. "Or you can leave now."

Rand exhaled dramatically, like he was being terribly inconvenienced and not actually receiving a great kindness from her. "Fine. Will you at least walk me there, Adrian? Then you can get back to that dhampir girl you knocked up."

Adrian scowled but didn't correct him. Lana was already retreating, leaving Adrian and me no choice but to walk with Rand. Nonetheless, I noticed her guards trailing at a respectful distance as the three of us made our way back toward the commune's front. Lana wasn't going to leave Rand unsupervised.

"How's your dad?" Rand asked Adrian companionably. "And your mom?"

"Not living together," Adrian replied. "I figured you knew that."

"Nate doesn't talk to me anymore. No one does. I have to get all my information through secondhand gossip." He sounded terribly put out by that as well. This was someone who felt sorry for himself a lot, I realized.

"Maybe that's something you should think about," Adrian remarked evenly. "If 'no one' is talking to you, maybe they're not the problem. Maybe you are."

He shot Adrian a wry look. "Don't act so high and mighty. I told you—I heard about you. You and your . . . human wife." Rand came to a sudden halt as it dawned on him. His gaze fell on me, then turned back to Adrian. "Wait . . . her? The

Alchemist? And you're just . . . out in public like this? No shame at all?"

Adrian remained remarkably calm. "Her name is Sydney. And we have nothing to be ashamed of. Humans and Moroi used to marry. They still do in the Keepers. Sydney and I love each other. That's all that matters."

Rand shook his head in disbelief. "Well, welcome to the family then, Sydney. At least this way I'm not the most scandalous anymore." He glanced back at Adrian. "I tell you, though, our aunt would be rolling in her grave if she knew what you'd done."

"I think she'd be okay with it. I know her pretty well," said Adrian. A moment later, he seemed to realize what he'd said. "I *knew* her pretty well, that is." I watched him carefully, trying hard to determine if it had been an honest slip of the tongue. Ever since he'd admitted hearing his aunt in his head to me, he'd been reticent about elaborating on how often she spoke to him. Seemingly unfazed, he kept his attention on Rand now. "Why weren't you at her funeral?"

Rand shrugged and slowed his pace as we came to a stop in front of a building labeled GUESTS. "I don't like funerals. That, and there wasn't enough time to get back by the time I heard. I was in Europe when it happened."

"Russia?" I asked. I'd spent a fair amount of time in Russia and was pretty sure I would've remembered seeing someone as obnoxious as Rand Ivashkov in the Moroi circles.

"France," Rand corrected. "I haven't been in Russia in a while."

"You were there at least once," Adrian pointed out. "If Dimitri really is your son."

Rand straightened himself up. "He is, and I was there lots of times. That family never appreciated me, though. So I stopped coming around."

Adrian eyed him carefully. "Really? That's all there is to the story? Despite his badass exterior, Dimitri's a pretty forgiving guy. I guess you'd have to be, to go on with life after being a Strigoi. But you? He's pissed off at you."

Rand looked away from us. "His mother and I stopped getting along. Boys overreact to that kind of thing, that's all." He stepped up onto the cabin's porch. "You coming in? Might as well claim your room now before the other guys staying overnight show up."

"We're not staying here," said Adrian.

Rand gestured to the darkening western sky. "You're here for the night. This is their only free guesthouse. Where else you going to stay?"

Adrian and I exchanged brief glances. Staying overnight hadn't come up in any of our planning. "Not here," he said adamantly. "Not with you."

"Dismiss me all you want, but I've made the best of what I've got," Rand said angrily. "I never fit in, never played by their rules, and one by one they rejected me. That'll happen to you, just wait. That's the price of marrying *her*. You lost everything you could have had, could have been, as an Ivashkov. Soon you'll see what it's like, drifting from place to place."

"We have to go check on my friends," Adrian told him, taking my arm and steering me away. "Nice running into you."

"You're a terrible liar, boy," Rand called after us.

"Is he right?" I asked quietly, once we'd put some distance between the guest cabin and us.

"That I'm a terrible liar? No. I'm a fantastic liar."

I came to a halt, forcing him to as well. It was dark enough that our only light came from strategically placed lanterns along the camp's main path. "Adrian, I mean what he said about me . . . did I really cost you all that? We always talk about me being on the run from humans, but you gave up the life of a royal to—"

"Sydney," Adrian interrupted, cupping my face in his hands. "Never, ever think like that. I don't regret anything we've faced. Being with you is the best thing that's ever happened to me, the one perfect decision I've made in a lifetime of fumbling and poor judgment. I'd go through it all again to be by your side. Never doubt that. Never doubt how I feel about you."

"Oh, Adrian," I said, letting him wrap me in his arms, surprised at the bubble of emotion welling up within me.

He held me tightly. "I love you. If anything, I can't believe you gave up everything you did to be with me. You changed your whole life for me."

"My life didn't even begin until I met you," I told him fiercely.

Adrian pulled back and looked at me closely, shadows on his face. "When you see someone like him, like Uncle Rand, does it make you nervous? That I might turn out like that?"

I felt my eyes widen. "No," I said adamantly. "You're nothing like him."

I could tell from Adrian's face he wasn't so certain and was in danger of falling into one of those terrible depressions of his. His recent spirit usage with Nina would only make him that much more vulnerable. Adrian might not have any doubts about me and our love, but the future Rand had predicted—us bouncing around with no place to live—might very well be a real one. That scared me, and it had to scare Adrian too. With great effort, I watched as he tried to force his dark thoughts away and put on a cheerier expression.

"Well, I guess on the bright side of all of this, I can celebrate a new family member."

I'd nearly forgotten the startling revelation about him and Dimitri. "Is it really true? How could you have not known that?"

Adrian gave a rueful headshake and began walking again. "From what I've heard about Uncle Rand's 'activities,' he might very well have dozens of illegitimate children around the world. Why not Dimitri?"

"It just seems weird Dimitri wouldn't have said anything before this," I remarked.

"That surprised me too," admitted Adrian as Diana's cabin came into view. "Though to be honest, I never thought of him having a father. He just seems like the kind of guy who sprung into being fully grown up. Or, if I was going to picture a dad for him, I guess I'd just go with a gray-haired version of him, complete with duster."

I laughed at that and followed him up to the cabin's porch. Someone called for us to enter when we knocked, and we found Rose and Dimitri sitting in the cabin's little living room. Diana had apparently left. Olive was lying on a bare-bones sofa, looking pale. "Is he gone?" asked Dimitri. His tone clearly told us which *he* was being referred to.

Adrian and I sat down together on a wooden bench. "No," I said. "He's staying in their guesthouse and seemed to think we would too."

"I can think of a dozen forms of torture I'd rather undergo than spend a night under the same roof as him," said Dimitri, deadpan.

"I'm sure it won't come to that," Adrian replied.

"Olive says we can stay here for the night," Rose explained. "If you don't mind making a bed on the floor."

"Considering the alternative? No problem." Adrian fixed his gaze on Dimitri. "When were you going to break the news that we're one big happy family?"

A pained expression crossed Dimitri's face. "I honestly didn't know."

Adrian threw up his hands. "Come *on*. You've got, what, two or three sisters? That guy was obviously around a lot. It never occurred to you that Rand Ivashkov might be related to another Ivashkov you knew?"

A smolder of anger shone in Dimitri's eyes. "He never told us his full name. He was always just Randall. We knew he was an American royal who frequently came by on business. We never asked questions. My mother liked him . . . for a while."

"He mentioned that they stopped getting along," I noted. "He claimed he wasn't appreciated."

That smolder in Dimitri's eyes turned into a flame. "Wasn't appreciated? He shoved my mother around when he'd been drinking and didn't get his way."

Those words drew even Adrian up short. "Then what happened?" he asked softly.

Dimitri didn't answer, but Rose did. "Dimitri shoved him back," she replied.

Silence fell, broken only by Olive shifting on the couch. She'd been listening quietly, her face creased with discomfort.

Adrian regarded her with a look I'd come to know by now, one that somehow managed to be both focused and distracted. He was viewing her aura. I'd tried chastising him about aura viewing for a while but had finally given up. It was so second nature to him, he didn't even realize he was doing it half the time. It really did use only a little spirit, according to Sonya, so I tried to pick my battles over larger expenditures.

"Are you okay?" Adrian asked Olive with concern.

"I don't feel well," she said. She slid her hand down her stomach. "Some pain. I've had it throughout the whole pregnancy."

"Your colors are all over the place—different from earlier. It's almost like looking at two people's auras blurred together." Adrian's eyebrows shot up. "Are you in labor?"

She looked startled at the thought . . . but also afraid. "I . . . I'm not sure. The pain's worse than usual, but it's still more than a month before I—"

The deep booming of a large iron bell rang out through the air. Rose and Dimitri were on their feet in an instant. "What's that?" she demanded.

Dimitri pulled a silver stake from his belt. "Strigoi warning. We have the same system back in Baia." He ran to the door, Rose close on his heels. Before leaving, he gestured to the fireplace. "Build a fire. If any Strigoi come in, throw them into it."

He didn't elaborate on how exactly we were supposed to accomplish that, with brute force or Adrian's spirit, but they were gone before I could question them. Adrian and I met each other's gazes, the new threat spurring us to action. With only a small spell, I made the fire in the hearth suddenly double in size. Fire was our best weapon against Strigoi, and while I could summon it out of thin air, having a ready source would aid both Adrian and me.

Olive cried out as the flames rose. I turned to her. Pain contorted her features as she rested a hand on her stomach. "Are you okay?"

"I think . . . I think the baby might be coming after all," she gasped out.

Adrian blanched. "When you say 'coming,' do you mean now or kind of in the near future?"

The question was ridiculous enough to momentarily draw her from her pain. "I don't know! I've never had one before!"

Adrian looked up at me. "So . . . um, you know how to do this, right? Deliver a baby?"

"What?" I asked. Panic seized me now. "Why would you even think that?"

"Because you're so good at everything else," he said. "All I know is what I've seen in movies. Boil water. Tear up sheets."

As usual, I clung to logic to try to calm myself. "You could boil water for sterilization. But the sheets? That's not really—"

A scream from outside interrupted my babbling. Adrian moved his body protectively to shield Olive, and I summoned a fireball to my palm. We all stared wordlessly at the dark window, unable to make out what was happening. We heard shouts and another scream, making my imagination run wild.

"I wish Neil was here," Olive whispered.

"Me too," I said, thinking I'd feel a lot better with him standing by the door with a silver stake.

Adrian squeezed Olive's hand. "You're going to be fine. Sydney and I will protect you. Nothing's going to come through that door that we don't want."

Just then, the door burst open and Rand Ivashkov appeared, face frantic.

"What's happening out there?" I demanded.

He slammed the door shut behind him and sank into a chair. "Strigoi. Dimitri told me to come stay here with you guys." He eyed Olive's state uneasily. "In case you needed help."

"Not unless you've got a secret medical degree you've been hiding from the family," snapped Adrian.

"How many Strigoi are there?" I asked.

Rand shook his head. "Not sure. Probably only a few or we'd all be dead by now. But a few can do a lot of damage if they get the drop on you."

Olive made a small cry of pain, and we turned back to her.

"Another contraction," I noted.

"At least it's been a few minutes. Maybe he'll wait until this is all over," Olive replied.

"He? You know it's a boy?" Adrian asked.

"Not for sure," she admitted. "But I just have a hunch."

"I believe in hunches," Adrian said seriously.

Another scream sounded, and I tried to provide a distraction for Olive. I might not know everything about labor and delivery, but stress like this couldn't be good for a pregnant woman. "What are you going to name him?" I asked her.

Adrian followed my lead. "Adrian Sinclair has a nice ring to it," he said.

Olive's eyes, full of fear, watched the window and door, but her lips curled into another smile at the joke. "Declan."

"Nice Irish name," I said.

"It would work," Adrian conceded. "Declan Adrian Sinclair."

"Declan Neil," she corrected.

I wondered how Neil would feel about having someone else's child named after him. In the nonstop chaos that had ensued since we'd arrived, there'd been no opportunity to talk to Olive about the circumstances that had driven her here to the commune. And as we continued our anxious vigil, it seemed unlikely we'd discuss matters anytime soon. Conversation dried up as time passed. All we could do was watch and wait. The sounds outside eventually quieted, and I didn't know whether to be reassured or more alarmed. Equally disconcerting was that Olive's contractions kept getting more frequent. I wondered if we should be boiling water after all.

The door opened again, and I nearly hurled the fireball at the newcomer until I saw it was Rose. Her face was streaked with blood and dirt. "We got them," she said. "None of our people died, but there are a lot of injuries. Their doctor's away right now, and we were wondering, Adrian, if you could . . ."

She couldn't finish, but I knew what she wanted. Adrian did too. He turned from her to me, his face full of pain.

"Sydney—"

"She said no one's dead," I interrupted.

"Some might be close," he countered. "Especially if the doctor's away."

I glanced back at Rose. "Are there people who might die?"

She hesitated. "I don't know. Some are clearly in pretty bad shape, though. I saw a lot of blood when I was back at their infirmary."

Adrian began moving toward the door. "That's it, then. I'm going to help." He paused to look back at Olive. "She needs someone too. Right now. The baby's coming. Sydney—"

"No, I'm coming with you. I know basic first aid," I said,

though my true motivation was to keep an eye on Adrian. "Rose, can you help Olive? Or get someone who can?"

The look on Rose's face showed she felt as completely unprepared for that as I was, but she gave a quick nod. "I'll try to find someone who actually knows what they're doing. There must be plenty of people who've helped with that before. But Sydney, are you sure you want to go? There's an Alchemist on the way to help destroy the bodies."

"An Alchemist?" Olive gasped out.

I froze, and suddenly, a whole new sort of panic took over. "On the way?"

"Not here yet," Rose concurred. "I think they said his name was Brad or Brett or something. Works out of Marquette."

"Don't risk it," Adrian told me. "Stay here."

I hesitated, knowing that was the smart thing to do. It would be idiotic to risk myself now after everything I'd done to avoid recapture by the Alchemists. Yet, at the same time, I was just as afraid of what might happen to Adrian if I left him alone to wield spirit. I shook my head. "Brad or Brett isn't here yet. I'll keep out of sight when he shows up."

Adrian's face told me he didn't like that plan, but Olive spoke before he could. "Is he like you?" she asked, more concerned than I would have expected. "An ex-Alchemist?"

I shook my head. "Not likely. He's probably the standard, analytical kind that thinks vampires are freaks of nature."

Olive looked even more alarmed, and I recalled her fear when she'd seen me earlier. Rose gave her a reassuring smile. "I know they don't always have the greatest personalities, but this one might be able to help with cleanup. Don't worry. It'll be okay. And in the meantime, I'm going to send someone to help with that baby." She fixed a hard look on Rand. "Wait with her until someone else gets here. Come on, you two."

Adrian and I followed her out into the darkened commune, and a feeling of dread settled over me, entirely different from what I'd felt during the Strigoi attack. The lanterns along the path made everything look extra sinister. We saw little evidence of the Strigoi until we reached Lana's cabin, where they'd gathered the injured. A dozen dhampirs were there, bloodied and beaten, but being tended to as best they could. Dimitri hurried over to us when we arrived.

"Thank you for helping," he said. "I know it's hard for you."

"It's not hard at all, actually," Adrian replied.

"Adrian," I warned. "Be smart about this. Only tend to the truly critical."

He gazed around, taking in all the dhampirs on makeshift cots. Rose was right that there was a lot of blood. Moans of pain filled the air.

"How can we choose who deserves healing?" Adrian asked softly. "Especially when they all just fought to keep us safe."

"I'll help you triage," I said.

Dimitri pointed at the far end of the room. "Some of the worst are down there. Whatever you can do will help. I've got to get back out there. Turns out one got away and is out in the woods. We're going after him."

"I'll go too," said Rose promptly.

Dimitri briefly touched her cheek. "I need you here. Help Sydney and Adrian."

"Help us later," I said. "Get someone for Olive now."

Rose's eyebrows shot up at that, and she hurried off to find Lana. Adrian and I settled into helping the injured. I tried to warn him again to use caution with his magic, but it wasn't easy. All he could focus on was the suffering around him—and how he wanted to fix it. He set into healing, using his spirit generously. He at least started with the critical ones Dimitri had pointed out. As for me, I began doing what I could with basic skills in the hopes that Adrian would see he didn't need to use spirit on everyone. I patched lacerations and gave water. I even gave pep talks. Most of the patients were conscious, and I worked hard to keep up a good bedside manner, assuring them all would be well. Every so often I'd pause to check on Adrian.

Mallory was among the injured, and she and another guard were pretty bad off, having lost lots of blood. Mallory also had a number of broken ribs, as well as some internal injuries, according to Adrian's read of her aura. A Strigoi appeared to have taken a chunk out of the place where her shoulder and neck met, and blood pooled from the wound, despite attempts to bandage it. She was one of the few unconscious ones, and it seemed hard to believe she'd been swooning over Rose and Dimitri only a few hours ago. Adrian made her his first priority, restoring her to almost complete health. I was glad for her but winced at the power that must have required. Wordlessly, he moved on to his next patient.

When he was halfway through her healing, Rose hurried up to me. "I sent someone to Olive. But you need to come with me now—upstairs. The Alchemist is about to come in."

I finished the bandage I was applying and gave one more warning to Adrian about caution. He nodded at me, and I wondered if he'd even heard my words. But there was no time to linger, not with an Alchemist about to walk in who could potentially undo all Adrian and I had done to win my freedom.

My heart raced as I followed Rose up to the second floor of Lana's cabin. I breathed a sigh of relief as we reached it. It was little more than a loft, but it kept me out of sight from those below. Unfortunately, it kept me away from what was happening downstairs as well.

"Rose," I said as she started to go, "you've got to make sure Adrian doesn't—"

A dhampir suddenly appeared in the doorway and beckoned Rose out urgently. I saw them speak in concerned whispers outside the door. Rose looked distressed and glanced my way, then followed the dhampir downstairs. That left me alone for the better part of an hour with nothing to do but pace and worry about what was happening. Finally, Diana came up to tell me the Alchemist had moved on to a different part of the camp and that I could come downstairs, as he had no reason to return to the infirmary.

I wasted no time in complying and was shocked to see that nearly every single person who'd been lying on the floor injured earlier was now up and about, looking healthy and well. Adrian was just finishing up a healing, and I stared, openmouthed, unable to believe what I was witnessing. "Adrian . . . what have you done?"

It took him several moments to turn to me, and when he did, I could barely believe the difference in him. He looked as bad as the patients had earlier—pale, sweating, eyes glazed. I caught hold of his arm, afraid he might faint from exhaustion.

"How many of them did you heal?" I whispered.

He swallowed and stared around vacantly. "I . . . I don't know. As many as I could . . ."

I clutched his hand, filled with a mix of anger and fear.

"Adrian! You didn't need to do that!" Glancing around, I noticed some people who'd had only light injuries—a few scratches or bruises—were completely unmarked now. I turned on him incredulously. "That was a waste of your energy! Most of these people would have healed on their own."

He seemed to be recovering a little of his bearings. "I could help them . . . why not? Once I started, it was just so hard to stop . . . what's the harm?"

Before I could even process that, Rose came up to us with a grave face. "You guys . . . there's something you should know. Olive's gone."

I was so focused on Adrian's wiped-out state, I thought I'd misheard. "What do you mean, she's gone?"

"She sneaked up on Rand and knocked him unconscious. Then she ran away before Lana got there to deliver the baby."

Adrian, though dazed, managed to focus on this seemingly improbable change of events. "Olive . . . knocked someone out . . . while she was in labor? How?"

"No idea," said Rose sadly. "But she's gone . . . probably fled out in the woods."

"In the woods," Adrian repeated. A new energy filled him as panic set in. "In labor. In the dark. Is that Strigoi still out there?"

Rose's expression answered for her, and Adrian hurried to the door with me fast on his heels. "We have to go," he said. "We have to go find her now."

Rose tried to stop us. "Adrian, it's not safe to—"

Dimitri suddenly burst through the door. "We found her. We found all of them. You have to come, Adrian. You have to come now."

We followed without question, and I struggled to keep up

with the others and their longer strides. Rose came too. "Did you find the Strigoi?" she called as we passed the commune's center.

"Yes. There." Dimitri gestured to two dhampirs dragging a dead Strigoi's body. They brought it to where three other Strigoi were piled. A human guy knelt by them, pouring the contents of a small vial over the bodies. The Alchemist, I realized. I angled myself so that Rose was between us. Fortunately, he was engrossed in his work.

"Then what happened?" asked Rose.

"He got to Olive first," he explained. "She'd already had the baby—out in the woods. She hid him there. We found him too. He's fine—small, but fine."

Adrian and I were still so overwhelmed by the course of events that we couldn't respond, but Rose was ready with more questions. "Why are we going to her? Why didn't you bring her in?"

Dimitri led us out of the commune and into a wooded area. "I was afraid to move her. I thought it best to leave her where she was until Adrian could heal her."

Adrian grimaced. "You guys, I . . . I don't know if I have enough spirit left to do it. If you can stabilize her until I recover . . . or if she's not that bad . . ."

Dimitri made no response as we trekked out into the deep forest past the commune, but his expression said that she was, in fact, that bad. My stomach sank as the implications hit me.

We finally reached a clearing in the woods. Lana and two other dhampirs stood there holding lanterns. We hurried up to them and found Olive propped up against a tree, a small bundle held close to her with one arm. When I got a good look at her, I understood why they'd been afraid to move her. Her face was so white, she could've passed for Strigoi herself. Her arm—the one not holding the baby—was nearly torn from her. The side of her head looked as though it had been slammed hard against something, and everywhere, everywhere, there was blood. Her eyes were closed, her breathing shallow.

Adrian focused on her for several moments, and then shook his head, his face full of despair. "I can't," he murmured, nearly choking on the words. "I can't even bring up her aura. I'm out . . . I'm out of magic."

Olive's eyelids fluttered at the sound of his voice. "Is that . . . is that Adrian?"

He knelt down beside her. "Shh, don't strain. You need to rest so I can build my magic back up and heal you."

She managed a harsh laugh, and a small trail of blood leaked from her lips. "I'm beyond any magic, even yours."

"Not true. I just need it back."

"No time," she croaked out. "But I need . . . to talk to you. Alone."

"Olive, you need to rest," Adrian insisted, but the words sounded hollow. We both knew she was right about time. Her life was bleeding out in front of us.

The baby in her arms began to cry.

"Go," Dimitri ordered the others, shooing them away. To Adrian and me, he said, "Give her what comfort you can."

I gave a weak nod, but mostly I was trying not to start crying.

"Take him," Olive said, when the others had left. She thrust the baby toward Adrian.

I was pretty sure he'd never held a baby in his life, but as his arms went around the tiny bundle, the baby quieted. I leaned over to get a better look. He was so tiny as to seem unreal. A fuzz of dark hair covered his head, and he looked up at us with astonishingly alert eyes. He was wrapped in someone's jacket, and Adrian attempted some half-hearted rocking.

"Shh, there you go. There you, Declan. Declan Neil Sinclair."

"Raymond," Olive said. She paused and coughed up more blood. "Declan Neil Raymond."

"Neil's last name," I said.

"You have to take him to Neil," she told us. "When I'm gone."

"Don't talk like that," Adrian said, sounding as though he were having trouble keeping sobs from his voice.

With her good arm, she clutched Adrian's sleeve. "You don't understand. He *is* Neil's. Neil's his father."

Arguing dhampir genetics seemed pointless, given her state. Maybe she was so out of it, she believed Neil was the father. Maybe she was speaking figuratively. From what I'd seen at Court, Neil loved her so much, he'd probably adopt the baby as his own anyway. "Of course," I said gently, simply wanting to pacify her.

She was fading fast, but a spark of anger glittered in her eyes. "No, I mean it. He's Neil's. I've never been with anyone else."

"Olive," Adrian said, not unkindly, "that's impossible."

"No," she repeated. She closed her eyes, and for a moment, I feared the worst. Then they fluttered open again. "I was only with Neil. Just once. And when I found out . . . I was so scared. I don't know what happened . . . it must have something to do with me being restored. With all the spirit that was in me. I've been so afraid if anyone—Moroi or Alchemists—knew, they'd want to take the baby. Experiment on him, like Sonya does. So I hid. Hid from them all. Even N-Nina." Her voice caught on her sister's name, and she paused to breathe, which seemed to be causing more difficulty.

What she was saying was impossible. Two dhampirs couldn't make a dhampir. It went against the fundamental rules of the world. And yet, if she believed that . . . I suddenly remembered her panic upon meeting me and then later, when she found out another Alchemist was coming. "That's why you ran," I said. "You were afraid of the Alchemist."

She gave a weak nod and opened her eyes again. "You know how they are. I don't know how this is possible, but they'd want to know. They'd take him. Please, Adrian. Sydney. Don't let them. Or the Moroi authorities. Keep him secret until he gets to Neil. Then Neil will hide him. Neil will keep him safe. But promise me . . ." Her eyes closed, and her head tilted. "Promise me . . . you'll . . . keep Declan safe . . ."

"Stay with us," Adrian said urgently. My own vision was blurred with tears. "A little longer. Spirit's coming back to me. I know it."

Declan stirred in Adrian's arms and began to cry again. Olive's eyes open a slit, and she smiled. "So sweet," she said softly. Her eyelids fell closed again, and all the tension went out of her body as she slumped forward.

"There," Adrian gasped out. "I've got it . . . a spark of spirit . . . enough to see auras . . ."

I clutched his arm and felt tears running down my cheeks. "Adrian . . ."

"The baby's is so bright," Adrian said. There were tears on his face now too. "Like a star. But in her . . . there's nothing. No aura left to see . . ."

CHAPTER 11
ADRIAN

WE WERE STILL STANDING OUT IN THE WOODS, and I was still holding Declan. Amazingly, he'd gone to sleep, blissfully unaware of what a confusing and heartbreaking world he'd just been born into. Sydney leaned against me, and I put an arm around her as best I could while still keeping a firm grip on Declan. Rose and Dimitri stood nearby, watching with stricken faces as Olive was gravely taken away.

"We need to act fast," I said, keeping my voice soft. "If we're going to honor her wishes."

Sydney looked up at me and blinked back tears. "You don't really think—that is, do you believe her? About Neil?"

I didn't answer right away. "I saw them at Court. You did too. When this whole thing started, it was impossible for me to believe she'd been with another guy. Now I understand. And when I look at him—at Declan—well, it's hard to explain, but there's something special about him. His aura. It's like he's got this light dusting of spirit, kind of like what Sonya and

I kept trying to create. He's got it naturally."

Sydney's breath caught. "If that's the case, a lot of people are going to be interested in him."

"They can't know about him," I said adamantly. "Olive was right about that, and I owe it to her to keep him secret. It's the least I can do since I failed her."

"Adrian—"

I wouldn't let Sydney finish. "We have to hide him. Will you help me?"

Her face was filled with concern for me, but she didn't hesitate in her answer. "You know you don't need to ask."

I kissed the top of her head. "We're going to need help." I beckoned Rose and Dimitri to come forward. They approached immediately.

Rose swallowed, her dark eyes shining with tears. "Adrian, I'm so sorry. There was nothing anyone could do."

Well, remarked Aunt Tatiana, *you could've done something if you hadn't been so careless with spirit.*

"No time for that," I said briskly. "I need your help. What'll happen to Declan now? You know these kinds of places, Dimitri. What's the protocol when the mother dies? I need to know if we can take him."

"Who's Declan?" asked Rose.

I nodded down at the baby in my arms, still wrapped in someone's coat.

Dimitri's face was hard to read. "If she had family living here in this camp, he'd go to them. I'm sure we could also contact her family on the outside, whoever's left of them. There's a tradition . . ."

"Yes?" I prompted.

173

He studied the baby uncertainly before continuing. "There's an old tradition among dhampirs, especially those living in dangerous places and in uncertain conditions. Whomever the mother first gives the baby to becomes its guardian. Like I said, it's old, but I'm guessing that's why Olive was so insistent about seeing you and why Lana hasn't tried to take him from you yet. I'm sure as soon as you tell her—"

"No," I interrupted. "That's perfect."

"You . . . want this baby?" asked Rose, making no attempt to hide how improbable she found the idea.

"I want to get the baby out of here," I said. "I want as few people to know about him as possible. Or that I'm taking him." I thought back to who'd been around, Lana and the two warrior dhampirs. I wasn't sure if anyone else had been there when Olive had been found. "Can you talk to Lana? Tell her we're taking the baby to Olive's family but that it's being kept quiet? And tell her not to mention my involvement to anyone. If we don't make a big deal about any of it, most of these people will assume we're taking him to his next of kin. But I'd prefer if he was as unmemorable as possible. I don't want anyone else seeing him or thinking too much more about him."

Rose and Dimitri exchanged understandably perplexed looks. "Adrian, what's going on?" asked Dimitri.

I shook my head. "I can't tell you. Not yet. But believe me when I say this baby's life may depend on what we do now. Will you help us?"

That was a hard argument for them to go against—and it wasn't a lie either. Because as we walked back toward the heart of the commune, my power gradually began creeping back. And each time I tuned into Declan's aura—looking closely, almost at the cellular level—I could see that infusion of spirit. It's unlikely anyone would notice it unless they were really looking for it.

And I understood with a shocking clarity why Olive had been afraid. Why she'd turned her back on everyone she knew and run off to a hole in the woods. What had happened, what I was holding in my arms, shouldn't exist. Two dhampirs couldn't make another dhampir. It went against one of the most basic rules of biology in our world. It was impossible, yet here it was.

He was a miracle.

But Olive had been right that there were people who'd want to study Declan, who'd want to possibly lock him up and experiment. And while I was ready to acknowledge that his birth was a wondrous, joyous thing, I wasn't ready to let his life be a series of experiments and finger-pointing—especially when his mother had died to protect him from that.

Dimitri spoke to Lana privately, and either because of that dhampir tradition or his own reputation (maybe both), she acceded to all our requests. She gave us a vacant cabin to stay in until dawn. When we asked for supplies, she sent them via Rose or Dimitri so that Declan would have as little exposure to others in the commune as possible. I needed him to be out of their minds. I needed them to forget him.

Of course, that meant Sydney and I were in charge of his care that night. And in a few short hours, I learned more than I'd ever expected to about babies. She was able to look up some information on her phone, taking comfort in logic and facts. The signal out here was bad, though, and sometimes we found it was easier to take a guess on something than wait for an answer. Declan, fortunately, was a forgiving guy and proved pretty accommodating as we figured things out together. He was patient as Sydney and I painstakingly read the instructions on the can of formula Lana sent. He made little complaint when I initially put his diaper on backward. When he grew tired again and started crying, I had no instructions to follow. Sydney gave a helpless shrug when I looked at her. So I just walked him around the living room, crooning classic rock songs until he dozed off and could be set down.

Rose, who'd stayed with us off and on but looked more terrified of the baby than a Strigoi, watched me with amazement. "You're kind of good at that," she remarked. "Adrian Ivashkov, baby whisperer."

I looked down at the sleeping baby. "I'm making it up as I go along."

"Are you ready to tell us what's going on?" she asked, her face growing grave. "You know we just want to help."

"Not yet. But if we can leave when Dimitri gets back, that'd be—"

Sydney's phone chimed with a text message. She looked surprised that anyone would be reaching out to her until she took a look at the display. "It's Ms. Terwilliger. She's mobilized the witches in Palm Springs. They're ready to start searching."

Rose stood up. "For Jill?"

"For Alicia, technically, but also for Jill," said Sydney. "She says we can join them . . ." She looked at me uncertainly, and I could guess her thoughts. We'd made this Michigan detour because we had time to pass while waiting for things to be ready for us in Palm Springs. Having a baby in tow hadn't been part of anyone's plan.

Sydney, Jill, now Declan, remarked Aunt Tatiana. *So many people counting on you. So many people to let down if you fail.*

"I hope you're including me in that 'we,'" said Rose fiercely. "I'm ready to bring Jill home."

"Palm Springs," I murmured, still rocking Declan. "That might be perfect. We can hide him away there."

"We can't take a baby on a witch hunt," warned Sydney.

I nodded in agreement. "Here. Take him, he's asleep."

Sydney carefully lifted Declan from my arms and looked at me quizzically as I reached for my phone. I had a bad signal too, but it was good enough to get a call out to my mom.

"Adrian?" she answered in a panic. "Where are you? I've been so worried, ever since that Nina girl had a fit! Are you okay?"

"Yeah . . . well, no. It's complicated. But I need you to meet me in Palm Springs as soon as you can. I'm going there soon. Can you do that?"

"Yes . . ." she began uncertainly. "But—"

"I can't tell you what's going on," I said swiftly. "Not yet."

"I know, darling. That wasn't what I was going to ask. I was wondering what I should do with the cat and the dragon while I'm gone?"

Good question. "Oh. Um, see if Sonya will watch them."

I disconnected and saw that Dimitri had stepped back inside. "We're going to Palm Springs?" he asked.

"Time to look for Jill," said Rose.

"If you're up for it," I added.

Dimitri held up a car seat with one hand, which was almost comical. "We can go whenever you're ready. Lana gave us this and swears it's easy to install."

Rose laughed at that. "Oh, this I've got to see, comrade. Dimitri Belikov, badass god, installing a baby's car seat."

He smiled good-naturedly, and we scurried around,

gathering up things. Sydney had to call Jackie back, and since my hands were full, she handed Declan off to Rose. "Just rock him," I said, seeing her panic.

Rose blanched but complied, earning laughter in return from Dimitri. "Rose Hathaway, notorious rebel, showing her maternal side."

She stuck her tongue out at him. "Enjoy it while you can, comrade. This is as close as you'll ever get to it."

I nearly dropped my bag as a startling thought occurred to me. Olive had said she and Neil had been together before he'd been injected with spirit. That meant whatever had happened to bring about Declan's conception had been the result of her being restored from being a Strigoi. Would that apply to Dimitri as well? Did that restoration only work on women? Rose and Dimitri were laughing now, joking because children were an impossible future for the two of them . . . but did they realize they might actually be capable of such a future? Did they want it?

You hold a lot of power over them, Aunt Tatiana whispered. *Power to make or break their future happiness.*

"Adrian?" asked Rose, seeing my astonished face. "You okay?"

"Yeah," I said, slowly moving again. "Just trying to get used to all this."

When we finally made our way out, with Declan in my arms once more, it was impossible to entirely avoid notice as we walked through the rest of the community. People were out and about, trying to recover from the terrible aftermath of the Strigoi attack. Most were too caught up in their own affairs, but a few saw me and wanted to talk to me—because I'd healed them.

"Thank you, thank you," exclaimed Mallory the guard, hurrying up and catching my arm. "They told me how bad I was. I might not have survived if it wasn't for what you did!"

If I hadn't done it, would Olive still be alive? I wondered. But I smiled instead and stammered out how glad I was that Mallory was doing well. When she called for a couple of her friends who'd also been injured to come over, I quickly handed Declan back to Sydney. "You two stay out of sight," I whispered. A baby and an ex-Alchemist were too memorable, and that was the last thing we needed right now.

Sydney complied, hastily getting away from my fan club and me, with Dimitri shadowing her. "Meet at the car," he called back.

I nodded and then turned back to those I'd healed. I accepted their gratitude as graciously as I could, but all the while, I couldn't shake the idea that Olive should have been among them. A few mentioned her, expressing how sad they were at her loss, but no one asked about the baby. When they finally dissipated, I thought I was free, but then another voice called my name. I turned and saw Lana working toward me.

"Damn shame about what happened here," she said, her eyes filled with grief. She seemed to have aged years in the day I'd known her. "I wish it had been different."

"Me too," I said.

"Dimitri didn't tell me what's going on, but I'm respecting his wishes—and yours. I don't know what all the secrecy's about, but I saw Olive's face when she was speaking to you, just before she passed." Lana paused and ran a hand over her eyes. "Something was eating her up, that much was obvious, and she trusted you with it—and the baby. That's good enough for me. I'm happy to help however you need."

"Do it by forgetting we were here," I said quietly. "Us and the baby."

"Fair enough," said Lana. She cleared her throat. "But I do have one uncomfortable question."

Only one? asked Aunt Tatiana.

"What would you like done with the body?" Lana asked.

I started. It wasn't anything I'd even thought about. Olive was gone. I'd literally seen the light of her aura go. That I'd be asked to deal with this hadn't even crossed my mind.

"Um, what would you normally do?"

Lana shrugged. "We could have the body sent to her family for burial or cremation. Or to a place in Houghton, if you wanted it dealt with sooner. The Alchemist left some of that chemical behind. The one that dissolves bodies. Said we could use it if we needed to."

My stomach lurched. The idea of Olive's body undergoing what a Strigoi's would was nauseating, especially after everything she'd gone through to redeem herself from that existence. And yet . . . I'd seen what that chemical could do. It would completely destroy what was left of Olive—destroy that she'd ever had a baby. I closed my eyes and felt the world sway around me.

"Adrian?" queried Lana. "You okay?"

I opened my eyes. "Use the chemical. It's what she would've wanted."

Lana arched an eyebrow at that, but I couldn't elaborate. I couldn't tell her that Olive wouldn't have wanted to risk her body being sent to a funeral parlor or back to her family, where people would learn she'd given birth and ask questions. Olive had died to keep Declan a secret. This was another terrible part of that legacy.

"Okay," said Lana. "And I meant what I said—I'll keep this under wraps. My people will too. I'll make sure it stays quiet. This group knows how to keep a secret."

"Thank you. For everything." I started to turn, but she caught my arm.

"Oh, what should I tell your uncle? He was asking about you."

My uncle was no one I wanted to talk to—especially since I was sure he was someone who couldn't keep a secret. I didn't want him asking me about Olive or what would become of her son. "Don't tell him anything," I said. "Just that I left."

Another long day of travel followed, made even more complicated by having an infant around who required feeding every two hours. We couldn't get a flight out of Houghton, so Dimitri drove us to Minneapolis—with frequent stops along the way—until we could finally camp out at the airport there and catch a last-minute flight to LAX. Throughout all of this, Sydney and I split our attention between taking care of Declan and making contact with the people in Palm Springs. I verified that Neil had made it there, per our earlier arrangements, but I didn't tell him anything that was going on, not about Olive or Declan. And until I spoke to him, I also had to keep Rose and Dimitri in the dark, as much as I hated it. I just didn't feel they should know the truth before Neil did.

"Is this your first?"

"Huh?"

Our plane was descending into Los Angeles, and I was doing my best to rock a fussing Declan while belted into my seat. In lieu of any proper baby toys, Sydney was trying to distract him by shaking a set of keys over him, even though she claimed to have read some article about how newborns couldn't actually see very far. The question had come from a little old lady sitting across the aisle from us. She nodded at Declan.

"Your first baby," she clarified.

Sydney and I exchanged glances, not entirely sure how to answer that. "Uh, yeah," I said.

The old woman beamed. "I thought so. You both are so attentive! So concerned. But don't worry. It's not as hard as you think. You'll get used to it. You two look like natural parents. I bet you'll have a dozen!" She cackled to herself as the plane touched down.

By the time we reached Palm Springs, Declan was the only one of us who wasn't wiped out. None of us had really had a decent night's sleep in days, but we kept on powering through as best as we could. Dimitri once again took it upon himself to drive and delivered us to Clarence Donahue's house, which provided a relatively safe haven—and also a much-needed source of blood for me. Clarence Donahue was a reclusive old Moroi who'd helped us in the past, and he was delighted to see us when his housekeeper showed us into his living room. I was delighted to see my mother sitting there with him.

"Mom," I said, wrapping her in a huge embrace.

"My goodness," she said, when I was reluctant to let her go. "It's only been a few days, dear."

"A lot's happened in that time," I told her honestly, thinking of how much life and death I'd witnessed in those days. "And I think a lot's going to go down when Sydney checks in with some of her friends. It's going to keep the rest of us pretty busy, and, uh, there's something I need your help with."

I stepped to the side and revealed Sydney, carrying Declan asleep in his car seat.

My mom stared at the baby in confusion, then looked at Sydney, and then turned to me wide-eyed. "Adrian," she exclaimed. "That's not—I mean, how is it possible—"

"He's not mine," I said wearily. "His name is Declan, and I'm taking care of him for a friend. I might need your help watching him while we go after Jill, though. There's no one else I can trust."

As though he knew his name, Declan opened his eyes and regarded us solemnly. I honestly wasn't sure how my mother was going to respond to this request. Dhampirs had always been in subservient roles to her, and she'd freaked out when I'd brought Rose home on a date. After she'd accepted my marriage with Sydney, I'd once commented to her that she'd have to accept the idea of dhampir grandchildren. My mom had shrugged off the topic, saying, yes, of course she understood that, but I'd wondered if she'd been pushing that off for another day's worries. How would she react now to caring for a dhampir child?

I carefully lifted Declan out of the seat and was astonished when my mother snatched him away. "Look at you," she crooned, swaying him in his arms. "Such a handsome little boy. The handsomest little boy."

I remember when you used to be her handsomest little boy, remarked Aunt Tatiana.

My mom dragged her gaze from him. "You should change him into some lighter clothes," she told me. "Those pajamas are too heavy for this climate."

"Um, those are all we have," I said. I pointed to a grocery

bag Rose had set down. "Really, his worldly possessions are all in there."

"Where's he going to sleep?" my mother asked.

"He's just been using the car seat."

She sighed loudly. "Oh, Adrian. This is just like the time you brought home a neighbor's puppy and seemed surprised when you found out you'd have to feed it every day."

"Hey," I retorted. "We've fed this little guy plenty of times."

"Sydney, dear," my mother added, "I expected more sense from you, if not Adrian. Surely you know that a baby needs all sorts of things."

Sydney was momentarily stunned, and I couldn't blame her. I was pretty sure my mother had never called her "dear" before, and I think Sydney was at a loss as to whether to feel flattered by the endearment or chastised for her lack of "sense."

"Yes, Mrs. Ivashkov," said Sydney at last. "That's why we wanted you out here while we got things settled. We know you'll get him all he needs."

"You're Mrs. Ivashkov now," corrected my mom. "Call me Daniella."

That was another surprise to Sydney, and she was saved from her shock by her phone ringing. "It's Ms. Terwilliger," she said, answering it and walking out of the room. She returned a few minutes later, face excited.

"The local witches are going to start searching tomorrow at dawn," she told us once she'd disconnected. "I've got the location to meet. Eddie and N-Neil will join us. Until then, we'll just lay low."

She tripped a bit over Neil's name, her eyes falling on Declan as she spoke. I understood how she felt. At some point, once things were stable, Neil was going to have to find out he was a father. The concept still made me reel. You'd think after everything I'd come to terms with—Strigoi being restored, the dead brought back to life—that I could take two dhampirs creating a baby in stride. But I couldn't. It was still too strange, too beyond how I'd centered my world.

My mother surprised me then by handing Declan back to me. "If you two are stuck inside and nothing else is happening this evening, then I need to do some shopping before everything closes so that he can be properly taken care of."

I took a little offense at the words. I honestly thought we'd done a pretty decent job of taking care of him in the last twenty-four hours. Maybe he only had one outfit, but it was mostly clean, and I was putting his diapers on correctly now. Plus, he was always fed as soon as he showed any signs of hunger. For someone who'd spent most of his adult life fearful of getting girls pregnant, I thought my unexpected paternal trial was turning out reasonably well.

But I knew what she meant, and part of the reason I'd wanted her to come was for her insight. After all, she'd raised a baby to adulthood, and I hadn't. "Not much left in my account," I told her. Both of us had been cut off by my dad. "But I'll give you my debit card, and you can use it as far as it'll go."

"Perhaps I may be of assistance," offered Clarence, getting to his feet. With the help of his snake-headed cane, he hobbled over to an ornate wooden box on a shelf in the wall. I'd seen that box a hundred times while I'd been in his home. What I hadn't seen was him ever open it, and my jaw nearly hit the floor when he lifted the lid and revealed stacks of one-hundred-dollar bills. He handed what had to be at least a thousand dollars to my mom. "Will this be enough for the young master, Lady Ivashkov?"

My mother actually had the audacity to deliberate. "It's a start," she declared magnanimously. She turned to Rose and Dimitri. "Now. Which one of you is going to drive me?"

Surprisingly, Rose volunteered. Although still uneasy around Declan and babies in general, she seemed kind of excited about shopping for one. Sydney looked disappointed at not being able to join them but made no arguments. With Alicia and the Alchemists on the loose, Sydney couldn't leave a secure location like this without good reason. She contented herself by holing up in a guest room and prepping some spells that would be of use in the search for Alicia tomorrow. That left Dimitri and me to babysit, which seemed like the setup for some sort of wacky sitcom.

"They really are amazing, aren't they?" he mused, admiring Declan as he slept in my arms. "Someone so small . . . who will have such enormous potential. Good, evil. Great acts, small acts. What will it be? What will he become?"

I wouldn't have known the answer for anyone, let alone for a child born because of the incredible magic used to restore his mother from an undead state. As Dimitri spoke, I was surprised to see a deep, heartfelt longing in his eyes. He and Rose might have teased each other about babies, yet underneath it all, he seriously and desperately would love a child of his own, I realized. With a few words, I knew I could change his entire world if I told him the truth about Declan, that Dimitri might very well be able to have a son or daughter of his own. It might only have been the result of lucky timing that he and Rose hadn't conceived yet. That the possibility was out there was something they needed to know.

He would be indebted to you, Aunt Tatiana murmured. *Since you've known him, you've always chased him, always been second to him. With Rose. With great deeds. But if you told him he could have a child with her, he would get down on his knees and weep at your feet.*

The power was in my hands, and the temptation to tell him nearly overwhelming . . . but I bit my lip. I couldn't. Not until Neil knew.

When my mom and Rose returned, I was astonished to see they'd become fast friends. I was also amazed at the quantity of merchandise they'd managed to buy in so short a time. A bassinet, a gazillion clothes, toys, and a whole bunch of products for babies I hadn't even known existed. Sydney looked it over with a critical eye and immediately began double-checking product reviews on her phone.

"This will get him by for now," my mother announced. "But of course he'll eventually need a full-size crib, once he's bigger. And although that car seat is adequate for now, we saw several that would be much more suitable."

"We saw some with cup holders and sunshades," added Rose.

Sydney nodded in agreement. "He'll definitely need a sunshade."

I knew it was pointless telling them Declan wouldn't be in our care by the time he needed a cup holder. When it came to the strong-willed women in my life, I found it was sometimes easiest to nod and agree with whatever they dictated was best. That being said, Declan did seem much more comfortable sleeping in a real bed that night, and the rest of us stood around admiring him after he'd fallen asleep.

"Sweetest baby ever," my mother said with a sigh.

"You mean second sweetest, right?" I corrected. I was a little surprised at how quickly she'd taken to him, but then again, perhaps I shouldn't have been. Her whole life had been thrown into upheaval, between leaving my father and supporting my unorthodox marriage. Here, in Declan, she had a project that she could throw herself into—something far more meaningful and substantial than her cross-stitch and less weird than a dragon or a witch's cat.

More importantly for us that night, my mother was more than willing to take on the responsibility of Declan's overnight feedings. Part of this was because she was still on a nocturnal schedule from Court. But she could also tell that the rest of us were exhausted, and being woken every couple of hours probably wasn't in our best interests if we wanted to be alert and ready for a possible encounter with Alicia tomorrow. After all, her whole point in that twisted scavenger hunt had been to wear Sydney down.

"I hope we find her," said Sydney as she got into bed that night. "Can you even imagine? This could all be over by this time tomorrow. We find Alicia. We find Jill. Everything goes back to normal—well, whatever passes for normal with us."

I slid into bed, enjoying the luxury of stretching out after having pulled my last nap in a cramped airplane seat. It was also heady to have Sydney in relative privacy for a change. Clarence's home was so big that our guest room was isolated in this hallway, unlike the cramped quarters back in Court's guest housing. Sydney, dressed simply in shorts and a tank top, curled up against me, and I sighed happily. At last, a moment of peace with her.

"Adrian," she said, "we need to talk about what happened at the commune."

My hold on her stiffened. "A lot happened."

"I know, I know, and obviously we're dealing with the most important part—Declan. But we need to talk about what you did—that healing."

She blames you! hissed Aunt Tatiana. *She blames you for Olive's death!*

"You think I'm responsible for Olive dying?" I demanded.

"What?" said Sydney. "No. *No.* Of course not. Adrian . . . you don't blame yourself, do you? A Strigoi did that to her. There was nothing you could have done."

"Then why are you giving me a hard time about the healing?" I asked.

She exhaled. "I'm worried about the way it wore you out. You said you'd tone down your spirit use. That it was for the best."

"Actually," I said, "I don't know that I ever said that. I think *you* decided it and have been forcing it on me."

Her kind tone suddenly became a lot frostier. "'Forcing' it? Adrian, I'm trying to help you. You heard what happened to Nina with all that spirit use. I don't want you comatose like her!"

"I didn't use as much as her," I retorted.

"You drained yourself! That seems like a lot to me."

"Yeah, well," I said angrily, "there are a bunch of dhampirs back in Lana's camp who'd disagree with you. They're grateful for what I did."

But not Olive, whispered Aunt Tatiana. *She has nothing to say at all.*

"Adrian," said Sydney, obviously trying for calm, "I'm sure they are grateful, but we've been over this. You need to go back on your medication. You can't save everybody. You can't use spirit indiscriminately and ignore the cost to yourself. You're putting your life in danger."

"What kind of life would I have—what kind of person would I be—if I hoarded that magic and let others suffer? I can't, Sydney. If I see someone, and I can help, I'm going to. I can't sit by and abandon them!"

"And I can't sit by and let you keep hurting yourself," she cried, losing that calm again.

"I'm sorry," I mumbled, rolling over to my side. "I guess I can't change who I am."

Long moments passed, and finally she rolled onto her side too so that our backs faced one another. Icy silence fell. So much for a peaceful or romantic night.

She doesn't understand, Aunt Tatiana told me. *She never will.*

I need her to, I answered back in my head. *I need her in my life to understand and support me. Without her, I'm lost.*

You'll always have me, came the phantom response.

I tugged the covers more tightly over me, thinking with dread about how one of these days, I was going to have to deal with the elephant in the room—or rather, the dead queen in my head. I was fairly certain that if I went back on my medication, Aunt Tatiana would go away . . . but then, so would spirit. Was I ready for that again? Without spirit, I never would've been able to heal those dhampirs. I wouldn't be able to help in the upcoming rescue for Jill. Without spirit, what was I?

Spirit couldn't save Olive, remarked Aunt Tatiana. *It's overrated.*

"Shut up," I mumbled.

Behind me, Sydney stirred. "Did you say something?"

I rolled back over and kissed her shoulder. "I said I'm sorry. I love you."

CHAPTER 12

SYDNEY

I WENT TO BED FEELING UNSETTLED. Adrian had swung back too quickly from his opposing stance for me to believe he'd truly had a change of heart. When morning came, though, there was little opportunity for further discussion. Declan demanded our attention, and then, before long, it was time for us to go and help the others search for Alicia. Before joining the witches, however, Adrian and I first had a much-needed reunion with some of our friends.

We went to Adrian's old apartment with Rose and Dimitri, triggering another wave of nostalgia as I thought back to all the time I'd spent there. Long afternoons lounging around in Adrian's arms, before we were married, before we were constantly pursued . . . I'd thought we were living on the edge back then, but compared to what we faced these days, life had been deceptively simple.

Trey Juarez greeted us at the door, his easy grin growing even bigger as he took in Adrian and me. "Been a long time,

Melbourne. Or do I call you Ivashkov now?"

I returned his powerful embrace. When Adrian had left Palm Springs to live at Court, he'd given his apartment to Trey. "I'm still just trying to get you to call me Sydney," I told him. I introduced Rose and Dimitri to him and then glanced around the apartment, still the sunny yellow shade that Adrian had painted it. Eddie and Neil were there waiting for us, and I gave them hugs too. "Where's Angeline?"

"At Amberwood. She's got summer classes."

"Does she?" I asked in surprise. "I didn't know that. I thought she was just boarding there for the summer."

"She was," Trey agreed, a sparkle in his eyes. "And then I convinced her some extra studying would help her with classes in the fall."

"The fall?" I settled down on the couch, trying not to think of the times Adrian and I had curled up together on it. "I figured she'd go back to the Keepers."

"You should know her better than that," said Neil wryly "The queen agreed to fund her education as a way of thanking her for looking after Jill all this time." I almost didn't process his words. The sight of Neil reminded me of Declan, waiting back at Clarence's. Adrian and I had agreed it was best to wait to tell Neil the news, but it was a huge secret to be carrying.

"Angeline almost refused," added Trey. "Said she didn't deserve it since she'd let Jill slip away. But I convinced her Jill will want a well-educated guardian when we rescue her—and that Amberwood's not that far of a drive from UCLA."

I smiled, despite a pang of jealousy. Trey was going to college soon, something I'd been denied initially because I was part of the Alchemists. Now, being constantly on the run from them, it seemed unlikely I'd go anytime soon. "Look at you, setting a good example for others," I teased.

"Hey," he said, "I meant all of it. And we *are* going to get Jill back, right? Explain this lead you've got. Eddie said it's some girl you fought before?"

The light mood instantly shifted as we got down to business. "Her name's Alicia DeGraw," I explained, getting out my phone. "We don't entirely know where or how she's holding Jill, but it seems pretty clear now she's doing it as a way to get back at me. Her last clue led to the Salton Sea, and that's where Ms. Terwilliger's friends are going to help us search today." I showed him Alicia's picture, which Ms. Terwilliger had obtained from a friend of hers who'd known Alicia back when she was Veronica's apprentice. It had been taken a couple of years before I met Alicia, but she looked the same: hipster glasses, excessive accessories, and bobbed, pale blond hair.

Trey's eyes widened. "I know this girl." Seeing our astonished looks, he hastily amended: "That is, I've seen her. She came here looking for you and Adrian. I told you guys . . . but I never caught her name."

Vaguely, I recalled Trey mentioning a girl who'd come by asking for Adrian and me during the time I'd been held captive by the Alchemists. We'd been so preoccupied by other things— like escaping with our lives from the Alchemists—that the incident had slipped our minds.

"She was here?" exclaimed Eddie.

"Only long enough to ask for Sydney and Adrian," Trey said. "And use the bathroom."

Realization hit me. "And I bet I left a comb or brush in there. That's how she got my hair to key that spell to me."

Many of our friends only knew bits and pieces of the story and the chase Alicia had led us on, so I took a moment to catch everyone up and give a full rundown. Eddie was glowering by the time I finished.

"It's been driving me crazy being in town, knowing I might be so close to Alicia and not able to do anything," he said. "But Ms. Terwilliger insisted we search with the other witches."

"You could've shaved in your downtime," suggested Adrian helpfully.

"I understand," I told Eddie, ignoring Adrian's snark. "I haven't liked the delay either, but getting them to help us will give us an extra layer of protection against Alicia. There's no telling what magical traps she might have laid."

"Are you sure she wants you to come to the Salton Sea?" asked Dimitri. "You think that clue was meant to be taken literally?"

"All her other clues were very specific," I said. "So, yes, I think that was her initial plan . . . however, we've delayed a few days by keeping me away. That may have undone whatever she originally wanted, which is good and bad. It means she's been thrown off . . . but it also means she may just come up with something new that we aren't expecting. Our hope is that we can find some clue at Salton today that might put us on the right track."

"I don't even know her, and I hate her already," remarked Rose.

I glanced at the time. "Let's hope we can find her so you can tell her in person. It's time to go."

Our group mobilized and set out in two different cars, off to meet Ms. Terwilliger and the other witches at a Salton Sea state park. The sky was overcast with gray clouds, hinting of a rare rainy summer day ahead. When I saw the group that Ms. Terwilliger had assembled, I was awestruck. At least two dozen witches stood before us.

"I feel bad," I murmured to Ms. Terwilliger, stepping away from the others. "Getting all these people involved."

She pushed her glasses up and smiled at me. "It's like I told you in the Ozarks: This is a problem for the entire magical community. You have nothing to feel bad about. It's Alicia's fault, not yours."

I sighed. "I just hope waiting to come here was the right course of action."

"While you were magically exhausted, just like she wanted you to be? No, Sydney. All you would've been doing is giving yourself to her. Even if we don't find her today, at least you've had a chance to rest and prepare for what's next."

I simply nodded, certainly not about to tell her that my last few days with Adrian had been anything but restful. Maybe I was no longer magically exhausted, but I was certainly mentally drained. Hopefully that wouldn't hurt in the hunt for Alicia.

Coven members I'd met at my initiation had all turned out, dropping whatever it was they'd had planned today in order to track down Alicia. Maude, Trina, Alison, and others whose names had slipped my mind in the last several months. Equally astonishing was that members of other covens had also come to join us, verifying Ms. Terwilliger's insistence that this was indeed a problem for the entire magical community.

"We're certainly not going to leave a mess like this for a newcomer like you to deal with alone," snapped Inez Garcia, coming up to me as I started to turn from Ms. Terwilliger. Inez was perhaps the most surprising addition of all today. She was a venerable old witch notable both for her powers and her refusal to join any coven. She was the witch Ms. Terwilliger had gone to about the wooden box. Her acerbic wit was also legendary, though she'd taken a mild liking to me (which was about as much as she liked anyone). Catching sight of Rose and Dimitri chatting near Trey, Inez gave a small snort of amusement. "No surprise you've got dhampirs with you. What happened to that Moroi boy you had in tow last time? The one with the nice cheekbones?"

"Oh, he's over there," I said, flushing slightly. "I, uh, married him."

Inez's pointed eyebrows rose. "Did you now? Well, good for you."

Maude, one of the senior witches in the Stelle, called everyone to attention. We gathered in a big circle as she cast a spell that created a miniature map of the Salton Sea on the ground in front of us. The plan was simple, for now, mostly because we didn't know for sure what to expect. Between Ms. Terwilliger's magical recruits and the "muscle" I'd provided with Trey and the dhampirs, we had nearly thirty people. We were going to divide into smaller groups to investigate as much of the shoreline as possible. Some parts were easier to get to than others, so today's goal was checking out the public areas. Theoretically, Alicia would've had the same limitations. The groups were divided up based on those who had strong affinities to detect magic in general and those who were good at casting spells to detect hidden enchantments. The dhampirs were distributed among the groups, just in case physical force was needed. Ms. Terwilliger wanted Adrian and me to stay with her, and Eddie insisted on remaining with us as well. Although Jill was his main priority, he still felt responsible for us.

It looked as though Ms. Terwilliger's predictions were spot-on, that Alicia might very well have abandoned her plan when I didn't immediately take the bait. If she had left a magical trap around, she'd also done a great job of eradicating all trace of it. Our search parties scoured all the public areas we could, checking some of them twice, without finding anything. Undaunted, we took a small break for lunch and then reconvened to explore the less accessible regions around the lake. Even getting into those areas required magic—mostly invisibility spells—and that took a fair bit of coordination. As evening rolled around, however, those clandestine searches proved as fruitless as the easier ones. No sign of Alicia or magical traps.

Maude and Ms. Terwilliger thanked the other covens for their help and sent them home for the night. "Maude and I are going to run a few errands to gather some spell components that might be useful," Ms. Terwilliger told me. "I'd like to lay some protective spells around where you're staying, just to be safe—unless you and Adrian would like to stay at my place?"

I smiled at that, thinking of Declan. "Things are a little complicated right now. I'd better stick to Clarence's."

"Fair enough," she said, "especially with those dhampirs of yours around. I like you having that extra protection, just in case Alicia attempts something we don't expect. In fact . . . well, I have another suggestion to help you out. I'd like you to stop by Malachi's home on your way back. You remember how to get there, of course?"

"Malachi Wolfe?" I asked, as if she could be referring to any other Malachi.

She nodded. "I've already spoken to him. He'll lend you a weapon—just in case. I trust your magic but would feel better with something extra guarding your back."

I didn't like the idea of a gun, but Ms. Terwilliger had a point. When it came to Alicia, we couldn't take any chances. I glanced back at my gathered friends. "No need for all of us to go—especially since one of us should get home and check on your mom, Adrian." I could tell from his expression that he understood my meaning perfectly—that it was actually Declan we needed to check up on.

"Well, as much as I'd love to see Wolfe, it's probably better you go to him, in case he demands another 'skill test' before letting you borrow a weapon," said Adrian. "I'll get back home to Mom. You guys . . ." He glanced at the dhampirs.

"I'll go with Sydney," said Eddie. "I want to finally meet this guy." He'd taken our lack of results today hard, so I was surprised to see him enthused about anything.

Of course, Malachi Wolfe had become legendary among my friends—most of whom had never met him and were only going off of the stories Adrian and I had told about our time in the Wolfe School of Defense. In fact, it was clear from Trey and Neil's faces that they wanted to come with Eddie and me, but Trey needed to pick up Angeline and had come out to the Salton Sea in Neil's rental car. The two of them decided to get that straightened out while Rose and Dimitri went with Adrian. That left Eddie and me, and after telling our friends goodbye, we set out for Malachi's compound on the outskirts of Palm Springs.

"Are the Chihuahuas really trained to attack?" he asked.

I couldn't help but grin. "That's what Wolfe claims. We've never seen them in action, though."

"I can't wait to see his nunchucks."

"Do *not* touch them," I warned. "Or any weapon, without permission. If he approves of you, he might lend you something too."

Some of Eddie's humor faded. "I really hate that it's come to you needing to borrow a weapon. I hate that it's come to any of this." He sighed in dismay. "I know Ms. Terwilliger warned us Alicia might have moved on, but I was really, really hoping we'd find some sign of her today."

"I know," I said in dismay. "I wanted that too. But if she had to scramble and change her plans, the odds are good she got careless. We just need to take advantage of that and beat her before her next move."

"And each day we wait is another day of God-knows-what for Jill."

The despair in his voice made my heart ache. "I know," I told him sadly. "I know."

Malachi's compound was a series of stark, industrial-looking buildings on a large, grassless lot well off the highway. We pulled into the long gravel driveway, and I saw some of Eddie's earlier enthusiasm return as every fantasy about Malachi's bizarre lifestyle slowly unfolded. The sun was just touching the horizon, making everything even creepier as shadows fell. I smiled to myself, remembering the first time Adrian and I had visited, unsure if we were walking into a self-defense class or an abduction.

I knocked at the door of the main house and wasn't surprised to hear the frantic pitter-pattering of little Chihuahua feet, followed by a cacophony of frenzied yelping. "Oh, man," breathed Eddie. "There really is a herd of them." I'd seen Eddie fearlessly face down an attacking Strigoi, but he took an uneasy step back at the sound of the canine charge.

I grinned and turned toward the door, waiting for Malachi Wolfe himself to answer. Slightly unstable and very unorthodox, Wolfe had nonetheless been a good friend to Adrian and me—and more than a friend to Ms. Terwilliger. That last part still made me squirm a bit, but after everything Adrian and I had endured, I was more convinced than ever that everyone needed someone to love—even scattered sorceresses and eyepatch-wearing self-defense instructors.

When no answer immediately came, I knocked again. This drove the dogs into a louder frenzy, but Wolfe still didn't materialize. "Weird," I said.

"Didn't you text him before we left?" asked Eddie.

"Ms. Terwilliger did," I replied. I glanced over at the other buildings, looking for movement. "He said he had some weapons in mind for me. Maybe he's getting them out." I stepped back to the ground and headed toward where I knew Wolfe kept a stockpile of weapons. "I hope he's not going to try to pass off that blowgun again."

Eddie's face lit up as he followed me across the sandy ground. "Blowgun? Are you seriously—"

His words were lost as a mailbox suddenly exploded beside us. Without missing a beat, Eddie pushed me down and rolled us away from the worst of the heat and flames. Gravel and hard ground scraped at my skin, but it was certainly better than the alternative. Eddie kept himself positioned protectively over me as we both carefully lifted our heads and peered around, taking in the fiery wreckage.

"What the hell?" he asked.

Another explosion erupted from the ground beside us. No flames this time, but the rocks that flew up from it were as good as shrapnel, and I cried out as a particularly sharp one bit into my arm. I pointed at the closest building.

"There!"

Before he could stop me, I ran toward it, casting a spell of unseen force that shattered a window. An ear-piercing alarm blared out. No surprise Wolfe would have this place wired. The question was whether his paranoia would extend to having that alarm system monitored by the police or not.

Eddie followed me through the window, and I found we were in the building that had served as a training area for my self-defense class. It was wide and open, lined with mirrors and cases of weapons. I sized up the room, looking for the safest position. Eddie, meanwhile, ran straight for one of the cases. After waffling between a bola and some brass knuckles, he went with the bola, swinging it around with practiced ease as he warily backed up and kept an eye on the window we'd broken. I called up my favorite spell, summoning a fireball to my palm.

"Is it Alicia?" Eddie yelled, making his voice heard over the alarm.

"I'd guess so," I called back. I'd sensed a human magic in those explosions, and unless there was yet another witch after me, Alicia seemed like the logical choice. With my non-fireball hand, I managed to text the most recent contact in my phone: Ms. Terwilliger. I could only manage a short message and hoped it would convey the severity of the situation: *help*.

I should've known Alicia wouldn't settle for the opening we'd made into the building. The main door suddenly exploded in a shower of sparks and wood. A silhouette appeared in the doorway, and without verifying its identity, I hurled my fireball. The figure held up a hand, and the fireball smashed harmlessly against an invisible barrier. When it cleared, the figure moved forward, and I finally came face-to-face with Alicia. She gave me a cold smile.

"Hello, Sydney, nice to see you again. Surprised to see me alive?"

I called another fireball to my hand. "It was never my intent to kill you." Even I realized how lame that sounded, considering all I'd done to her, and she gave a harsh laugh.

"Really? What exactly was the point of stabbing me and leaving me in a burning house?"

Before I could respond, Eddie charged her, swinging his bola in the air. With a flick of the wrist, she made a wall of mirrors beside him shatter. I saw it coming but wasn't quite fast enough in dismissing my fireball in a favor of a shield for him. I deflected part of the damage, but some of the glass embedded itself in him, particularly his bare arm. I saw a brief flash of pain pass over his features, but he didn't stop moving. Alicia shattered another mirror, and this time, I had an invisible shield squarely in place to protect him. He released the bola, but despite its perfect aim and fast speed, she anticipated it and blew it away with a wave of invisible force.

"Where's Jill?" I yelled at her.

A cruel smile twisted over Alicia's features. "You'd love to know that, wouldn't you?"

Eddie picked up a piece of broken glass and came running toward her, wielding it like a knife. "I swear, if you've hurt her—"

"Oh, honestly. As if I'd waste my time hurting her." Alicia took out a pinch of powder from her pocket, throwing it at

Eddie and shouting an incantation I didn't know. I wasn't able to intercept this one in time, and the magic seized Eddie. Like that, he froze in place, midstride and holding the glass shard menacingly in his hand.

"What have you done to him?" I cried.

"Relax, Sydney," Alicia said. "He's still alive. Just like your little Moroi friend—for now."

"Take me to her!" I demanded.

Alicia laughed. "Sorry, Sydney. You'll never see her again. She's going to have to suffer through a few more psalms . . . and you? You're just going to suffer . . ."

The floor under my feet rippled. I staggered and fell to my knees but was able to throw a fireball at Alicia before I completely lost my balance. My aim was spot-on, but she lifted her hands to cast what I suspected was another shielding spell. The incantation she spoke was Greek, one I hadn't heard before either. The fireball hit another unseen wall, but rather than shatter, the flames rebounded and came back toward *me* in exactly the same path. I yelped and managed to get out of its way just in time. I was spared, but the fireball hit a cabinet instead, engulfing it in flames. The fire spread quickly, making me wonder what kind of varnish Wolfe used. At the same time, the alarm finally stopped blaring.

"Mirroring spell," Alicia said gleefully. "Very useful. Be careful what you cast."

She meant it as a taunt, but there was truth in it that made me hesitate before I planned my next course of action. It was too long a delay, as she soon cast what I recognized as the same spell that had frozen Eddie. That one was too complex for me to fully follow, but it gave me the opportunity to dodge and block it. I then opted for a different kind of freezing—a literal one, as I sent a wave of ice her way. It wasn't nearly as lethal as a fireball, but it also wouldn't add to the already-spreading fire. Alicia responded with the mirror spell, sending the ice back my way. I ducked, and the ice landed in part of the burning room beside me. Rather than diminish the fire, however, it simply made the smoke grow thicker.

"You must be getting tired," she teased.

She was right. I still had plenty of magic in me, but this active combat was exhausting. Ms. Terwilliger's words came back to me: *She wants an easy fight.* That's what Alicia was doing, trying to wear me down with magic so she could cast the spell that finished me. With the stolen life and magic she had, this battle wouldn't exhaust her as quickly.

"Alicia, we don't have to fight," I said. "Please. Let's stop this and get out of here before this place burns down. Tell me where Jill is, release Eddie, and we can be on our way."

"Stop this? After you tried to kill me?"

"I only—"

Not caring about making the flames worse, Alicia hurled another fireball at me. I was tempted to try the mirroring spell and send it back to her, but she was too close to Eddie for my comfort.

"You're too much of a threat, Sydney," she said as I neutralized the fireball with a water spell. "I can't allow you to leave. I'm going to let this building burn down around you, just like you left me to burn in that house."

The floor rippled beneath me again, causing me to fall once more. She began speaking a complicated incantation, one I recognized as the start of the spell that had frozen Eddie in place. That was her plan. Make me into a living statue and leave me in this burning building, paralleling what I'd done to her. Desperately, I scrambled to my feet, needing to get out of the way of the spell. As she finished speaking, I saw something incredible: Malachi Wolfe, standing in the doorway to the burning room. His eye patch was on his right eye (it changed from day to day), and there were pieces of rope around his wrists and ankles as though he'd been bound.

I couldn't replicate the statue spell on my own, but I'd heard the mirroring spell enough to feel good about that. I spoke the words and felt the magic engage in me. Alicia's eyes widened in alarm as she attempted to move out of the way of the rebounding spell. What she hadn't seen, however, was the herd of Chihuahuas running into the room with Wolfe. He'd spoken a word to them and pointed at her, and they swarmed around her feet, causing her to stumble and preventing her from moving away quickly. The statue spell seized her, and suddenly, she was as frozen as Eddie, except far less graceful looking. He was like some noble warrior, ready to strike. She was mid-fall, staring in disbelief at the yipping pack of Chihuahuas swarming her frozen feet.

"Would've been here sooner," growled Wolfe, calling the pack off with a quick gesture. "But that bitch tied me up. Had to wait for the dogs to gnaw through my ropes."

"Quickly!" I said, running toward Eddie. "Help me get him out of here." I coughed from the thickening smoke and glanced at Alicia, her pretty face frozen in a snarl of dismay. "Help me get both of them out of here."

Between Wolfe and me, we managed to drag the frozen forms out before the building came down. We got them to

Wolfe's main house as the fire department showed up, followed almost immediately by Adrian, Trey, Ms. Terwilliger, and a few of the witches from the lake. Adrian pulled me into an embrace.

"Are you okay?" he asked. "When Jackie called me, I didn't know what to expect."

I rested my head against his chest, reassured by his touch. "Fine. I got lucky. Really lucky. But Eddie—"

One of the witches from a coven I didn't know produced some dried flowers that she spread over Eddie as she chanted a Latin spell. Moments later, Eddie came to life again, still in mid-jump. He stumbled as he landed, looking around in surprise when he wasn't where he expected. Adrian and I astonished him further by sweeping him into a group hug.

"You'll have to unfreeze Alicia too," I said in dismay. "We need to find Jill."

Ms. Terwilliger frowned. "That's unfortunate. This is actually a very neat way to deal with her. You didn't get any indication where Jill was beforehand?"

I shook my head and released Eddie. "No. She admitted Jill was alive 'for now' but didn't elaborate." I thought back, trying to replay each word amid the chaos. Although it had been nice to hear Alicia confirm Jill was alive, we'd already gotten a sense of that through our spells. It wasn't as useful as I'd hoped. "And she said something about Jill listening to psalms."

It made as little sense to Ms. Terwilliger as it had to me, and she gave a great sigh, exchanging glances with some of the other witches. They didn't look thrilled about releasing Alicia either. "Well, once the fire department's finished, we'll have to create a secure circle and release her to get some answers."

Trey, who'd been standing off on the sidelines, suddenly

cleared his throat. "You might not have to. I think I know where she's at—or, well, at least who's holding her." All eyes shifted to him in astonishment, but he didn't flinch under the scrutiny. "I think the Warriors of Light have her."

CHAPTER 13

ADRIAN

"WHAT DOES SALMON HAVE TO DO with the Warriors?" I asked.

Sydney shot me a wry look. "Psalms, not salmon. And I don't know the connection." She regarded Trey expectantly. "They're a kind of religious poem, right? From the Bible?"

He nodded. "Yes. Well, that is, the ones the Warriors like to quote all the time aren't actually in the Bible. They've made up a bunch of their own. But they recite them a lot on formal occasions, before meetings . . . stuff like that. If Alicia said Jill was hearing them, she's probably being held by them somewhere. Believe me, they'd love nothing more than to hold a Moroi captive."

Eddie turned toward Jackie incredulously and pointed at Alicia. "Unfreeze her like you did me! We need answers, and we need them now! Before it's too late for Jill!"

I'd never seen him so worked up and was tempted to calm him with compulsion. Jackie remained remarkably unruffled.

"I'm certainly not going to release her here—if we do it, it'll be with a dozen other witches to secure her. And even if we do, don't expect her to be forthcoming."

"She's right," said Sydney slowly. "Even if we free Alicia, we don't know that she'll tell us anything."

"I'll make her talk," insisted Eddie. "Or Adrian could compel her."

Sydney didn't look thrilled about that, but in my head, Aunt Tatiana was chomping at the bit. *Yes! Yes! We'll compel her into telling us things she doesn't even realize she knows!*

"There are spells to protect against that, and Alicia's wily enough to have taken that precaution." Jackie glanced at one of her witch friends. "What do you think? What time span would weaken her?"

The witch regarded frozen Alicia with a critical eye. "I'd leave her like that for a week, honestly. But if you're in a rush . . ." She eyed Eddie before turning back to Alicia. "I'd say forty-eight hours."

"Forty-eight hours!" exclaimed Eddie. "Jill might not have forty-eight hours if the Warriors are holding her! They could be performing some execution ritual as we speak!"

Jackie remained undaunted. "Being in that frozen state strips you of energy. Two days like that, and she'll be physically and magically burned out. Much easier to question. Even then, I still wouldn't free her unless we're in an extremely secure location with extra backup. She's too unpredictable."

"Two days is too much," Eddie reiterated. I couldn't help but share his dismay. Sydney, however, looked thoughtful.

"Alicia will be less of a threat and maybe easier to interrogate by then," she said slowly. "And in the meantime, we might be able to get some faster answers about the Warriors."

"How?" Trey and I asked together.

"From Marcus," Sydney said. "Or rather, from one of his contacts. She's undercover in the Warriors. She might be able to uncover something before we could get it out of Alicia anyway. Let me check with her and Marcus. If they can't dig up anything in twenty-four hours, the witches will release Alicia for questioning."

No one seemed thrilled by that compromise, but they agreed to it. We all finally dispersed, with Eddie going to stay with Trey while Sydney and I returned to Clarence's house. Sydney called Marcus along the way to explain the situation, and he promised to get back to her as soon as he could. When we arrived at Clarence's, Rose and Dimitri were chomping at the bit to know what had happened. I let Sydney fill them in while I went to my mom and Declan. He'd only been in my life for a couple of days, but I was surprised by how much I ached to see him, even though he did little more than sleep. After the turbulent events of the day—and the panic I'd felt upon learning Sydney had faced Alicia alone—Declan's presence was soothing.

Marcus called Sydney back a couple of hours later, saying he had news and would come to Palm Springs immediately to deliver it in person. Marcus was as much a wanted fugitive as Sydney, though, and in his usual cautious way, he arranged for a meeting away from both Clarence's and Trey's the next day.

The place he chose was a Mongolian restaurant outside of town. Rose and Dimitri, after much coaxing, agreed to wait at Clarence's for an update so as not to create too large a crowd. We had Trey and Eddie join us, though, because Trey had useful insight about the Warriors and because no force on earth could keep Eddie from making plans about Jill. When we walked into the restaurant, Sydney exhaled in relief.

"Good. He brought Sabrina with him."

I'd met Sabrina briefly but didn't know her well. She was about my age and had been an undercover member of the Warriors of Light for years. Her first meeting with Sydney had involved holding Sydney at gunpoint, which didn't thrill me, though we knew now that Sabrina had been trying to protect Marcus. Over time, we'd come to respect her and the important job she did. She didn't agree with the Warriors' philosophy, yet she'd remained among them because the intel she provided was so useful to others. I certainly hoped it'd be useful today.

"Good news and bad news," said Marcus, which wasn't exactly the opening we'd been hoping for. "The good news is that we're pretty sure the Warriors do have Jill. The bad news is that we don't know exactly where she is."

Eddie crossed his arms. "Time to free Alicia and get some answers."

"Not necessarily," said Sabrina. Her long blond hair was pulled up into a high ponytail today, and she looked very much like an ordinary girl, not someone posing as a member of a fanatical anti-vampire group. "My guess is that Alicia doesn't know where Jill is either. She most likely caught Jill and delivered her to the Warriors, then let them hide her away somewhere. I snooped around and found reports of a 'high-profile Moroi prisoner,' but they aren't even revealing her location to members in our own group. They might work with someone like Alicia, but they wouldn't trust her much."

The news wasn't cheering me up, and Eddie shared my

frustration. "Then what do we do if your own people don't know where she is?" he demanded.

"Well," said Sabrina. "*Someone* knows. Just not someone at my level."

Marcus nodded as he swallowed a bite of his stir-fry, which by my estimation seemed to contain entirely meat and no vegetables.

Primitive, sniffed Aunt Tatiana.

Hey, lay off, I told her. *Being a dashing fugitive probably requires lots of protein.*

"We have some ideas to get to that someone," Marcus said. "The first is to ask the Alchemists to do it. We know they have ties to the Warriors."

"For all we know, they're working with them," said Eddie. "They have in the past."

"On some things," Sydney said slowly. "But not on this. They don't want to risk the Moroi going into chaos. They want Jill back. They wouldn't stand by if she was a prisoner."

"Agreed," said Marcus. His eyes met mine. "That, and they might intervene simply because they won't like the Warriors overstepping their bounds. They're nothing if not control freaks, and they aren't going to like that the Warriors worked with a witch to interfere with the Moroi. Of course, that means someone has to tell them the Warriors have Jill."

"It doesn't have to be one of you," Eddie said, catching the unspoken message between Marcus and me. "Heck, I'll do it."

"They might not believe you," I said, smiling at his vehemence. "They might not even believe *me.*"

Trey had been quiet while discussing the group he'd once been a member of, but he finally spoke up now. "There's also a good chance the Warriors will deny it, even if the Alchemists do come asking about it. They're kind of obsessed with control too. They might be difficult out of spite."

"You're right," said Sabrina. "Which is why we have one more option."

There was a warning note in her voice that put me on alert. "Which is?"

She exchanged glances with Marcus and then turned to Sydney. "The Warriors are going to be initiating some new members next week. You could go undercover and then try to infiltrate the higher tiers of power to find out where Jill's at." She spoke in a rush, as though that might help reduce the overall absurdity of the suggestion.

"You want me to join the Warriors?" Sydney exclaimed.

"No," said Eddie and I in unison.

"You'd just be participating in their recruitment," said Sabrina, as though that were some kind of reassurance. "It's like an orientation."

"Or a sorority rush," said Marcus, which really didn't improve things.

Trey shook his head in dismay. "I know what you're talking about, and it's crazy." He turned to the rest of us. "They round up a bunch of potential recruits, bring them in secret to a Warrior compound, and make them compete in all kinds of ordeals to prove their worth. Remember when I had to fight my own cousin?"

The Warriors had once held Sonya captive and used her as part of a ceremony meant to "test" its young members. Along with fighting his cousin, Trey had then been expected to kill Sonya. He hadn't planned on going through with it, and those plans went awry anyway when a group of guardians disrupted the whole ceremony to bust Sonya out. Sydney had also caused a fair amount of chaos, and the Warriors certainly weren't her fans.

"The Warriors know Sydney's face," Eddie reminded us. "She can't do it. Send me. I wouldn't mind throwing a few of those freaks around. I've already had lots of practice."

"You have," agreed Marcus, "but Sydney's had a bit more practice with breaking and entering to retrieve intel. And they probably know your face too."

Sydney frowned. "Can we both go? I wouldn't mind the backup, and I've got a few tricks that could disguise us."

Are you going to sit by and let them go ahead with this? Aunt Tatiana asked me.

I turned to Sydney in amazement. "Are you seriously considering this? I mean, I'm all for crazy plans, but this is out there even for me."

Sabrina frowned in thought. "The Warriors usually just sponsor one person, but I've occasionally seen someone present two. If you could disguise yourselves, I could get you both in."

"Then send me and Sydney," I said.

"No way," said Eddie. "I'm in much better condition to beat those freaks up. No offense, Adrian." I started to say I could protect her with spirit but knew she wouldn't like that.

"You should stay behind, Adrian," agreed Sydney. "You could try to compel answers out of Alicia when the witches unfreeze her. No one but you can do that."

I opened my mouth to protest but couldn't think of anything to say. Sydney had me cornered and knew it. I wanted to go with her, but not because I had a concrete plan for dealing with the Warriors—I only had a gut instinct to protect her. But she was right about Alicia. We could give the witches their two days while Sydney went undercover with the Warriors. Hopefully that would weaken whatever compulsion protection Alicia had put upon herself.

"You're endorsing me using spirit?" I asked in amazement.

"No," she admitted. "I'm hoping they can get answers out of her through other means. But if they can't, I have a feeling you'll use compulsion regardless."

"You're a wise woman, as usual," I told Sydney.

She smiled at that, but I could tell she wasn't happy with the idea at all. With a sigh, she turned back to Sabrina. "How much trouble will you get in for this? For bringing two spies in? Because obviously we aren't really going to stay with the Warriors."

Sydney had a point. What she and Eddie were volunteering for—infiltrating some barbaric initiation ritual—was dangerous, but we couldn't forget Sabrina's role in this. She was playing a game with a very volatile group and could ultimately face more risk.

"Depends on if you guys get caught or not." Sabrina offered a tight smile that didn't reach her eyes. "So don't get caught, okay?"

Trey looked grimmer and grimmer as the planning progressed. "But this only happens if you can't convince the Alchemists that the Warriors are holding Jill. If you can convince them, they can hopefully do the heavy lifting so you don't have to get involved with any of this madness."

"Hopefully," agreed Marcus. "But in the meantime, we should prep Sydney and Eddie on what to expect if they do go with Sabrina."

Sabrina proceeded to give us a rundown on how she planned to sneak Sydney and Eddie in. The whole thing sounded awful the more she described it, and I again wanted to ask Sydney not to go. I realized me wanting to protect her from those dangers was akin to her asking me to hold back on spirit. Both were dangerous courses of action . . . yet how could we not, when Jill's life was at risk?

There's no good answer, declared Aunt Tatiana morosely. *And no good will come of any of this.*

Lunch wound down with plans being finalized and Sydney intending to get some magical disguise help from her witch connections. Sabrina got a call summoning her back to the Warriors earlier than she'd expected. She grimaced and stood up. "I'll be in touch soon, when I get a few more details about the recruitment. Can one of you drop Marcus off at his safe house?"

"We'll do it," Sydney said, preempting Eddie and Trey. "We'll talk to you guys later."

Our group dispersed, and Sydney and I led Marcus to the rental car we'd been driving since coming back to Palm Springs. It was a convertible, a bonus upgrade given to us by the company, even though we hadn't asked for it.

"Nice," said Marcus. "Great day to have the top down." He glanced over at me. "Er, maybe not."

After yesterday's gray, Palm Springs was back to its sweltering summer conditions, ones I certainly didn't want to expose myself to. Sunlight didn't kill Moroi, the way it did Strigoi, but it could certainly be uncomfortable for us if we were out in it long enough. Moments like this reminded me of the differences between Sydney and me. She loved the sun, and a life with me kept her from it.

"You can put the top down if you want," I said casually, tossing Sydney the keys.

She gave me a weak smile, guessing my thoughts. "Nah, I'd rather have air conditioning."

I smiled back, knowing she was lying. Sometimes, lounging in bed, she and I would discuss plans for a future dream house. We'd decided we'd build a screened-in porch, airy enough for me to still enjoy the heat but covered enough to block the worst of the light. I always teased her I'd serve her lemonade out there. It would be the perfect place for us—the meeting of worlds. But at the moment, it was hard to imagine a future like that.

Marcus gave her directions to an apartment complex that actually wasn't that far from where I used to go to school at Carlton on the other side of town. As she drove us onto the highway, I dialed someone that few Moroi were lucky enough to have in their phone's memory. I was even more surprised when she answered on the first ring.

"Hello, Adrian," said Lissa.

"Were you waiting by the phone for me?" I teased.

"I was waiting for Christian to call me, actually. But I'd rather hear from you—at least if you're calling to say you've got Jill."

"Afraid not," I said, feeling a pang at the loss. "But I've got some news that might be of use. We have good evidence that the Warriors of Light are holding Jill."

Lissa clearly hadn't expected that. "What? I thought it was some witch who hated Sydney. If the Warriors have her, then this isn't just about some vendetta anymore. Those people like to kill vampires for fun."

"It sounds like Alicia gave Jill to them for holding. Now Sydney has a convoluted plan to try to find out where Jill's being held, but if the Alchemists could put some pressure on the Warriors instead, it'd save us a lot of trouble," I told her. "The only problem is, Sydney can't exactly call them up and ask."

"But I can," guessed Lissa.

"You're very charming and persuasive," I told her. "Plus you've got a *little* bit more influence than we do."

"I'll see what I can do," she replied, sounding exhausted at the thought. I didn't blame her. Diplomacy would exhaust me too, especially when dealing with assholes like the Alchemists. "They're going to want to know what 'good evidence' we've got."

I hesitated, thinking of Sabrina. "We can't exactly give our source up. Can you just tell them it's an anonymous tip and have them look into that?"

"I'll try," said Lissa. "But you know how they are."

"Yes," I agreed. "I certainly do. Good luck—and thanks."

"Nothing to thank me for. Jill's my sister."

I disconnected and was just in time to see Sydney drive right past the apartment complex Marcus had indicated. "Hey," I said, recognizing it from my Carlton days. "You missed it."

Her expression had darkened. "I didn't miss the guys in suits snooping around the side of the building." Her eyes lifted to the rearview mirror, and she sighed. "Or the black car that just peeled out of the building's lot and is now following us."

"Damn it," said Marcus. "They found out I came to town. I thought that place was secure."

I turned in my seat, craning my neck to see what Sydney had. Sure enough, a black Escalade was doing some pretty aggressive maneuvering to get into our lane. Sydney made an abrupt turn that caused me to grip the door, and the Escalade followed suit. The precious, fragile sense of freedom I'd allowed myself to enjoy since leaving Court dissipated like smoke on the wind.

"Sorry, you guys," said Marcus. "They must have spotted me when I came in this morning."

Sydney made another surprise turn, one that the Escalade got honked at for copying. Her face was filled with tension, and I knew she had to be working hard to remain as calm as she looked. This was the nightmare she'd lived with for so long: the Alchemists finding her again. "Don't feel so bad," she told Marcus. "After everything that's gone down in Palm Springs, they probably keep eyes and ears here regularly. For all we know, you weren't even spotted. Someone could've seen Eddie and decided to do some snooping. He's a person of interest to them too." She shook her head. "The real issue is how to lose them."

"Get back on the highway and take the first downtown exit," Marcus said.

Going back into a congested area makes no sense, hissed Aunt Tatiana. *They'll take Sydney again!*

"Shouldn't we get on the open highway and try to outrun them?" I asked.

"We'd never be able to do it," he said. "Besides, they'd probably get backup, and we'd find a few more of those coming after us."

Sydney exited as directed, pointing us toward the city center. Ahead of us, I could see some of the most crowded corridors of downtown, narrow streets packed with cars while pedestrians and outdoor tables filled the sidewalks.

"I'm guessing you're playing on the fact that the Alchemists don't like to make a scene," Sydney remarked. "But remember, they *did* chase us—quite openly—down the Strip in Las Vegas." She'd been in a wedding dress at the time, making us stand out that much more. "They'll do what they've got to do."

Marcus nodded. "I know. But they'll still avoid too much of a show if they can. Really, my main goal is getting to my escape car."

"Your escape car?" I stared, dumbfounded. "You have an escape car?"

He flashed me a smile. "I'm Marcus Finch. Of *course* I have an escape car. It's accessed by an underground tunnel that comes out of Miguel's Taqueria."

"Underground—" Sydney shook her head. "Never mind. That's six blocks from here, and we're about to get stuck because of lights and slow cars." The cars in front of us came to a stop as the traffic signal turned red.

"Correction," said Marcus, suddenly unbuckling his seat belt. "*They're* about to get stuck because of lights and a stopped car. Everyone get out." Immediately, I realized what was about to happen, and he confirmed it when he put his hand on the door's handle. "You guys know how to be evasive. Meet me at Miguel's—but don't let them follow you there."

He was out of the car in a flash, and a couple of seconds later, so were we, once Sydney had shifted the car into park. He tore off down one side of the street, losing himself in the crowds of tourists and lunchgoers without looking back. Some might have considered it abandonment, but Marcus knew us well enough by now to trust we knew what to do in situations like this. Be unpredictable. Hide among crowds and businesses. Meet back up when we'd lost them.

That was assuming, of course, that they even followed us. There'd been two cars between them and us on the road, so there was a chance they might not have seen us ditch our car. When the light turned green and traffic didn't move, they would figure out that something had gone wrong. The question was how far Sydney and I could get before then and whether they'd follow Marcus or us.

They followed us, of course.

"Faster," I said, clutching her hand as we tore off down the sidewalk.

A series of honks let me know when the light turned green, as angry drivers found themselves unable to get around our abandoned car. Shouts behind us were a tip-off that something else was awry, and when I glanced back, I saw a man and woman in beige suits barreling down the sidewalk toward us, oblivious to the pedestrians in their way. So much for not making a scene.

Ahead of us, the sidewalk looked even more packed than usual as people clustered around something. Great. Not the slowdown we needed. Another quick look behind me showed the Alchemist man—who was nearly as tall as me—gaining ground. I approached the crowd and saw they had stopped to admire displays of clothing that a shop had set out on the sidewalk as part of some sort of promotion. Dresses, gauzy scarves, and more created a brightly colored display that made even the most indifferent passerby stop and admire it. Sydney and I squeezed our way into a group of women admiring a purple silk dress and saw the Alchemists mere feet behind me.

Sydney glanced around, and a smile unexpectedly crossed her lips. She spoke a magical incantation that was lost in the noise of the street, but the power it invoked had an immediate effect. All of that beautiful clothing around us exploded into rainbow-colored wisps of fabric. It rained down around us, making it nearly impossible to see. Chaos ensued as people cried out in wonder, unsure if it was an attack or some sort of publicity stunt.

"Come on," she said, picking up the pace again.

As we ran away, I also heard an especially loud cry of dismay from someone I recognized—Lia DiStefano. This was her shop, which explained Sydney's sly smile. I felt a *little* bad . . . but also kind of not. Lia had made a gorgeous dress for Sydney once, a red gown inspired by ancient Greek styles. Sydney had been so beautiful in it, I'd thought I was dreaming. I had to give Lia credit for that. On the other hand, Lia had been so desperate to have Jill model for her that she'd covertly published an ad with Jill—the one that Alicia had included in the box Jackie had brought to Sydney. I didn't entirely know the relationship between Alicia, the Warriors, and how that ad had connected them to Jill, but there was no question that the ad had put Jill at risk.

"Sorry, Lia," I muttered as I raced past her shop. "Next time, don't recruit models you aren't supposed to use."

A block away was a florist's shop I'd been in once before. Without checking to see if we'd been followed, we quickly darted in through its door, which was propped open to enjoy the afternoon heat. Immediately, the overwhelming fragrance of roses and lilies surrounded us. Bouquets of every color filled the shop, but I looked past all of that for what I'd remembered seeing the last time I was here: a back door. The shop had two entrances, one that faced the main thoroughfare out front and this second one that led to parking in the alley behind the businesses. I nodded and smiled at the surprised florist, then hurried Sydney through to the back door as though what we were doing was perfectly normal.

In the alley, I paused and dared a peek through the door's window, waiting to see if an Alchemist came bursting into the shop. No one did, so I crossed my fingers that destroying Lia's display had caused enough confusion to cover the rest of our journey. Sydney and I ran down the back alley, past the doors of more businesses, some of which were public and some weren't. When we reached the back door for Miguel's Taqueria, it read DELIVERIES ONLY. I knocked anyway, wondering how we would explain my presence to whoever answered.

The guy who opened the door, however, didn't seem surprised at all to see us. He waved us inside. "You must be Marcus's friends."

We entered and found ourselves in the entryway to the kitchen, which smelled delicious. A cook flipping a quesadilla glanced up, nodded like our presence was totally normal, and returned to his work. Meanwhile, our guide led us to a nearby storage room lined with shelves of food. There was a bona fide trapdoor in the floor. He opened it up, and down below, holding a flashlight, was Marcus. He waved up at us.

"How do you know Marcus?" I asked as I started to climb the rungs down.

My guide shrugged. "He did me a favor once."

That seemed to be the story of Marcus's life. We thanked the guy and then made our way down. Just as Marcus had said, there really was a tunnel. We hurried through it with little conversation, emerging into a utility shed in a park a few blocks away. We saw no signs of pursuit in the tunnel or up above, and

Marcus felt secure enough to lead us to a parked blue Chevy. He produced some keys from his pocket and unlocked the door.

It wasn't until we were on the road that he finally spoke. "Well," he said. "I've got good news and bad news. The good news is that you don't have to keep making the Alchemists think you're at Court. The bad news is, the Alchemists know you aren't there anymore."

CHAPTER 14

ADRIAN . . . AGAIN

ONCE I KNEW WE WERE MOMENTARILY SAFE from the Alchemists, the first thing I had to do was secure Declan and my mom.

"Where are you?" I asked her when she answered the phone. I was sitting in the backseat while Marcus drove us to what he swore really was a safe house. Sydney was in the passenger seat, sending text updates to pretty much everyone we knew.

"I'm at Clarence's," replied my mother. "Where else would I be?"

I breathed a sigh of relief. "Good. You need to stay there for a while—do not leave. Do you have enough supplies for Declan?" I thought she'd gone overboard in her initial shopping. Now I was grateful.

"Well, yes, I suppose, though he doesn't seem terribly fond of those pacifiers I bought. I might need to find a different—"

"Do not leave," I repeated. "The house is almost certainly being watched. The Alchemists know we're here."

Immediately, my mother grasped the severity of the situation. "Are you all right?"

"We're fine—we got away. But they'll watch all our hangouts now to see if we go there. They'll know we aren't back at Clarence's, and that's fine. But they also probably don't know you and Declan are there, and we need to keep it that way. Stay inside."

She fell silent for several moments. "Adrian, there's something . . . unusual about Declan, isn't there?"

"Special," I corrected. "He's very, very special. And for now, it's best if the Alchemists don't know he exists. If they want to chase after Sydney and me, fine. But he needs to stay off their radar."

"I understand," she said. "If we need anything, I'll either have it shipped here or send Rose and Dimitri for it, assuming they can leave?"

I hesitated. "Yes. The Alchemists have no interest in them. They might be curious about why they're in town, but they won't break into Clarence's house or anything to find out, not without some other provocation. Other Moroi and dhampirs have stayed with him before. Can I talk to one of them?"

After some shuffling, Rose answered. "I can tell by your mom's face that something went wrong."

"The Alchemists know Sydney and I are here," I told her. "They managed to track Marcus when he came to town and stumbled into us in the process."

I couldn't be certain, but I think Rose swore in Russian. "So what's the plan?"

"We're on our way to an allegedly safe place," I told her. "From there, Sydney's going to investigate the Warriors, and I'll eventually interrogate Alicia."

"I want to be in on that," Rose said promptly.

"I know, but I really, really need you guys to stay with my mom and Declan. I was just telling her that she can't leave the house. I don't think the Alchemists know she's in town, and I'm hoping it stays that way. But if something weird happens, I need you guys to protect them."

"What do you mean, 'something weird'? Why would anyone care about them?" Rose, like my mom, was beginning to suspect something odd was happening.

"I can't tell you," I said. "Just trust me—it's important. At least one of you needs to stay with them at all times. If there's a way you can safely meet me when I talk to Alicia, we'll make it happen. But in the meantime, promise me you'll take care of them."

A long silence followed, and I could guess why. Rose, like everyone else, wanted to find Jill. With so many potential leads, it was understandable that she'd much rather be involved with that mission than literal babysitting. But Rose had seen enough at the commune—and was enough of my friend—to finally accede. "Okay. We'll keep an eye on them. But if there's anything we can do to find Jill—anything at all—"

"I'll let you know," I promised. I disconnected and looked around. "Is this it?"

We'd left the urban sprawl of Palm Springs, going off into the desert to a place that made Wolfe's compound look downright civilized. A small, lone cabin sat alone on a scrubby landscape, and the car's tires kicked up clouds of dust as we turned toward it on a sandy dirt road.

"Yup," said Marcus.

"Well, it's certainly remote," noted Sydney. "But is it safe?"

"Safe as we'll get for now," Marcus assured us, pulling the car up to a stop outside the house. "No one followed us here. No one knows of my connection to these people."

We got out of the car and followed Marcus to the door. He had to knock three times—getting progressively louder—before the door finally opened. A fifty-something guy with scraggly hair and round-lensed glasses peered up at us, squinting at the sunlight like a Moroi might have. His face brightened with recognition. "Marcus, man, been a while!"

"Good to see you too, Howie," Marcus replied. "My friends and I need a place to stay. Is it okay if we crash here?"

"Totally, totally." Howie stepped aside so we could enter. "Come on in, man."

"Howie and his wife, Patty, grow and sell all sorts of herbs," explained Marcus.

I inhaled deeply as I walked around the living room, which could have come straight out of 1971. "Especially one herb in particular," I added.

"Don't worry," said Marcus, his lips quirking into a smile. "They're good people."

Sydney wrinkled her nose. "Not going to do us any good to evade the Alchemists if we then get arrested in a drug raid."

Marcus was unconcerned. "That's the least of our worries. They'll give us a place to stay. And their kitchen's always well stocked."

That was true, at least. So long as we could survive on junk food, we'd be in no danger of going hungry anytime soon. I'd never seen so many boxes of Twinkies in my life. Patty was as dazedly friendly as her husband, assuring us we could make ourselves at home and stay as long we liked. The two of them probably spent most of their time in the basement or in the garden outside, growing the various plants they then consumed or sold. Once we were settled, they disappeared downstairs, leaving us to make plans. I learned then that while I'd talked to Rose and my mom, Marcus and Sydney had been gathering other info.

"Sabrina got back to Marcus. She's going to take Eddie and me to the Warriors late tonight," Sydney said. "Very late. We apparently have to arrive at dawn. Ms. Terwilliger's going to come out beforehand with Eddie to help with some spells and prepare us."

"I hope it goes without saying that Eddie will be careful in coming here," said Marcus. "By now, the Alchemists probably have eyes on everyone you know in the area."

"He'll be careful," she said confidently. "He knows how to avoid being followed." She turned back to me. "Ms. Terwilliger will then take you with her, for when the witches unfreeze Alicia. Promise me you'll be careful, Adrian. Go easy on her. Only use as little compulsion as necessary. Remember, the odds are good she may not even know where the Alchemists are holding Jill."

Go easy on her? Even though I knew Sydney had meant that as a way of looking out for me, it was impossible to imagine. How could I go easy on the woman who'd kidnapped Jill? Who was the reason Jill might very well be suffering at the hands of those madmen? Sonya had been in bad shape when she'd been rescued from the Warriors, and they'd had Jill much, much longer.

Alicia will pay, Aunt Tatiana promised in my head.

To Sydney, I said, "I'll see what I can do."

My phone rang, and I felt a dry sort of amusement at the display. "Not many people can claim to talk to the Moroi queen twice in one day. Hello?"

"Adrian?" came Lissa's voice. "What have you done?"

"Why do you assume I've done anything?" I asked.

Lissa sighed. "Because an angry Alchemist bureaucrat just called, pretty worked up about how you and Sydney are at large in Palm Springs! They made it very clear they aren't going to pull any punches in trying to get her back. I thought you guys were lying low."

"We were, we were," I said. "It was kind of an accident. But we're safe for the time being."

"Well, try to stay that way. On the bright side, I was able to get through to someone to ask about the Alchemists possibly putting pressure on the Warriors."

Hope filled me. It would save Sydney from infiltrating the Warriors and me from interrogating Alicia if the Alchemists could just rescue Jill for us. "And?" I asked.

"It's what I feared—they want more proof. I mean, the person I talked to made some vague comments about making 'inquiries,' but I didn't really feel like he was taking me seriously. I think he thinks I was using it to deflect from you and Sydney being outside of Court."

My hopes fell as I looked at Sydney across the room. She was trying to sit in an overstuffed beanbag chair. The thought of her going off to sneak around the Warriors' compound made me ill. It had been one thing when she'd left with Eddie and Ms. Terwilliger, but now she was walking right into the hands of some of our enemies. What if she was found out? What if the Warriors tried to renew their friendship with the Alchemists by using her as a bargaining chip? What if the Warriors decided to make an example of the woman who'd married a vampire?

No good can come of any of this, Aunt Tatiana reiterated.

"I'll keep working on them, though," Lissa continued, oblivious to my churning thoughts. "And I assume you guys are doing your own things to get answers?"

"So it seems," I said.

"Well, let me know if I can offer any help. I talked to Rose earlier, and it sounds like you've already got her working on something. Feel free to use her and Dimitri and Neil however you can if it'll help get Jill back."

Lissa's tone sounded perfectly innocent, and I realized Rose must have kept the news of Declan secret even from her best friend. It made me grateful but also drove home the precariousness of Declan's situation. Lissa's mention of Neil also reminded me that we still hadn't yet had a chance to sit him down and explain what's going on. Too many complications just kept coming up.

The rest of the day was spent waiting for Jackie and Eddie to come by. Marcus, who'd spent so much of his life on the run, seemed perfectly at ease cooped up in the cabin's small living room. Sydney and I, who'd grown used to our freedom, short as it was, had a harder time. We made all the plans we could with our friends remotely, and then mostly tried to pass the time. Despite the private location, we were hesitant to go outside. The house's one TV was in the basement, and the secondhand smoke coming out of there was strong enough to keep us away. That left a stack of old *Reader's Digest*s as our remaining entertainment.

"There's a car pulling up," said Marcus later that evening. He'd been standing near the window, occasionally looking out the drawn curtains. A frown crossed his face. "I don't see Jackie or Eddie."

Sydney leapt up and joined him at the window. After a few moments, her tension faded. "It's okay. I know them."

Marcus opened the door, and two women I recognized entered. One was Maude, the senior member of Sydney's coven, who'd helped at the lake. The other was feisty old Inez, giving me a wink as she stepped across the threshold. Maude lingered at the door, keeping it open as though she expected someone else to come through. No one did, and after several seconds, she nodded for Marcus to close it. I knew enough from Sydney to realize someone invisible had entered, and as that realization hit me, the spell surrounding that person broke.

"Eddie," Sydney exclaimed, running to give him a hug.

He grinned back. "You guys okay?"

"Fine," I said. "Just stocking up on carbs and waiting for the next phase of craziness to start."

"You're sure no one followed you?" asked Marcus, tugging the curtains around the front windows closer together.

"Positive," said Eddie. "We met up in a public place, and the Alchemists sent to watch me never even knew I left with these two."

Inez was sizing up our surroundings with a critical eye and didn't look impressed. "Jaclyn sent us since she couldn't get away from your friends. They've staked out her house."

"The Alchemists aren't my friends," Sydney retorted.

"Well, whatever they are, they're a pain in the ass," Inez said. "But we told her we'd help you, so here we are."

"Thank you, ma'am," Sydney said, adorably polite as ever. "I know what an inconvenience it must be."

Maude smiled kindly at her. "It's not as inconvenient as

some people would have you think." She set down two large tote bags, stuffed to overflowing with mysterious ingredients. "Now then. I understand we need to make you stronger."

"Do you?" Sydney asked in surprise.

Inez pushed up the sleeves of her rose-printed dress and peered into one of the bags. "That's what Jaclyn says. Says you're going to be getting in fights or some such nonsense."

"Well, yeah, but I just figured I'd use the evasive techniques Wolfe taught me."

"Wolfe?" Inez snorted in disgust. "That hippie that Jaclyn's dating? Believe me, smarts and 'evasive techniques' are fine if that's all you've got to rely on, but if you get a chance to be the baddest and strongest, *always* be the baddest and strongest."

There were a number of things wrong with what she'd said, starting with her referring to Wolfe—who owned more weapons than anyone I'd ever met—as a hippie.

Inez carefully took out an innocuous-looking canteen from the bag. "What's that?" I asked.

"A very special and complex potion," said Maude. "One that several of us worked on for most of today."

As she spoke, I took note of the dark circles under her eyes and fatigue in her voice. Sydney saw it too. "You didn't have to do that . . ." she said.

"We did," said Maude simply. "Cleaning up after Alicia is our responsibility—and if that involves preparing you for these bizarre acts of brutality, we'll help you do it."

"What's in it?" I asked. The scope and randomness of human magic was still kind of amazing to me. Plus, focusing on it distracted me from thinking about Sydney and "bizarre acts of brutality."

"You're happier not knowing," Maude told me. "Now then. We need to finish off the spell by—"

We heard the sound of a door opening. A moment later, the beaded curtain separating the living room from the kitchen rustled, and Howie stepped through. He looked surprised to see additional people here and blinked a few times, as though ascertaining that we were all real and not some hallucination. I imagined in his life, that was a distinction that had to constantly be made. And, considering my increasing interactions with Aunt Tatiana, it was something I could relate to.

"Hey, man, Marcus," he said, pushing up his glasses. "Didn't know you had more people over, man. We're looking for the Doritos. Have you seen the Doritos?"

Marcus pointed to an end table by the couch. Howie brightened as he lifted the Doritos bag, then turned dismayed when he saw it was nearly empty. "You were up here eating them around lunchtime," Marcus reminded him.

Howie looked pleasantly skeptical. "I was?"

"Yeah," I confirmed. "You said you were watching some mutant-shark movie that was on commercial."

"Trey was watching that earlier today too," remarked Eddie in a too-casual way that made me think Trey hadn't been the only one watching it.

"Was it a double feature with *Raptorbot Rampage?*" Sydney asked dryly.

Howie held up a warning finger. "That stuff's not made up, you know. Real life is stranger than fiction, man. The government's hiding it from us."

"Totally," said Marcus, steering Howie back toward the beaded curtain. "Why don't you take some cookies back down

235

in the basement instead? I think I saw some Nutter Butters in the kitchen."

Marcus got our host situated and then sent him on his way. None of the rest of us spoke until we heard the basement door close again. Eddie remarked, "Real life *is* stranger than fiction."

"Tell me about it," Sydney said, turning back to the canteen. "What do I have to do?"

"Drink it," said Inez. "We mixed in some Tang to help it taste better. Emphasis on 'help.'"

"But first we finish the spell," said Maude. She and Inez linked hands, forming a circle around where the canteen sat on a table. I'd heard Sydney recite spells enough to recognize the sound of Latin. I'd also learned enough to know that most of the spells she used were simple ones with immediate results. The kind these witches were dealing with now—spells with multiple parts that required multiple magic users—were heady, and Sydney's awed expression reflected as much. When they finished the chant, Maude handed the canteen over to Sydney with a flourish. "Bottoms up," said Maude.

Sydney unscrewed the lid and grimaced at what she saw inside. I was standing near her and shared her disgust. The concoction smelled like wet rope . . . and Tang.

"The faster you drink it, the better," added Inez. "Plugging your nose wouldn't hurt either."

Sydney did both, but none of it stopped her from gagging. "It better not come back up," warned Inez. "Because we don't have any more of it."

Sydney winced and shook her head as she handed the canteen back. "It's staying down. What now? Am I really stronger? Mostly I just feel like I want to brush my teeth." She certainly hadn't sprouted giant muscles nor begun compulsively pumping iron.

"And how much stronger?" asked Eddie eagerly. "Like lift-up-a-car stronger?"

Maude smiled. "Sorry to disappoint, but no. For one thing, that would attract too much attention, and you probably don't want that. For another, our power has limitations. We can't go around creating gods. I'd say . . ." She glanced between Eddie and Sydney speculatively, her smile growing. "I'd say you're strong enough to hold your own with a dhampir in an arm wrestling match."

"I would kind of love to see that," I admitted. Eddie's face said he would as well.

Sydney groaned. "Really? That's so barbaric."

Eddie leaned over and propped his arm up on the table that had previously held the canteen. "Come on, Mrs. Ivashkov. Let's do this. Besides, if you're squeamish about arm wrestling, how are you going to handle going head-to-head with the Warriors?"

He had a point, at least based on the stories Sabrina had told us. Sydney stood opposite him at the table and mirrored his arm position. Their arms clasped, and Marcus counted them down, looking nearly as excited as Eddie. To my astonishment, when they started, Eddie didn't immediately slam her hand down as I'd expected. His eyes widened, as did his grin. He increased his effort and began making progress. Gritting her teeth, Sydney pushed back, and amazingly, she soon took the upper hand, so to speak.

"It's so strange," she said. "I can feel the strength within me . . . as though it's both part of me and yet not part of me. Like it was something I put on. Like clothing." Ultimately,

Eddie pushed his strength to its limit and finally defeated her, but not without her holding her own for a while. I held up her arm triumphantly, like a victor at a boxing match.

"My wife, ladies and gentlemen. Beauty, brains, and now brawn."

"Awesome," said Eddie, in a rare moment of delight. "How long will that last?"

"Four days," said Maude, looking apologetic. "Like I said, we can't create gods."

"Four days," Sydney repeated. "Sabrina's taking us later tonight. So we've got three and a half days to find out what the Warriors are hiding about Jill."

"Or just kick everyone's ass the first day so they leave you alone after that," suggested Marcus helpfully.

Noting the second tote bag the witches had brought, I asked, "What else is there besides super strength?"

Maude began unpacking the bag's contents. "Jackie says we need to do some appearance changes too."

"I've done those kinds of spells before," Sydney told them. "You don't need to do anything more."

"Hush, girl," snapped Inez. "You need to conserve your strength for whatever madness you're getting involved in. Besides, maintaining a sustained spell of change is no easy task. You ever done it for a week?" She glanced at Eddie. "For two people?"

"No, ma'am," Sydney admitted.

Maude tossed Sydney two boxes of hair dye in "Burnished Chestnut." "One for each of you," she said. "You can do it after we leave. The less we have to change with magic, the better."

Eddie took one of the boxes and raised an eyebrow. He made

no complaint, however. Some guys would've thrown a fit about having to dye their hair, but not Eddie. I supposed when you vanquished evil undead creatures as part of your normal life, a little salon treatment in no way threatened your masculinity.

The rest of the bag contained what I recognized as standard spell components: herbs, crystals, powders. Maude and Inez began building a spell circle on the table, and I realized I was watching another complicated act of magic that had required multiple people and parts. Sydney realized it too.

"So much," she murmured to me. "They're helping so much."

"Take it," I replied, squeezing her hand. "You're worth it. Jill's worth it."

When their materials were ready, Inez set two silver rings in the middle of it all. She glanced at Maude. "Are you ready?"

Maude nodded and walked over to Sydney, wielding a wand. Reluctantly I stepped away from her, remarking, "How come you never wave a wand?"

Sydney smiled back. "Despite the clichés, witches rarely use wands. They're necessary for detailed work or if part of the wand contains an element that can focus or amplify the magic." She eyed the crystals on the wand Maude held up to her face. "I'm guessing focus here."

"Correct," said Maude. "Now hold still and close your eyes." She recited a Greek verse, and a faint glow lit the wand. A moment later, she touched the tip of Sydney's nose with it. Slowly, carefully, Maude moved the wand around, going on to Sydney's eyelids, then her cheekbones and chin. Each place the wand touched, it was like Maude was airbrushing a picture, changing each of Sydney's features. Her cheekbones rounded a little, her face grew narrower. They were small, subtle changes, but taken all together, the results wholly altered her. Even with her normal hair color, I doubted anyone would've recognized her. Soon even Sydney's tattoo disappeared. The biggest shock of all was when Maude stepped back and told Sydney to open her eyes. What had once been brown were now as vivid a blue as Marcus's.

I couldn't help a gasp, and Sydney turned to me with a sheepish smile. "Still recognize me?"

"I'd know you anywhere," I said gallantly.

"I wouldn't," said Eddie.

Immediately, Maude directed her attention to him. "Your turn. Close your eyes."

He did, and she repeated the spell. I watched in wonder as his face changed appearance every place the wand passed. When she was finished, he no longer looked like the Eddie I knew, but he certainly looked like he could be related to the new Sydney.

"Can I see?" asked Eddie excitedly.

"Wait," said Inez, taking the wand from Maude. "We have to act quickly to save the spell." She waved the wand over the rings and chanted in Greek again. Sparks jumped between the wand and the rings. When she finished, she gave one ring to Eddie and one to Sydney. They slipped them on, and Sydney's breath caught.

"Strange . . ." she murmured. "I feel like something just locked into place."

"Those rings bind the spells to you now," said Maude. "Take them off, and your original appearances will return. Otherwise, they should last for about a week."

"That's your real deadline," added Inez. "You can probably

hide when your strength's gone. But when your face comes back, the jig is up. Then you really will have to rely on your smarts to explain that away."

Her voice was as sarcastic and crotchety as always, but underneath, I could tell she was worn out. A quick aura check proved as much. The magic they'd just performed here had been substantial, and it was only part of what had been started earlier today with the help of other witches. Sydney turned to Maude and Inez.

"I can't thank you enough for what you've done. Really. This means so much to me and—"

"No need to gush," interrupted Inez. "We know you're grateful. And you should be. But now you need to prove it and go clean up Alicia's mess. Save your friend."

Sydney straightened up. "I will, ma'am."

The witches gave a few more last-minute instructions, both for Sydney and for me since I'd be joining them later to release Alicia, and then went on their way. Eddie and Sydney made a beeline for a mirror and exclaimed in amazement at their change in appearance. They had previously been mistaken for siblings, and now they just looked like a different set of siblings. They had the same blue eyes, and Maude had done a neat job of making them look pleasantly average. Hopefully it would ensure no one gave them a second glance.

I'd just finished helping them dye their hair "Burnished Chestnut"—a shade that was dark brown with a faint red cast—when Sabrina showed up. Her normally cocky persona faltered a bit as she took them in. She'd grown used to a number of weird realities, but human magic wasn't something she'd had a lot of experience with.

"Incredible," she murmured, looking back and forth between their faces. "I'd never think it was you. You could walk right past the Alchemists now."

Marcus, watching with amusement, crossed his arms and leaned back into Howie's overstuffed sofa. "Maybe your friends can hook me up with that spell once in a while. Going incognito would be pretty handy."

"I'll let them know," Sydney said. To Sabrina, she held up the hand wearing the silver ring. "Are there any rules about jewelry? Will they let us wear these in?"

"They should," she said. "They'll search for weapons or anything else they think is suspicious. Cell phones too—they don't want any way for people to track you. You'll go blindfolded when I take you in."

"Sounds a lot like when I went to their arena," Sydney remarked. She took off her engagement and wedding rings and walked over to me. "I don't want anything to happen to these while I'm there."

I clasped both of her hands in mine. "It's not the rings I'm worried about."

A faint smile crossed her lips, and even though the face was different, there was a feel to that smile that was uniquely Sydney. "I'll be fine . . . but I want you to hold on to these for me until I get back."

"Deal," I said in a low voice that only she could hear, "but I get to put them back on you."

"Okay," she said.

"On my knees," I added.

"Okay."

"And we both have to be nake—"

"Adrian," she said warningly.

"We'll discuss the terms later," I said with a wink. But I felt a pang in my heart as I squeezed the rings and let go of her hands, hating the danger she was about to walk into. Her appearance might be different, but her aura shone to me like no one else's— so brave, despite the dangers ahead. I wanted so badly to go with her but knew there was nothing I could do there. My biggest help would be with Alicia when the witches unfroze her.

"We should grab something to eat and then hit the road," Sabrina said.

"Hope you like Orcos and cheese puffs," Eddie told her.

We ate a bizarre meal of junk food while Sabrina elaborated on a few more things for us. "We're going to Calexico, down by the border," she said. "But you're not supposed to know that. We have to keep up appearances. Once we go in, we'll probably be separated, but I'll be around. They'll also let me keep my phone, so I can send messages to Marcus."

"And you'll then update me, right?" I said.

Marcus gave me a tight smile. "Right. Don't worry. Sabrina will look after them."

It was a hollow reassurance, since we all knew things could go very, very badly at the Warriors' place and that Sabrina would probably be able to do very little. In her usual way, Sydney was more concerned about me as they were leaving. "Be careful, Adrian. I want to find Jill too but not at the cost of losing you."

"It'll be remedial compulsion," I assured her. "You're the one walking into a hornet's nest."

"This is what we do," she said simply. "You have your job. I have mine." She stood on her tiptoes to give me a light kiss on the cheek. No way was I settling for that. With a quick maneuver, I swept her into my arms and gave her a long, deep kiss goodbye, not caring about the witnesses. When she finally pulled back, that new face was blushing in a very Sydney way, but she stayed in my arms.

"I can't say I didn't expect that," she admitted.

"This is it," I told her. "We're on the verge of getting Jill back. Once we get that, we'll secure our freedom and finally get that happily ever after."

How exactly are you going to manage that? demanded Aunt Tatiana. *Living back at Court? With those Keepers in Michigan?*

I had a feeling Sydney was full of the same questions, but she didn't speak any of them aloud. Instead, her face showed only love and hope as she gave me another parting kiss. The next thing I knew, Sabrina was ushering them out to her car to begin this bizarre adventure. I stood with Marcus in the doorway, gazing off into the night, even after they were gone.

"I hope this is a good plan," I said to him, my heart aching.

Marcus sighed, and for once, his usual optimistic expression looked weary. It must be hard constantly convincing people that every risky thing he came up with would pay off.

"Good doesn't enter into it," he admitted. "It's the only plan we've got."

CHAPTER 15
SYDNEY

CALEXICO WAS A LITTLE LESS THAN TWO HOURS AWAY, which made for a long and strange journey. When we were halfway there, Sabrina stopped to blindfold us, per Warrior protocol. For the rest of the trip, she repeated information we'd already memorized, information that we could never get enough of as we braced ourselves for this strange endeavor. I managed to hold on to that Zen state, focusing solely on Jill and my purpose here, remaining empty of all emotion. I especially tried hard not to worry too much about Adrian. I knew if I did, I'd falter. Instead, I took in Sabrina's advice and insight, meshing it with what I knew I had to do. I felt oddly cool and detached.

Then we reached the Warriors' compound.

Sabrina warned us it was coming as the car slowed for the compound's gate. I heard the window roll down. "Sabrina Woods," she said, "bringing two potential recruits."

"Two, huh?" a gravelly voice responded back, sounding more amused than concerned.

Sabrina herself remained perfectly calm. "I didn't bring any last year. Making up for it, I guess."

"Take 'em to the holding area," came the response.

The window rolled up, and Sabrina slowly accelerated. A heavy exhalation of relief was the only sign that she was more nervous about this endeavor than she'd let on. I heard the tires crunching on gravel, and a minute later, the car came to a stop. She turned it off and opened her door. "Everyone out," she said.

She guided us from the car toward the sound of people speaking. Here, at last, our blindfolds were removed. The desert landscape was scrubby and barren and contained a collection of ramshackle buildings. It kind of reminded me of Wolfe's setup, except much more rundown. Two hulking guys with guns strapped to them were chatting amiably with each other in front of the door to a large building, though their faces hardened when they saw us approach. Sabrina repeated what she'd said at the gate, adding this time, "They're brother and sister."

One of the guys seemed to like this. "This is a family organization, after all."

That wasn't exactly what came to mind when I thought of the Warriors, but I gave him a smile I hoped came across as tough and cool. The guards patted us down, searching us for weapons or tracking equipment. Their examination was brisk and thankfully not lewd in any way. Eddie and I had made sure to leave our phones with Howie, and after finding nothing suspect, one of the guards waved us on through the door behind them. Sabrina started to follow, but a guard shook his head.

"They go on alone," he said. "You go through the spectators' door on the other side."

Sabrina had warned us we'd eventually get separated, so I tried not to let my panic show as she gave us a casual farewell and wished us luck. Eddie and I stepped through the doorway, which led us into an open, dusty arena not unlike where I'd been when the Warriors were holding Sonya. It looked as though it was originally intended for baseball or soccer, but something told me that wouldn't be happening today.

A few dozen other people lingered in the arena. Some were in groups, some were pointedly solo and eyeing everyone else as potential enemies. Some looked like ordinary people you'd run into at the mall. Others practically had "Yes, I want to join a fanatical vampire-hating group" stamped across their foreheads. All of them were around our age, give or take a few years. The gender split was almost even, slightly favoring guys. Out in the stands, other people were beginning to filter in and take seats. I caught sight of Sabrina and gave her a quick nod before turning my attention back to Eddie.

"She said things start at sunrise," I told him. To the east, the sky was a burning orange, and the rest of it carried a light purple hue. "Technically, we're already there."

"Your guess is as good as mine as to how this'll unfold," he said, his sharp dhampir eyes scanning rapidly around as he spoke. Even in casual situations, his natural tendency was to watch for threats. In a high-stakes situation like this, he was constantly on edge.

"I just hope we're able to—"

My words were cut off by the sound of a trumpet. We all turned in its direction and saw three men wearing yellow robes and golden helmets. I stiffened, earning a quick look of concern from Eddie.

"What's wrong?" he whispered. "I mean, aside from the obvious."

"I know two of them. Master Angeletti and Master Ortega. They were at the last gathering."

"Remember, they can't recognize you."

I nodded, but seeing those familiar faces set me on edge. I expected at any moment one of them would point in my direction and declare me an enemy, sending all of these wannabe recruits my way.

But the two masters paid me no more attention than they did any of the other recruits. When the third man—the trumpeter—stopped playing, Master Angeletti spoke, his voice still deep and his gray beard still scraggly. "Do you see that?" he asked, raising his hands toward the rising sun. "That is why we are here, what gives us all life. The sun. The light. We were born to the light, born to goodness. It reminds me of one of my favorite psalms:

> Humans are born into the light
>
> Shining good, shining bright
>
> Only evil thrives at night
>
> Let us banish them from our sight."

I nearly choked with laughter, hearing poetry I probably could've written when I was ten years old. But Master Angeletti's face was full of rapture as he spoke, and the other Warriors nodded along approvingly, like he was quoting one of Shakespeare's sonnets.

"That is the natural way of things," Master Angeletti told us. "Those who thrive in darkness are not part of the divine plan. They are evil and unnatural, and it is the job of our army to eliminate them and save mankind."

Beside him, Master Ortega took a turn. "All of you are here because you have shown interest in eradicating that darkness and because your sponsors think you may be worthy to join us. But make no mistake: *We* will be the ones to decide who truly deserves to serve among us. It will not be easy. You will be tested and scrutinized, your very soul examined. If any of you are afraid or know you won't have the stamina to face what's to come, I invite you to leave now."

Silence fell as he looked around expectantly. A few of the other recruits shifted their stances, but no one made any motions to leave.

"Very well then," boomed Master Ortega. "Let the trials begin!"

If I'd ever wondered about the fundamental difference between the Alchemists and the Warriors, I soon had my answer. Whatever their flaws, the Alchemists were almost always adherents of the think-first-act-later mindset. The Warriors? Not so much.

Once the opening formalities were out of the way, Master Ortega handed things over to the recruiting director—who, to my complete astonishment, turned out to be Chris Juarez: Trey's cousin. I hadn't seen him since the Warriors had held Sonya, and Trey didn't really talk much about his family after they'd disowned him. Trey had humiliated them by dating a dhampir. Chris had apparently walked the straight and narrow, earning this esteemed position. He strutted out in front of us now, dressed simply in jeans and a muscle shirt that showed off his well-built physique.

"You wouldn't be here if you weren't interested in ridding the world of evil," he told us. "And we'll eventually determine just *how* interested you are. But before we get to that, we need to see if you can hold your own if it comes down to facing that evil. Are you afraid of pain? Are you afraid of getting dirty? Are you afraid of doing whatever it takes to keep humanity in the light?" His volume grew louder with each shouted question, stirring spectators and recruits alike into a frenzy. Some of the people standing near Eddie and me shouted back answers. One guy simply let out a primal battle scream that earned cheers from those in the stand. Me, I mostly tried to show excitement and interest, as opposed to the actual shock and disgust I felt.

While Chris had been speaking, other Warriors had been setting up the arena with an odd assortment of items: wooden boxes, tin cans, buckets, cinder blocks. I wondered if there was some sort of obstacle course in the works. When they finished that task, they came out to all the recruits and gave us each a wooden heart attached to a cord. My assumed name—Fiona Gray—was written on it. Eddie, going by Fred Gray, also received one.

"This represents your heart—your life," said Chris. "Right now we need to know who wants this the most—who's willing to do whatever it takes to be the victor. Ladies, please step aside and take seats over there." He pointed to a section of the stands. "You guys, go find spots wherever you want."

I met Eddie's eyes briefly as we turned to each other before parting. "Good luck," I said.

"No luck needed with this lot," he replied.

I smiled at that and sat down beside a surly looking girl who was about a head taller than me and nearly as muscled as Chris. There were about thirty male recruits, and they scattered throughout the arena, taking positions they thought would be most strategic. Some stood on the crates, some staked out items that looked like they could be made into weapons—like the cinder blocks. Eddie based his position on those of the other combatants, selecting a place that gave him space and a good vantage.

"For the next hour," Chris announced, "your goal is to collect as many of your opponents' hearts as possible, by any means necessary. Everything in this arena is fair game. Any tactic is fair game—though we do ask that you try not to kill anyone. The six competitors with the most hearts at the end of the hour will advance. If at any time you feel incapable of going on, simply retreat over to that bench"—he pointed at another section of the stands, where a man in a red hat stood—"and place both palms down. That will release you from the challenge, and Bart will give you any first aid needed."

Bart, in a plaid shirt and ripped-up jeans, didn't strike me as someone who'd had any official medical training, but maybe appearances were deceiving.

My stomach was in knots as Chris asked if there were any questions and checked to make sure everyone was ready. Sabrina had warned us there'd be some sort of physical competition, but she hadn't known the specifics. They changed year to year so that no sponsor could warn their recruits in advance. Apparently, the Warriors wanted things to stay fair, which seemed ironic considering the drugged and worn-down state they'd had Sonya in before bringing her to an attempted execution.

Chris held up his hand to mark the start, and a tense silence filled the air. Eddie leaned forward, squarely in his zone, eyes sharp and body ready. "Begin!" yelled Chris, bringing his hand down.

What followed next was chaos.

The guys fell on each other like a pack of dogs fighting for a scrap of meat. Some went for full-on bodily contact, attempting to throw each other to the ground and steal hearts. Other competitors took a more savage approach, hurling cinder blocks and wielding other debris as weapons. Most of my attention stayed on Eddie, who took a calmer approach and waited for people to come after him. His strength wasn't initially obvious, and many thought he'd be easy prey. Their mistaken beliefs were soon corrected as he dispatched one attacker after another, knocking them out with precision punches and kicks—then collecting their hearts afterward. Losing your heart didn't mean you were out of the competition. If you could recover your heart—or simply have a majority at the end of the hour—it was all good. Some of those Eddie took hearts from attempted recovery. Others moved on to seemingly easier foes.

My real heart—the one in my chest—thudded as I watched Eddie. I needed him to stay in the competition. I needed us both to. So far, there didn't seem to be any cause to worry. He was clearly faster and stronger than most people out there, plus he had the seasoning and experience to make use of his gifts. Others, though strong, had no real skills and simply relied on brute force—which proved effective in some cases. I saw one guy slam a wooden plank into another's knee, causing the victim to crumple in pain and scream as he fell. His attacker snatched away the victory heart, ignoring his opponent's pleas for help in getting to Bart and first aid. Eddie happened to be passing by at the time and paused to help the fallen guy get to the bench.

Another guy—the one who'd let out the earlier primal

scream—was also making pretty short work of his competition. His muscles bulged grotesquely, making me wonder if he took steroids or simply lived in a gym. He apparently had some fans in the audience, because they shouted his name each time he captured a heart. "Caleb! Caleb! Go, Caleb!"

Caleb flashed a malicious grin at his fans as he stormed through the arena, looking for new prey. Although his own strength was powerful unaided, he still sometimes utilized a cinder block as an asset. I wasn't alone in gasping when he slammed it into some guy's head, instantly knocking the guy to the ground. Caleb swept up the three hearts his victim wore and went on his way. Bart himself came out to drag the fallen back to the safety of the stands, and I didn't really start breathing again until I saw the poor guy limply move an arm.

Two other guys had arrived together, like Eddie and me, and were teaming up to take out foes and split the hearts between them. It was a smart strategy, and I wished Eddie and I could've utilized it. The Warriors had some outdated hang-ups about men and women, and although there were female competitors, Sabrina had explained that girls in the Warriors were often kept out of the line of danger and relegated to milder roles. I wasn't sure if I should applaud the Warriors for showing some sign of consideration or be offended that they didn't think women could keep up with men in bloodthirsty brutality.

As the hour wound down, about half of the competitors were gone from the fray, off getting whatever medical attention Bart could administer. A few guys were clearly dominant: notably Eddie, Caleb, and the twosome. Those remaining were trying to pick off each other or go after one of the leaders. Chris shouted a five-minute warning, and one guy, desperately realizing he was nearly out of the running, made a frantic charge at Caleb in the hopes of securing a massive stash of hearts. Caleb knocked him away like he was a fly, then kicked him when he was down on the ground, despite the guy's pleas to stop. "Just take them! Just take them!" The guy on the ground frantically tried to pull the hearts off his head and hand them over while Caleb just kept kicking. The nausea in my stomach reared up again until Caleb finally left the guy in peace. He stalked off, his gaze falling on Eddie, but thankfully, Chris called time just then. Everyone leaned forward, eager to find out the results.

Unsurprisingly, Caleb and Eddie had the most, followed by three other guys I hadn't paid much attention to. The two who'd worked together were tied for the sixth-place spot. I wondered if the Warriors would accept seven victors, but after deliberating with the masters, Chris selected only one as the winner. He congratulated the other, encouraging him to try again next year. I hadn't noticed the guy who'd won—Wayne—doing anything particularly different from his friend in fighting. Wayne was, however, much bigger and better built. Something told me the Warriors put a lot of emphasis on physical appearances, probably assuming that he who looked the strongest would be the strongest.

That didn't bode well for me, because when the girls were called up—thirteen of us—it was clear I was the smallest and least buff-looking of them all. Things worsened when Chris announced that only two girls would advance and that they would be determined based on whoever had the most hearts at the end of the hour. Eddie and I exchanged brief glances across the arena at that. Two girls? That wasn't much of a safety net, especially when it was imperative that I, more than Eddie, stick around to search out information about Jill's whereabouts. He gave me a tight smile and nodded encouragingly, seeming to say, "Well, then, just make sure you've got the most hearts."

Right. No problem.

Seeing the guys compete first had given us some sense of what the best strategy might be. We positioned ourselves in the arena, a number of the girls immediately moving toward potential weapons. I saw a few of them eye me, as the smallest, and I readied myself for defense. In some ways, I welcomed it, as that was what I'd focused on the most with Wolfe. But defense wouldn't win me any hearts. I wasn't violent by nature. Offense was second nature to Eddie, and he'd had an easier time slipping into that role.

Chris started the match, and chaos once again ensued. Two girls immediately headed for me. Blood pounded in my ears, and a cool sense of purpose slowly slid into place as I drew on all of Wolfe's lessons. I stayed out of their reach, ducking their brutish and often clumsy advances. It seemed to frustrate them when I didn't prove to be an easy victim, and eventually they got in each other's way. With a snarl, they turned on each other, both falling into the dirt in a tangle of hitting and hair pulling. One emerged victorious, carrying the other's heart, and charged toward me. Finally, I allowed myself to give in to the fight and astonished her with a punch that sent her stumbling backward as my magic-infused strength coursed through me. I had that same strange sense as before that the strength was both part of me and yet not part of me, but soon I fell into its rhythm. After a few more failed attacks, the girl yielded and gave me her hearts.

I looked around, uncertain of my next move. I knew I

needed to just go up and attack someone, but it was still a weird and unfamiliar sensation. *You're playing a role, Sydney*, I told myself. *Get into it. Don't feel bad—remember what these people are. What they might have done to Jill.*

I was spared from choosing my next victim when another girl decided my earlier victory was a lucky break. A similar process followed, with me engaging in a long game of self-defense. *The best fight is the one you avoid*, Wolfe had always said. I led my foe on a merry chase, and when she finally grew impatient and lunged for me, I was able to trip her up and effectively pin her to the ground. Her ankle twisted as she went down, and I was able to take her heart with little resistance. It was also clear she was out of commission, and although I felt a little guilty about that, I was relieved to be responsible for an injury that would only require a little recuperation. Based on the screams of those around me, others wouldn't be so lucky.

That left me with three hearts, and I felt rather proud. A glance over at Eddie, sitting near the other male victors, told me I shouldn't feel so cocky. He gestured frantically, the message loud and clear: *Pick up the pace.* My pro-defense tactic was keeping me safe but not racking up the hearts. A quick reconnaissance told me others had more hearts than I did, but before I could choose my next course of action, the decision was taken from me.

The girl who'd sat near me, the big bulky one, came at me full force. We collided and fell to the ground. Her fist closed around the cords around my neck, and she pulled, nearly choking me in the process. That magical strength surged within me, and with one big push, I knocked her off of me and scrambled to my feet. She too rose and eyed me speculatively, clearly surprised at the hidden force beneath my small exterior. Chris shouted the five-minute warning. I braced for the tall girl to come at me, but then, with a quick shrug, she turned away and headed toward someone else. It took me only a moment to understand why. She clearly had the most hearts of any girl. With time nearly up, she wasn't going to risk losing them to someone who'd surprised her with a big show of strength. She'd play it safe and let the clock run out. A few other girls were in contention for second place and suddenly grew more frenzied in their attacks.

Me? I was squarely in third—except there was no third place.

I met Eddie's eyes again and saw true concern now. Then, my gaze slid to the person sitting beside him in the stands: Caleb, smug and secure in his position. Without thinking twice, I strode over and jerked Caleb up by his shirt. That magical strength burned through me, matching us far more evenly than we would ever have been in normal circumstances. Catching him by surprise gave me an extra edge. I landed a punch that would've made Wolfe proud and then kicked at his knee. I didn't break anything, but Caleb did trip and fall to the ground. I quickly pulled the hearts from around his neck and sidestepped as he swung a fist toward me and roared in rage. Eddie jumped up, quick to defend me, but by then, Chris was calling time.

He hurried over to us, frowning at the unorthodox behavior. "What the hell do you think you're doing?" he demanded.

"Winning," I said. I held up my original three hearts with the mass I'd stolen from Caleb. "You said the winning girls would be picked based on whoever had the most hearts at the end of our hour. That's me."

Chris flushed at being trapped in his words. "Yeah, but—"

"And you said any tactic is fair game."

"But—"

"And," I continued triumphantly, "you asked if we were willing to do anything in the fight against evil. I am. Even if it means facing someone bigger and stronger—which those vampiric demons obviously will be." I waved a dismissive hand at the other female competitors, who were staring openmouthed. "What's the point of going up against them?"

A shocked silence hung around us—then it was replaced by laughter. Master Angeletti made his way toward us through the stands, careful not to trip on his golden robes. His face was filled with mirth. "She has a point, Juarez. She outsmarted you, and I say if she can do that—and take down our biggest male competitor—she's earned her spot."

Caleb turned beet red. "I didn't give her all I had. She's just a girl."

Master Angeletti waved him off. "Relax. You can still stay. This girl—what's your name?"

"Fiona, sir. Fiona Gray."

"Fiona Gray can have one of the female spots. It looks like the other goes to that young lady over there." Master Angeletti nodded to the tall girl, the one who'd played it safe in letting the clock run out. Her name was Tara, and although she didn't look thrilled to see me declared a victor, she made no complaint so long as she got her spot. It was the girl who would've been second place who spat out a series of obscenities my way. That seemed to amuse the Warrior authorities, but they held fast in their decision. She and the other defeated recruits were dismissed.

We victors were then treated to a banquet in our honor, back in what served as the compound's mess hall. The seven of us were seated at one table, while the seasoned Warriors filled others. Personally, I would've preferred a shower, but at least I got the chance to sit by Eddie again. He and I grinned and nodded over our plates of ribs as the others relived key moments from the earlier matches and talked about how we were "totally" going to annihilate real vampires. Most of the others seemed impressed by what I'd done to Caleb and got a good chuckle out of it. He, however, clearly wasn't amused. Throughout the meal, he shot several dark looks over to where Eddie and I sat, and I hoped I wouldn't regret my last-minute save in the arena.

After lunch, the Warriors decided they'd tested our penchant for brutality enough—for now, at least—and that it was time to see what kind of personalities we had. We were called one by one to come speak to the high masters and a select group of Warriors about our intentions going forward. They brought us in by alphabetical order, meaning I went before Eddie and wasn't able to get any sort of warning of what was to come. This, at least, was pretty consistent from year to year, and Sabrina had briefed us on what to expect: mostly a lot of interrogation during which we'd affirm how much we hated vampires.

What I wasn't expecting was how much it would remind me of re-education.

Once I was seated in front of the masters and all-male council, they directed my attention to a large screen hanging on the wall. An image of happy, ordinary-looking Moroi appeared.

"What do you see?" asked Master Angeletti.

My heart caught in my throat, and suddenly, I was back in

that underground prison, strapped into a chair with Sheridan's pretty but cruel face gazing down at me.

"What do you see, Sydney?"

"Moroi, ma'am."

"Wrong. You see creatures of evil."

"I don't know. Maybe they are. I'd have to know more about these particular Moroi."

"You don't need to know anything except what I've told you. They are creatures of evil."

And then she'd tortured me, dipping my hand an acidic solution that felt like it was burning my flesh off, forcing me to endure the pain until I would finally agree with her and repeat that they were creatures of evil. The memory was so intense, so vivid as I sat there with the Warriors that my skin started to crawl again. The room felt like it was closing in, becoming a prison just as re-education had been, and I worried I would faint in front of them.

"Fiona?" asked Master Angeletti, tilting his head at me. Although stern-faced, there was an indulgence to his voice, as though he thought I might be intimidated by their presence. "What do you see?"

I swallowed, again paralyzed by fear of my past. As my silence persisted, the other Warriors began looking at me curiously. *It's an act, Sydney!* I frantically told myself. *You did it then, you can do it now. This isn't re-education. You aren't trapped, and Jill's life is on the line.*

Jill.

It was the thought of her name, the memory of her clear and innocent face that drew me back to life. I blinked and focused back on the screen.

"Evil, sir," I said. "I see evil things that have no part of the natural order."

And so it began. I answered in the ways Sabrina had prompted me, not that I needed much coaching. I just had to answer like I would have in re-education. I recited a cover story we'd come up with, about how my brother Fred and I had been attacked by a Strigoi one night and barely gotten away with our lives. I explained how we'd tried telling the authorities, but no one would believe us. We'd known the truth of the evil we'd seen and spent the next few years searching for help, until finally we'd met Sabrina and learned of the Warriors' quest.

When the interview finished, the Warriors were smiling reassuringly, pleased with my answers. I smiled back, but on the inside, I was a mess. I could barely stop myself from shaking or losing myself to the memories of that terrible time. I gave Eddie an encouraging nod when I was released back to the waiting room with the others, and then I sank into a chair, grateful that no one seemed interested in talking to me. I was able to sit and space for a while, steadying my breathing and shaking off the memories. He returned a little while later, irritated by their line of questioning but overall relaxed.

"Psychos," he muttered to me, keeping a smile on his face for the sake of the others in the room. "I stuck to the story, and they took it well."

"Same here," I said, envious of how easy it had been for him. He didn't have the baggage I had.

Once everyone had been interviewed, it was time for dinner and another banquet back in the mess hall. As we ate, Master Ortega recited a psalm and gave a long sermon about the glory of humanity and the light and how we were all doing such a great job in fighting the good fight. It was a variation of what I'd heard with the Alchemists, even before re-education, and I wondered if I'd ever be free of groups of people trying to impose their beliefs on me. Fortunately, we were given some personal time afterward, and Sabrina came over to talk to us in a corner of the room. Other sponsors were meeting with their recruits, so nobody took it amiss.

"Hanging in there?" she asked quietly. We nodded, and she gave me a wry smile. "Ballsy move, going after Caleb."

"I thought they'd appreciate the moxie," I replied.

"Yes and no," she said. "Taking on a challenge like that does score you some points, but there are those who just don't like anyone breaking the rules."

"Sounds familiar," I said, thinking of the Alchemists.

"What'll happen now?" asked Eddie.

Sabrina glanced around and shrugged. "Not much tonight. There are separate dorms for men and women, so everyone'll go to bed soon. That'll be your chance to look around, Sydney. I checked out the facilities earlier today, and there aren't a lot of locked doors to deal with. You said those were a problem, right?"

"Right," I agreed. Invisibility spells could hide me but wouldn't do any good if someone saw a door opening by itself. "And security cameras."

She shook her head. "There are none of those. Most security's on the perimeter of the compound. They want to keep others out and all of us in. Moving around—if they can't see you—shouldn't be too difficult for you. The areas they want protected have armed guards, which hopefully you can slip past."

"Hopefully." It was amazing that we could discuss armed

guards as minor obstacles. "Except I'm just not sure where I'm going."

"I am," she said. "I found out while scouting around. If you look out the window behind me, you'll see a big gray building. That's the women's dorm. To its right is the men's dorm, and to the right again is the building where the masters have their headquarters. That's where you'll find your answers."

Eddie and I both glanced at the window indicated. He frowned. "I hate that this is all on you. I feel useless."

I touched his arm reassuringly. "You're my backup," I said. "I feel better having you here."

"And we may need your help when it's time to get out," added Sabrina.

I noted her use of "we." "You'll be coming with us?" I asked.

"When you guys disappear, I'll get in trouble for bringing false recruits—even if they don't think I'm part of a conspiracy, they'll accuse me of being sloppy. I don't want to deal with that. And honestly?" She sighed. "I'm ready to be done with this job. I'll help Marcus some other way."

Our free time wrapped up, and everyone was sent off to their dorms. Chris advised us recruits in particular to get some sleep because we had a "big day" tomorrow. I tried not to grimace. I was already sore and scraped up from today, and my work wasn't even over.

As I entered the girls' dorm, I found that Sabrina had been right. There were a lot of open doorways connecting halls and rooms. Because there was no air conditioning, many windows were left open as well. Curtains were hung in the room doorways to provide privacy, and those didn't even touch the floor. It was *almost* a dream come true for someone needing to sneak around invisibly, especially since there were so few women around to begin with, meaning most of the dorm wasn't in use.

Unfortunately, my room wasn't empty. Someone had had the brilliant idea to put Tara and me together. She glowered at me as we got ready for bed and made a few seemingly idle threats about how she'd prove to everyone that she was the superior candidate. She didn't seem like she'd attack me in my sleep, though. The problem was that I couldn't risk her waking and seeing my bed empty—then reporting me. That meant I had to cast a sleeping spell on her, something I'd never done before.

I waited until she seemed to be sleeping naturally, then I crept out into the dark room. The curtain hanging in our doorway hung down about two-thirds of the way, allowing some light from the hall to shine in. I studied Tara's sleeping form and braced myself for the spell. It didn't require a lot of strength, exactly, but it did require some complex calculations. It almost worked like a drug. The amount of magic required was dependent on the person's size. In the dim lighting, I hazarded a guess at how much she weighed. One hundred sixty? Casting too weak a spell could risk her waking early, and I couldn't have that. So I erred on the side of caution and cast as I would for someone weighing two hundred pounds.

Her breathing deepened as the magic flowed through her, and her features seemed much more relaxed. Maybe I was doing her a favor. Maybe a night of solid sleep would help her in tomorrow's competition. Little did she know she'd soon be the only girl competing. Backing away, I cast my own spell, wrapping my body in invisibility. I put as much magic as I could into it, making sure it would last a while and not be easily broken.

Once that was in place, I knelt in front of the curtained doorway and crept under, careful not to disturb the fabric. Out in the hall, a guard with a gun stood nearby, stifling a yawn. He clearly didn't expect much of a disturbance tonight. I walked past him easily, right over to an open window, and climbed out into the darkness, off to explore the depths of the Warriors' camp.

CHAPTER 16

ADRIAN

I HAD TROUBLE SLEEPING after Sydney left. I couldn't shake my fears about what kind of dangers she was walking into and how I couldn't be there to protect her. It didn't matter that she was brave and clever and competent—and probably better at protecting me than I was her. The urge to look out for her was just too strong.

I also had trouble sleeping because my bed was a giant beanbag.

"You sure you don't want the couch?" asked Marcus.

I shook my head and gave the beanbag a couple of half-hearted punches to get it into shape. "You take it," I said. "I don't know if I could fall asleep under any conditions."

He grinned. "Howie probably has something to help you sleep."

"No thanks," I said with a snort.

Marcus shut out the lights and curled up on the mustard yellow couch. Silence fell, aside from the occasional faint strains of "Mr. Tambourine Man" coming from the basement. I shifted a few times, trying to get comfortable but having little success. I tried to turn my thoughts from Sydney toward thinking about tomorrow, when I'd be helping the witches interrogate Alicia. Those weren't exactly calming thoughts, but they at least helped me channel my emotions into something besides anxiety. Before she'd left, Maude had said someone would come and pick me up tomorrow evening to take me to where Alicia was being held. Apparently, they were busy securing a location and also trying to figure out a way to slip Ms. Terwilliger out without the spying Alchemists following her.

Amazingly, despite all the crazy conditions, I did finally fall asleep. And even more incredibly, I found myself being swept into a spirit dream by someone else. As a lush tropical garden slowly materialized around me, I knew who the dream's creator was even before she appeared.

"Hello, Sonya," I said.

She emerged from behind a honeysuckle bush, wearing casual gardening clothes but with her red hair immaculately styled. "Adrian," she said, by way of greeting. "You're hard to find in sleep these days. I can't tell what schedule you're on."

"Not much of any," I admitted. "Haven't had much sleep, really. We've been busy."

"I've gathered as much. Rumor has it the Alchemists know you left Court now."

"Afraid so." I leaned against a palm tree. "You could have called if you wanted to talk."

She nodded. "I know. But I wanted to chat face-to-face. There was also something you could only see in a dream. Or rather, someone."

It took me a moment to realize what she meant. "Nina."

Sadness filled Sonya's features. "Yes. Her waking condition hasn't changed very much. She's not exactly comatose, but she's also not particularly responsive. If you put food in front of her, she'll eat it. Turn on a shower, she'll stand under it. But she makes few decisions that aren't initiated for her. And she never talks."

The shock of that news made me reel, and I used a small bit of spirit to create a bench to sit on. "Is there any hope for improvement?" I asked.

"I don't know." Sonya sat beside me. "I mean, I'm praying there is. I never want to say there's no hope. But that spirit overload . . . it was too much, with too little preparation. She was in such a fragile state already from excessive use and in no way prepared to handle what she summoned. The scarring from it was formidable."

My heart plummeted. "I should have stopped her somehow."

"I don't think you could have, Adrian. She was intent on doing whatever she thought she had to do to find her sister."

I hesitated, almost afraid to speak my next words. "I found her. I found Olive and learned why she ran. But . . . well, the story doesn't exactly have a happy ending."

Sonya didn't press me for details. "I'm not sure I'd tell her that."

"Tell her?" I asked.

"Yes. That's part of the reason I wanted to talk to you. When Nina wouldn't respond in person, I tried reaching her in spirit dreams. That didn't work either at first. Then I was able to—in a way. I'll show you."

She fell silent and stared off at a clearing in the garden. After several moments of intense concentration, a huge rectangular block of stone appeared. A small opening was cut into it, but that opening was covered in bars. I stood up and peered inside, gasping at what I saw. Nina sat there in the small stone cell, on the floor, wrapped in shadows.

"Nina!" I exclaimed.

She stared off at the stone wall, saying nothing, her face expressionless.

"Nina? Can you hear me?"

Sonya came to stand beside me. "I think she can, but I just don't think she's capable of responding."

I gestured to the portable stone prison around her. "Where did this come from?"

"Her mind," replied Sonya. "This is how she sees herself: trapped. But honestly? The fact that she appears this way at all is promising. Before, there wasn't enough of her mind to form any sort of connection with. I'm hoping, in time, that she'll advance further, so I try to talk to her either in person or in dreams. I thought you'd like to know, in case you want to visit as well."

"I do," I said, still coming to terms with the shock I felt at her condition. Even while imprisoned and tortured, Sydney's mind had remained strong enough to connect at the spirit-dream level. What kind of damage had been done to Nina to put her in this state? Was this the danger I was courting with my continued spirit use?

"I think it's good for different people to talk to her," said Sonya carefully. "But I think certain topics are best avoided until she's recovered. Like unhappy endings."

She didn't need to elaborate for me to understand. Knowing

the truth—that Olive was dead—was probably not going to be therapeutic for Nina's immediate recovery. I nodded and stepped back up to the stone cell's window.

"I'm glad to see you again, Nina. There's so much I want to tell you. A lot of it's about Olive. And some of it . . . some of it's really incredible." I smiled as Declan came to mind. "You're definitely going to want to hear about it, so you need to come back to us soon, okay?"

There was no response or change of expression, not even at the mention of Olive's name.

"It'll take time," said Sonya, gently touching my arm. "But all of this helps."

"Thank you for letting me know about her," I said. As my gaze shifted back to Sonya, it hit me that she too would probably be very interested in knowing about Declan. I didn't know for certain, but I had a sneaking suspicion that the way spirit was infused in him was exactly the feat she was trying to replicate for her vaccine. If she could see him, she might make incredible progress—and yet, that was exactly what Olive had been trying to avoid. It was what she'd died for.

"What is it?" asked Sonya, seeing my scrutiny.

I gave her a weak smile. "Nothing. There's just a lot going on."

"I can imagine—and I won't keep you. I just wanted you to know Nina's progress and see how you could talk to her."

"Thanks," I said, giving a Sonya a small hug. "I'll keep checking in with her. Let me know if she wakes in the real world."

The dream dissolved, and I returned to my own sleep, surprising myself when I slept in to almost noon at Howie's.

When I woke, another meal of junk food followed. I'd never wanted a salad so much in my life. I also learned from Marcus that Sabrina had sent an update from the Warriors' compound. They were all inside and safe, and so far, their cover was holding.

That news got me through the day until evening came around, and an unknown car pulled up outside our safe house. I could see Marcus starting to freak out until I recognized Neil in the driver's seat.

"Jackie Terwilliger sent me to fetch you," he explained. "I helped get her out earlier and shake the Alchemists who were watching her house. She's getting things ready for Alicia now."

At the mention of Alicia's name, his expression darkened. She had that effect on people. "I'm kind of surprised I get to be the 'lucky' one to witness her interrogation," he added. "But with Eddie off on some mission, and Rose and Dimitri doing something mysterious at Clarence's, I'm the only free guardian around."

"Did you talk to Rose and Dimitri?" I asked casually.

"I saw them," said Neil. "And your mum, I stopped by this morning. That's a cute little fellow she's taking care of, by the way. Is he part of the reason Rose and Dimitri are sticking around? I got the impression Rose *really* would have liked to come with me."

I hesitated. Neil still didn't know that he was a father—or that the girl he loved was dead. It was a huge, burning secret he deserved to know, but again, I was struck by the poor timing. I certainly wasn't going to bring it up in front of Marcus. And it didn't really seem right to mention it as a "by the way" en route to interrogating Alicia.

"It's a long story," I said simply. "I'll fill you in later."

"Fair enough," said Neil. Guardians were used to secrets and a need-to-know basis. He could take it stride—though he also didn't realize that this secret hit so close to home.

I told Marcus to keep me updated as soon as he learned anything about Sydney and Eddie's progress at the Warriors' compound. After stocking up on a few snacks from Howie's kitchen—though honestly, I was kind of sick of it all by now—Neil and I headed back to the civilization of Palm Springs. Along the way, he mentioned that he'd heard Nina was sick, and I again had to tread very carefully about the extent of my involvement. Naturally, Neil also wanted to know if I'd obtained any news of Olive, especially in light of her sister's condition. I played it vague, saying I hadn't been able to make contact, hating that I had to lie to him. Disappointment showed in his face, and I realized I was going to hate having to tell him the truth as well—at least about Olive.

I soon learned from him that we were going to the home of Maude, the Stelle's leader. Not only was she not under Alchemist surveillance, she also apparently had a bona fide dungeon in her house. At least that's what Inez told me when we arrived.

Maude, overhearing as she passed by, rolled her eyes. "It's not a dungeon, Inez. It's a wine cellar."

We were standing in Maude's living room, waiting for a few other coven members to show up. Inez sniffed in contempt. "It's underground and has stone walls," she retorted. "*And* it doesn't have wine racks."

"I haven't gotten them installed yet," explained Maude.

"I just call it like I see it," said Inez.

Jackie strolled over to us. "Well, regardless, it's incredibly useful right now. Underground rooms are excellent for containing magic. We can create a circle to prevent Alicia from attempting anything nefarious, and then you can work your own brand of magic, Adrian. Ah, here are the others."

A few more newcomers entered, bringing the total number of witches up to fourteen. According to Jackie, there were a bunch of sacred numbers in spell craft, but to offer the best protection against Alicia, a circle of thirteen was needed, as well as someone to work other spells. After two days in that frozen form, Alicia was probably weakened, but after all the times she'd surprised us, no one wanted to take any chances.

With everyone here, we headed down into the basement. There, I found Alicia frozen in exactly the same form she'd been at Wolfe's. I also found myself agreeing with Inez.

"It is kind of dungeon-esque," I murmured to her. "Who uses stone this dark for a wine cellar? I'd expect something more Tuscan."

"I know, right?" she whispered back.

Thirteen witches linked hands and formed a circle of protection around Alicia, chanting spells that would supposedly keep all human magic locked inside. Maude, separate from the circle, then used the same herbs and incantations that had freed Eddie at Wolfe's compound. Staring at Alicia, frozen in the awkward defensive position Sydney had trapped her in, I couldn't help but suddenly share in the witches' initial reluctance to free her. She'd tried to kill Sydney, steal Jackie's power, and left Jackie's sister in a coma. She'd also captured Jill and turned her over to the Warriors—simply as a way to get back at Sydney. Really, Alicia deserved to be left a statue forever.

But then we'd never get answers.

Maude's spell completed, and as it did, she slipped outside the circle to stand by Neil and me. We watched as Alicia came to life again, her legs buckling as the muscles suddenly had to learn to function once more. Yet even as she crumpled to the floor, a snarl crossed her features, and she held up her hand, sending bolts of light out from her. They hit an invisible wall formed by the thirteen and dissipated harmlessly.

"You can't hold me forever," she cried. "And as soon as I'm free again, I'll make all of you pay!"

I leaned toward Maude, pitching my voice low. "She has a point. What *will* happen to her?"

"Don't worry," she murmured back. "Just as you Moroi have your own prisons, we have ours." Clearing her throat, she stepped forward so that she remained outside of the circle but was still in Alicia's field of vision. "What happens to you now will depend on how cooperative you are, Alicia. We can make life comfortable as you're brought to justice—or very unpleasant."

Alicia expressed what she thought of that by sending a fireball in Maude's direction. It too was absorbed, and I thought she should consider herself lucky their protective wall didn't bounce things back to her.

Maude crossed her arms and regarded Alicia unflinchingly. "We understand you played a part in the disappearance of a young Moroi girl. Tell us where you took her."

For a moment, Alicia looked surprised at the question until she noticed me standing off to the side of the circle. She chuckled. "Where is Sydney? Is she too afraid to face me again?"

Don't let her talk to you like that! ordered Aunt Tatiana.

With a small amount of spirit telekinesis, I made Alicia's arms suddenly snap against her sides, as though she were in a straightjacket. Her eyes widened in astonishment when she tried to lift them and couldn't. "Sydney has more skill and integrity than you ever will," I said. "You're lucky you won't have to face her again. Now tell us where you took Jill. We know she's with the Warriors. Where?"

"Tell us, and we'll send you off to your trial as a well-treated prisoner," added Maude. "Otherwise, we'll put you back in that inert state."

"It'll take more than threats or parlor tricks to get me to tell you where she's at." Alicia shot me a malicious grin. "You might have caught me, but that's one battle Sydney won't win. You'll never see that Moroi brat again."

If she hurts Jill . . . Aunt Tatiana didn't finish her threat, and she didn't need to. Anger—fueled by my raging aunt—welled up in me, and I forcibly pushed it down, needing a cool head. "Enough games," I said. I released her arms and redirected my spirit into compulsion. "Tell us where Jill is."

Alicia's eyes started to glaze over, her jaw going slack . . . then, amazingly, she shook it off. Her features hardened again. "I'm not that easy to control," she said.

"She may have bolstered herself with potions," Maude told me. Jackie had hinted at this as well, that Alicia might very well have given herself all sorts of magical protection, including against compulsion. "It won't last forever. A few more days, and it should all be gone."

I gritted my teeth and upped my spirit use. "No. We're getting answers today." With renewed magic, I focused on Alicia again. "Tell us where Jill is."

Again, Alicia looked defiant, but this time she had more difficulty standing against me. "With . . . with the Warriors."

"We know that," I said. "Where? Where are they holding her?"

Trying to compel her was like trying to open a door that someone was pushing back against on the other side. Both of us were throwing all we had into it. Her will and whatever potion she'd taken were strong, but I believed my powers were stronger. Again, I increased the amount of spirit channeling through me, knowing that an average-willed person would have been bent to my will by now. Sydney's warnings echoed back to me, about not going crazy with spirit use, but I pushed on anyway. We needed answers.

"Where are the Warriors holding her?" I demanded.

Alicia was visibly sweating now, fighting hard against my power. "In . . . in Utah," she blurted out at last. "St. George. A compound there. But you'll never get to her! You'll never get through to her!"

"Why?" I asked, pushing hard with the compulsion. "Why?"

"Too . . . many . . . obstacles," she said, pale and trembling.

"Tell me everything," I ordered.

She remained obstinate, and I was ready to compel her even more. One tidal wave of spirit, and I was certain I could have her on her hands and knees, begging to tell me all she knew.

Do it! ordered Aunt Tatiana. *Make her pay! Make her your slave!*

I was ready to . . . but then, unexpectedly, an image of last night's dream meeting with Sonya came back to me. Or, more specifically, an image of Nina in her cell came back to me. I recalled Sonya's words about the scars of spirit use and remembered my promise to Sydney to keep things in check.

Sydney couldn't have foreseen this, Aunt Tatiana argued.

You're stronger than Nina. You won't end up like her.

No, I told that phantom voice. *I won't risk it. I'll keep my word to Sydney.*

With great reluctance, I released the compulsion and spirit directed against Alicia. She slumped, this time simply from mental exhaustion.

"That's enough for us to go on," I said. "We can find this place in St. George." Whether it would be through Sydney's sleuthing, the Alchemists giving in and helping, or even Sabrina's insight, it couldn't be that difficult now that we had a city. I would've liked to know more about the "obstacles" in place, but I wasn't going to burn myself out when she probably just meant crazy Warriors and their weapons. The guardians could handle that. They had before.

"Do you need anything else from her before we freeze her up again?" asked Maude.

Alicia's eyes went wide. "You said I wouldn't be frozen if I cooperated!"

"That wasn't exactly cooperating," replied Maude coolly.

I shook my head. "That should be enough. If we need more, I'll let you know."

"No!" shouted Alicia. Fireballs formed in her hands, and she began futilely hurling them at the invisible barrier. "I won't go into that state again! I won't! You can't—"

But Maude was casting beside me, and a minute later, Alicia was frozen in place again, her fireball-hurling stance even more ridiculous than her last one. The witches disbanded the circle, and Jackie came over to speak to me.

"Are you sure you got everything you needed from her? I felt you wanted to ask her more."

"I did," I admitted. "But her defenses were strong. I'll pass the St. George information to my contacts and see what they can find out."

Jackie nodded. "Very well then. I also spoke to Maude. If you'd like, you're welcome to stay here at her house until the next move in this plan. It'll put you a little closer to the action, and from what I hear, she has a lot more room than the last place you were staying."

"Hopefully more produce too," I added. I glanced at Neil. "You're the security expert. Is it safe?"

"I believe so," he said after a moment's thought. "No one followed any of us. And if it's fine with her, I'll stay on too to look after you."

We thanked Maude for her hospitality and stayed out of the way as the witches wrapped things up. Apparently, Alicia would eventually be transported to a magical trial and prison, but for now, she'd remain in the wine cellar/dungeon. Neil and I, thankfully, had guest rooms upstairs. I sent the St. George info to Marcus and then finally decided it was time to break some hard news, since it looked like Neil and I would be waiting around together for a while.

"Neil . . ." I began, when we were alone in his room. "We need to talk."

"Sure," he said easily. "Is it about Jill?"

"Nothing at all to do with her, actually." I gestured to the bed. "Maybe you should sit down."

Neil frowned, alerted by my tone. "I'll stand, thanks. Just tell me what's happening."

I crossed my arms, as though I could protect myself from all the anguish I was about to dredge up. Until then, I didn't realize how I'd been fighting to keep it from crushing me.

"Neil, there's no easy way to say this . . . and I'm so sorry to be the one telling you . . . but Olive died two nights ago."

Neil made no sound at all, but his face went white, so white I thought he might pass out. "No," he said at last, after several long moments of agonized silence. "No, that's impossible." He shook his head adamantly. "No."

"A Strigoi killed her," I said. Whereas I'd initially struggled to find words, I now suddenly found myself rushing forward, unable to stop. "She was staying in a dhampir commune. In Michigan. A small group of Strigoi attacked it, breaking through the wards somehow. We think they got a human to pull one of the warding stakes up. Regardless, they got in, and Olive was caught when she was running away and—"

"Wait," interrupted Neil. In the blink of an eye, his stricken face had turned hard and skeptical. "Olive wouldn't run away from a fight. Certainly not from a group of Strigoi. She of all people would stand her ground."

That terrible agony ripped through me. "She was running away to protect her baby. Declan—the baby my mom is taking care of."

Another heavy silence filled the room as the weight of those words sunk in. I wished then that I'd waited for Sydney. She would have done a more eloquent job explaining this.

"And it wasn't even the Strigoi she was running from," I said, when Neil only continued to stare at me in shock. "Neil, the baby, Declan . . . he's yours. Your son. You're the father."

Disbelief returned to Neil's features, but this time it was more stunned than angry. "We both know that's not true," he said. "Was that . . . was that why she ran? Did she think I'd judge her? We had no real commitments, not truly. I was crazy about her, it's true, but there was just—"

"The one time, I know," I finished. "But that's all it took. Somehow, something happened to her when she was restored from being a Strigoi that let her conceive a baby with you. I didn't believe it either until I looked at him more closely with my magic. There's definitely a spiritual, I don't know, residue on him. It's crazy, I know. But he *is* yours."

Neil sat on the bed, so still he could have been a statue. I understood his grief and sat beside him. "Neil, I'm so sorry."

"Olive's dead," he said numbly. He looked up at me and blinked back tears. "If what you're saying is true—if somehow, through some sort of magic, that baby is mine, then why didn't Olive tell me herself? Why'd she run away?"

"Because she was afraid of that magic," I said. "And she was afraid of what people would say or do—both the Moroi and the Alchemists. She hid him to protect him from being treated like a freak of nature, and I promised to help protect him."

Neil stared blankly for several moments, and then I think hearing about *protection* woke up his better instincts. "Who knows? Who knows about D-Declan?"

"About his true nature?" I gestured to myself. "Only me and Sydney. Rose and Dimitri know he's Olive's, as do a couple of people back at the commune. That's it. We thought it was safest that as few people know about him as possible. If they knew that somehow, probably through Olive being restored, dhampirs could have kids . . . well, it'd shock a lot of people. Some would be happy, some curious. They'd all want to learn more about him, and that's not what Olive wanted."

Neil remained silent and nearly as motionless as Alicia had been.

"Neil?" I said, a little unnerved by his shell-shocked state. "It's going to be okay. I'll help you. We'll make sure Olive's wishes are honored—that Declan lives a happy, normal life. Once this business with Jill is over, we'll get you and Declan together and—"

"No," said Neil, suddenly coming to life. He looked up at me sharply, and though his expression was hard, there was a terrible sadness in his voice. "I can't ever see him again."

CHAPTER 17
SYDNEY

THE WARRIORS' COMPOUND WAS QUIET and still as I crept through the night. Trey and Sabrina had said the Warriors could have wild parties when they wanted, but when curfews and discipline were laid down, everyone obeyed. That was certainly the case now. Most people were tucked away in their dorms, and the people who passed me as I crept invisibly toward the masters' headquarters were those on patrol. None of them seemed to expect much to happen overnight, and they made their rounds with relaxed confidence.

Another open window allowed me to slip inside the masters' building easily, right in front of a guard assigned to watch at the front door. Inside, I found mostly quiet and empty rooms, and like in my building, most of the doorways were open. There were, of course, a few rooms with real doors, and as luck would have it, it was in one of those that the masters chose to have a meeting. At least, that's what I assumed was going on. Two guards were posted in front of a closed door, and I could hear muffled voices behind it. Noting its position, I went back outside and circled around to it, hoping I'd find its window open to allow me to climb in and spy. When I reached it, I found it only partway open, enough to let in air in the hot night but not enough for me to climb through. Sabrina had said one of the masters usually carried pertinent information about their organization at all times—sometimes in hard copy or sometimes on a laptop, depending who it was and how tech savvy he was. My plan had been to rifle through said information in the hopes of finding where Jill might be held. For now, I'd have to start with eavesdropping.

As it turned out, I'd arrived just in time for the beginning of their meeting, which I initially thought was a stroke of luck. It meant I hadn't missed anything. Unfortunately, it meant I had to endure a lot of preliminary material—including more of those absurd psalms. Then someone got sidetracked and started asking about baseball scores. All the while, I was conscious of my invisibility. It was long lasting, but not *that* long lasting, and it was a relief when the group finally started talking about the business of the day.

"All in all, it was a strong showing," a voice I recognized as Master Angeletti's said. "We had a good turnout, and they put on a commendable show."

"Some were a little out of line," a sullen voice grumbled. I knew that one too: Chris Juarez.

Master Angeletti laughed. "Still put out that that girl tricked you? I say more power to her. We need more thinkers around here."

"Not too many." That was Master Ortega.

"No, no, of course not," said Master Angeletti. "But if we're going to be dealing with the Alchemists more, we need to be able to outsmart them."

My ears pricked at that. The Alchemists? I'd once done some reconnaissance for Marcus and discovered that there were indeed Alchemists and Warriors working together, but Marcus had yet to learn the full extent of how deep that relationship went.

"We've already outsmarted them," said Master Ortega. "We've gotten them to do business with us."

"Yes, but don't get too comfortable with that arrangement," said a new voice that must have been one of the council members. "Didn't you say you got a call about that girl, Alfred?"

"Yes, yes," said Master Angeletti, not sounding particularly concerned. "But it was just preliminary. One of them claimed they'd gotten a tip we might be holding her, but I think they were just covering their bases. I checked with the guards, though, and they said there was no sign that anyone had been snooping around or was coming for her. I'll keep logging everything here, though, just so we've got a trail if anything happens."

I didn't know what he meant until I heard the click of fingers typing on keys. I tensed, waiting for them to elaborate about "that girl," but they switched topics, moving on to more about the trials. Nonetheless, excitement surged through me. Sabrina had been right. There was a computer or laptop in there that Master Angeletti was apparently keeping records on. Was there other information about "that girl" recorded? I didn't know for sure if they were referring to Jill, but it was promising, as was the laptop's existence. I needed to make obtaining it my goal. That wasn't going to be easy, seeing as how I had no idea how long this meeting was going to last or if Master Angeletti would leave his laptop behind when it ended. I was mentally listing all the possible distractions I might cause when the Alchemists came up in conversation again—in a way I totally didn't expect.

"Well, just be careful," Master Ortega was saying in response to someone else. "Don't screw up this deal with the Alchemists. If your contact can really deliver on what he's offering, we won't have to focus so much on the candidates' physical prowess. We can make our recruits as strong as we like."

"I still don't like it," muttered another unknown council member. "We're dabbling in unholy substances."

"Not if we purify those substances first," said Master Angeletti. "And use the strength they give us to fight back against the evil."

I frowned as I tried to determine what they might be referring to. "I've seen what these substances can do," remarked Chris. "I saw them when they were used at my cousin's school. If the Alchemists really do have more of them, they're letting them go to waste if they aren't using them in the fight against evil."

"The Alchemists fight evil by cataloguing it," chuckled someone.

"Don't make those kinds of comments around our contact," warned Master Ortega. "He's already hesitant about doing business with us. His people won't like it if they find out what he's doing."

"I know what I'm doing," snapped Master Angeletti. "And believe me, I'm paying him enough to get over any hesitancy he might have."

The conversation drifted back toward a discussion of the

recruits, analyzing each of us according to what the Warriors saw as our pros and cons. I only half listened, my mind spinning with the other shocking piece of news I'd heard. Based on what Chris had said, it sounded as though they were talking about using vampire blood to create performance-enhancing tattoos on humans. A surge of those had occurred at Amberwood Prep, resulting in both athletic and academic prowess. The problem was, the results of those tattoos were unpredictable and often had illicit side effects. The ring had been shut down when I'd helped uncover its mastermind: Keith Darnell. He'd been sent off to re-education, reprogrammed, and now toed the line with nearly robotic loyalty.

Or did he?

The Warriors had kept referring to "he" as their contact. I'd known of no other Alchemist participating in such activity . . . was it possible Keith had broken free of some of that programming? Was he now making a secret deal with these psychopaths, one that would give their fighters superhuman strength?

Again, I heard those clicking keys, driving home the importance of getting a look at what was on that laptop. I considered a few options that might allow me a chance to peek at it, but I soon rejected those. The Warriors might act like they were from the Middle Ages, but it was very likely Master Angeletti locked his laptop when he left it. I might need technical assistance to view it. That, and I really wanted more than just a peek. If he logged notes on all their meetings, kept track of important calls and transactions . . . well, the possibilities for what that laptop could hold were endless. Rescuing Jill was my main priority, but I might very well walk out of this with information that could show us a whole lot more.

Abandoning the masters' meeting, I used more invisibility magic to break into other dorms and smuggle out Sabrina and Eddie. Neither was asleep when I found them, and we managed to find a secluded spot behind a storage shed to talk.

"You were right," I told Sabrina. "Master Angeletti does log his information on a laptop. And I heard what sounded very much like a suspicious reference to them holding Jill."

Eddie perked up. "Then what are we waiting for? Let's go take it."

"Actually, that's kind of what I had in mind," I said. "I mean, maybe there are more delicate ways to go about this, but do we have that kind of time? We've lost so much with Jill." I turned to Sabrina. "Marcus hinted that you were prepared for if your cover was ever blown. Is that true?"

She arched an eyebrow. "You plan on blowing it?"

"Not if I can help it," I said. "But the end result of all this is going to be the laptop gone and Eddie and me never finishing the recruitment. If they link us to the theft, they'll link us to you. You could be in trouble."

"Understood," she said. "If I leave this gig with a prize like his laptop, it'll be worth it."

"I just worry about them coming after you," I said.

Sabrina remained unfazed. "Don't worry about me. These guys aren't as connected as the Alchemists, and I know how to avoid them. Now, what's your plan?"

"Kind of simple, really," I admitted. "Create a big distraction. Steal the laptop in the chaos."

She looked a little disappointed, probably because she'd

been expecting something more sophisticated and stealthy. And really, if I'd had the time to concoct a more elegant plan, I would have. Eddie, meanwhile, had no problem with my idea. It was straightforward, which he liked.

"Fire?" he suggested.

"I considered it. But with as close as these buildings are . . ." I gestured around at how tightly packed in everything on the compound was. "Well, I don't like these guys, but I don't want to kill all of them if a fire gets out of hand. So, believe it or not, I'm going to take a page out of Alicia's book. Spell book, if you want to get technical."

"Alicia probably would burn this place down around them," he pointed out.

"Probably. But she does have less violent methods. While I was waiting around in Palm Springs, I looked up some of the spells she used on us. Most were pretty advanced, but I think I could pull off the fotianas."

"The what?" asked Sabrina.

"Think of them as annoying mutant fireflies," Eddie told her.

I nodded in agreement. "I feel like a swarm of them would be a pretty good distraction—enough to get the masters out of their meeting. Then I can grab the laptop, and we can all run out of here in the chaos. Sabrina, do you think you'll be able to get out and get your car ready?"

"Sure. The gate guards won't stop me. And if there's a big enough uproar, I can claim I'm getting weapons from my car and that Eddie's helping me." Seeing our surprised looks, she rolled her eyes. "Come on. You don't think everyone here has weapons stashed in their car?"

The question then came down to whether I could pull off

Alicia's spell. I'd committed the spell to memory after reading about it, but magic was a lot more than just memorization. Summoning supernatural creatures wasn't an easy task, especially with no physical spell components to aid me. I spoke the words, concentrating on the power within me, and felt the magic flare up in response. The spell I'd read about had an element of control to it—a way for the caster to direct the fotianas to do the caster's bidding. I'd planned on having the fotianas do some steady loops of the compound, enough to be distracting and steer everyone's attention from the masters' meeting room but not degenerate into complete chaos.

Unfortunately, things didn't quite work out as I'd planned.

It took a lot more strength and energy than I'd expected to cast the spell, and although I pulled it off—barely—I couldn't actually maintain control. A swarm of fotianas materialized in front of me, hovering there for a moment before suddenly scattering off and flying around the compound at insane speeds and in wildly different directions. We stared after them, gaping.

"Were they that fast at the robot museum?" asked Eddie, eyes wide.

"I don't think so," I said. "I may not have cast it perfectly. I also didn't mean to summon quite so many."

If we'd wanted chaos, though, we got it. The fotianas instantly attracted attention, spinning and twirling around the compound, leaving trails of light behind. And, just like at the museum, the fotianas stung those they came into contact with. Screams and shouts rose up almost immediately, and with them, a cry I hadn't expected.

"Armageddon! Armageddon is upon us! Warriors, take up arms!"

Sabrina gasped, and I turned to her in surprise. "They mean that figuratively, right?" I asked.

She shook her head frantically. "Are you kidding? These people? It's what they've been preparing for. I didn't think they'd take this as a sign, though!"

"Look!" Eddie pointed toward a group of Warriors hurrying in our direction. Panic surged into me. How had they linked the fotianas to us?

"The storage shed," explained Sabrina, steering us away from it. "That's what they're going for. They do Armageddon drills to get ready for this, and the weapons they use are in here."

Sure enough, the mob of Warriors paid us no attention and huddled around the shed as they waited for it to be unlocked. As soon as that happened, someone began passing out swords and maces to the waiting throng. Once armed, they tore off back into the compound's center, swinging madly against the fotianas, which they'd termed "demons of hell."

"Well," I said, having to shout amid all the noise, "they're certainly distracted. Can you guys have the car ready while I go for the laptop?"

Sabrina nodded, but Eddie said to me, "Let me come with you."

"Easier for me to slip in and out alone," I replied.

"Sydney—"

"Eddie," I said firmly, "I can handle this. You have to trust me. Go with Sabrina and be ready to speed away as soon as I get through the gates."

I thought he might still protest, but at last, he yielded. The two of them took off for the gate, and I ran back to the masters' meeting room, having to dodge frenzied armed Warriors and fotianas along the way. Fortunately, things were so chaotic that no one paid any attention to one lone recruit. They probably thought I was lost and confused. In fact, the odds might be good that they'd assume our disappearance was out of fear and never link Sabrina and us to the missing laptop.

As I'd hoped, the masters had run out of their meeting when the commotion started. I got into the empty room easily and nearly whooped with joy when I saw the laptop sitting out. As I'd suspected, the screen was locked, but that'd be a problem for later. I picked it up and turned to the door—where I nearly ran right into Master Angeletti. He stood there stunned for a moment, his eyes going from my face to the laptop and then back to me.

"What do you think you're doing?" he sputtered out, blocking the exit.

So much for not implicating ourselves in the laptop's theft. I deliberated for only a moment. If my cover was already blown, I might as well go all the way. Summoning back Malachi Wolfe's training, I wound up and punched Master Angeletti, landing a hit he clearly hadn't expected. I'd totally forgotten about the strength spell the witches had laid on me. With the extra power behind my punch, he went flying back several feet, landing flat on his back. Groaning, he put a hand to his head but didn't come after me as I sprinted over him and hurried back out through the compound.

No one stopped me as I headed toward the main gate. The Warriors were too busy swinging their weapons at the fotianas, shouting about the last battle and sending their enemies to hell. The gate guards had abandoned their posts to join the fray, and

I slipped out easily, happy to find Sabrina's car running and ready for me. I tumbled into the backseat, and she had her foot on the gas before I could even manage to shut the door.

"You got it?" she asked, once we were speeding away.

"Got it," I confirmed, fastening my seat belt. "But it, uh, wasn't as covert as I hoped. You might want to go with that staying-away-from-them plan after all."

She snorted. "No problem there, especially if that laptop pays off."

I hugged it to me. "Let's hope so. Where are we going to take it?"

"To Marcus, of course."

Marcus was still staying at Howie's cabin in the desert, and it was nearly sunrise when we reached it hours later. I was hoping Adrian would still be there, but when we walked into the living room, we found only Marcus on the couch, eating an oatmeal cream pie for breakfast and leafing through a copy of *Reader's Digest*. "I think he's staying with those witches of yours," he explained, immediately handing over my cell phone.

I, in turn, gave him the laptop. "Know anyone who can get into it?"

Marcus grinned. "Our host, actually."

I stared stupidly for a moment. "Howie?"

"Yup. Believe it or not, he used to work in computers before 'retiring' to the herb business. I'll give it to him right away." Marcus disappeared through the beaded curtain.

I promptly dialed Adrian, and it went to voice mail. It was hard to say what schedule he might be on, and if it was anything human, he might very well still be asleep. Stifling a yawn, I decided that didn't seem like too bad of an idea after my all-night venture. Eddie and Sabrina were on the same page, and Marcus assured us he'd make sure no one bothered us while we camped out in the living room. I fell asleep almost instantly and woke a few hours later to the sound of Eddie and Marcus whispering. Sabrina was still asleep, curled up on the beanbag chair.

"What's up?" I asked quietly, walking over to join Marcus and Eddie.

"Howie got in pretty easily," said Marcus. "Master Angeletti wasn't that big on security. I've spent the last hour or so perusing some of the files."

"Did you find anything about where they're holding Jill?" I asked eagerly.

Marcus nodded. "That's what I was just telling Eddie. It's all here—well, almost. They mention her, talk about how long she's been held, have schematics for the place they're holding her. There are even specifics on the terms they negotiated with Alicia."

"Terms?" I asked.

"Apparently, they cut some sort of deal. Alicia wanted her held a while—probably so that she had a bargaining chip with you—but the Warriors eventually want to use her in some sort of barbaric execution ritual."

My heart stopped. "Just like they did with Sonya."

"It would seem so," said Marcus grimly. "Per the deal they struck with Alicia, they only have to hold her for three more days."

I had to stop my jaw from dropping. "Three days?"

"We have to get there—now," said Eddie, his face like a thundercloud. I was inclined to agree.

Marcus shot him a look of sympathy. "That's the thing.

Remember I said we 'almost' had all the info on her? The one thing we don't have is the location of where they're holding her. They refer to it as their 'Judgment Day Complex.'"

I would've laughed if the situation wasn't so dire. "Stupid name. But it might be enough for the Alchemists to go on. I'll talk to them myself this time and see if I can get their attention."

"Oh," remarked Marcus. There was a dry smile on his face I couldn't fully interpret. "I've got something that might help with that. Did you know the Warriors are buying enchanted vampire blood from rogue Alchemists?"

I thought back to what I'd overheard at the compound. "I did, actually. I was going to see if you could find anything on the laptop about it—I take it you did. Is Keith the one doing it again?"

"No," said Marcus, turning the screen toward me. "Here's a list."

I read it. "I see."

"Yup. I bet the Alchemists would be interested in that—and a number of other Warrior and Alchemist interactions that have been going on."

I agreed with him, but before I could respond, my phone rang, showing Adrian's number. "Hang on." I answered, relief surging through me. "Adrian, are you okay?"

He chuckled on the other end of the line. "Of course you'd ask that. *You're* the one who just went undercover with the Warriors, not me." He paused. "You are back from that, right?"

"I am, and we got what we needed—kind of. We have all sorts of details about where they're holding Jill, just not the actual geographical location."

There was a long pause. "Well, I'll be damned," he said.

"That was about the only thing we got from Alicia. It's in St. George. But we couldn't get any other info from her about the setup—not without, ah, extra force. She insinuated that there might be some obstacles there."

"St. George," I repeated. I wanted to sink to the ground in relief. "That's it. The last piece. We've got the rest—the layout, whatever obstacles she meant. Now we've just got to get everyone mobilized—only we've got three days to do it."

"Why three days?"

"Because they plan on killing her then, just like they were planning with Sonya. It was an arrangement they had for holding her for Alicia while she played her game with me."

More silence, but I could sense the shift in Adrian's tone. "Three days." I knew how hard it had to be for him. The thought of her trapped and undergoing torture was eating me up, and I didn't have nearly the bond he did with her.

"We'll get her," I said. "Don't worry. Now that we have all this, I'll make the Alchemists help. You contact the guardians see if Rose and Dimitri can organize that. And check on Declan while you're at it—"

"I have," he interrupted. "Checked on Declan, I mean. I think I'm driving my mom crazy with all my calls. They're fine. But Sydney . . . I told Neil."

My mind was spinning with plans for Jill, so that news drew me up short. "About Declan? What'd he say?"

"He's afraid to be around Declan. I mean, not afraid of Declan himself, but afraid that someone will string the truth about Declan's history together."

"But he's his father," I said lamely. "He has to be with him."

Adrian sighed. "That's what I told him! But Neil keeps

arguing that some spirit user might see they're related or that even a layperson might notice plain old physical resemblance and start asking questions. He says we can't show any sign that they have a connection or inspire anyone to do a genetic test—and he insists that that involves him keeping his distance. He offered to do everything in his power to help Declan otherwise. I swear, I think he'd rob a bank if he needed to."

My head reeled. "We'll talk him out of it. He's probably just in shock. Once he hears reason, he'll understand."

We disconnected, and I hoped my words were true. It made my heart ache that Neil would want to make such a sacrifice, even if—logically—I could understand what might make him think that way. But still. How could he deprive Declan of a father when he already had lost a mother? And what would become of Declan then?

Those were troubling questions for later. For now, I had to get things in motion with the Alchemists. I had Eddie drive me to the other side of Palm Springs, to a pay phone at a remote gas station. Tracking cell phones wasn't easy, but it wasn't beyond the Alchemists, and I wouldn't take any chances. Picking up the phone, I steeled myself to dial a number I hadn't called in a very long time but still had memorized. I just hoped I'd get an answer.

"Stanton here," came the familiar voice.

"Hello, Stanton. This is Sydney Ivashkov."

Silence met me, possibly from astonishment or initiating a track on the call. Maybe both.

"Hello, Sydney," she said at last. "Isn't this a pleasant surprise? I can't say I expected to hear from you."

"The pleasure's all yours, and I'm not repeating any of this, so listen closely. The Moroi need Alchemist backup to rescue

Jill Dragomir from the Warriors of Light. I'm sure you've heard this from Queen Vasilisa."

"Yes," she replied. "And I'm sure you've heard that our superiors have chosen not to participate, seeing as there's only been circumstantial proof the Warriors took the girl."

"Well, we've got evidence now, so you're going to convince them to participate," I said. "And if you do, I'll give you the names of four Alchemists who are selling charmed Moroi blood to the Warriors to make more of those strength-enhancing tattoos. In fact, I'll give you two of those names now: Edward Hill and Callie DiMaggio. Go investigate them. You've got one hour, at which point I'll call again—from another number, so don't bother staking out this one—and then you're going to tell me about how you'll be sending that backup to St. George, Utah, within the next twenty-four hours to help the Moroi rescue Jill. If she's rescued safely, I'll give you the other names. Talk to you then."

I hung up, and Eddie regarded me with awe. "That was pretty badass. But do you actually think it'll work?"

I followed him back to the car, hoping my gamble would pay off. We drove to a different part of town, to a restaurant called Pies and Stuff that Adrian and I used to frequent. Eddie and I waited there, neither of us speaking much as we munched on pie, both of us lost in our own thoughts. I knew Eddie was consumed by Jill and the three days. I was too. But I was also worried about Declan and Neil. I would've loved to go to Clarence's to check on the baby, but as long as the Alchemists were keeping watch there, I couldn't risk it.

When the hour deadline was up, I bought a souvenir for Adrian, for old times' sake, and then prepared to call Stanton again. Part of the reason I'd chosen Pies and Stuff was because they had a pay phone in their parking lot. "What'd you decide?" I asked when Stanton answered.

"We'll help you," she said grimly. "Your story checks out about those two. I've got a group going to St. George right now."

"Wow," I said, impressed in spite of myself. "You move fast. Do you know where to go in St. George?"

"We know about a Warrior camp there. We're going to scout it out and assess if it matches what you know."

"I've got records all about it that I can have sent to you," I told her. "The guardians—"

"Are also en route," she finished. "We've been in touch with them and will be coordinating our efforts to strike together to get the girl out. I expect it all to happen within the next day. I assume that's good enough for you."

"That's good enough for you to get the last two names," I replied. It was hard to keep my cool, considering how relieved I was to hear action was being taken for Jill. The fact that this was all finally happening—and so quickly—was exhilarating. "But if you want the rest of the information I have, you're going to have to work for it."

There was a long pause. Then: "What information would that be, exactly?"

"I have proof of other Warrior and Alchemist interactions, deals you probably don't know about. Deals I hope you don't know about." Stanton was a stickler for the rules, but I wanted to believe she was one of the better Alchemists. "I'll give you all that information too. *And* I'll make sure the Moroi don't know the dirt. You force them to put an awful lot of faith in your help . . . but I have a feeling they might not be so cooperative if they knew you've got people in the group working with the enemy."

"What do you want?" was all she asked. That told me a couple of things, most importantly that she knew it was very possible there were traitors in her midst.

"Amnesty for everyone we released from re-education. And an end to re-education, period."

There was a sharp intake of breath. "Impossible."

"What's the point of re-education, Stanton?" I demanded. "Half the time it doesn't work. There were people who'd been in there for ages. And even if it seems to work, you never really trust those people anyway. Like Keith. You're always watching. If you want to help protect humans from evil—the real evil, Strigoi—then there must be a better use of your resources."

"We can discuss this after we rescue Jill Dragomir," she said stiffly.

"No. We're discussing it now. Amnesty for everyone—including Adrian and me. When this is over, I want to go off with him, wherever we want, and live a normal life. I don't want to see Alchemists driving by or watching me in restaurants. I want to be left alone to pursue my own interests. In exchange, I will give you a copy of what I found on a very incriminating laptop owned by Master Angeletti of the Warriors. And I *won't* give a copy of that information to the Moroi—unless you violate the terms of this agreement."

Glancing up, I saw Eddie studying some posters on the door of Pies and Stuff, and I was glad he was out of earshot. He probably wouldn't like the idea of me withholding something that might be of interest to his people, but right now, I was negotiating for my life—and the lives of the other ex-Alchemists. I couldn't favor the Alchemists or the Moroi. I had to look out for everyone who'd simply been caught in the middle of their negotiations.

"I'll be honest," said Stanton at last. "Many questions have been raised internally about the usefulness of re-education—whether it's truly doing what we want. But I can't agree to your deal on my own. You should know that by now. I need to take it to the others. What I will promise you is amnesty for the rest of this endeavor in St. George. If you want to attend, you have my word you can without fear from the Alchemists. Then I'll let you know what the others have to say."

Something in Stanton's voice—as well as what I knew of her character—made me believe her. "Fair enough," I said. I tried to make my tone lofty, like I was doing her a great favor in making this concession, but in truth, I was anxious to get things under way.

It was time for us to bring Jill home.

CHAPTER 18

ADRIAN

"JUST LOOK AT HIM," I insisted. "Please."

"No," said Neil, turning away from the phone I held toward him. "If I look at him . . ." His voice choked, and he was unable to continue.

We were still at Maude's house, waiting for the next phase of action, and I was trying to get him to overcome the crazy idea that he needed to avoid Declan.

"Look," I said. "No one's going to think it's suspicious if you raise him. We all know you loved Olive. They'll think you're helping because of that—not because through some crazy twist of spirit, you two managed to change the world as we know it!"

Neil shook his head. "Hardly anyone even knows Olive had a baby. That's a good thing. You need to keep it that way—and keep me out of the picture."

We'd been over this a hundred times, and it was driving me crazy. If Neil had wanted to stay away from Declan, say, because he didn't like kids or was freaked out by fatherhood, I could've understood that more. But it was obvious Neil desperately wanted to see and be a part of Declan's life. I could hear the longing in his voice.

"We'll find a way," I said. "I swear it."

There was a haunted look on Neil's face. "Declan is a miracle," he murmured. "And he needs to be protected—and given a normal life. A happy, normal life."

"I want that too," I said wearily. "Believe me, I do."

"Adrian?" Maude's voice came through to where we were sitting on the back porch, enjoying the warm evening. "You have some guests."

In a flash, Neil and I were back inside, my heart racing. Sure enough, there was Sydney, standing in the living room and back to her normal appearance. I swept her into my arms, spinning her around so much that she laughed and told me to set her down before she got dizzy. I cupped her face in my hands.

"You're okay," I said happily.

She gave me a teasing punch. "You knew I was."

"A phone call is different from seeing," I said. I pressed a kiss to her forehead. "I mean, I knew you were competent and brave and awesome, but, well . . . it's still not easy having your wife off risking her life with a bunch of vampire-hating freaks." I reached into my pocket. "Oh, and don't forget this." I got down on my knees and slipped on her diamond and ruby rings, which I'd been holding on to while she was away. "As promised. I mean, except for the naked part. But we can worry about that later."

I expected a chastising "Adrian," but she smiled, her face filled with love and happiness. She took my hands and helped me up, looking as though she might even kiss me, until she remembered we had an audience. Flustered, she stepped back and crossed her arms in an attempt to look professional. Eddie and Marcus looked amused by all of this. Neil, oddly, looked intrigued as he glanced back and forth between Sydney and me.

"Time to get back to business," she said.

"It's happening," said Eddie eagerly. "We're getting Jill back."

"What's the plan?" I asked. Once I'd called and told Rose and Dimitri the information about Jill and the Alchemists, I'd lost track of what was happening. I knew Sydney had been part of the strategizing, though.

"The Alchemists have confirmed that the place they knew about in St. George is the same as the one in the records we had on the laptop. So they and the guardians are analyzing all the schematics to make sure they've got a solid course of action," Sydney explained.

I felt a bit of smugness at that. Alicia had been so cocky that we wouldn't be prepared to go for Jill, but she hadn't counted on Sydney's sleuthing. I was proud of myself for holding back in truly turning on the spirit. In fact, I'd been very cautious of it the last couple of days, and amazingly, Aunt Tatiana had stayed mostly quiet.

"We also currently have amnesty, so we can move around freely and go join them in St. George," Sydney said, nodding to me. "Not that you and I'll do much as far as action, but we can at least monitor things and be there when Jill's released. Neil, Eddie, and some of the others will be at the actual rescue."

"I look forward to it," said Neil, a dangerous edge in his voice. Eddie's fierce expression answered for him.

"We'll all get more details once we're in St. George," continued Sydney. "We can hit the road as soon as everyone's ready. It's about a six-hour drive, and we should end up there right about the time the raid is scheduled to happen."

"I'm ready to go any time," said Neil.

"Me too," I said. "Just give me two minutes to gather my things."

Sydney followed me to Maude's guest room and watched as I shoved my spare clothes and laptop into the tote bag I'd been hauling around on this adventure. "Rose called me," she said, shutting the door. "She and Dimitri wanted to see if it was okay for them to go to St. George—leaving your mom and Declan at Clarence's. I told them it was. I hope that's all right."

I paused, momentarily alarmed, then gave a slow nod. "Yeah, I think so. The Alchemists will have given up watching your hangouts, now that they know where you're headed. And really, as long as no one's looking for Declan . . ."

"That's what I thought too," agreed Sydney. "Though I could tell Rose was dying to know why we've been so secretive about him."

I slung my bag over my shoulder and put my free arm around her, noticing that she had a small bag tucked in the crook of her elbow. "I think we should tell them when this is over—and once we've figured things out with Neil. They're trustworthy . . . and they deserve to know. You know what it means for them."

"I do. Plus, whatever we end up doing to help Declan and Neil . . . well, I think we're going to need a few allies. They're good ones to have. I don't suppose Neil's changed his mind?"

"No," I said in exasperation. "He still keeps wanting to take the moral high ground, saying it's best for Declan."

"We'll talk him out of it," she said. "Once this is all over and Jill's back."

"Once Jill's back," I reiterated. The floodgate holding back all the emotions I felt about Jill threatened to burst. "God, I can't believe we're so close. It's been so long, and I've been so worried about her."

Sydney squeezed my hand. "I know, I know. And we're almost there."

"I wanted to rip Alicia apart," I admitted. "For what she'd done. I wanted to pulverize her with spirit."

"You didn't, did you?" asked Sydney, her eyes widening.

I exhaled. "No. I wanted to, but no. I kept it in check. I only used as much spirit as I needed. And I've been keeping it under control ever since."

The smile that lit Sydney's features warmed me all over. "I'm so proud of you, Adrian. I know it can't be easy."

"It's not," I admitted. "But I'm trying. And I think I can do it—I think I can control myself. I don't need the meds. I can just hold back on spirit."

Her smile faltered, like she might disagree, but then she surprised me by saying, "I'll support you and be there for you, whatever you choose to do, for the rest of our lives." She handed me the bag under her arm. "I got you a gift. Well, it's kind of for both of us."

I opened it up and found a coffee mug from Pies and Stuff. "Oh, man, I can't believe you went without me," I teased.

"This is for us," she said. "The first thing to put in our new home together. I'm working out something with Stanton to buy our freedom. When this is all over, we're going to have a life together, Adrian. A real one."

Love for her threatened to overwhelm me. I set down all my bags and drew her into my arms. That silly mug suddenly took on monumental significance, and looking down at her, at the face I loved so much, I could see the future she described, a future together where we could accomplish anything. Going back on meds seemed a small price for that. I didn't need spirit so long as I had Sydney.

I pressed her gently against the door and kissed her, allowing myself to briefly forget everything waiting for us outside this room. For now, there was just the two of us and this one perfect moment of togetherness.

"You make me believe anything is possible," I whispered.

"I told you before, we're the center," she said. "And the center will hold."

I kissed her again, more deeply, and it was with great reluctance that we finally had to draw apart again. "I'm all for a real home," I said, brushing hair from her face, "but before that, can we *please* have a real honeymoon?"

"Gladly," she murmured, kissing me one more time. "As soon as we have Jill, everything's going to change."

I held her tightly. "Then by God, let's go get Jill."

The four of us hit the road to St. George, driving overnight to get there in time. We tried to take turns and get rest, but it was hard. Honestly, by this point, I felt like schedules and "daytime hours" were just suggestions in my life. I was happy to be with Sydney again, and she and I found ourselves catching up on what we'd missed during our time apart. She wouldn't elaborate on what deal she was attempting with Stanton, but she spoke confidently about that future home we both wanted so much.

We made good time, arriving at the Alchemists' and guardians' makeshift command center just before dawn. And as much as I hated to admit it, the Alchemists proved useful. In less than a day, they'd found a vacant office building and filled it with Alchemists and computers. They had cameras and satellite info on the Warriors' compound, as well as scouts already in place on-site, reporting back with information on the Warriors' state of affairs and security measures.

A gruff guy named McLean was in charge of the Alchemists' soldiers, and he and Dimitri—who'd gotten there a few hours ago—were working surprisingly well together organizing the attack. Everyone assured us it would be simple, relatively speaking. Our forces outnumbered the Warriors'. If the initial raid came on strong, without warning, there should be no reason we wouldn't triumph. Sydney and I exchanged uneasy glances, knowing things were rarely as easy as they seemed, but we tried to be optimistic. We hoped this would be simple. We needed it to be, and we sent Dimitri, Rose, Eddie, and Neil off in high spirits, leaving us nothing to do but wait around for updates.

It felt strange for me, though, not to be out there. I'd spent so much of the last month worried for Jill but unable to act while trapped at Court. Then, when we'd gotten our lead on Alicia, I'd had to stay behind at first in order to cover for Sydney. Now, finally, we knew where Jill was, and I was staying behind again. It was maddening. Ever since I'd brought Jill back from the assassination attempt, I'd felt as though her life were in my hands. Even though I knew a compound of armed fanatics was best breached by trained guardians and Alchemists, I couldn't shake the feeling I should be out there.

"It's okay," Sydney said gently, coming to rest a hand on my arm. "I feel useless too, but they're the experts. And once they get her out, we'll be among the first to see her."

"I know," I said. I slipped an arm around her. "Patience just isn't always one of my better traits."

As I was speaking, Sydney's gaze wandered to something behind me, and I turned to look. It was her father and Zoe, entering the command center. They too froze for a moment, and then Zoe took a few steps forward, her face breaking into a smile, until a sharp rebuke from her father drew her up short.

"Zoe," he barked.

"My own sister can't come see me, Dad?" Sydney asked. "Afraid I'll taint her?"

He flushed. "I heard you cut some kind of deal with Stanton. It wouldn't have happened if I were in charge."

"How are you, Zoe?" Sydney asked, directing her attention to the youngest Sage sister. "You okay?"

Zoe cast an uncertain look at her father and then gave a slow nod. "Yeah. You?"

"Come along," ordered their father. "Let's see how this operation is progressing."

Zoe gave Sydney one last glance and then reluctantly followed Jared Sage to where some Alchemists were monitoring communications from the team raiding the Warriors' compound. Sydney broke from me and went after them. "I want an update too," she said. But when she reached the group huddled around the two people in charge of communications, Sydney waited until her father was distracted, asking someone a question. She touched Zoe's sleeve and gently drew her back a few steps toward us.

"I never thanked you for not reporting me, back in the Ozarks," said Sydney softly.

Zoe shook her head but kept an anxious eye on their dad. "It's the least I could do. Sydney, if I'd had any idea what you had to go through there, I never would've turned you in. I thought they were going to help you. Honestly." Tears brimmed in her eyes.

"How do you know what happened there?" I asked. Last I knew, the full details of what detainees in re-education endured wasn't widely known.

Zoe didn't answer right away, and from the uneasy way she regarded me, it was clear she hadn't quite come to terms with a vampire brother-in-law. "Carly told me," she said at last. "She heard it from some guy who helped you out. I think she's dating him?"

Sydney and I exchanged surprised looks. "Marcus?" we asked in unison.

"Yeah," said Zoe. "I think that's his name."

"That sly dog," I muttered. It had been apparent when he and Carly met that he had a crush on Sydney's older sister, but I'd had no idea he'd pursued her.

"I'm glad you're talking to Carly," said Sydney. "Do you ever talk to Mom?"

Zoe shook her head. "No. I wish I could, but Dad won't let me. And he made sure the terms of the divorce were pretty absolute."

There was a misery in her voice that both Sydney and I picked up on. "Do you want out?" Sydney asked urgently. "Do you want to be free of them?"

"Not yet," said Zoe. Seeing Sydney's skeptical look, she

continued: "No, I'm serious. That's not fear talking. I still believe in the cause . . . but I'm not always happy about some of the methods. That doesn't mean I'm ready to give up. I want to keep learning and working with them . . . and then, who knows?" Her face fell a little. "I wouldn't mind seeing Mom again, though."

"Zoe!" thundered Jared. He'd just noticed her talking to us. "Get over here and—"

"I'm getting a report in," exclaimed the Alchemist on communication. She was sitting beside a guardian who was sharing the monitoring duty. They were both in headphones, with laptops in front of them, and he gave a nod of agreement. "Both teams are in—but there are apparently mines on the property."

Sydney clenched my hand, and a terrible silence descended on all of us as we waited for more. Alicia's face came to mind, taunting that we'd never get through to Jill.

"Mines have been bypassed," the guardian said several minutes later. We all exhaled in relief, only to tense up once more. "They're engaging the enemy combatants now."

Even with the headphones' dampening, I could hear the crackle of urgent dispatches from those raiding the compound, as well as what sounded like gunshots. Sydney leaned against me again, one of her hands resting on the little wooden cross necklace I'd painted for her long ago. Minutes felt like hours, and through it all, I just kept thinking, *I should be there, I should be there*.

Why? sneered Aunt Tatiana. *What good would you be without spirit? Your wife wouldn't let you use it there, remember?*

A grin suddenly broke over the guardian's face as he

listened to the latest message. "They're in. The upper levels of the compound have been seized. All combatants detained." He paused as more information came in. "No casualties on our side." In a surprising moment of solidarity, he and the Alchemist high-fived, but I couldn't share their joy, not yet.

"Do they have Jill?" I demanded. "Do they have the princess yet?"

The guardian shook his head. "They're going for her now. She's being held in the basement, but they did some heat sensing, and there's only one person there. All evidence points to a Moroi of her size."

I drew Sydney to me in a crushing embrace, burying my face against her hair. "It's over. It's finally over." I wasn't one for tears, but I felt them coming to my eyes at the thought I'd soon be reunited with Jill.

"I— Yes. What's that?"

I turned to the Alchemist in headphones and realized he was talking to someone on the other end, not to us. A frown creased his features, and then he looked up at us. "Someone wants to speak to you, Mrs. Ivashkov."

Out of the corner of my eye, I saw Sydney's father glare at the name.

"Me?" Sydney asked, accepting the headphones handed over to her. She put them on and sat on the chair, joining a conversation we could only hear half of. "What do you mean? I see . . . are there any markings? Any objects? Okay . . . no, you could be right. Just wait . . . I'll come. Yes."

She stood up and took the headphones off. "What's going on?" I asked.

"That was Eddie," she said. "He was with the group about

to raid the basement, but then, at the last minute, he made them stop at the entrance."

"Why?" asked Zoe.

Sydney met my eyes. "He said it smelled like Ms. Terwilliger's house."

For a minute, I thought she was suggesting Jackie was there, and then I caught on to the inference he'd made. "You think there's some kind of magic use going on down there?"

"Alicia was the one who caught Jill for them," Sydney remarked. "It's possible she left some kind of trap in place. It would also explain why there were no Warriors on guard down there."

"Probably because they all ran up to fight in the initial assault," her dad said.

Alicia's words echoed back to me: *You'll never get to her! You'll never get through to her!* A feeling of dread settled into my stomach. "No, there's something there."

"They've suspended things until I can get out there to look," said Sydney. Her eyes met mine. "You coming with me?"

There was no need to ask, and we both knew it. A guardian drove us out to the site, which was outside of the city proper. No surprise there, as fanatics tended not to build their strongholds in civilized areas full of other people who might call the police. Desert terrain dominated, albeit in a different way from Palm Springs. The rocks and ground were a red that looked striking in the setting sun, with little patches of scrubby vegetation here and there. The compound itself was a wide, one-story building surrounded by barbed wire. Alchemists and guardians patrolled the area side by side, and I could see where they had rounded up and contained the enemy Warriors. Dimitri met us as we got out of the car.

"This way," he said, gesturing forward. "We think there are still mines in the area. I'll take you on a path I know is safe."

We followed him over the rocky ground, into the enclosure, past the glaring prisoners. The building itself was as stark as a military barracks, and as far as I could tell, it had served no purpose except to hold prisoners and as a hangout to discuss crazed anti-vampire schemes. It chilled me seeing it all.

A stairwell in the center of the building led downstairs to an underground level, and there, we saw Eddie, Neil, and Rose waiting at the bottom. Sydney and I followed the stairs down and found ourselves standing in a long concrete corridor that stretched off into darkness. A few doors could be seen branching off, but I had no idea what was beyond them. Beside me, Sydney winced.

"Reminds me of a primitive version of some of the re-education levels," she murmured, shuddering.

Thinking back to when I helped rescue her, I could understand what she meant. That facility had also contained vast halls with mysterious doors, though it had had a much more clinical feel to it. It had all been sterile and lit with stark fluorescent lighting. This, meanwhile, was more like a dirty, medieval dungeon in the wilds of Utah. It made me sick to think of Jill being inside.

"We think Jill's just down there," said Rose. "That's what the Alchemists' equipment detected. I want to go in and get her, but Eddie . . ." It was clear she didn't share his fears.

He looked a little embarrassed but held his ground. "I just can't shake the feeling something's off here. Why not have guards on their most valuable prisoner? And do you smell that?"

Sydney nodded, and I had to agree. "It does smell like Jackie's house," I remarked.

"Someone's burned incense here," said Sydney. "Though it's not something you'd see Ms. Terwilliger using very much. Vetiver. Black lotus." She frowned and scanned around. "There. There are some ashes down the hall. That's where it was burned."

I started to investigate, but she held me back.

"Wait," she said. She held up her hand and spoke words in a language I didn't know. After several seconds, glowing symbols appeared in the ceiling above where the ashes were. Sydney studied them intently until they faded away, and then she exhaled in dismay. "Damn."

I rarely heard her swear and didn't think that boded well.

"What is it?" I asked.

"There's a demon here," she replied in a tone that was far too casual for that kind of pronouncement. "It looks like Alicia summoned one to stand guard."

"Hopper's technically a demon," I offered.

Her face was grim. "Not that kind, I'm afraid. This is a senicus." Seeing our blank looks, she asked, "Have you ever heard of a hydra in Greek mythology? It's kind of like that. Kind of. Serpentine, lots of heads. But these heads spit boiling acid."

I'd taken Greek mythology in high school and actually paid attention to it. "Do the heads grow back too?" I asked.

"Not if you destroy them with fire," she said.

"Do we need a flamethrower?" asked Neil.

Sydney held out her palm, and a ball of flame appeared. "No need."

Rose's eyes widened in wonder. "Whoa. Will blades still hurt this thing?"

"No," said Sydney. "It has a magical hide that'll protect it. I'm the only one who can really take this thing out. What you guys need to do is get Jill out of here while I distract it. Someone needs to sneak past it while it's engaged. Fire's the only way to destroy this thing, and I don't want Jill trapped here if things literally go up in smoke."

Once again, I was feeling useless. Sydney might be a pro at wielding fireballs, but that didn't mean I wanted her taking on this hydra-demon-thing alone. "What should I do?"

"Nothing," she said. "Get out of here."

She thinks you're incompetent! hissed Aunt Tatiana. *She thinks you'll be in the way.*

"Sydney, let me help," I insisted.

Sydney's eyes weren't even on me as she scrutinized the corridor, probably gauging the range of her fireballs and how flammable the whole thing was. "Adrian, there's nothing you can do here. Stay safe in case Jill needs help when she gets out."

Do you hear that? asked Aunt Tatiana. *She doesn't think you're capable of anything!*

My temper started to flare, and I nearly agreed with Aunt Tatiana until I took a moment to mentally replay what Sydney had said. *No, she's right*, I told the phantom in my head. *If Jill's injured, I need to conserve my power. No repeats of Olive.*

Aunt Tatiana disagreed. *You don't need to conserve! You can do it all!*

Trying to shut out that internal voice, I kissed Sydney and drew her into a brief embrace. "Be careful," I murmured. "And if you do need me, I'll be close by."

"Not too close," she warned. "This thing spits acid. I can't have you injured."

"Understood," I said, before Aunt Tatiana could raise a protest about how Sydney was coddling me.

I took up a position on the staircase, allowing me a quick escape if need be but also giving me a good vantage on the action about to take place. I hadn't argued with Sydney, but Jill's health wasn't the only thing I was concerned about. Along with Sydney, the dhampirs were putting themselves at risk. I wanted to be on hand in case any of them were injured in this escapade. After a heated argument, the three of them decided on a plan. Eddie and Neil would wait with me as backup while Rose slipped into the corridor alone. Each of the guys wanted to go, but she pointed out that she was smaller and faster. She also argued that all of them, plus Jill, trying to get back past the demon would make for tight quarters. It was hard for the guys to fault her logic, and Sydney concurred that with fireballs flying, it'd be easier for her to have fewer people to worry about.

So Eddie and Neil reluctantly came to wait by me, and Rose hovered just behind Sydney. "Time to summon it," said Sydney nervously. "It'd come on its own if I crossed those runes, but I'd rather bring it out on my own terms." She held up her hands and spoke an incantation that once again made the markings in the ceiling glow. Only this time, a creature materialized below it.

I understood then why a hydra had been her closest comparison. From the waist down, the demon walked on two legs just like we did—albeit with scaly skin and talons in its feet. From the waist up, it had several sinuous tentacles extending from its torso, as well as five snakelike necks and heads. All of them were hissing and glaring at Sydney. I felt fear churn in my own stomach at the sight of it and almost wished for the time when the only monsters I knew about in this world were Strigoi. Despite the terror that thing inspired, I still felt an overwhelmingly protective urge to help Sydney. It wouldn't matter if my own life was at risk. I'd gladly sacrifice it for hers.

Do it! Do it! exclaimed Aunt Tatiana. *Throw something at it!*

"There's nothing to throw," I said. "And Sydney's got this."

"Hmm?" asked Eddie.

I'd spoken out loud again and shook my head. "Nothing."

Sydney held her ground, staring down the snake-demon in front of her as though she did this every day and hadn't unexpectedly walked into one's lair now. A fireball came easily to her fingertips, and she hurled it without preamble at one of the serpentine heads. Her aim was good—except that the snake was just too fast. In the blink of an eye it had swerved its head and dodged. One of the other heads spit a glob of bright green goo that landed on the concrete floor and began eating away at the surface. I didn't want to think about what that stuff would do to flesh.

Sydney threw and missed again, but her gaze remained steely. "I'll get a hit in eventually," I heard her tell Rose. "And that's when you make your move."

Rose was braced beside her, ready to pounce. The two of them made a striking combo, one dark and one golden, both utterly fearless in the face of this danger. They were beautiful in their deadliness.

Sydney's next fireball struck a head. The creature reared back in pain, all of its surviving heads screaming. Rose used that as her chance, sprinting past the creature and keeping to the opposite side of the cement corridor. The demon still noticed her and started to turn, but a direct fireball hit drew its angry attention back to Sydney. Some of its tentacles were short and stubby, but a few were quite long and occasionally made dangerous grabs for her—meaning she had to dodge both those attacks and the acid. She managed it more deftly than I could have, evading the strikes with a skill Wolfe would have applauded.

"Too close," muttered Neil, after Sydney just barely sidestepped some acid.

"She's got this," I said. And as though on cue, another fireball blasted into one of the snake heads, leaving a charred husk behind.

"What's taking Rose so long?" demanded Eddie.

I didn't have an answer for that. She'd disappeared into the darkness, and none of us knew what was beyond that. She could have twenty doors to look in. Or maybe they were locked. Or Jill could be tied up or in chains. None of us knew for sure, and that uncertainty was hard on the rest of us.

Sydney had just annihilated a third snake head when I heard Eddie give a sharp intake of breath. In the shadows beyond the creature, I could just make out Rose, with another figure leaning heavily on her for support. The other person's face was buried on Rose's shoulder, but there was no mistaking the tangle of long, light brown hair. My heart jumped to my throat.

Jill.

Rose was obviously waiting for an opening to get back through, and a shift in Sydney's stance told me she'd seen them behind the demon. She threw a fireball wide, one that wasn't specifically aimed at a head but which forced the creature to rear toward the side of the corridor. Rose recognized her opportunity and hurried forward, half dragging Jill along the way. A cluster of tentacles made contact with Rose's leg, and

I stopped breathing—but then a rapid and well-placed fireball took out a fourth head. The creature let go and turned its wrath on Sydney as Rose broke through and got Jill to the stairs.

In a flash, Eddie and Neil were at her side, helping Rose bring her up. My stomach twisted as I took in the sight of Jill, and I had an unwelcome sense of déjà vu back to the time when we'd finally found Sydney in the depths of the re-education center. Jill's condition was similar. She'd lost a considerable amount of weight, and her skin was pale, even by Moroi standards. She was in dirty, rumpled pajamas—what she'd been kidnapped in, no doubt—and it looked as though they hadn't really let her bathe either. Her pupils were slightly dilated, which confirmed they'd given her some kind of drug that had interfered with me reaching her in dreams.

"Are you okay?" I asked. I drew spirit into me, prepared to heal her.

"N-no, don't do it," she warned. Even drugged, the bond must have still been working. That, or she simply knew me well enough by now to guess what I'd do. It took her a few seconds to form the rest of her words. "I . . . I'm just weak. Hungry. They gave me animal blood."

My stomach turned at that. Moroi could survive on animal blood, but "survive" was about the kindest way you could put it. We'd stay alive but lose a lot of strength and energy. There were always stories that popped up once in a while about some Moroi family that got trapped without a feeder for a week or so and had to feed off animals. They'd emerge weak and debilitated, making for sensational headlines in Moroi news. I couldn't even imagine what shape Jill must be in after a month of that. It explained why she could barely stand.

Still, the instinct was there to help her anyway, to give her a boost with spirit. "No," she said sharply, again anticipating me. "Just get me to a feeder. And get someone out to the back of this property. There's a shed there with another basement prison."

"I'll take her to a feeder," said Eddie, starting to move her up the stairs. Rose helped by supporting Jill's other side.

"I'll go find the other Moroi," said Neil, starting to move ahead of them. He paused and glanced back at Sydney. "Unless you need me?"

I shook my head. "I'll get her out of here. Go help the others."

The dhampirs and Jill disappeared, leaving me alone to look after Sydney. That snake demon was down to one head, but I noticed now that there was smoke in the corridor. One of her fireballs must have hit a door and found something to ignite.

"We need to get out of here," I yelled to her. "That fire might spread. Jill's safe."

"I'm not leaving this guy to run rampant!" Sydney shouted back. A well-placed fireball nearly took out the remaining head, but the creature dodged at the last second, missing the hit by barely an inch. It roared in fury, and one of its tentacles shot out more quickly than Sydney could anticipate. It caught her by her feet, knocking her to the ground, and with equal speed, the demon hurried over, its last head rearing up in triumph as it prepared to drench her in acid.

Do something! Do something! Aunt Tatiana screamed at me.

But there was nothing to telekinetically throw, no plants to summon like Sonya might do. This was the waking world, not a dream. Spirit was not a combat magic, but in the space of a heartbeat, I still knew I had to act. Sydney—my heart, my love, and my wife—was seconds away from death. I would have gladly thrown my body in front of hers, but there was no time for that either. I had only a millisecond to decide, so I pulled out my last spirit trick.

"Stop!" I ordered.

Spirit burned through me, and I sent a wave of compulsion into the demon, attempting to bend its will to mine. I'd never done anything like that. I didn't even know if it could be done. The creature actually paused, however, making me think it had both sentience and the ability to be controlled. Emphasis on *ability*. Because even though the creature momentarily restrained itself, I could feel my hold slipping, and it snarled again, ready to strike Sydney. The more strong-willed a person was, the harder it was to compel them. Demons must be in an entirely different class, because I was already amped up on spirit and was just barely having an effect.

More, more! said Aunt Tatiana.

I drew on greater reserves of spirit, pulling everything out of me, all my energy and life, all my resolve. It was more than I'd used in the dream with Olive, nearly as much as I'd used to bring back Jill. Spirit filled every part of me, making me greater than I'd ever thought I could be, nearly godlike. I turned that power on the demon, exerting my control as I issued my commands: "Let her go! Back up!"

The demon obeyed.

Its tentacles released Sydney, who scrambled away and got to her feet. Fire filled her palms, and with the demon in my thrall, it made an easy target for her to finish the last head. Once that one was destroyed, the rest of the creature's body disintegrated into a fine black dust. Spirit still burned brightly within me, though, making me feel exhilarated and unstoppable. Sydney hurried to my side and shook my arm.

"Adrian, let it go," she said. "It's done. You did it. Release the magic!"

No one has ever possessed power like this, Aunt Tatiana told me. *Can you feel it? Don't you feel alive? Why would you ever want to let this go?*

She was right. With this kind of power, I could do great things. Strigoi, the Warriors, even demons: None of our enemies stood a chance. We didn't need silver stakes or Sonya's vaccine. I could do it all. I would save our people singlehandedly.

"Adrian, Adrian!"

For a moment, I didn't know whom the voice belonged to. I was too lost in my power, power that was burning me up. A face moved into my smoky vision, a human with blond hair and brown eyes, but I didn't know her either.

"Adrian," she cried again. "Let it go. Please. Release the magic—for me."

For me, she'd said.

But who was she? Then, at last, the intoxication of spirit faded enough for me to know. Sydney. Sydney, my wife. She was the one looking into my face, looking so completely terrified.

Ignore her, said Aunt Tatiana. *This is the magic you were born to wield!*

Sydney squeezed my hand. "Adrian, please. Release the magic."

I could feel spirit starting to obscure my mind again, starting to blot Sydney out, starting to destroy all of my higher reasoning, just as it had Nina's. I wanted to let go, but it was hard when that power gave me such a heady, glorious feeling.

You are a god, Aunt Tatiana told me. *I'm so proud of you.*

"Adrian," said Sydney. "I love you."

Those words, that voice, had more power over me than any phantom ever could. And then, just before spirit could blot her away again, I let go of the magic.

CHAPTER 19

SYDNEY

I KNEW WHEN IT HAPPENED. I saw it in his eyes, a sudden coming back to himself. At least I hoped he was coming back to himself. I had no idea what kind of power he'd used to command an otherworldly demon, but I knew what massive amounts of spirit did to those who wielded it.

"Sydney," he gasped out, sagging into me.

I nearly wept in relief. "Yes. Come on, let's go."

The door I'd accidentally hit was burning merrily now, and I didn't know how these lower rooms connected to the main floor. I didn't want to risk everything collapsing down around us. Adrian seemed a little addled, and I had to guide him to the stairs. A panicked part of me kept thinking back to what he'd told me about Nina, how spirit had left her incoherent. *He knew me*, I told myself. *He knew me*. As long as we had that, I had to believe everything would be okay.

We made it upstairs, where a cluster of guardians anxiously waited at the stairwell's entrance. They'd been under strict orders not to interfere, but it was clear that went against their natures.

"Get everyone out of here," I said to the guardian closest to me. "There's a fire down there, and I don't know how far it's spread. And make sure there are no weapons left up here." These were the Warriors, after all. I didn't want a new disaster brought on because of explosives accidentally igniting.

Adrian and I made it outside, and I guided him past the busy guardians and Alchemists, as well as the Warrior prisoners. Out near where we'd parked, I caught sight of some familiar faces and made them our destination. Rose, Dimitri, and Eddie stood by Jill, who was sitting in a folding chair next to another chair. That chair's occupant was starting to get up and be led away by a guardian, and I recognized the vacant expression of a feeder.

"Wait," I called. "Adrian needs blood too."

Jill leapt to her feet, still looking weary and bedraggled, but with much more life and color in her face than when I'd seen her in the basement. Despite everything she'd just been through, she hurried forward to help Adrian sit. I didn't know if he actually needed blood, but he'd just been through a big ordeal of his own, and blood usually had a curative effect on Moroi. He hadn't said a word to me since my name earlier, and I couldn't shake the panic that spirit might have finally claimed him for good. The feeder offered his neck, and Adrian automatically leaned over and bit down. I looked away, not sure I'd ever be entirely comfortable with this part of vampiric life.

"He's in there," said Jill, holding my hand, her green eyes looking even wider than usual with her face so gaunt. "He'll be okay."

I nodded and tried to hold back tears. "You should be

resting," I told her. My heart was tied up with Adrian, but it hit me then just how much she'd endured. The fact that she could stand here and be concerned for someone else was a testament to her strength. "Oh, God, Jill. I can't even imagine what you must have gone through. I'm so sorry we couldn't get to you sooner. Did they hurt you?"

She shook her head and managed a weak smile, though I could see the anguish in her eyes. "Most were too nervous to be around me that long. Alicia had some kind of time conditions set on that spell . . . with that creature. There was a short period each day, around sunrise, when someone could come into my cell, drug me, leave food and blood, and then get out. They never stayed long—I think they were too afraid of being trapped in there with me."

"I'm so sorry," I said again. "I wish we could have saved you sooner."

Jill hugged me. "I know you were trying. I was able to see a lot through the bond and—"

"Jailbait?"

The feeder was stepping away, and Adrian was looking in our direction, his expression alert and clear. Jill cried out and ran into his arms, tears shining on her face. My own tears fell then, unable to stop themselves in the wake of this reunion.

"You're okay," he breathed, cupping her face. "You're okay. I was so worried. You have no idea. I thought I'd failed you—"

Jill began to cry harder. "You've never failed me. Never."

I wanted to throw myself in Adrian's arms as well but waited so that they could have this moment. The love Adrian and I shared was powerful, and I knew it would sustain us for the rest of our lives, no matter what was to come. But the love he and Jill shared, this sibling-like affection born from spirit, was powerful too. I knew how it had eaten him up to be away from her.

The sound of a car door caught my attention. I looked over to the other side of the makeshift parking lot just in time to see my father and Zoe getting out of a car—with Stanton. After a quick glance to ascertain Adrian and Jill were fine without me, I walked over to intercept the Alchemists.

"Sydney," said Stanton, by way of greeting. "It seems everything's worked out in this operation of yours. I presume you'll give me those other two names?"

"Charlene Hampton and Eugene Li," I said promptly.

Stanton repeated them to herself and immediately reached for her cell phone. "Very good. I'll see to it they're looked into."

"What about the rest of our deal?" I demanded.

"Not much time has passed," she reminded me. "But I was able to get an intermediary decision—for you. The other Alchemist leaders have agreed to leave you alone. You and your, uh, husband may go off into the world and do whatever it is you plan on doing." A small frown in her otherwise proper delivery was the only indication of how distasteful she found that prospect.

"You mean it?" I asked. "Adrian and I are free? No one spying on us or looking over our shoulder?" My dad's jaw dropped.

"As free as anyone is in this world," she said ruefully. "Honestly, I think it was a relief to some of them. You're an awful lot of trouble, Sydney Ivashkov."

I couldn't help but smile. "And what about the others? The other detainees?"

"Amnesty for them as well—if you turn over the information," she added. "I can't make any guarantees about the future of re-education. That's a more complex issue."

It didn't seem that complex to me, but freedom for me and the others who'd suffered through re-education was a huge boon—if the Alchemists held true to it.

"I meant what I said about my questions concerning the re-education issue," Stanton told me. "It is one I plan on pursuing. We do need to have disciplinary systems in place—like in the case of the tattoo emergence—but obviously, there are lines we might be able to better redefine."

"Thank you, ma'am," I said. Again, I hoped I was right in my read of her, that she was telling the truth. "I'll have the laptop's contents sent to you."

"Excellent. Now excuse me a moment while I deal with Ms. Hampton and Mr. Li." She dialed a number on her cell phone and strolled away, leaving me in a slightly awkward situation with my dad and Zoe.

"I don't know what you've pulled over her," my dad growled. "But there's no way the Alchemists are going to let you just get away with this abomination of a life. Some might think it's okay, but others won't."

"That's true," I said. "But Stanton clearly thinks it's okay. And I firmly believe people like her will make a strong enough argument to ease up on me and some of the others who no longer want to be part of the Alchemists. In fact, you're going to help her make that case."

Fury sparked in his eyes. "Never."

"Because here's the thing, Dad," I told him, continuing as though he hadn't spoken, "I got Stanton to help with this rescue by giving her four names of people who were working with the

Warriors to make more of those illicit tattoos. I gave her four—but I had five. And I think you know who the fifth was."

"I have no idea," he said immediately.

Zoe gave him a shocked look. "What? You didn't—you couldn't have—"

"The proof is there," I said. "The laptop we recovered has records of meetings and orders you made with some of the Warriors. Now, if you're lucky, the Alchemists who were already busted won't turn you in to try to save themselves. And if you're cooperative, *I* won't turn you in either."

"Cooperative," he scoffed. "What does that mean to someone like you? Someone who's thrown away all the moral lessons you were raised with—"

"It means," I interrupted, "that you're going to support Stanton in revising re-education and holding to this deal with me. And it also means you're going to restructure the custody arrangement so that Zoe gets to see Mom."

My dad clenched his hands into fists. "You've no right to dictate any of this! I won't go along with this blackmail."

"Fine," I said. "Then I'll go tell Stanton there's one more person she needs brought in. And don't forget, even if they get rid of re-education, she *did* say they'd still need disciplinary measures in place for instances like this."

"Dad, how could you?" exclaimed Zoe. "You know how many people those tattoos hurt!"

"You don't understand," he said. "It's the Warriors who'd be getting them. It doesn't matter what happens to them."

I nodded with mock solemnity. "I'm sure that hypocritical argument will hold up well with Stanton. The Alchemists *love* gray areas. They certainly prefer that to black and white."

"Sydney?" I heard Adrian call. I turned and gave him a quick wave before turning back to my dad and Zoe.

"Those are my terms. Comply, and I'll make sure there's no mention of your name when I turn the info over to Stanton. And if not . . ." I left it hanging, letting my father's imagination do the work for him. As he stood there in shock, I gave Zoe a fast hug. "Good seeing you. Get a message to me if he doesn't let you see Mom—though I'll probably find out before then."

Leaving them, I went back over to where my friends were. Only Dimitri and Neil were missing. Adrian intercepted me, sweeping me into his arms. "Sydney," he breathed into my ear. "I'm so sorry I lost it down there."

"You didn't lose anything," I said fiercely, wrapping my arms around his neck. "You held it together. You brought yourself back and did the right thing."

"I didn't feel like I had it together," he said softly, holding my gaze. "There was a minute there—I didn't know you—I didn't know anything, except how the power felt. And Aunt Tatiana was there, screaming in my head. She's still there, even while I'm talking to you. I think . . ." He took a deep breath. "I think I'm definitely ready to go back on my meds. I don't know what'll happen if a time comes when I need spirit and can't use it . . . but there's no way I can risk losing myself like I almost did today. I can't be like Nina. Like Avery."

I buried my face into his chest. "You won't be. You already have proven you aren't. You stepped back when they couldn't. And whatever happens, you won't have to face it alone. I'll help you." Tears came to my eyes again, and this time, they were tears of happiness. "I think we did it—I think we might be free of the Alchemists. I've been wheeling and dealing, and . . . well,

I don't know if it'll work, but it looks like it might. And . . ." I started laughing, realizing I was babbling. "I don't know what's coming next, but I do know we'll be together."

Adrian caught my left hand with his, letting our wedding rings shine together in a glittering display of rubies and diamonds. "That's all that matters, Sage-Ivashkov. Well, that and me having to put the smackdown on Castile if he doesn't finally get his act together with Jill."

I turned to where Eddie was sitting with Jill, holding her hand and speaking earnestly. I laughed again. "I think you'd lose in a smackdown with him, no offense. But fortunately, I think he's finally coming around."

I watched Eddie and Jill a few more moments, unable to hear what they were saying. From her shining face, it was good news. She touched his unshaven face and smiled, apparently liking the scruffiness Adrian always teased him about. Leaning into Adrian, I sighed happily, feeling at peace with the world for the first time in a very long time. We sat there, holding each other, for several peaceful minutes until we saw Dimitri approaching.

"Any news?" I asked, lifting my head.

"Take that feeder," Dimitri told another guardian walking behind him. The man hurried to obey. "We found more Moroi."

"The others being held," said Jill. She glanced between Rose and Eddie. "I told you guys about them. Are they okay?"

"Yes," said Dimitri. "Malnourished, like you. But they'll be all right. Neil played a huge role in rescuing them. They were in a very difficult, almost cavern-like prison that required a fair amount of climbing."

"Neil's a good guy like that," Adrian said. "Where is he?"

Dimitri looked perplexed. "I actually thought he was coming back here." He touched his earpiece. "Does anyone have a visual on Neil Raymond?" We all watched in silence as Dimitri waited for a response. At last, he shook his head. "No one's seen him."

Adrian and I exchanged glances, the same thought hitting us. "Get everyone looking for him," Adrian said. "Now. If you don't find him right away, I have a feeling you won't ever."

Dimitri looked astonished by that declaration but nonetheless ordered a camp-wide search for Neil. Eddie looked both concerned and confused. "Do you think he's hurt? Or captured?"

I shook my head. "I think he saw an opportunity. And we have to stop him."

But we were too late, and after an hour, nothing came back from Dimitri's searches. Neil had performed his heroics and then disappeared.

"He knew," Adrian said. "He knew that as soon as this was over, I was going to start a hard sell on Declan. This is my fault."

"What are you talking about?" asked Rose. She could tell something was afoot and had been waiting not so patiently during the search. "Is Declan okay?"

"He's fine," Adrian said, but again we exchanged looks, neither of us able to give voice to our fears. If we'd lost Neil, what was going to happen to Declan? Adrian shook his head. "I'll find Neil in a dream."

"Adrian," I warned. "You just said—"

"I know, I know," he said with a groan. "But we have to find Neil. You know why."

Here it was, spirit threatening us again. "Even if you find

him in the dream world, that's no guarantee he'll come back to us in the waking one," I reminded Adrian.

"Will someone please tell me what's going on?" asked Eddie. "Why wouldn't Neil come back?"

I laced my fingers with Adrian's. "Let's just get back to Declan. Then we'll figure out what to do about Neil."

Even though they didn't know the whole story, Rose, Dimitri, and Eddie wanted to go back to Clarence's with Adrian and me in the hopes of tracking down Neil. Jill wanted to as well, but she was taken away to Court, both to be under Lissa's protection and to receive further medical treatment. I could tell it was agonizing for Eddie to part with her, but Neil was his friend, and they'd saved each other's lives more than once. I pretended not to see as Eddie kissed Jill goodbye and promised to see her soon.

Back at Clarence's, we found things as we'd left them. Clarence was resting in his room, and Daniella was in the living room, going on about how Declan needed pajamas made of organic cotton rather than "God-knows-what" kind of cotton. She told us, much to our complete astonishment, that Neil had been by.

"What?" exclaimed Adrian.

"Just this morning," she said. "Came by and held the baby for a while. Didn't say much. Then he was on his way. I thought you knew."

I had picked up Declan and was cradling him in my arms, surprised that I'd missed his warmth and, for lack of a better term, baby scent. Adrian stood by me and shared my surprise. "We had no idea," he said.

"He left this," Daniella added. She handed over a sealed

envelope that Adrian tore into immediately. Inside was a handwritten letter that Adrian opened so that we both could read it.

Adrian and Sydney,

I know each of you have your own ways of figuring out where I am. If that's the course of action you choose to take, nothing I do can stop you. But, I'm begging you, please don't. Please let me stay away. Let the guardians think I've gone AWOL. Let me wander the world, helping those I can.

I know you think I should stay with Declan. Believe me, I wish I could. I wish more than anything that I could stay and raise Olive's son—my son—and give him all the things he needs. But I can't shake the feeling that we'd never be safe. Someday, someone might start asking about Olive and her son. Someone might connect the baby I'm raising to him, and then her fears would be realized. News of his conception would change our world. It would excite some people and scare others. Most of all, it'd make Olive's predictions come true: people wanting to study him like a lab rat.

And that's why I'm proposing that no one finds out he's my son or Olive's. From now on, let him be yours.

No one would question you two raising a dhampir. After all, your own children will be dhampirs, and from what I've seen, you two are smart enough to find a way to convince others he's your biological child. I've also seen the way you two love each other, the way you support each other. Even with as challenging as your relationship has been, you've held true to yourselves and each other. That's what Declan needs. That's the kind of home Olive wanted for him, the kind I want for him.

I know it won't be easy, and walking away from this is one of the hardest things I've had to do. If a day comes when I can feel convinced that it's safe, beyond a doubt, for me to be in his life, then I will. You can use one of those magical methods of yours to find me, and I swear I'll be there at his side in an instant. But until then, so long as the shadow of others' fear and scrutiny hangs over him, I beg you to take him and give him the beautiful life I know you can give him.

Best,
Neil

Adrian's hands were shaking as he finished reading the letter. Tears had formed in my eyes, and I was forced to blink them back. "He's right," I finally said. "We *can* find him with my magic. You don't even need to use spirit."

Adrian folded up the letter and took Declan from me. "But he's also right about the risks."

"What he's asking is big . . ." I began. Neil was right that no one would question us having a dhampir child, but that didn't mean the complications weren't endless. Our own lives were already uncertain. I sank down on the couch, still holding Declan, my mind reeling.

When Adrian had first proposed to me, I'd been nervous, not for lack of love but because being a nineteen-year-old bride had never been in my plans. And being a nineteen-year-old mother? That was definitely not in my plans. But then, was anything turning out the way I'd expected? I studied Declan's face, loving all the little perfect details but also fully aware that if I committed to him, any attempts at salvaging the future I'd wanted—a home with Adrian, college, normality—were going to be seriously thwarted. And yet, how could I abandon Declan?

I looked up at Adrian. "I don't know what to do. I don't have the answer." I realized those weren't words I uttered very often.

Adrian took a deep breath and glanced at those around us. "I think . . . I think maybe we need to ask for some help with this."

I understood the suggestion and considered it. The fewer people who knew the truth about Declan, the better. But what was being asked of us was too big for us to shoulder alone. We needed allies we could trust in deciding Declan's future, and glancing around at those gathered—Rose, Dimitri, Eddie, and Daniella—I realized these were the people we could count on. "Okay," I told Adrian.

"Can somebody finally tell us what's going on?" Rose cut in impatiently.

Adrian took a deep breath, bracing himself for the monumental story he was about to tell. Everyone else had gone very still and very silent, as though sensing the gravity of what was to come. "What I'm about to say is going to change everything you think," Adrian said. He focused on Rose and Dimitri. "You two in particular are about to get your worlds rocked."

EPILOGUE

ADRIAN

"IS THAT THEM?" MY MOTHER CALLED. "I thought I heard the door."

"It had better be," I said, taking a pan out of the oven and carefully setting it on the counter. "This roast is at peak deliciousness. I'm not waiting for them to dive in. It would be a crime. A declaration of war against fine cuisine everywhere."

My mother, used to my theatrics, smiled. "Sydney's not here yet either."

"Oh," I said. "Well, I'll wait for her."

Eddie stuck his head in the kitchen, his face alight. "They're here."

I took off my oven mitts and apron and strolled out to the living room to see the guests who'd just come into the living room of our small rented house. I hadn't seen Rose and Dimitri in almost a year and a half, right around the time Jill had been rescued from the Warriors in St. George. They looked the same as ever, gorgeous and formidable, as they stamped snow off their boots and gave us big smiles. Jill, who'd traveled with them, had already thrown herself into Eddie's arms and was kissing him.

"Whoa, hey," I said. "It hasn't been *that* long since you saw each other. Control yourselves."

It had actually been about a month since they'd been together, which I knew probably felt like an eternity to them. They'd been dating ever since her rescue from St. George, but she had had to go back to Court to finish her education while Eddie stayed with us. So their relationship had become a long-distance one over the last year, with her visiting us on breaks or him going to Court when he could get another guardian to stay with us.

Jill flushed pink and extracted herself from Eddie long enough to give me a hug. "I've missed you so much!" she said.

"I've missed you too," I told her warmly. Every time I saw her, I was astonished to see how much she had transformed from an awkward girl into a poised princess of the Dragomir line. "But you've got to admit, I've been pretty good about updates. And I send you pictures every week."

She grinned. "I know, I know. It's just a little different not being with you like I used to."

I planted a kiss on her forehead. "Better for both of us that way, Jailbait."

I'd held good on my word to Sydney. I'd gone back on my meds, silencing both spirit and Aunt Tatiana. It had also quieted the bond between Jill and me. She still had a sense of me but no longer the intimate view into my heart and mind like she'd once had. Before I could say more to her, a plaintive wail made its way to us.

"The little master awakes," I said. "Be right back."

I sprinted out of the room and up the stairs, to the bedroom that doubled as both a nursery and Eddie's room. I had high enough royal rank to finally be assigned my own guardian, and Eddie, in that noble way of his, had pulled strings to be assigned to us. I'd initially protested because I wanted him to stay at Court and have a semi-normal dating life with Jill. Eddie, however, felt obligated to be with us—both out of friendship to Sydney and me and for all the times Neil had helped him. We'd offered to turn the house's small study into Eddie's own bedroom, but he always ended up sleeping in Declan's room anyway.

"Hey, buddy," I said, walking over to the crib. Declan stood there in fire truck pajamas, watching me seriously with big brown eyes. His dark curls were tousled from sleep, but he beamed as I approached and lifted him out. "Did you have a good nap? We have guests, you know. Aunt Jill is back."

Declan leaned his head against me and yawned, not responding. He was only a year and a half and not much of a conversationalist. Only a few of us knew his true age, however. To the rest of the world, we said he was just over a year old.

That was because we were also telling the rest of the world that he was my and Sydney's son.

Neil had been convinced it was the only way to give Declan a chance at an ordinary life, and we'd finally respected Neil's wishes to stay in hiding. There was no other family to care for Declan; Nina had never recovered. Even if we'd passed Declan off as Olive's son, whom we were raising on her behalf, there might still be too many questions about his father. But if we, a Moroi and a human, said we had a dhampir son, there was no reason for anyone to think we weren't telling the truth.

And so Sydney and I had dropped out of contact with everyone for a while, finally telling the world we had a baby a few months after his supposed birthday. We claimed she'd gotten pregnant right after being rescued from re-education, and then we'd said he came early. We stayed away from people enough that we were able to fudge the dates and make it all seem plausible. If we seemed secretive in our actions, most people assumed it was because we were still nervous about the Alchemists. They'd held good on their word to leave us alone so far, but everyone understood why we might be wary.

It had also helped that we'd had excellent allies. There was no way Sydney and I could've pulled all this off without our friends. Rose and Dimitri had helped cover for us back at Court. My mom had been huge in helping watch Declan so that Sydney and I could still pursue other interests. Eddie had also helped take care of him, along with offering us much-needed protection. He was also the only one of us who'd finally gotten in touch with Neil in whatever undisclosed location he was at. Neil still kept his distance but had recently allowed Eddie to send updates and pictures, and our hope was that someday Neil and Declan could be back in each other's lives.

"Look at him!" squealed Jill when I came down the stairs. "He's gotten so big!"

Even Rose and Dimitri got in on the baby admiration. Whereas we'd seen Jill recently, it had been months and months since their last visit. Declan was probably a giant to them. "We should've brought him a silver stake," Dimitri said. "I'm surprised Eddie hasn't taught him already."

Eddie, his arm resting on Jill, smiled. "We work on it right after morning nap."

The living room door opened again, and Sydney stepped through, snowflakes in her blond hair, a backpack over one shoulder, and a paper bag in her arms. I quickly handed Declan to Jill and took the bags from Sydney. Inside the paper one, I saw French bread and some fruit. The backpack felt like it had a hundred books in it, which was probably true. She smiled up at me as she took her heavy coat off.

"Sorry I'm late," she said. "The roads were bad."

Underneath the coat, she wore a red wool dress and a nametag reading SYDNEY IVASHKOV, STUDENT DOCENT. "Exciting times at the museum?" I asked.

"Always," she said, giving me a brief kiss on the lips.

"Better be careful in that dress," I said. "Someone might mistake you for a work of art."

After we'd moved here last year, Sydney had been ready to throw herself into the job market to support us, and that's when we'd had our first real fight that didn't involve something supernatural. I'd been insistent she finally go to college. She'd said it could wait until our finances built up. Fortunately, another good friend had come through for us: Clarence. With his ample fortune, he'd been more than happy to send us regular stipends—in fact, we'd had to limit him so as not to attract too much attention. But between those payments and student loans, Sydney had finally achieved her dream of studying ancient art at a local university. She'd even nabbed an internship at their museum.

Recently, I'd also been able to help our family income with . . . my own job.

❦

Sometimes that seemed like the most surreal part of all. Me, Adrian Ivashkov, earning an ordinary living. After all the bizarre ups and downs I'd had with money, going from a spoiled kid with unlimited funds to a guy cut off by his father, it seemed unreal sometimes that I now got by with an hourly wage like everyone else. Equally astonishing was how much I'd grown to like it. I'd honestly never expected to get a job with my art degree—if I even finished it. There just weren't that many jobs demanding artists and certainly not ones that needed people with incomplete art degrees. While helping out a neighbor one day, though, I'd learned her daughter's preschool was looking for a part-time art teacher. At that level, my degree didn't matter so much, just my enthusiasm for teaching art to kids. Incredibly, I'd turned out to be pretty good at it—though maybe it was just my natural-born immaturity that allowed me to relate to kids. I'd found a few other preschools and pitched myself to them too, eventually gathering enough part-time positions to contribute substantially to our family's income.

The original place liked me so much that the director had told me if I finished a bachelor's degree in education, I could come work a full-time teacher's position with better pay and solid hours. Sydney hadn't pressured me to go back to college, but when she'd heard that, her eyes had lit up, and I had a feeling she'd be working my college tuition into her master budget.

I'd never seen this budget plan, but it apparently accounted for a lot of things. So far, it managed to support the five of us in the rented house and had a timeline in place for when we'd be able to afford a house of our own, more education for her and me, and eventually Declan's education. It was pretty impressive that she could make all of this work, but then, I'd learned to expect impressive things from her.

She hugged all our guests and then took Declan from Jill. Pretending he was our dhampir son might have started off as an act, but it had become reality as far as we were concerned. Sydney loved the little guy fiercely and, like the rest of us, would do anything for him. She kissed the top of his curly head and was rewarded with a smile. "*¿Cómo estás, mi amor?*" she asked, carrying him off to the kitchen to check dinner.

Rose turned to me. "Did she just speak to him in Spanish?"

"Yeah," I said. "She only speaks to him in Spanish, actually. It was in some parenting book she read about kids learning a second language."

"We should eat," my mother said, shooting me a wry look. "Otherwise a crime against fine cuisine might be committed."

That was another thing I'd taken upon myself, along with my collection of jobs: cooking. And it turned out I wasn't so bad at that either.

Later, when dinner had wound down and we were all around the table, I found myself gazing around and unable to believe this was how my life had turned out. Never would I have guessed I'd fall so comfortably into the role of husband and father. Never would I have guessed I'd be married to a human. And I certainly wouldn't have guessed I'd be so happy without spirit.

After we'd rescued Jill and agreed to raise Declan, we'd had to make a very quick decision about where to run off to with our newly bought freedom. Northern Maine had won out. Close to civilization but far enough that it wasn't so easy for someone to sneak up on us. I still woke conflicted sometimes, feeling guilty for loving Declan so much, being so glad I was able to call him my son. And always, always, I felt guilty for not saving Olive, for not having rationed my spirit that night.

But the past was gone, and all I could do now was honor Olive's wishes and give Declan as normal a life as possible. So far, we seemed to be pulling that off. He had no idea there was anything different about himself. Only a handful of people knew he wasn't actually my son. Even fewer than that knew the truth of his remarkable parentage. Everyone here at this Christmas gathering was in that elite group. All knew about Declan's past, and all were committed to protecting his future.

Thinking about that, my gaze rested on Rose and Dimitri, sitting together at one end of the table. We'd told them about Declan because the odds were good they too were in the same situation as Olive and Neil. Both Dimitri and Olive had been restored from being Strigoi, and whatever feat of spirit had allowed Olive to conceive with another dhampir would likely apply to Rose and Dimitri also. Unlike us, however, they weren't going to be able to go off and cover up the miracle. Their lives were too visible. If they had a child together, everyone would know . . . and the revelation would come to light. Both of them knew this, but what their future plans were, I still didn't know.

Well, I soon learned *one* plan of theirs.

"Holy crap," I said. While staring off at Rose and Dimitri, a brilliant flash had caught my eye—a flash on Rose's finger.

"What's that?" I exclaimed. "Did you rob Lissa's crown jewels?"

Rose, in what was a rare look for her, actually appeared flustered. "Maybe it's too much."

Dimitri brought her hand up to his lips and kissed the top of it. "No, it's perfect."

Jill clapped her hands in delight. "An engagement ring!"

"Hold up," I ordered. "Show the goods."

With Dimitri grinning, Rose complied, holding out her left hand for the rest of the table to see. It was a remarkable piece of work. A large, perfectly cut round diamond was set into a lacy square of platinum filigree that was edged in tiny blue opals. It was a statement ring if ever there was one, and a wholly unexpected choice.

"Did you pick that out?" I asked Dimitri. Honestly, I would have expected him to bend a piece of steel with his bare hands and present her with that.

"He did," said Rose, her normal good humor returning. "He kept telling me that once I turned twenty, it was just a matter of time before he proposed. I told him if he did, he better make it a rock star ring—nothing subtle."

"That's pretty rock star," said Eddie. "How long ago did this happen?"

"About a month," said Dimitri. "I got her to wear it but can't get her to set a date."

She grinned. "All in good time, comrade. Maybe when I'm thirty. There's no hurry. Besides, surely Christian's going to propose to Liss one of these days. We don't want to overshadow them."

Dimitri shook his head in exasperation, but he kept smiling. "You've always got an excuse, Roza. One of these days . . ."

"One of these days," she agreed.

We stayed up late catching up with everyone and then finally dispersed for bed. Rose and Dimitri were camped out in the living room, and Jill had made the study her bedroom, just as she always did when she visited. Declan had passed out a while ago, and once I made sure he was resting comfortably in his crib, I made my way to my own bedroom. This house we'd been renting was an old Victorian, and our bedroom was in the turret, which was off to the house's side and practically its own wing. I loved the room's round shape and privacy. It made me feel like we were in our own castle.

Seeing as Jill had taken over Sydney's usual studying place, I wasn't surprised to find Sydney on our bed surrounded by books now, wearing a short robe. "You changed," I said, shutting the door behind me. "I was hoping to see some more of that red dress."

She smiled up at me and closed a textbook entitled *Minoan Art and Architecture*. "I thought you'd like this better. But I could go put it back on if you want."

I helped her stack up the books and move them off the bed so that I could sit beside her. "That depends," I said, running a hand over her leg. "Is there anything on under it?"

"Nope. Probably I should change." She pretended to get up, and I caught her hand, pulling her down and rolling her to her back.

"Don't even think of it." She wrapped her arms around my neck, and I noticed she still had on her rings, which reminded me of our guests' big news. "I'd been wondering how Rose and Dimitri would handle having kids or not," I remarked. "But I guess that's a question that won't be decided for a while, seeing as how he can't even get her to the altar."

Sydney laughed. "I think he'll get her there sooner than you think. She talks a good game, but I bet she'll give in eventually. I did."

"Yeah, but Belikov's not nearly as charming as I am. Or as good a cook. It's an uphill battle for him."

"Maybe you can give him some pointers," Sydney teased.

"Maybe," I agreed. I brought my mouth down and kissed her, amazed at how one touch from her always set me aflame. Even after long days, whenever I came home to her, I always felt alive and energized. I'd worried once we weren't always on the run and living life on the edge that the passion might fade between us. If anything, stability—and, most importantly, freedom—had ignited it even more. The sentiment I'd had last year had been confirmed: I didn't need spirit. I just needed Sydney. I slid my hand to the sash in her robe and discovered she'd tied it with some sort of sailor's knot that only she could undo. "Oh, come on," I groaned.

"Sorry," she said, laughing again. "I didn't even think about it. Honest."

"I believe you," I said. I paused to kiss the nape of her neck. "You're the smartest girl I know. You can't help knowing everything and being constantly brilliant—and I wouldn't have it any other way." I kissed her lips again, but after several moments, she pulled back slightly.

"Hey," she murmured. "There are people in the house."

"There are *always* people in the house," I reminded her. "That's why we escaped up here to the castle tower. Escape plan number . . . hell, I don't know. I lost count. We haven't had to come up with some dreamy escape plan in a while."

Sydney trailed her fingers down the side of my face. "That's because we're living it, Adrian. This is the only escape plan we need."

"Are you sure?" I asked, propping myself up on one elbow.

I tried to put on a thoughtful, speculative expression. "Because there are things that could be tweaked. Like a bigger house. Or maybe—"

"Adrian," she interrupted. "Didn't you just say I'm brilliant and know everything? Then trust me on this."

"Always," I said, letting her pull me back down to her. "Always."

GO BACK TO WHERE IT ALL BEGAN....

Vampire Academy

TURN THE PAGE TO READ THE

FIRST CHAPTER . . .

ONE

I FELT HER FEAR BEFORE I heard her screams.

Her nightmare pulsed into me, shaking me out of my own dream, which had had something to do with a beach and some hot guy rubbing suntan oil on me. Images—hers, not mine—tumbled through my mind: fire and blood, the smell of smoke, the twisted metal of a car. The pictures wrapped around me, suffocating me, until some rational part of my brain reminded me that this wasn't *my* dream.

I woke up, strands of long, dark hair sticking to my forehead.

Lissa lay in her bed, thrashing and screaming. I bolted out of mine, quickly crossing the few feet that separated us.

"Liss," I said, shaking her. "Liss, wake up."

Her screams dropped off, replaced by soft whimpers. "Andre," she moaned. "Oh God."

I helped her sit up. "Liss, you aren't there anymore. Wake up."

After a few moments, her eyes fluttered open, and in the dim lighting, I could see a flicker of consciousness start to take over. Her frantic breathing slowed, and she leaned into me, resting her head against my shoulder. I put an arm around her and ran a hand over her hair.

"It's okay," I told her gently. "Everything's okay."

"I had that dream."

"Yeah. I know."

We sat like that for several minutes, not saying anything else. When I felt her emotions calm down, I leaned over to the nightstand between our beds and turned on the lamp. It glowed dimly, but neither of us really needed much to see by. Attracted by the light, our housemate's cat, Oscar, leapt up onto the sill of the open window.

He gave me a wide berth—animals don't like dhampirs, for whatever reason—but jumped onto the bed and rubbed his head against Lissa, purring softly. Animals didn't have a problem with Moroi, and they all loved Lissa in particular. Smiling, she scratched his chin, and I felt her calm further.

"When did we last do a feeding?" I asked, studying her face. Her fair skin was paler than usual. Dark circles hung under her eyes, and there was an air of frailty about her. School had been hectic this week, and I couldn't remember the last time I'd given her blood. "It's been like . . . more than two days, hasn't it? Three? Why didn't you say anything?"

She shrugged and wouldn't meet my eyes. "You were busy. I didn't want to—"

"Screw that," I said, shifting into a better position. No wonder she seemed so weak. Oscar, not wanting me any closer, leapt down and returned to the window, where he could watch at a safe distance. "Come on. Let's do this."

"Rose—"

"Come *on*. It'll make you feel better."

I tilted my head and tossed my hair back, baring my neck. I saw her hesitate, but the sight of my neck and what it offered proved too powerful. A hungry expression crossed her face, and her lips parted slightly, exposing the fangs she normally kept hidden while living among humans. Those fangs contrasted oddly with the rest of her features. With her pretty face and pale blond hair, she looked more like an angel than a vampire.

As her teeth neared my bare skin, I felt my heart race with a mix of fear and anticipation. I always hated feeling the latter, but it was nothing I could help, a weakness I couldn't shake.

Her fangs bit into me, hard, and I cried out at the brief flare of pain. Then it faded, replaced by a wonderful, golden joy that spread through my body. It was better than any of the times I'd been drunk or high. Better than sex—or so I imagined, since I'd never done it. It was a blanket of pure, refined pleasure, wrapping me up and promising everything would be right in the world. On and on it went. The chemicals in her saliva triggered an endorphin rush, and I lost track of the world, lost track of who I was.

Then, regretfully, it was over. It had taken less than a minute.

She pulled back, wiping her hand across her lips as she studied me. "You okay?"

"I . . . yeah." I lay back on the bed, dizzy from the blood loss. "I just need to sleep it off. I'm fine."

Her pale, jade-green eyes watched me with concern. She stood up. "I'm going to get you something to eat."

My protests came awkwardly to my lips, and she left before I could get out a sentence. The buzz from her bite had lessened as soon as she broke the connection, but some of it still lingered in my veins, and I felt a goofy smile cross my lips. Turning my head, I glanced up at Oscar, still sitting in the window.

"You don't know what you're missing," I told him.

His attention was on something outside. Hunkering down into a crouch, he puffed out his jet-black fur. His tail started twitching.

My smile faded, and I forced myself to sit up. The world spun, and I waited for it to right itself before trying to stand. When I managed it, the dizziness set in again and this time refused to leave. Still, I felt okay enough to stumble to the window and peer out with Oscar. He eyed me warily, scooted over a little, and then returned to whatever had held his attention.

A warm breeze—unseasonably warm for a Portland fall—played with my hair as I leaned out. The street was dark and relatively quiet. It was three in the morning, just about the only time a college campus settled down, at least somewhat. The house in which we'd rented a room for the past eight months sat on a residential street with old, mismatched houses. Across the road, a streetlight flickered, nearly ready to burn out. It still cast enough light for me to make out the shapes of cars and buildings. In our own yard, I could see the silhouettes of trees and bushes.

And a man watching me.

I jerked back in surprise. A figure stood by a tree in the yard, about thirty feet away, where he could easily see through the window. He was close enough that I probably could have thrown something and hit him. He was certainly close enough that he could have seen what Lissa and I had just done.

The shadows covered him so well that even with my heightened sight, I couldn't make out any of his features, save for his height. He was tall. Really tall. He stood there for just a moment, barely discernible, and then stepped back, disappearing into the shadows cast by the trees on the far side of the yard. I was pretty sure I saw someone else move nearby and join him before the blackness swallowed them both.

Whoever these figures were, Oscar didn't like them. Not counting me, he usually got along with most people, growing upset only when someone posed an immediate danger. The guy outside hadn't done anything threatening to Oscar, but the cat had sensed something, something that put him on edge.

Something similar to what he always sensed in me.

Icy fear raced through me, almost—but not quite—eradicating the lovely bliss of Lissa's bite. Backing up from the window, I jerked on a pair of jeans that I found on the floor, nearly falling over in the process. Once they were on, I grabbed my coat and Lissa's, along with our wallets. Shoving my feet into the first shoes I saw, I headed out the door.

Downstairs, I found her in the cramped kitchen, rummaging through the refrigerator. One of our housemates, Jeremy, sat at the table, hand on his forehead as he stared sadly at a calculus book. Lissa regarded me with surprise.

"You shouldn't be up."

"We have to go. Now."

Her eyes widened, and then a moment later, understanding clicked in. "Are you . . . really? Are you sure?"

I nodded. I couldn't explain how I knew for sure. I just did.

Jeremy watched us curiously. "What's wrong?"

An idea came to mind. "Liss, get his car keys."

He looked back and forth between us. "What are you—"

Lissa unhesitatingly walked over to him. Her fear poured into me through our psychic bond, but there was something else too: her complete faith that I would take care of everything, that we would be safe. Like always, I hoped I was worthy of that kind of trust.

She smiled broadly and gazed directly into his eyes. For a moment, Jeremy just stared, still confused, and then I saw the thrall seize him. His eyes glazed over, and he regarded her adoringly.

"We need to borrow your car," she said in a gentle voice. "Where are your keys?"

He smiled, and I shivered. I had a high resistance to compulsion, but I could still feel its effects when it was directed at another person. That, and I'd been taught my entire life that using it was wrong. Reaching into his pocket, Jeremy handed over a set of keys hanging on a large red key chain.

"Thank you," said Lissa. "And where is it parked?"

"Down the street," he said dreamily. "At the corner. By Brown." Four blocks away.

"Thank you," she repeated, backing up. "As soon as we leave, I want you to go back to studying. Forget you ever saw us tonight."

He nodded obligingly. I got the impression he would have walked off a cliff for her right then if she'd asked. All humans were susceptible to compulsion, but Jeremy appeared weaker than most. That came in handy right now.

"Come on," I told her. "We've got to move."

We stepped outside, heading toward the corner he'd named. I was still dizzy from the bite and kept stumbling, unable to move as quickly as I wanted. Lissa had to catch hold of me a few times to stop me from falling. All the time, that anxiety rushed into me from her mind. I tried my best to ignore it; I had my own fears to deal with.

"Rose . . . what are we going to do if they catch us?" she whispered.

"They won't," I said fiercely. "I won't let them."

"But if they've found us—"

"They found us before. They didn't catch us then. We'll just drive over to the train station and go to L.A. They'll lose the trail."

I made it sound simple. I always did, even though there

was nothing simple about being on the run from the people we'd grown up with. We'd been doing it for two years, hiding wherever we could and just trying to finish high school. Our senior year had just started, and living on a college campus had seemed safe. We were so close to freedom.

She said nothing more, and I felt her faith in me surge up once more. This was the way it had always been between us. I was the one who took action, who made sure things happened—sometimes recklessly so. She was the more reasonable one, the one who thought things out and researched them extensively before acting. Both styles had their uses, but at the moment, recklessness was called for. We didn't have time to hesitate.

Lissa and I had been best friends ever since kindergarten, when our teacher had paired us together for writing lessons. Forcing five-year-olds to spell *Vasilisa Dragomir* and *Rosemarie Hathaway* was beyond cruel, and we'd—or rather, *I'd*—responded appropriately. I'd chucked my book at our teacher and called her a fascist bastard. I hadn't known what those words meant, but I'd known how to hit a moving target.

Lissa and I had been inseparable ever since.

ALSO BY RICHELLE MEAD

Bloodlines

LOVE AND LOYALTY RUN DEEPER
THAN BLOOD . . .

 /BloodlinesBooks

VAMPIRE ACADEMY

DON'T MISS THE MAJOR FILM

The International Bestselling Series

FORBIDDEN TEMPTATION LIES BEHIND THE IRON GATES

 /vampireacademynovels